PENGUIN POETS IN TRANSLATION

GENERAL EDITOR: CHRISTOPHER RICKS

HOMER IN ENGLISH

The Greeks attributed both the *Iliad* and the *Odyssey* to a single poet whom they named Homer. Nothing is known of his life, though the main ancient tradition made him a native of the island of Chios, in the east Aegean. His date too is uncertain: most modern scholars place the composition of the *Iliad* in the second half of the eighth century BC.

GEORGE STEINER, the writer, critic and scholar, was born in Paris in 1929, and is the author of some twelve books, translated into as many languages. These include *The Death of Tragedy*, *Language and Silence*, *In Bluebeard's Castle*, *After Babel*, *Antigones*, *Real Presences* and several works of fiction. He has taught at both Oxford and Cambridge, and at the Universities of Geneva, Harvard, Yale and Princeton. He also edited *The Penguin Book of Verse Translation* and a collection of critical essays on Homer.

AMINADAV DYKMAN was born in Warsaw in 1958. Trained in classical philology and Hebrew, he came from Jerusalem to Geneva to work in comparative literature with Professor Steiner. He is the author of numerous articles and essays in the fields of ancient poetry, Slavonic studies and translation.

HOMER IN ENGLISH

Edited with an Introduction and Notes by
GEORGE STEINER

with the Assistance of AMINADAV DYKMAN

PENGUIN BOOKS

PENGUIN BOOKS

Published by the Penguin Group
Penguin Books Ltd, 27 Wrights Lane, London w8 5TZ, England
Penguin Books USA Inc., 375 Hudson Street, New York, New York 10014, USA
Penguin Books Australia Ltd, Ringwood, Victoria, Australia
Penguin Books Canada Ltd, 10 Alcorn Avenue, Toronto, Ontario, Canada M4V 3B2
Penguin Books (NZ) Ltd, 182–190 Wairau Road, Auckland 10, New Zealand

Penguin Books Ltd, Registered Offices: Harmondsworth, Middlesex, England

First published 1996
10 9 8 7 6 5 4 3 2 1

This collection copyright © George Steiner, 1996
The Acknowledgements on pages 356–7 constitute an extension of this copyright page

All rights reserved

The moral right of the author has been asserted

Typeset by Datix International Ltd, Bungay, Suffolk
Printed in England by Clays Ltd, St Ives plc
Set in 10/12.5 pt Monophoto Bembo

Except in the United States of America, this book is sold subject
to the condition that it shall not, by way of trade or otherwise, be lent,
re-sold, hired out, or otherwise circulated without the publisher's
prior consent in any form of binding or cover other than that in
which it is published and without a similar condition including this
condition being imposed on the subsequent purchaser

For Andrew Feldherr

vivite felices, memores et vivite nostri,
sive erimus seu nos fata fuisse velint.
                              Tibullus, III, v

CONTENTS

PREFACE

An anthology of this kind is always, in a sense, collective. I am indebted to the booksellers who have, over long years, helped me find English and American 'Homers'. To the public and university libraries, notably the Rare-Book Room of the Cambridge University Library, in which a good many of the rarer versions can be consulted. The difficult copy-editing of so various a text is due to my Penguin editors.

But, above all, I owe thanks to my younger colleague and collaborator Aminadav Dykman. His scholarship in the classics, his knowledge of European literatures and textual criticism, his fascination with the history of metrics, prosody and rhetoric have been invaluable. This book is also his.

GS

INTRODUCTION

The *Iliad* and the *Odyssey*, notably Book I of the *Iliad*, are the texts most frequently translated into English – where 'English' comprises not only the varieties of the language spoken and written in Britain since the late Middle Ages, but the entire global spectrum. If we include under 'Homer' the so-called *Homeric Hymns*, there is, more particularly during the eighteenth and nineteenth centuries, scarcely a single year in which some English-language poet, scholar, parson, schoolmaster or gentleman of classical attainments did not translate and, more often than not, publish out of Homer. The British Library lists under 'Homerus', not to mention my own personal collection – a passion dating back to my school-days – are very far from complete.

Starting with the *Seege of Troy* romance and the *Laud Troy Book* (which runs to more than 18,000 lines), the history of imitations, adaptations, sequels and translations is never-ending. We move from the alliterative verses of the anonymous *Gest Historiale of the Destruction of Troy* and a Scottish version attributed to John Barbour, to Lydgate's celebrated *Troy Book* and Caxton's *Recuyell of the Historyes of Troye*. Through these two texts, the 'matter of Homer' informs not only the foundations and growth of the arts of English narrative in verse and in prose, but the origins and dissemination of printing itself. Printing comes to England via a 'Troye Booke'.

Since the end of the Second World War, near to a dozen complete British-English and American-English *Iliads* and *Odysseys* have been published. Hardly has one appeared, when another is announced. Widely read translations, such as E. V. Rieu's, are reissued and revised. English-language 'Homers' thus decisively outnumber English renditions of the Bible. Unless I am mistaken, the 'translation act' which renders the Trojan war, the homecoming of Odysseus or the *Homeric Hymns* into medieval, Tudor, Elizabethan, Jacobean, Augustan, Romantic, Victorian or twentieth-century English, into the English of North America or the Caribbean, surpasses in frequency that of any other act of transfer into any other Western tongue and literature.

When we take into account the verse and prose romances, the plays (for example, Shakespeare's *Troilus and Cressida*), the lyric imitations and evocations (as in Tennyson), the fiction derived from the rape of Helen, the wrath of Achilles, the death of Hector, the fall of Troy, the enchantments of Circe, Penelope's web, the vengeance of Odysseus, the Homeric presences, the creative echo, from Caxton to Joyce and Derek Walcott, from Chaucer to Robert Graves and W. H. Auden, becomes almost incommensurable. And this is to omit the 'lives of the Homeric' in English art from medieval illuminations to Caro, or in music to the times of Walton's *Troilus and Cressida*, Britten's music for a radio dramatization of the *Odyssey*, or Tippett's *King Priam*.

But it is not only the numerical prodigality which arrests attention. It is the quality and diversity of the long lineage of translators and respondents to Homer. It is the complexity of modulation, the investment of vision which takes us from Lydgate and Caxton to *Ulysses* and *Omeros*. It is not only on Keats that Chapman's Homer exercised its uneven spell. What might Dryden's projected *Iliad* have been had he persisted beyond Book One? I do not see what English epic poem after *Paradise Regained* – and how abundant Homer is in Milton – rivals the authority and narrative sweep of Pope's *Iliad*. There are persuasive 'domesticities', as from a Flemish interior, in Cowper's *Odyssey*, in his treatment of 'that species of the sublime that owes its very existence to simplicity'. Shelley's *Homeric Hymns* exhibit both poetic virtuosity and a close knowledge of Greek lyric texts. What understanding of modern English and American poetry could set aside the translations, from the imitations of the *Iliad* and the *Odyssey* in Ezra Pound – that magical first *Canto*! – in Auden's 'Shield of Achilles', in Graves, in Robert Lowell, in Robert Fitzgerald or in that incandescent reading by

Christopher Logue? The sirens that sing of destruction and tempo-
rary relief to the fire-watcher on the London roofs in T. S. Eliot's
Four Quartets are those of the air-raid alarm; but they are also the
temptresses of Odysseus, their fatal music recaptured and, as it were,
amplified through Dante's use of the myth.

Nor is it only poets, playwrights, novelists who have mirrored
Homer into English, into Anglo-Irish, into American, Scottish or
West Indian branches of the language. It is philosophers or inquirers
into meaning such as Thomas Hobbes and I. A. Richards. It is
thinkers on society such as William Morris and Samuel Butler. It is,
in the legacy of Caxton and Ogilby, master-publishers such as
Rieu. We find prime ministers (the Earl of Derby's *Iliad* appears in
1864 and Gladstone makes repeated attempts at Homer). Ecclesiastics
and headmasters are legion. T. E. Lawrence prefaces his *Odyssey* in
lofty modesty. He is a man of war and survival. Unlike scholarly
rivals or detractors, he has killed his man in combat and undergone
extreme peril. These, he opines, are qualifications not altogether
impertinent to the task of voicing Homer. Also Graves could make
this claim. Before long, moreover, our catalogue will include more
women (four are represented in this anthology). Has Nausikaa not
been held to be the author of the *Odyssey*, has Simone Weil not
written one of the most challenging (though, to my mind, mis-
guided) commentaries on the *Iliad*?

The bare facts compel the question: Why? Why, distinctively
among other Western literatures, should those in the English lan-
guages generate a perennial ubiquity of translations from Homer,
of Homeric variants, re-creations, pastiches and travesties (these
extend from the Renaissance to a two-volume eighteenth-century
burlesque-erotic *Iliad* and *Odyssey* and the calypso lyrics of Lawrence
Durrell)? The recent and current multiplicity is striking. Till *Lady
Chatterley's Lover* (now, I suspect, beyond it), Rieu's *Odyssey* marks
the greatest single 'hit' in Penguin's publishing history. Not long
thereafter comes Richmond Lattimore's *Iliad*, hailed as exemplary.
Then we have Fitzgerald's inspired *Odyssey*. Lattimore feels obliged
to riposte with an *Odyssey* of his own. Fitzgerald, *à contrecœur* one
suspects, now adds his *Iliad*. Robert Fagles acclaims Fitzgerald's

achievement, only to present, a few years later, his own Homer. Not to mention Graves, Rees, Mandelbaum and many others. Today, the sequence shows no sign of slowing down. Inevitably, the cut-off point in this collection (1994) is arbitrary. This selection will be out of date when it appears. What induces twentieth-century commercial and academic presses to commission, edit and issue these costly, voluminous addenda to what is already, so richly, available?

The 'natural' national myth ought to have been Arthurian – as Malory, Milton, Tennyson or T. H. White variously supposed. Did, for Britain, the major Christian legends and typologies not lie to hand as they did on the continent of Europe? What Faustus after Marlowe in English literature to set beside Valéry's or Bulgakov's or Thomas Mann's? What Don Juan except Byron's? No, it is to Achilles and Odysseus, to the 'topless towers of Ilium' and the shores of Ithaka, it is to 'deep-browed Homer' that English-language sensibility turns and returns, incessantly, as if striving to appropriate to itself, to the native genius, material already, by some destined or elective affinity, its own. It is a *Ulysses* which Joyce writes when re-creating Dublin. It is an *Omeros* in which Walcott sings his profoundly Afro-Caribbean music of Eros, of masculine rivalries, of the spirit world and of the sea.

Again, I ask: Why?

The etymologically spurious identification of Britons with Roman descendants of Aeneas, which is to say with those who had battled for and emigrated from Homeric Troy, is medieval and, perhaps, even earlier. It is alive in Tudor historiography, iconography and symbolic perceptions of England's noble ascendancy. Logic suggests that this would have made Virgil and the *Aeneid* the talismanic reference rather than Greek Homer and his cruel paladins. And there *is* a significant Virgilian note in English literature, music and art (consider Dryden, Purcell or Turner). But it pales beside the centrality of the Homeric. A first thought might be this: there shines throughout the *Iliad* an idealized yet also unflinching vision of masculinity, of an order of values and mutual recognitions radically virile. In ways too inwoven, too manifold to be readily categorized, this vision matches, underwrites and images certain primary components in English consciousness and social history. The Homeric saga of warfare and masculine intimacies, with its formidable emphasis on competitive sports, seems immediate, as is no other text, to the boys' school, to the all-male college, the regiment and the club (configurations cardinal to British, not to Continental societies). This lyric masculinity aches in Keats's desire to be in the trench shouting with Achilles, no less than in the self-identification as Homeric heroes, as lovers before death, proclaimed by English subalterns and poets at Ypres or in that Homeric setting at the Dardanelles.

The topic is both insistent and elusive. As so often in the phenomenology of English sentiments, homoeroticism is, as it were, organic and organizing. In its Homeric context, this factor is sanctified by sacrificial bravery, by devotion to friendship and duty even more than in the Platonizing homoeroticism of the Victorians. What public schoolboy (until recently), what young officer in the Western Desert did not thrill, more or less consciously, to the remembrance of Hector's roar at the very edge of the Greek encampment, or to Achilles' lament over Patroklos – a thrill in which athletic prestige, masculine handsomeness, ambitious valour and a more or less diffuse homoeroticism animate, if this expression may be allowed, a singularly British 'puberty of the spirit'? What observation more in the tenor of the *Iliad* than that whereby the most testing and consequential of British victories on land, that at Waterloo, was said to have been won on the playing-fields of Eton? Remember the naked dead, in the Homeric manner, on English war memorials.

Most subtly, moreover, Homer's *Iliad* sustains a divided, even duplicitous focus. The doom of Hector and the desolation of Priam's city weigh as intensely as do the triumph of Achilles and of the Achaean host. This equable pathos, the balance held so justly, would appear to have struck native chords in British reception. The *Iliad* could be the only supreme tale of human valour and suffering in which we *can* have it both ways. Hector remains the archetype of the 'good loser', a pivotal configuration in English self-regard. Hector and Priam are the patrons of all Dunkirks. The epic appeals, at an inward level, to that now poignant code of 'fair play' which defined British mores to themselves and the world at large. 'What's Hecuba to him?' ruminates Hamlet. A Danish, not an English question.

The perennial spell exercised by the *Odyssey* could have its more obvious source. The Homeric tale is that of the sea and of all who go down to it in their 'dark ships'. It remains incomparable in its salt-savour, in its orchestration of tempests and of calms, in its nuanced articulations of the dialogue between sea and strand, wave and shore. Homer's is that wine-dark sea which Matthew Arnold heard on Dover Beach. Coleridge's Ancient Mariner, Poe's Gordon Pym, Conrad's seamen at the helm are descendants of peregrine Odysseus. As are the souls overboard or clinging to a raft in Melville. An island-civilization, sea-drenched and guarded by stormy waters at every crucial season in its history, will find in Homer's *Odyssey* not only a book of common prayer – 'may I endure this storm, may I reach the harbour' – but of shared adventure and global promise. Du Bellay's famous sonnet on Odysseus' homecoming from his *beau voyage* is magical; but it is lit by the soft streams in the Loire country. The sea is absent. It roils and thunders in Chapman's couplets. Its rages sing in the North Atlantic 'Homers' of Robert Fitzgerald or the West Indian marines of *Omeros*.

But these conjectures as to the unbroken hold of Homer on English tongues and literatures are probably inadequate. The empathies of vision and revision lie deep. The light from Achilles' helmet, from the eyes of the 'cat-like Penelope' (T. E. Lawrence's epithet), 'screams . . . across three thousand years'. That dizzying phrase is out of Christopher Logue's transmutation of the *Patrocleia*. It 'screams' in English as it does in no other language after Greek. From the beginnings of our literature to the present, to tomorrow. Whatever the underlying causes, this crowded vitality and constancy of echo offer a wealth of implications.

To borrow an image from plant genetics: the sequence of translations from Homer provides a unique radioactive tracer. By its luminescent progress, we can follow the development of the language, of its vocabularies, syntax and semantic resources, from root to stem, from its stem to its multiple branches and leaves. Every model of English lexical and grammatical observance is visible in this chain: all the way from the most ornate and experimental, as in Chapman or Joyce, to the 'basic English' purposed in I. A. Richards's narration of the fury of Achilles. The Homeric sequence is an inventory of metrical means: we find in it alliterative verse, rhyme royal, Spenserian stanzas, heroic couplets, iambic pentameter, blank and free verse. It exemplifies trials in quantitative and syllabic measures of every kind. That intricate subject, the evolution of English prose rhythms, of punctuation, also unfolds in the Homeric sequence. As does that of dialect, of regional idioms from the Scottish Lowlands and Lancashire to Trinidad and Boston.

This vivacity of structural illumination, of dynamic legibility, coursing through organic tissue, springs from the nature of translation itself. For it is in and through the process of translation that a language is made eminently self-aware. Translation constrains it to formal and diachronic introspection, to an explicit investment and enlargement of its historical, colloquial and metaphoric instruments. Simultaneously, translation puts a language under pressure of its limitations. It will solicit modes of perception and designation which that language had left underdeveloped, or had altogether discarded. An act of translation draws up a balance sheet, as it were, for the target language. When such an act engenders a continuity which extends from Anglo-Norman to English in its twentieth-century planetary variety, linguistic history and forms are writ large. There is, in consequence, a sense in which this collection is a concise chronicle of English.

Which chronicle begins tangentially. It is via Dares and Dictys, whom the Middle Ages took to be witnesses of the events at Troy, and via Benoît de Sainte Maure's *Roman de Troie* (running to 30,000 lines), that Ilium and Ulysses enter into Middle English. Chaucer knows of the *Iliad* only through Boccaccio. It is a Latin version of the Homeric material and, more especially, Virgil's complexly inflected view of Homer, which are fitfully available to Tudor England. We still are uncertain as to just how much Greek George Chapman knew as he addressed the original and the 'Prince of Poets' between 1598 and 1616. But the vital point is this: these are the years in which English is in the highest state of 'excitation', when it has been enriched, energized, made musical as never before or since by its encounter with a transcendent source-text in Wyclif, Tyndale and the Authorized Version. Now, in the *Iliad* and the *Odyssey*, this same language meets with immanence, with the concrete turbulence and blaze of simile in the Homeric world. It strives to match a swiftness of narrative, a strength of internal connections, an economy of impact (Helen passing the old men and casting silence on them) comparable with yet radically different from that of Scripture. In these very years, moreover, the language is called upon to enact a diversity of rhetorical, oratorical, political discourse which will, in analogue with Homeric exempla, enter into its own parliamentary practices.

In Chapman's *Whole Works of Homer*, notably in the fourteeners of his *Iliad*, English is spendthrift, inebriate with waste motion, at times precious and as yet uncertain of its coruscating force. It is also the language of Elizabethan and Jacobean drama, charged with sensory, corporeal thrust. At moments, it is already exact in that manual, pragmatic vein which is the virtue of English. At others, it comes armed with lyric sorrow. Homer, as Chapman construes and misconstrues him, makes the English language know itself and impels it to cast its lexical-grammatical net over a thronging prodigality of life:

> such a fire from his bright shield extends
> His ominous radiance, and in heaven imprest his fervent blaze.
> His crested helmet, grave and high, had next triumphant place
> On his curl'd head: and like a starre it cast a spurrie ray,
> About which a bright thickned bush of golden haire did play,
> Which Vulcan forg'd him for his plume . . .
>
> The faire scourge then Automedon takes up, and up doth get
> To guide the horse. The fight's seate last Achilles tooke behind,
> Who lookt so arm'd as if the Sunne, there falne from heaven, had
>   shin'd —

> And terribly thus charg'd his steeds: 'Xanthus and Balius,
> Seed of the Harpye, in the charge ye undertake of us,
> Discharge it not as when Patroclus ye left dead in field . . .'

So much to be said about the uses of Latinity to give 'ominous' coloration to this passage from the coda of *Iliad*, XIX. Note the adjective: we will hear it again in the most brilliant of later twentieth-century renditions. Chapman's astronomy has a theatrical logic. The shield's celestial radiance, the star with its 'spurrie' rays (an inspired concatenation), the fallen sun – each is a *figura* of Achilles' destiny. Observe the formidable placement of the adverb: the son of Peleus 'charges' his beloved steeds 'terribly', where that 'charge' signifies 'address', 'instruction', but evokes, inescapably, the 'charge in battle', the war-lunge of the chariot itself as well as the sombre image of the unloading of the fallen Patroclus ('Discharge').

> Next, his high Head the Helmet grac'd; behind
> The sweepy Crest hung floating in the Wind:
> Like the red Star, that from his flaming Hair
> Shakes down Diseases, Pestilence and War;
> So stream'd the golden Honours from his Head,
> Trembled the sparkling Plumes, and the loose Glories shed . . .
>
> *Xanthus and Balius!* of *Podarges'* Strain,
> (Unless ye boast that heav'nly Race in vain)
> Be swift, be mindful of the Load ye bear,
> And learn to make your Master more your Care:
> Thro' falling Squadrons bear my slaught'ring Sword
> Nor, as ye left *Patroclus*, leave your Lord.

Alexander Pope, of course; in an idiom which declares itself dismissive, indeed scornful, of Chapman's or Ogilby's. But which is itself under pressure as it seeks to map a linguistic terrain outside the Shakespearian and Miltonic precedents and in rivalry with the genius for narrated action in Dryden's poems and translations. There is a shorthand of learned, authoritative allusion in 'the red Star' signifying Mars. 'Honours' and 'Glories' are very nearly technically heraldic. That speed, which Matthew Arnold will place foremost among the requisites of Homeric translation, gathers pace towards the laconic climax: 'Nor, as ye left *Patroclus*, leave your Lord.'

Most thought-provoking, however, is the ample footnote on the lines immediately following. How, asks Pope, is one to excuse 'the extravagant Fiction of a Horse speaking'? (Shades of Swift.) Pope invokes 'Fable, Tradition, and History', the latter in the person of Livy. He cites the poignant translation of the passage by Mr Fenton (it is intriguing that we find no such text in what we have of Richard Fenton's works). Then comes Pope's trump card: Balaam's eloquent ass. With this biblical validation, the footnote opens on universality: Homer inhabited an 'Age of Wonders' in which good taste and sensibility were receptive of the miraculous. In voice and pedantry, this note is Nabokovian. But the issue is capital. The tensed energies of Pope's Homer result from a constant conflict between the archaic matter of the epic fable and the new criteria of Cartesian-Newtonian rationality, between the semantics of myth and a language whose ideals are those of the logic of the Enlightenment.

Augustan verse will not really resolve the contradiction. But by virtue of its clarity, concision and supple flow, the heroic couplet prepares the ripening of modern prose (this interaction is already manifest in Dryden). In regard to Homeric translations, this development is, throughout the nineteenth century, shadowed, as it were, by nostalgia for a lost poetic rhetoric and for the sonority of the Authorized Version:

And he lifted the stout helmet and set it on his head, and like a star it shone, the horse-hair crested helmet, and around it waved plumes of gold that Hephaistos had set thick about the crest . . . And terribly he called upon the horses of his sire: 'Xanthos and Bailos, famed children of Podarge, in other sort take heed to bring your charioteer safe back to the Danaan host, when we have done with battle, and leave him not as ye left Patroklos to lie there dead.'

So, with its debt to Chapman's distant find, 'terribly', the 1892

Lang, Leaf and Myers, life-preserver to generations of schoolboys eager for a 'trot', and 'Homer' to a wide general readership in the Victorian era and early twentieth century. But in recent decades, British and American poet-translators insist on the advantages of verse-forms, particularly under the impact of the scholarly discovery of Homer's oral and formulaic fabric. There is in these modern versions both a repudiation of prose – E. V. Rieu's publishing-triumph being implicitly or explicitly the 'target of rejection' – and an attempt at loyalty to the strangeness, to the remoteness of the Greek original:

> Then lifting his rugged helmet
> he set it down on his brows, and the horse-hair crest
> shone like a star and the waving golden plumes shook
> that Hephaestus drove in bristling thick along its ridge.
> And brilliant Achilles tested himself in all his gear,
> Achilles spun on his heels to see if it fit tightly . . .
> 'Roan Beauty and Charger, illustrious foals of Light-foot!
> Try harder, do better this time – bring your charioteer
> back home alive to his waiting Argive comrades
> once we're through with fighting. Don't leave Achilles
> there on the battlefield as you left Patroclus – dead!'

The speech-patterns of informal prose are audible in the relaxed verse (too much so in the clotted line on Hephaistos). Those 'ands', on which the narrative pulse depends, tell of the King James Bible, but also of Hemingway. Elsewhere in this episode, Robert Fagles has Achilles testing whether or not his heroic limbs 'ran free' in his new armour, where 'running free' helps define his method as translator. 'Gear' is American in flavour; Roan Beauty and Charger even more so. The bristling panoply worn in American football and the Kentucky stud-farms are close to hand. None the less, what lies in back of that 'spun on his heels' and the verb 'cinch' which Fagles uses when he describes Automedon's preparations of the horses for combat, is not only adherence to Homer: it is Logue's brio in this tempestuous finale to Book XIX.

The radioactive tracer which these successive versions allow us to

follow lights up not only the history of the English languages and
their interrelations. It also tells of the reciprocities 'in motion' as
between different translators and readers of Homer. Each translator
competes more or less openly with the great family of his predeces-
sors and contemporaries. Respectfully, polemically, mimetically or
not, he 'takes on' both Homer and the British or American 'Homers'
already in the field. He may do so in a spirit of indebtedness: T. E.
Lawrence using Palmer. In salutation: Fagles in respect of Fitzgerald.
Often the connection is corrective and agonistic: Cowper announces
his quarrel with what he takes to be the unjustified ornateness and
ponderous archaeology of Pope. Recent American poet-translators
articulate their critique of Lattimore's didacticism, of what they
judge to be the plodding academicism of his verse. E. V. Rieu
provokes the riposte of all those translators who believe that prose,
however fluent or robust, betrays the very essence of the *Iliad* and
Odyssey.

The interactions are always triangular: if the two epics form the
apex, the base and internal spaces are those of other translations –
even into other languages (Pope looks to the French precedent).
These spaces reflect and, in turn, generate the image we have not
only of Homer and the Homeric world, but also of the climate of
culture and taste in which the translations were commissioned,
published and read. Thus the Stuart Homer – cf. Ogilby's elaborate
biography of the blind bard! – is not that of Chapman and not, yet,
that of Dryden and Pope. Victorian and Edwardian versions docu-
ment British sentiments at the time, in reference to warfare, to
masculine bonds, to colonialism and the mastered sea. A cluster of
translations was 'set in motion' by Schliemann's spectacular excava-
tions at Troy and Mycenae. For a spell, Milman Parry's revolution-
ary demonstration of the formulaic conventions of oral epics
dominated the practice of translation. Now a certain reaction and
emphasis on Homer's innovative powers and operative freedom
have set in. But current 'Homers' all come after Moses Finley's re-
valuation of the socio-economic structures of the Homeric, pre-
Mycenaean background.

Augustan representations of political, social and psychological experience are, therefore, as crucial to Pope's Homer as the Vietnam-war aura is to Robert Lowell's selection from the *Iliad* or late twentieth-century ethnic, populist pluralism is to Walcott's *Omeros*. Compare Pope's Nestor, so evidently construed out of a characteristic eighteenth-century reverence for and satire on old age, with the figure of the gin-sodden sahib and garrulous expatriate in Walcott. Homeric Nestor moves behind both, but his masks are protean.

Such shifts in perspective determine the fascinating pendulum-swing in the relative placement of the two epics in their Anglo-American lives. For Pope and his forerunners, the *Iliad* stands supreme. It remains not only the unmatched font of the Western poetic imagination and the enduring model of sublimity. It is also a lasting manual of statecraft, of the arts of persuasion and of war. The *Odyssey* is felt to be an inspired offshoot, a later redaction, tainted with Mediterranean folklore and patches of pathos in which even early exegetes and translators intuit an almost 'feminine' fibre. Viewed through Virgil, the *Odyssey* often figures in neoclassical estimates as the begetter of the *Aeneid*, itself a sovereign text but not of the primal stature of the *Iliad*. As literary modes grow more introspective, as perceptions come to dwell on psychological motivations and the dramas of privacy, it is the *Odyssey* which looks pivotal. Here lie the germs of the novel. Read through Dante, it is Odysseus' fatal unrest which absorbs Tennyson. It is Circe, Calypso, the Sirens and patient Penelope who people Pre-Raphaelite and *fin de siècle* images. With Joyce's *Ulysses*, as Borges proclaims, time is reversed: Homer now comes after Joyce. Yet the experience of the Second World War produces a counter-current. The proud cities set ablaze, the chivalric heroism of the fighter-pilot or commando, restore Hector and Troy to felt immediacy. The sufferings of civilians at the bloody hands of their captors make of Hecuba and Andromache emblems all too familiar. English and American poet-dramatists turn back to 'the Trojan women' as do Hauptmann and Sartre on the Continent. Today, I would guess, the two epics are in active equilibrium of repute, though it may be that late twentieth-century moods are more at home in the subtle variousness and questionings of the *Odyssey*.

*

I believe our *Iliad* to be the product of an editorial recension of genius, of a wonderfully formative act of combination, selection and editing of the voluminous oral material. This recension would coincide with the new techniques of writing and of the preparation of papyrus or hides in quantities sufficient for so extensive an inscription. I take the editor of genius (or one of the editors, somewhat as in the case of the Authorized Version) to have been the *author* of the *Odyssey*. In older age, perhaps, and at some ironic distance. Though the motif is adumbrated in Achilles' complaint to Thetis in the *Iliad*, the flat declaration by Achilles in the Underworld of the *Odyssey* that he would choose a life even in abject servitude over one of heroic brevity, puts in drastic doubt the entire world-image of the earlier epic. And it seems to me that only some such relationship between our two texts, between compilation or redaction and composition, could have generated the sheer marvel of the moment in Book VIII of the *Odyssey* in which Odysseus, incognito, hears the minstrel Demodokos singing tales of Troy and of Odysseus' role therein.

The craft, the social functions of the several minstrels who appear in the *Iliad* and the *Odyssey* take us back to the beginnings of Western literature and, perhaps, music. The montage-effect, the mirroring inward in this Demodokos-episode (as in Don Giovanni's audition of a piece out of *Figaro* during his last supper!) are 'modern' and, indeed, 'post-modern'. The hybrid arc of Walcott's conception spans inception and modernity:

> ... A hot street led to the beach
> past the small shops and the clubs and a pharmacy
> in whose angling shade, his khaki dog on a leash,
>
> the blind man sat on his crate after the pirogues
> set out, muttering the dark language of the blind,
> gnarled hands on his stick, his ears as sharp as the dog's.
>
> Sometimes he would sing and the scraps blew on the wind
> when her beads rubbed their rosary. Old St. Omere.
> He claimed he'd sailed round the world. 'Monsieur Seven Seas'

> they christened him, from a cod–liver–oil label
> with its wriggling swordfish. But his words were not clear.
> They were Greek to her. Or old African babble.

Later, in the spirit of Borges's anti-chronology, the blind singer of Homeric songs hails:

>   . . . Anna Livia!
> Muse of our age's Omeros, undimmed Master
> and true tenor of the place! . . .

Who

> from the Martello brought one-eyed Ulysses
> to the copper-bright strand, watching the mail-packet
> butting past the Head, its wake glittering like keys

where that 'wake' again celebrates Joyce and those 'keys' adduce Joyce–Homer–Omeros' 'tenor' and the sung structure of the epic saga.

Mark the displacements of identity, the 'deconstructive' tactics of ghostliness in the Demodokos encounter. The minstrel in Book VIII is himself blind. (The early ascription of blindness to Homer is, I think, a move by the Homeridae, by the guild of the professional singers-reciters of both epics, to conceal from an increasingly sophisticated public the illiteracy of their begetter.) Demodokos cannot see Odysseus, who is 'invisible' through disguise. Who, on arrival at the Phaeacian court, has made of himself *outis*, the 'No one' who, by his act of de-nomination, of un-naming, had escaped from death at the hands of the Cyclops. The minstrel sings of a fierce quarrel between Odysseus and Achilles in the camp before Troy. The *Iliad*, as we have it, recounts no such incident. It might belong to one of the other epics in the Troy cycle. Or, more subtly, this bitter exchange at a banquet, which brings joy to the scheming heart of Agamemnon, might be Demodokos' invention, which is to say, an invention by the author of our *Odyssey*. In which case, the Odysseus of the epic is listening to, is witnessing his own modulation into fiction, into 'non-being', existentiality fading into the glow of timelessness. The mask, the persona in its original sense, is made shadow:

Thus sang the bard, but Ulysses drew his purple mantle over his head and covered his face, for he was ashamed to let the Phaeacians see that he was weeping. When the bard left off singing he wiped the tears from his eyes, uncovered his face, and, taking his cup, made a drink-offering to the gods; but when the Phaeacians pressed Demodocus to sing further, for they delighted in his lays, then Ulysses again drew his mantle over his head and wept bitterly.

(Samuel Butler)

T. E. Lawrence embroiders. His minstrel is 'very famous'. Odysseus 'with two strong hands drew the purple cloak over his head to hide his goodly face. He was ashamed to let the tears well from his deep-set eyes publicly before the Phaeacians.' Demodokos 'pours a libation to the God'. His verses 'are unalloyed delight' to the listening 'chiefs'.

Robert Graves was, *in propria persona*, a warrior and singer of tales:

> Odysseus
> with massive hand drew his rich mantle down
> over his brow, cloaking his face with it,
> to make the Phaiákians miss the secret tears
> that started to his eyes. How skilfully
> he dried them when the song came to a pause!
> threw back his mantle, spilt his gout of wine!
> But soon the minstrel plucked his note once more
> to please Phaiákian lords, who loved the song;
> then in his cloak Odysseus wept again.
> His tears flowed in the mantle unperceived:
> only Alkínoös, at his elbow, saw them,
> and caught the low groan in the man's breathing.

We have here a vignette out of Ossian and romantic 'bardolatry' which Graves deliberately entitles 'The Song of the Harper'. The tune is that of Weber or Berlioz, rather than of the street-singers plucking at a Balkan, Anatolian or North African stringed instrument, as we meet them in most recent anthropological-ethnographic portrayals of Homer. What one misses – even in Robert Fitzgerald – is the haunting intricacy of Odysseus' depersonalization, that 'ultra-modern' tension between the survivance and potential immortality of the hero when he becomes the object of a minstrel's art, and the concomitant eradication of this same hero from actual life. This tension vibrates throughout the *Odyssey* as it looks back to, as it selectively incorporates the *Iliad*. It gives to Odysseus' descent into the Underworld, to his dialogue with the great shades 'burning still' – as Fitzgerald memorably images the ghost of incensed Ajax – their critical ambiguity. I have already referred to Achilles' bitter repudiation of the heroic ideal: 'Do not make light of Death before me, O shining Odysseus. Would that I were on earth a menial, bound to some insubstantial man who must pinch and scrape to keep alive! Life so were better than King of Kings among these dead men who have had their day and died' (T. E. Lawrence). Derek Walcott presses the question even further, to include the poet's own claims and calling:

> There, in her head of ebony,
> there was no real need for the historian's
> remorse, nor for literature's. Why not see Helen
>
> as the sun saw her, with no Homeric shadow,
> swinging her plastic sandals on that beach alone,
> as fresh as the sea-wind? Why make the smoke a door?

Where 'smoke', I take it, signifies sacrifice and shadow, and where that 'door' leads both to Hades and to the West African and Voodoo figurations into which, seemingly without strain, Walcott metamorphoses the Nekya in the *Odyssey*.

To answer Walcott's teasing query – why not see the Helen, Hector, Odysseus, Agamemnon, King Priam in our fields of echo and recognition 'with no Homeric shadow'? We cannot, in fact, do so. No break is visible in the continuing history of translations, adaptations and imitations. The *Iliad* and the *Odyssey* are perennially active in the pulse of the English languages, in the texts and contexts of Anglo-Saxon self-definition. Once more, I ask: Why? Let me put forward one further conjecture.

The *auctoritas* of Shakespeare over the language, over the repertoire of our private and public perceptions and sense of the literary fact, is at once inspiring and despotic. At different times in the history of the English tongues, Shakespeare, to cite Edmund Gosse, threatens 'to suffocate' all who come after him or reduce them to mere echo. By contrast, the linguistic-cultural distance to the Homeric is at once talismanic and liberating. We revert to Homer as, in some ways, an unattainable dawn and model. But we are sufficiently remote and free from him to answer back creatively. We test our own means of narrative, of poetic pathos, of the presentment of the human and natural worlds, against that originating source – but it remains a source whose strangeness, whose indistinct horizons invite our freedom. Twice, in the prodigal course of our theme, the discrimination is drawn between the Homeric touchstone and Shakespearian prepotence. We need to reflect on Pope's 'Homer' in relation to Pope's editing of Shakespeare. We need to listen, even more closely than hitherto, to the play and flicker of analogies and contrasts as between *Ulysses* as a whole and the 'exagminations' of *Hamlet* in the early part of the book.

Moreover, the issue is not one of 'Homeric shadow'. It is, as Christopher Logue instructs us, one of noon-light. Logue does so in a vocabulary which goes back to Chapman – an 'ominous' radiance floods Achilles' heart – and which moves forward to audacities no previous translator had enlisted:

> The chariot's basket dips. The whip
>   fires in between the horses' ears,
>   and as in dreams or at Cape Kennedy they rise,
>   slowly it seems, their chests like royals, yet,
>   behind them in a double plume the sand curls up,
>   a yellow canopy,
>   is barely dented by their flying hooves,

> and wheels that barely touch the world,
> and the wind slams shut behind them.

Achilles' helmet is 'a welded cortex':

> Though it is noon, the helmet screams against the light;
> Scratches the eye; so violent it can be seen
> Across three thousand years.

Not only seen, I would say, but *heard*. As can be heard the swallow-cry twang of the great bow as Odysseus strings it for vengeance. Or the sudden silence of the old gaffers on the battlements of Troy, struck dumb by the beauty of passing Helen. Or the enigmatic song of the Sirens, as it hums through Western literature from Dante and Milton to Donne, from Donne to Rilke and Kafka. Each translator in turn has his 'eyes scratched' and blood stopped by the violence of that light 'across three thousand years', by that first and unsurpassed noon. But then, was not Homer blind?

This anthology is a *selection* from six and one half centuries of material. If it includes such evident summits of translation as the 'Homers' of Chapman, Dryden, Pope, Shelley or Logue, it also presents much that is of mainly historical or experimental value, which tells of the experience of past and present in Anglo-Saxon political, social and literary feeling. The contents range from the word-for-word, line-for-line interlinear technique (in which Walter Benjamin saw the secret ideal of all 'Adamic' translation) to distant evocations and inferences of the Homeric as in Auden's 'Shield of Achilles' or Hugo Manning's hints towards Odysseus 'the sea-fox'. I have given examples of Homeric travesty and burlesque, of the Homeric substance in lyric, prose-fiction and even dramatic genres. Appropriately, this harvest concludes with passages from the *Odyssey* specially translated for this volume by a younger American poet.

So much has been left out. Of the abundance of partial translations which cluster around Pope. Of the veritable 'pride' of Homeric versions after Matthew Arnold's famous challenge and critique. I have, regrettably, been unable to include examples of film-scripts based on adventures or heroes out of the *Iliad* and *Odyssey*. Nor has there been place for recent comic-book adaptations. Flaxman's illustrations to Homer exercised almost as much influence on British and American readings as did the translation by Pope or the Homeric *reprises* in Tennyson. More space could have been found for the long tradition of 'Homers for the young', of which Charles Lamb's retelling of the *Odyssey* is an enchanting example. I have not (yet) tracked down certain privately printed fragments of Homer translated, imitated by classically schooled officers on their way to the Dardanelles.

As this Penguin book goes to press, new 'Homers' in English and its planetary variants are appearing or have been announced as forthcoming. As in Odysseus' descent into Hades, the bright shades of the Homeric throng towards one, each with its accent, guise and story to tell. Women translators, who have already turned to Greek lyric poetry and tragedy, may now be at work. One is haunted by Robert Graves's dictum: 'There is one story, and one story only that has proved worth the telling.'

May this selection bring to its readers something of the joy that has gone into its gathering.

George Steiner
Geneva/Cambridge, January 1996

*

Editorial note. Line numbers (where available) of standard editions of English translations or poems are printed at the head of the extract; numbers within square brackets are the line numbers of the standard Greek editions.

Translators' and authors' birth and death dates have been supplied where known.

GEOFFREY CHAUCER (1340?–1400)

This magnificent echo of a distant, indirectly known *Iliad* was probably completed around 1385. Chaucer is adapting Boccaccio's *Il Filostrato*, 'The One Stricken by Love'. He expands his source by close to a third to create this 'litel myn tragedye'. Boccaccio himself adapts Guido delle Colonne's Latin version of Benoît de Sainte Maure's *Roman de Troie*. Cf. A. M. Young, *Troy and Her Legend* (1948) for a survey of the complex background.

Troylus and Criseyde I.134–61 *The story of the war*

The thinges fellen as thei don of werre
Betwixen hem of Troye and Grekes ofte,
For som day boughten they of Troye it derre,
And eft the Grekes founde nothing softe
The folk of Troye; and thus Fortune on lofte
Now up, now down gan hem to whilen bothe
After hire cours, ay whil that thei were wrothe.

But how this town com to destruccion
Ne falleth naught to purpos me to telle,
10 For it were here a long digression
Fro my matere, and yow to long to dwelle.
But the Troian gestes as thei felle,
in Omer, or yn Dares, or in Dite,
Whoso that kan may rede hem as thei write.

But though that Grekes hem of Troye shetten,
And hire cyte bisegede al aboute,
Hire olde usage wolde thei not letten
As for to honoure hire goddes ful devoute;
But aldermost yn honour out of doute,
20   Thei hadde a relyk hight Palladion
That was hire tryst aboven everichon.

And so bifell, whan comen was the tyme
Of Aperil, whan clothed is the mede
With newe grene of lusti ver the pryme,
And swoote smellen floures white and rede,
In sondry wyses shewed, as I rede,
The folk of Troye hire observaunces olde,
Palladiones feste for to holde.

II.176–210 *Hector and Troylus*

'Of Ector nedeth it no more for to telle:
In al this world ther nys a bettre knyght
Than he, that is of worthinesse welle,
And he wel more vertu hath than myght.
This knoweth many a wis and worthi wyght.
The same pris of Troylus I seye –
God help me so, I knowe not swyche tweye.'

'Be God,' quod she, 'of Ector that is soth.
Of Troylus the same thing trowe I;
10   For dredeles, men tellen that he doth
In armes day by day so worthily,
And bereth hym here at hom so gentilly
To every wight, that alle prys hath he
Of hem that me were levest preysed be.'

'Ye sey right soth, ywys,' quod Pandarus,
'For yesterday whoso hadde with hym ben,
He myghte han wondred upon Troylus,
For nevere yet so thikke a swarm of ben
Ne fleygh, as Grekes gonne fro hym flen,
20 And thorugh the feld in every wightes ere
There nas no cry but "Troylus is there!"

'Now here, now ther, he hunted hem so faste,
Ther nas but Grekes blood, and Troylus.
Now hym he hurte, and hym al down he caste;
Ay wher he wente, it was arayed thus:
He was hire deth, and lyf and sheld for us;
That al that day ther dorste noon withstonde,
Whil that he held his blody swerd in honde.

'Therto he is the frendlyeste man
30 Of gret estat that evere I sawh my lyve,
And wher hym lyst, best felawshipe kan
To suche as hym thenketh able for to thryve.'
And with that word tho Pandarus as blyve
He tok his leve and seyde, 'I wol go henne.'
'Nay, blame have I, myn uncle,' quod she thenne.

IV.29–56 *The Trojans suffer heavy losses*

Liggyng yn ost, as I have seyd er this,
The Grekys stronge aboute Troye town,
Byfel that whanne that Phebus shynyng is
Upon the brest of Hercules lyoun,
That Ector with many a bold baroun
Caste on a day with Grekes for to fighte,
As he was woned, to greve hem what he myghte.

Not I how longe or short it was bytwene
This purpos and that day they fighte mente,
10 But on a day, wel armed, bright and shene,
Ector and many a worthi wight out wente,
With spere yn honde and bygge bowes bente,
And in the berd, withouten lenger lette,
Hire fomen in the feld anon hem mette.

The longe day, with speres sharpe ygrounde,
With arwes, dartes, swerdes, maces felle,
They fyghte and bryngen hors and man to grounde,
And with hire axes out the braynes quelle.
But in the laste shour, soth for to telle,
20 The folk of Troye hemselven so mysledden
That with the worse at nyght homward they fledden.

At whiche day was taken Antenor,
Maugre Polydamas or Monesteo,
Santippe, Sarpedon, Polynestor,
Polyte, or eke the Trojian daun Rupheo,
And other lasse folk as Phebuseo;
So that for harm that day the folk of Troye
Dredden to lese a gret part of hire joye.

V.953–94 *Criseyde to the lustful Diomede*

As she that hadde hire herte on Troylus
So faste that there may non it arace,
And strangely she spak and seyde thus,
'O Diomede, I love that ilke place
Ther I was born, and Joves, for his grace,
Delivere it soone of al that doth it care.
God, for thi might, so leve it wel to fare!

'That Grekes wolde hire wrath on Troye wreke,
If that thi myghte. I knowe it wel, ywys.
10   But it shal not bifallen as ye speke.
And God toforn, and ferther over this,
I wot my fader wys and redy is,
And that he me hath bought, as ye me tolde,
So dere; I am the more unto hym holde.

'That Grekes ben of heigh condicion
I wot ek wel; but certeyn, men shal fynde
As worthi folk withinne Troye town,
As konnyng, and as parfit, and as kynde
As ben bitwyxen Orcades and Inde.
20   And that ye koude wel youre lady serve,
I trowe ek wel, hire thank for to deserve.

'But as to speke of love, ywys,' she seyde,
'I hadde a lord, to whom I wedded was,
The whos myn herte al was, til that he deyde;
And other love, as help me here Pallas,
Ther in myn herte nys, ne nevere was.
And that ye ben of noble and heigh kynrede,
I have wel herd it tellen, out of drede.

'And that doth me to han so gret a wonder
30   That ye wol scornen ony womman so.
Ek God wot, love and I ben fer asonder!
I am disposed bet, so mot I go,
Unto my deth to pleyne and maken wo.
What I shal after don, I kan nat seye;
But trewelich, as yet me lyst not pleye.

'Myn herte is now in tribulacion,
And ye in armes bisy day by day.
Hereafter, whan ye wonnen han the town,
Peraunter thanne so it happen may

40   That whan I se that nevere yit I say,
        Than wol I werke that I nevere wroughte.
        This word to yow ynough suffisen oughte.

V.1732–92 *Troylus' grief and the envoi of the poem*

        What shulde I seyen? I hate, ywys, Criseyde,
        And God wot I wol hate hire everemore.
        And that thow me bysoughtest don of yore,
        Havynge unto myn honour ne my reste
        Right no reward, I dede al that the leste.

        'If I dede ought that myghte lyken the,
        It is me lef; and of this treson now,
        God wot that it a sorwe is unto me.
        And dredles, for hertes ese of yow,
10   Right fayn wolde I amende it, wist I how.
        And fro this world almyghti God I preye
        Delyvere hire soon – I kan no more seye.'

        Gret was the sorwe and pleynte of Troylus,
        But forth hire cours Fortune ay gan to holde:
        Criseyde loveth the sone of Tydeus,
        And Troylus mot wepe in cares colde.
        Swich is this world, whoso it kan biholde.
        In ech estat is litel hertes reste.
        God leve us for to take it for the beste!

20   In many cruwel batayle out of drede
        Of Troylus, this ilke noble knyght,
        As men may in these olde bokes rede,
        Was sen his knyghthod and his grete myght.
        And dredles, his yre, day and nyght,
        Ful cruwely the Grekes ay aboughte;
        And alwey most this Diomede he soughte.

And ofte tyme I fynde that they mette
With blody strokes and with wordes grete,
Assayinge how hire speres weren whette;
30   And God it wot, with many a cruwel hete
Gan Troylus upon his helm to bete.
But natheles, Fortune it nought ne wolde
Of others hond that eyther deyen sholde.

And yf I hadde ytaken for to writen
The armes of this ilke worthi man,
Than wolde ich of his batayles enditen,
But for that I to writen first bygan
Of his love, I have seyd as I kan –
His worthi dedes, whoso list hem here,
40   Red Dares, he kan telle hem alle yfere –

Bysechyng every lady bryght of hewe
And every gentil womman, what she be,
That al be that Criseyde was untrewe,
That for that gylt she be nat wroth with me –
Ye may hire gilte in other bokes se;
And gladlyer I wol write, yf yow leste,
Penelopees trouthe and goode Alceste.

Ne I sey not this alonly for these men,
But most for wommen that bytraysed be
50   Thorugh false folk – God yeve hem sorwe, amen! –
That with hire grete wit and subtilte
Bytrayse yow. And this commeveth me
To speke, and yn effect yow alle I preye,
Beth war of men, and herkneth what I seye.

Go litel bok, go litel myn tragedye,
Ther God thi makere yet, er that he dye,
So sende myght to make yn som comedye.
But litel bok, no makyng thow n'envye,

But subgit be to alle poesye,
60   And kys the steppes where as thow seest pace
Virgile, Ovyde, Omer, Lukan, and Stace.   (c.1385)

ROBERT HENRYSON (c.1425–c.1506)

Two manuscripts exist of this poem and a sixteenth-century version appended to a fifteenth-century copy of Chaucer's *Troilus*. Some scholars assign our poem to the 1460s or 70s.

Follows closely on Chaucer: Diomede the seducer, Troilus the courtly lover. But the doom of Cresseid modulates into a bleak moralism. Both poets refer to their texts as 'tragedies'. For Henryson there is the fruit of self-knowledge. The doom of Troy and that of Cresseid are finely conjoined.

'The Testament of Cresseid', 452–602

'O Ladyis fair of Troy and Grece, attend
My miserie, quhilk nane may comprehend.
My frivoll Fortoun, my Infelicitie:
My greit mischeif quhilk na man can amend.
Be war in tyme, approchis neir the end,
And in your mynd ane mirrour mak of me:
As I am now, peradventure that ye
For all your micht may cum to that same end,
Or ellis war, gif ony war may be.

10   'Nocht is your fairnes bot ane faiding flour,
Nocht is your famous laud and hie honour
Bot wind Inflat in uther mennis eiris.
Your roising reid to rotting sall retour:
Exempill mak of me in your Memour,

Quhilk of sic thingis wofull witnes beiris,
All Welth in Eird, away as Wind it weiris.
Be war thairfoir, approchis neir the hour:
Fortoun is fikkill, quhen scho beginnis & steiris.'

Thus chydand with hir drerie destenye,
20   Weiping, scho woik the nicht fra end to end.
Bot all in vane; hir dule, hir cairfull cry
Micht not remeid, nor yit hir murning mend.
And Lipper Lady rais and till hir wend,
And said: 'quhy spurnis thow aganis the Wall,
To sla thy self, and mend nathing at all?

'Sen thy weiping dowbillis bot thy wo,
I counsall the mak vertew of ane neid –
To leir to clap thy clapper to and fro,
And [leve] efter the law of lipper leid.'
30   Thair was na buit, bot furth with thame scho yeid
Fra place to place, quhill cauld and hounger sair
Compellit hir to be ane rank beggair.

That samin tyme of Troy the garnisoun,
Quhilk had to chiftane worthie Troylus,
Throw jeopardie of weir had strikken doun
Knichtis of Grece in number [mervellous;]
With greit tryumphe and laude victorious
Agane to Troy [richt] royallie thay raid
The way quhair Cresseid with the lipper baid.

40   Seing that companie, thai come all with ane stevin;
Thay gaif ane cry and schuik coppis gude speid;
Said: 'Worthie lordis, for Goddis lufe of hevin,
To us lipper part of your almous-deid!'
Than to thair cry nobill Troylus tuik heid;
Having pietie, neir by the place can pas
Quhair Cresseid sat, not witting quhat scho was.

Than upon him scho kest up baith hir ene –
And with ane blenk it come into his thocht
That he sumtime hir face befoir had sene.
50   Bot scho was in sic plye he knew hir nocht;
Yit than hir luik into his mynd it brocht
The sweit visage and amorous blenking
Of fair Cresseid, sumtyme his awin darling.

Na wonder was suppois in mynd that he
Tuik hit figure sa sone – and lo now quhy:
The idole of ane thing in cace may be
Sa deip imprentit in the fantasy
That it deludis the wittis outwardly,
And sa appeiris in forme and lyke estait
60   Within the mynd as it was figurait.

Ane spark of lufe than till his hart culd spring
And kendlit all his bodie in ane fyre:
With hait fevir ane sweit and trimbling
Him tuik quhill he was reddie to expyre;
To beir his scheild his breist began to tyre;
Within ane quhyle he changit mony hew,
And nevertheles not ane ane-uther knew.

For knichtlie pietie and memoriall
Of fair Cresseid, ane gyrdill can he tak,
70   [Ane purs of gold, and mony gay jowall,]
And in the skirt of Cresseid doun can swak;
Than raid away and not ane word [he] spak,
Pensive in hart, quhill he come to the toun,
And for greit cair oftsyis almaist fell doun.

The lipper folk to Cresseid than can draw
To se the equall distributioun
Of the almous; bot quhen the gold thay saw,
Ilk ane to uther prevelie can roun,

And said: 'Yone lord hes mair affectioun,
80 How ever it be, unto yone lazarous
Than to us all: we knaw be his almous.'

'Quhat lord is yone,' quod scho, '– have ye na feill –
Hes done to us so greit humanitie?'
'Yes,' quod a lipper man, 'I knaw him weill;
Schir Troylus it is, gentill and fre.'
Quhen Cresseid understude that it was he,
Stiffer than steill thair stert ane bitter stound
Throwout hir hart, and fell doun to the ground,

Quhen scho ovircome, with siching sair and sad,
90 With mony cairfull cry and cald: 'Ochane!
Now is my breist with stormie stoundis stad;
Wrappit in wo, ane wretch full will of wane!'
Than swounit scho oft or scho culd refrane,
And ever in hir swouning cryit scho thus:
'O fals Cresseid and trew knicht Troylus!

'Thy lufe, thy lawtie and thy gentilnes
I countit small in my prosperitie,
Sa elevait I was in wantones
And clam upon the fickill quheill sa hie.
100 All faith and lufe I promissit to the
Was in the self fickill and frivolous:
O fals Cresseid and trew knicht Troilus!

'For lufe of me thow keipt gude continence,
Honest and chaist in conversatioun.
Of all wemen protectour and defence
Thou was, and helpit thair opinioun.
My mynd in fleschelie foull affectioun
Was inclynit to lustis lecherous:
Fy, fals Cresseid! O trew knicht Troylus!

110 'Lovers be war and tak gude heid about
Quhome that ye lufe, for quhome ye suffer paine:
I lat yow wit thair is richt few thairout
Quhome ye may traist to have trew lufe agane –
Preif quhen ye will, your labour is in vaine.
Thairfoir I reid ye tak thame as ye find,
For thay ar sad as widdercock in wind.

'Becaus I knaw the greit unstabilnes,
Brukkill as glas, into myself, I say,
Traisting in uther als greit unfaithfulnes –
120 Als unconstant and als untrew of fay –
Thocht sum be trew, I wait richt few ar thay:
Quha findis treuth lat him his lady ruse!
Nane but myself as now I will accuse.'

Quhen this was said, with paper scho sat doun,
And on this maneir maid hir testament:
'Heir I beteiche my corps and carioun
With wormis and with taidis to be rent:
My cop and clapper and myne ornament,
And all my gold, the lipper folk sall have
130 Quhen I am deid, to burie me in grave.

'This royall ring set with this rubie reid
Quhilk Troylus in drowrie to me send,
To him agane I leif it quhen I am deid
To mak my cairfull deid unto him kend:
Thus I conclude schortlie, and mak ane end:
My spreit I leif to Diane quhair scho dwellis,
To walk with hir in waist woddis and wellis.

'O Diomeid, thou hes baith broche and belt
Quhilk Troylus gave me in takning
140 Of his trew lufe!' And with that word scho swelt.
And sone ane lipper man tuik of the ring,

Syne buryit hir withouttin tarying.
To Troylus furthwith the ring he bair
And of Cresseid the deith he can declair.

Quhen he had hard hir greit infirmitie,
Hir legacie and lamentatioun,
And how scho endit in sic povertie,
He swelt for wo and fell doun in ane swoun;
For greit sorrow his hart to brist was boun:
150 Siching full sadlie said: 'I can no moir –
Scho was untrew and wo is me thairfoir.'   (1460s/70s)

JOHN LYDGATE (?1370–1452)

This text was composed between 1412 and 1420. It is a vastly
enlarged version, in decasyllabic couplets, of Guido delle Colonne's
Historia Destructionis Troiae of *c.*1287. We know of two early
printed editions of Lydgate in 1513 and 1555. Caxton incorporates
Lydgate in his famous *Recuyell of the Historyes of Troye*, printed in
Bruges in 1475. He provides Prologues and Epilogues.

The Troy Book, Prologue, 145–75 Caxton states the high
calling of the writer

Til after sone Appollo lyst nat tarie
To take soiour in the Sagittarie.
Whyche tyme I gan the prolog to beholde   *Then, in 1413,*
Of Troye Boke, I-made be dayes olde,   *I lookt at the*
Wher was remembrid, of auctours vs be-forn,   *Prolog of the*
Of the dede the verreie trewe corn,   *Troy Book*
So as it fil seuerid from the chaf;
For in her honde they hilde for a staf   *written by truthful men*

The trouthe only, whyche thei han compyled
10   Vn-to this fyn, that we wer nat begyled
Of necligence thoruȝ forȝetilnesse.
The whiche serpent of age by processe
Engendred is fersly vs tassaille,
Of the trouth to make vs for to faille;
For ner[e] writers, al wer out of mynde,   *Without writers*
Nat story only, but of nature and kynde
The trewe knowyng schulde haue gon to wrak,   *knowledge would*
And from science oure wittes put a-bak,   *have died:*
Ne hadde oure elderis cerched out and souȝt
20   The sothefast pyth, to ympe it in oure thouȝt,
Of thinges passed, for-dirked of her hewe,
But thoruȝ writyng þei be refresched newe,   *they enable us*
Of oure auncetrys left to vs by-hynde;
To make a merour only to oure mynde,
To seen eche thing trewly as it was,   *to see things*
More bryȝt and clere þan in any glas.   *as they really*
For ner her writyng nowe memorial,   *were,*
Dethe with his swerde schulde haue slay[e]n al,   *and stop Death*
And y-dymmed with his sodeyn schoures   *dimming the*
30·   The gret[e] prowes of thise conquerouris,   *brightness of*
And dirk[ed] eke the briȝtnesse of her fame.   *heroes' fame.*

II.7852-75 *A woman is the cause of all this war*

How liȝt þe cause, for whiche so many man   *And the cause*
Hath lost his lif in meschef pitously;   *of the deaths of*
And ȝit no man can be war þer-by –   *so many men*
Almost for nouȝt was þis strif be-gonne: *was almost nothing,*
And who list loke, þei han no þing wonne
But only deth, allas, þe harde stounde!
So many knyȝt cauȝt his deþes wounde
Wiþ-oute recure or any remedie.
And for a woman, ȝif I schal nat lye,   *just a woman!*

10 Gan al þis strif, it was þe more pite,
 þat so gret meschef or aduersite
 Of mortal slauȝter euer schulde tyde!
 Bet had ben to haue set a-side   *They should*
 Swiche quarellis, dere I-now amyte,   *have dropt*
 To haue lete passid or þe vengaunce bite: *their quarrel.*
 For wisdam wer to cast a-forn and se
 ȝif swiche sclaundris myȝt eschewed be
 Or þe venym gonne for to ripe;
 For þow[ȝ] þat men with hornys blowe & pipe
20 Whan an hous is fired in his hete,   *But when once*
 Of þe sparkle to late is to trete,   *a house catches*
 þat causid al: wherfore, at þe gynnyng *fire it's no good*
 þe remedie is put of euery þing,   *bothering about*
 As euery wiȝt may deme in his resoun. *the first spark.*

III.5423–74 *Priam's lament for slain Hector*

 But now, allas! how shal I procede   *How can I tell more*
 In þe story, þat for wo and drede   *of my story,*
 Fele myn hond boþe tremble and quake, *when my hand trembles*
 O worþi Hector, only for þi sake,   *for Hector's sake?*
 Of þi deth I am so loth to write.
 O who shal now help me to endyte,
 Or vn-to whom shal I clepe or calle? –
 Certis to noon of þe mvsis alle,   *No Muse will help me.*
 þat by accorde singen euer in on,
10 Vp-on Pernaso, besiden Elycon,
 So angelik in her armonye,
 þat tonge is noon þat may specefie   *Their angelic harmony fits*
 þe grete swetnes of her goodly song;
 For no discorde is founden hem among,
 In her mvsik þei bene entvnyd so –
 It syt hem nouȝt for to help in wo,   *not a theme of woe.*

Nor with maters þat be with mournynge shent,
As tragedies, al to-tore and rent,
In compleynynge pitously in rage
20 In þe theatre, with a ded visage –
To hem, allas! I clepe dar nor crye, *I dare not appeal*
My troubled penne of grace for to guye – *to my Muse.*
Nouþer to Clyo nor Callyope,
But to Allecto and Thesyphone, *I turn to the dire Furies,*
And Megera, þat euere doth compleine,
As þei þat lyve euere in wo and peyne
Eternally, and in turment dwelle
With Cerberus, depe doun in helle, *who dwell in Hell.*
Whom I mote praie to be gracious
30 To my mater, whiche is so furious.
For to a whiȝt þat is compleynynge,
A drery fere is riȝt wel sittynge;
And to a mater, meynt with hevynes,
Acordeth wel a chere of drerynes
To ben allyed, as by vnyte.
Wherefore, helpe now, þou woful Nyobe, *Help me, Niobe,*
Som drery ter, in al þi pitous peyne,
In-to my penne dolfully to reyne;
And helpe also, þou cruel Yxioun, *Ixion,*
40 And Belydes, þat doth þe boket gon;
And with þi stoon helpe þou, ȝeȝiphus, *Sisyphus*
And in þi riuer, helpe eke Tantalus, *and Tantalus,*
þat for hunger haste so huge pyne,
þis woful pleint helpe me for to fyne, *to pen my plaint for the*
Me to forthre doth ȝoure besynes.
For now þe stok and rote of worþines,
Of knyȝthod grounde, of manhod sours & wel, *Source of*
þat to-forn alle bare a-weie þe belle *Manhood,*
Of dorynge do, þis flour of hiȝe prowes – *Hector!*
50 And was exaumple also of gentilnes,
þat neuere koude don amys nor seie,
Allas, Hector, allas! why shuldestou deie!

IV.6513–35 *Menelaus rescues Helena in burning Troy*

Oute of þe temple longinge to Minerue,
From Grekis swerd her lyues to conserue.
And Menelay toke þe quene Eleyne   *Menelaus takes Helen.*
In-to his garde, for whom so grete a peyne
Bood in his hert many day to-forn,
By whom, allas! þe cite is now lorn.
And Grekes ay were besy in her Ire   *The Greeks slay, burn,*
To sleen and kylle, & cruelly to fire
On euery side and to bete doun
10 Palais & house & walles of þe toun:
þei spare nouȝt, for al goth to þe fire,   *and spare nothing.*
So feruent hate brent in her desire
Of olde enuie auenged for to be,
þat þei ne lefte with-Inne þe cite
No þing vnbrent; and also Ylyoun   *Ilion is overthrown.*
Was in þis rage turned vp-so-doun.
þer maked wern noon excepciouns,
Only outake þe possessiouns   *But the goods of*
Of Anthenor (euele mote he fare)   *Antenor and their*
                                          friends are preserved.
20 And Eneas, whom þe Grekis spare,
As þei to hem were bounde by her oþe.
And þus þe Grekis, furious & wroþe,
Han *al* þat day robbed and y-brent . . .

IV.7058–108 *Lydgate's magnificent comparison between the lamentation of the Hebrew Prophets and that owed to fallen Troy*

Certis, I trowe nat olde Ieremye,   *Neither Jeremiah,*
þat so be-wepte þe captiuite
Of þilke noble rial chefe cite
Ierusalem, and his destruccioun,
With al þe hole transmygracioun

Of þe Iewes; nor þou Eȝechiel,   *Ezekiel,*
þat were þat tyme þat þe meschef fel
Vn-to þe kyng y-called Sedechie,
In Ba[b]ilon, & for þi prophesie
10 With stonys were cruelly y-slawe;
Nor he þat was departed with a sawe, –
ȝe boþe two, þat koude so compleyne, –
Nor Danyel þat felt so gret[e] peyne   *nor Daniel,*
For þe kynges transmutacioun
In-to a beste, til þoruȝ þe orisoun
Of Daniel he restored was
To mynde ageyn, & ete no more no gras: –
ȝet verrailly, þouȝ ȝe alle þre
With ȝoure weping had alive be   *had they been alive,*
20 And present eke at þe destruccioun
Of þis noble worþi royal toun,
To haue beweiled þe meschef & þe wo,
And þe slauȝter at þe sege do
On ouþer party in ful cruel wyse, –
Alle ȝoure teris myȝt[e] nat suffise   *could have mournd*
To haue be-wepte her sorwes euerychon,   *enuf the sorrows*
Be tresoun wrouȝt, as wel as be her foon!   *of Troy.*
Here-of no more; for it may nat availle.
But like as he þat gynneth for to saille
30 Ageyn þe wynde, whan þe mast doþ rive,
Riȝt so it were but in veyn to strive
Ageyn þe fate, bitterer panne galle,
By hiȝe vengaunce vp-on Troye falle,
Nor to presvme her furies, sharpe whette,
Ceriously in þis boke to sette:
So gret a þing I dar not vndirtake,   *I can't do it.*
But evene here a pitous ende I make   *So here I end the*
Of þe sege, after my symplesse;   *Siege of Troy,*
And þouȝ my stile, blottid *with* rudenes,
40 As of metre, be rusty and vnfiled,
þis ferþe boke, þat I haue compiled

    With humble hond, of her þat doth me quake,

    Vn-to ȝoure grace holy I betake,   *and commit it to*

    Of ȝoure merci no þing in dispeir,   *your mercy.*

    So as I can, makyng my repeir   *I'll now tell you*

    To þe Grekis, & no lenger dwelle,   *the adventures of*

    Her aventures of þe se to telle,   *the Greeks in*

    In þer resort home to her contre;   *their journey home,*

    And how [þat] þei þere received be, –

50   Only of support, so ȝe not dispise, –

    þe fi[f]the boke shortly shal deuise.   *in my 5th Book.*

Epilogue to Book III *Caxton's summary of the Homeric tradition*

Thus ende I this book whyche I haue translated after myn Auctor as nyghe as god hath gyuen me connyng to whom be gyuen the laude ⁊ preysyng / And for as moche as in the wrytyng of the same my penne is worn / myn hande wery ⁊ not stedfast myn eyen dimmed with ouermoche lokyng on the whit paper / and my corage not so prone and redy to laboure as hit hath ben / and that age crepeth on me dayly and febleth all the bodye / and also be cause I haue promysid to dyuerce gentilmen and to my frendes to adresse to hem as hastely as I myght this sayd book / Therefore I haue practysed ⁊ learned at my grete charge and dispense to ordeyne this said book in prynte after the maner ⁊ forme as ye may here see / and is not wreton with penne and ynke as other bokes ben / to thende that euery man may haue them attones / ffor all the bookes of this storye named the recule of the historyes of troyes thus empryntid as ye here see were begonne in oon day / and also fynyshid in oon day / whiche book I haue presented to my sayd redoubtid lady as a fore is sayd. And she hath well acceptid hit / and largely rewarded me / wherfore I beseche almyghty god to rewarde her euerlastyng blisse after this lyf. Prayng her said grace and all them that shall rede this book not to desdaigne the symple and rude werke. nether to replye against the sayyng of the maters towchyd in this book / thauwh hyt acorde not vnto the translacion of other whiche haue wreton hit / ffor dyuerce men haue made dyuerce bookes / whiche in all poyntes acorde not as Dictes. Dares. and Homerus for dictes ⁊ homerus as grekes sayn and wryten fauorably for the grekes / and gyue to them more worship || than to the troians / And Dares wryteth otherwyse than they doo / And also as for the propre names / hit is no wonder that they acorde not / ffor somme oon name in thyse dayes haue dyuerce equyuocacions after the contrees that they dwlle in / but alle acorde in conclusion the general destruccion of that noble cyte of Troye / And the deth of so many noble prynces as kynges dukes Erles barons. knyghtes and comyn peple and the ruyne irreperable of that Cyte that neuer syn was reedefyed whiche may be ensample to all men duryng the world how dredefull and Ieopardous it is to begynne a warre and what hormes. losses. and deth foloweth. Terfore thapostle saith all that is wreton is wreton to our doctryne / whiche doctryne for the comyn wele I beseche god maye be taken in suche place and tyme as shall be most nedefull in encrecyng of peas loue and charyte whyche graunte vs he that suffryd for the same to be crucyfied on the rood tree / And saye we all Amen for charyte. (1412/20)

ARTHUR HALL (1563–1604)

This work is *rarissima*, having appeared in only one edition. But although it is a translation from the French of Hugues Salel, Hall's is indeed the very first English 'Homer'. We have been unable to consult the text directly and borrow a few brief samples from H. G. Wright: *The Life and Works of Arthur Hall of Grantham*. Hall uses a seven-foot line.

Tenne Bookes of the Iliades of Homer I.197–200 [184–7]

To thy Pauillion wil I send tricke Brysida to bring
Thy best beloued, that al men knowe how pusuanter a King
I am than thou, and that henceforth none be so hardie bolde
To put vp head to matche with me, by whom I be controlde.

I.560–62 [565–7]

Go sit you downe, and talke no more so fonde and foolishly,
Least moued I, with my fistes I giue you banging lawes,
And in such sort, as no God here can saue you from my
       clawes.

V.307–10 [284–5]

                    O Diomede the deed now is it done,
Wherby I justly judge my selfe the happiest vnder sunne,
This blow so deepe it pierced hath thy side, and pretie poke
Of guts, as die of force thou must, receiuing thus the stroke.

V.525–8 [475–7]

I see not one, no, no, like Dogges, whom Lion seekes to teare
They leaue the here in daunger great, and runne away for
       feare.
They leaue not thee, but vs also, who here are come not
       strest
In thys quarrell to spend our bloud, and thro haue done our
       best.

WILLIAM SHAKESPEARE
(1564–1616)

Scholars tend to assign the composition to late 1602. The question of Shakespeare's sources remains vexed. Did he draw on a Latin and/or French 'Homer'? He drew on his beloved Ovid. Possibly on Chaucer and Lydgate. Assuredly on Henryson. Some scholars take into (improbable) account eight possible translations: five in Latin verse or prose, two in French and Arthur Hall's translation from the French of Books I–X of the *Iliad*. The real question is this: did or did not Shakespeare know, use the 1598 version of *Seauen Bookes of the Iliades* by Chapman (the 'rival poet' of the Sonnets)? Shakespeare's dramatization of the Greek council of war, of Hector's challenge, of the encounter between Ajax and Hector *do* seem indebted to Chapman. Certain possibly pertinent motifs not yet available in Chapman are omitted by Shakespeare. But even close verbal study of the two texts leaves the matter equivocal. And Shakespeare's overwhelming 'invention' of the episode of the killing of Hector shows his characteristic intuitions beyond any certain source or precedent.

Troilus and Cressida , First Quarto *The Prologue, 1–31*

In Troy there lyes the Scene: From Iles of Greece [*The Prologue . . .*
The Princes Orgillous, their high blood chaf'd   *chance of Warre.*]
Have to the Port of Athens sent their shippes
Fraught with the ministers and instruments
Of cruell Warre: Sixty and nine that wore
Their Crownets Regall, from th'Athenian bay
Put forth toward Phrygia, and their vow is made
To ransacke Troy, within whose strong emures
The ravish'd *Helen, Menelaus* Queene,
10   With wanton *Paris* sleepes, and that's the Quarrell.
To *Tenedos* they come,

And the deepe-drawing Barke do there disgorge   *Barkes*
Their warlike frautage: now on Dardan Plaines
The fresh and yet unbruised Greekes do pitch
Their brave Pavillions. *Priams* six-gated City,
Dardan and *Timbria, Helias, Chetas, Trojen,*
And *Antenonidus* with massie Staples   *Antenorides*
And corresponsive and fulfilling Bolts
Stirre up the Sonnes of Troy.   *Sperr up*
20   Now Expectation tickling skittish spirits,
On one and other side, Trojan and Greeke,
Sets all on hazard. And hither am I come,
A Prologue arm'd, but not in confidence
Of Authors pen, or Actors voyce; but suited
In like conditions, as our Argument;
To tell you (faire Beholders) that our Play
Leapes ore the vaunt and firstlings of those broyles,
Beginning in the middle: starting thence away,
To what may be digested in a Play:
30   Like, or finde fault, do as your pleasures are,
Now good, or bad, 'tis but the chance of Warre.

Act II, ii, 101–214 *Cassandra and the Trojan leaders*

Enter Cassandra with her haire about her   (*Enter Cassandra raving.*)
          eares
    CASSANDRA. Cry *Troyans*, cry.
    PRIAM. What noyse? what shreeke is this?
    TROYLUS. 'Tis our mad sister, I do know her voyce.
    CASSANDRA. Cry Troyans.
    HECTOR. It is *Cassandra*.
    CASSANDRA. Cry Troyans cry; lend me ten thousand eyes,
And I will fill them with Propheticke teares.
    HECTOR. Peace sister, peace.
    CASSANDRA. Virgins, and Boyes;   *elders, canst but clamours:*
          mid-age & wrinkled old,

10   Soft infancie, that nothing can but cry,
Adde to my clamour: let us pay betimes
A moity of that masse of moane to come.
Cry Troyans cry, practise your eyes with teares,
Troy must not be, nor goodly Illion stand,
Our fire-brand Brother *Paris* burnes us all.
Cry Troyans cry, a *Helen* and a woe;
Cry, cry, Troy burnes, or else let *Helen* goe.
        [*Exit*]
        HECTOR. Now youthfull *Troylus*, do not these hie strains
Of divination in our Sister, worke
20   Some touches of remorse? Or is your bloud
So madly hot, that no discourse of reason,
Nor feare of bad successe in a bad cause,
Can qualifie the same?
        TROYLUS. Why Brother *Hector*,
We may not thinke the justnesse of each acte
Such, and no other then event doth forme it,
Nor once deject the courage of our mindes;   *mindes*,
Because *Cassandra's* mad, her brainsicke raptures   mad:
Cannot distaste the goodnesse of a quarrell,
30   Which hath our severall Honours all engag'd
To make it gracious. For my private part,
I am no more touch'd, then all *Priams* sonnes,
And Jove forbid there should be done among'st us
Such things as might offend the weakest spleene,
To fight for, and maintaine.
        PARIS. Else might the world convince of levitie,
As well my under-takings as your counsels:
But I attest the gods, your full consent
Gave wings to my propension, and cut off
40   All feares attending on so dire a project.
For what (alas) can these my single armes?
What propugnation is in one mans valour
To stand the push and enmity of those
This quarrell would excite? Yet I protest,

Were I alone to passe the difficulties,
And had as ample power, as I have will,
Paris should ne're retract what he hath done,
Nor faint in the pursuite.
    PRIAM. *Paris*, you speake
50 Like one be-sotted on your sweet delights;
You have the Hony still, but these the Gall,
So to be valiant, is no praise at all.
    PARIS. Sir, I propose not meerely to my selfe,
The pleasures such a beauty brings with it:
But I would have the soyle of her faire Rape
Wip'd off in honourable keeping her.
What Treason were it to the ransack'd Queene,
Disgrace to your great worths, and shame to me,
Now to deliver her possession up
60 On termes of base compulsion? Can it be,
That so degenerate a straine as this,
Should once set footing in your generous bosomes?
There's not the meanest spirit on our partie,
Without a heart to dare, or sword to draw,
When *Helen* is defended: nor none so Noble,
Whose life were ill bestow'd, or death unfam'd,
Where *Helen* is the subject. Then (I say)
Well may we fight for her, whom we know well,
The worlds large spaces cannot paralell.
70   HECTOR. *Paris* and *Troylus*, you have both said well:
And on the cause and question now in hand,
Have gloz'd, but superficially; not much
Unlike young men, whom *Aristotle* thought
Unfit to heare Morall Philosophie.
The Reasons you alledge, do more conduce
To the hot passion of distemp'red blood,
Then to make up a free determination
'Twixt right and wrong: For pleasure, and revenge,
Have eares more deafe then Adders, to the voyce
80 Of any true decision. Nature craves

All dues be rendred to their Owners: now
What neerer debt in all humanity,
Then Wife is to the Husband? If this law
Of Nature be corrupted through affection,
And that great mindes of partiall indulgence,
To their benummed wills resist the same,
There is a Law in each well-ordred Nation,   well-orderd
To curbe those raging appetites that are
Most disobedient and refracturie.
90 If *Helen* then be wife to Sparta's King
(As it is knowne she is) these Morall Lawes
Of Nature, and of Nation, speake alowd   nations,
To have her backe return'd. Thus to persist
In doing wrong, extenuates not wrong,
But makes it much more heavie. *Hectors* opinion
Is this in way of truth: yet nere the lesse,
My spritely brethren, I propend to you
In resolution to keepe *Helen* still;
For 'tis a cause that hath no meane dependance,
100 Upon our joynt and severall dignities.
     TROILUS. Why? there you toucht the life of our designe:
Were it not glory that we more affected,
Then the performance of our heaving spleenes,
I would not wish a drop of *Trojan* blood,
Spent more in her defence. But worthy *Hector*,
She is a theame of honour and renowne,
A spurre to valiant and magnanimous deeds,
Whose present courage may beate downe our foes,
And fame in time to come canonize us.
110 For I presume brave *Hector* would not loose
So rich advantage of a promis'd glory,
As smiles upon the fore-head of this action,
For the wide worlds revenew.
     HECTOR. I am yours,
You valiant off-spring of great *Priamus*,
I have a roisting challenge sent among'st

The dull and factious nobles of the Greekes,
Will strike amazement to their drowsie spirits,
120 I was advertiz'd, their Great generall slept,
Whil'st emulation in the armie crept:
This I presume will wake him.
          [*Exeunt*.]

Act V, viii, 1–22 *The killing of Hector*

   Enter Hector.   (*Scene viii.*
  HECTOR. Most putrified core so faire without: *Another part of*
Thy goodly armour thus hath cost thy life.   *the plains.*)
Now is my daies worke done; Ile take good breath: *take my breth:*
Rest Sword, thou hast thy fill of bloud   (*Puts off his helmet*
     and death.   *and hangs his shield*
   Enter Achilles and his Myrmidons.   *behind him.*)
  ACHILLES. Looke *Hector* how the Sunne begins to set;
How ugly night comes breathing at his heeles,   *heeles:*
Even with the vaile and darking of the Sunne.   *darkning . . . Sunne,*
To close the day up, *Hectors* life is done.
  HECTOR. I am unarm'd, forgoe this vantage Greeke.
10 ACHILLES. Strike fellowes, strike, this is the man I
     seeke.   (*Hector falls.*)
So Illion fall thou: now Troy sinke downe;   *thou next, come Troy*
Here lyes thy heart, thy sinewes, and thy bone.
On *Myrmidons*, cry you all a maine,   *Myrmydons, and cry*
Achilles hath the mighty *Hector* slaine.
   [*Retreat*.]
Harke, a retreat upon our Grecian part.   *a retire upon*
  GREEKE. The Trojan Trumpets sounds   (*One:*) *The Troyans*
     the like my Lord.   *trumpet sound the*
  ACHILLES. The dragon wing of night ore-spreds the earth
And stickler-like the Armies seperates   *separates.*
My halfe supt Sword, that frankly would have fed,
20 Pleas'd with this dainty bed; thus goes to bed.   *dainty baite thus*

Come, tye his body to my horses tayle;
Along the field, I will the Trojan traile.
    [*Exeunt.*]
    Sound Retreat.   [*Sound Retreat. Shout.*]
    [*Shout.*]   (1602)

GEORGE CHAPMAN (*c.*1560–1634)

The extent and depth of Chapman's knowledge of Homeric Greek remain uncertain. But it is with Chapman that Homer enters the language in something of his own voice. At many points, this translation is unsurpassed by virtue of its poetic energy and linguistic resource. Keats's famous salute, to be found later in this volume, is fully justified. As are the positive observations on Chapman in Coleridge, Matthew Arnold and Saintsbury. Chapman defines his ideal in lines 120–42 of 'To the Reader'. His lapidary project – 'With Poesie to open Poesie.' – could be the motto of our entire enterprise.

The text goes through several states between the *Seven Bookes* of 1598 (which seem to have swept Hall from the field) and the completed *Iliads* of 1611. At first the epic is viewed in a moralistic-heroic perspective, centred on the exemplum of Achilles. But Chapman's reading evolves and grows subtler. We can follow an evaluative shift towards Hector and Ulysses. Metrical units are treated syllabically. Gradually, Chapman achieves mastery over the awkward fourteener. At his best, he comes to echo movingly 'Homer, Prince of Poets'.

Homer's Iliads III.153–77 [143–60] *Helen on the ramparts*

Thus went she forth and tooke with her her women most of
    name,
Aethre, Pittheus' lovely birth, and Clymene, whom fame
Hath for her faire eyes memorisd. They reacht the Scaean
    towrs,
Where Priam sat to see the fight with all his Counsellours,
Panthous, Lampus, Clytius and stout Hicetaon,
Thimoetes, wise Antenor and profound Ucalegon –
All grave old men, and souldiers they had bene, but for age
Now left the warres; yet Counsellors they were exceeding
    sage.
And as in well-growne woods, on trees,   *Old men and their weake*
    cold spinie Grashoppers   *utterance most aptly*
10   Sit chirping and send voices out that   *compared to Grashoppers*
    scarce can pierce our eares   *and their singing.*
For softnesse and their weake faint sounds; so (talking on the
    towre)
These Seniors of the people sate, who, when they saw the
    powre
Of beautie in the Queene ascend, even those cold-spirited
    Peeres,
Those wise and almost witherd men,   *Helen's beautie moves*
    found this heate in their yeares   *even the oldest.*
That they were forc't (though whispering) to say: 'What man
    can blame
The Greekes and Troyans to endure, for so admir'd a Dame,
So many miseries, and so long? In her sweet countenance
    shine
Lookes like the Goddesses'. And yet (though never so divine)
Before we boast, unjustly still, of her enforced prise
20   And justly suffer for her sake, with all our progenies,

Labor and ruine, let her go: the profit of our land
Must passe the beautie.' Thus, though these could beare so fit
    a hand
On their affections, yet when all their gravest powers were
    usde
They could not chuse but welcome her, and rather they
    accusde
The gods than beautie.

IV.456–83 [429–56] *Battle is joined, Mars encounters Athene*

The rest went silently away, you could not   *The silence of the*
    heare a voice,   *Greeke fight.*
Nor would have thought in all their breasts they had one in
    their choice –
Their silence uttering their awe of them that them contrould,
Which made ech man keep bright his arms, march, fight still
    where he should.
The Troyans (like a sort of Ewes pend in a   *The Troyans*
    rich man's fold,   *compared to Ewes*
Close at his dore till all be milkt, and never baaing hold,
Hearing the bleating of their lambs) did all their wide host fill
With showts and clamors, nor observ'd one voice, one baaing
    still
But shew'd mixt tongs from many a land of men cald to
    their aid,
10 Rude Mars had th'ordring of their spirits   *Mars for the Troyans,*
    – of Greeks, the learned Maid.   *Pallas for the Greekes.*
But Terror follow'd both the hosts, and   *Discord the sister of Mars.*
    Flight, and furious Strife,   *Virgil the same of Fame.*
The sister and the mate of Mars, that spoile of humane life.
And never is her rage at rest: at first she is but small,
Yet after (but a little fed) she growes so vast and tall

That while her feet move here in earth, her forhead is in
    heaven.
And this was she that made even then both hosts so deadly
    given.
Through every troope she stalkt and stird rough sighes up as
    she went;
But when in one field both the foes her furie did content
And both came under reach of darts, then darts and shields
    opposd
20 To darts and shields, strength answerd strength. Then swords
    and targets closd
With swords and targets, both with pikes; and then did
    tumult rise
Up to her height; then conqueror's boasts mixt with the
    conquerd's cries;
Earth flow'd with blood. And as from hils, raine waters
    headlong fall
That all waies eate huge Ruts which, met in one bed, fill a
    vall
With such a confluence of streames that on the mountaine
    grounds,
Farre off, in frighted shepheards' eares the bustling noise
    rebounds:
So grew their conflicts, and so shew'd their scuffling to the
    eare,
With flight and clamor still commixt, and all effects of feare.

VIII.480–97 [542–65] *Star-like, the Trojans encamp in the night-field*

This speech all Troyans did applaud, who from their traces
    losde
Their sweating horse, which severally with headstals they
    reposde

And fastned by their chariots; when others brought from
    towne
Fat sheepe and oxen instantly, bread, wine, and hewed
    downe
Huge store of wood. The winds transferd into the friendly
    skie
Their supper's savour, to the which they sate delightfully
And spent all night in open field. Fires   *Ignes Troianorum*
    round about them shinde.   *astris similes.*
As when about the silver Moone, when aire is free from winde
And stars shine cleare, to whose sweete beames high prospects
    and the brows
10 Of all steepe hils and pinnacles thrust up themselves for
    showes
And even the lowly vallies joy to glitter in their sight,
When the unmeasur'd firmament bursts to disclose her light
And all the signes in heaven are seene that glad the shepheard's
    hart;
So many fires disclosde their beames, made by the Troyan
    part,
Before the face of Ilion and her bright turrets show'd.
A thousand courts of guard kept fires, and every guard
    allow'd
Fiftie stout men, by whom their horse eate oates and hard
    white corne,
And all did wishfully expect the silver-throned morne.

XI.358–85 [401–33] *Odysseus isolated in battle*

Now was Ulysses desolate: feare made no friend remaine.
He thus spake to his mightie mind: 'What   *Ulysses to himselfe.*
    doth my state sustaine?
If I should flie this ods in feare, that thus comes clustring on,
Twere high dishonour: yet twere worse to be surprised
    alone.

Tis Jove that drives the rest to flight; but that's a faint excuse.
Why do I tempt my mind so much? Pale cowards fight
    refuse:
He that affects renowne in warre must like a rocke be fixt,
Wound or be wounded: valour's truth puts no respect
    betwixt.'
    In this contention with himselfe, in flew the shadie bands
10 Of targateres, who sieg'd him round with mischiefe-filled
    hands.
·As when a crew of gallants watch the wild muse of a Bore,
Their dogs put after in full crie, he rusheth on before,
Whets, with his lather-making jawes, his crooked tuskes for
    blood
And (holding firme his usuall haunts) breakes through the
    deepned wood,
They charging, though his hote approch be never so abhord:
So to assaile the Jove-lov'd Greeke, the Ilians did accord
And he made through them: first he hurt, upon his shoulder
    blade,
Deiops, a blamelesse man at armes, then sent to endlesse
    shade
Thoon and Ennomus, and strooke the strong Chersidamas,
20 As from his chariot he leapt downe, beneath his targe of
    brasse,
Who fell and crawld upon the earth with his sustaining
    palmes
And left the fight. Nor yet his lance left dealing Martiall almes,
But Socus' brother by both sides, yong Charops, did
    impresse.
Then Princely Socus to his aide made brotherly accesse
And (coming neare) spake in his charge: 'O great Laertes'
    sonne,
Insatiate in slie stratagems and labours never done,
This houre or thou shalt boast to kill the two Hippasides
And prize their armes, or fall thy selfe in my resolv'd accesse.'

XVI.143–52 [156–66] *The Myrmidons pour into the fray*

And when ye see (upon a *A simile most lively*
mountaine bred) *expressive.*
A den of Wolves (about whose hearts unmeasur'd strengths
are fed)
New come from currie of a Stagge, their jawes all blood-
besmeard,
And when from some blacke water-fount they altogether
herd,
There having plentifully lapt with thin and thrust-out tongs
The top and clearest of the spring, go belching from their
lungs
The clotterd gore, looke dreadfully and entertaine no dread,
Their bellies gaunt, all taken up with being so rawly fed:
Then say that such in strength and looke were great Achilles'
men
10   Now orderd for the dreadfull fight

XVI.762–93 [829–61] *The dialogue between Hector and the dying Patroclus*

And thus his great Divorcer brav'd: 'Patroclus, *Hector's insultation*
thy conceit *over Patroclus, being*
Gave thee th' eversion of our Troy, and to thy *wounded under him.*
fleete a freight
Of Troyan Ladies, their free lives put all in bands by thee:
But (too much priser of thy selfe) all these are propt by me.
For these have my horse stretcht their hoofes to this so long a
warre,
And I (farre best of Troy in armes) keepe off from Troy as
farre –

Even to the last beame of my life – their necessary day.

And here (in place of us and ours) on thee shall Vultures
    prey,

Poore wretch. Nor shall thy mightie Friend affoord thee any
    aid,

10   That gave thy parting much deepe charge. And this perhaps
    he said:

"Martiall Patroclus, turne not face nor see my fleete before

The curets from great Hector's breast, all guilded with his
    gore,

Thou hew'st in peeces." If thus vaine were his far-stretcht
    commands,

As vaine was thy heart to beleeve his words lay in thy hands.'

He, languishing, replide: 'This proves thy   *Patroclus, languishing,*
    glory worse than vaine,   *to Hector.*

That when two gods have given thy hands what their powres
    did obtaine

(They conquering, and they spoiling me both of my armes
    and mind,

It being a worke of ease for them) thy soule should be so
    blind

To oversee their evident deeds and take their powres to thee –

20   When, if the powres of twentie such had dar'd t' encounter
    me,

My lance had strew'd earth with them all. Thou onely doest
    obtaine

A third place in my death, whom first a harmfull fate hath
    slaine

Effected by Latona's sonne: second, and first of men,

Euphorbus. And this one thing more concernes thee; note it
    then:

Thou shalt not long survive thy selfe; nay, now Death cals
    for thee,

And violent fate. Achilles' lance shall make this good for me.'

Thus death joyn'd to his words his end; his soule tooke
    instant wing,
And to the house that hath no lights descended, sorrowing
For his sad fate, to leave him yong and in his ablest age.
30 He dead, yet Hector askt him why, in that prophetique rage,
He so forespake him, when none knew but great Achilles
        might
Prevent his death and on his lance receive his latest light?

XVIII.173-95 [203-29] *The cries of Achilles stem the Trojan onrush*

And straite Minerva honor'd him, who Jove's shield clapt
    upon
His mightie shoulders, and his head girt with a cloud of gold,
That cast beames round about his browes. And as when
    armes enfold
A citie in an Ile, from thence a fume at first appeares   *Simile.*
(Being in the day), but when the Even her cloudie forehead
    reares,
Thicke show the fires, and up they cast their splendor, that
    men nie,
Seeing their distresse, perhaps may set ships out to their
    supply:
So (to shew such aid) from his head a light rose, scaling
    heaven.
And forth the wall he stept and stood, nor brake the precept
    given
10 By his great mother (mixt in fight), but sent abroad his voice,
Which Pallas farre off ecchoed – who did betwixt them hoise
Shrill Tumult to a toplesse height. And as a voice is heard
With emulous affection, when any towne is spher'd   *Simile.*
With siege of such a foe as kils men's minds, and for the
    towne
Makes sound his trumpet: so the voice from Thetis' issue
    throwne

Won emulously th' eares of all. His brazen voice once heard,
The minds of all were startl'd so, they yeelded; and so feard
The faire-man'd horses that they flew backe and their chariots
    turn'd,
Presaging in their augurous hearts the labours that they
    mourn'd
20 A litle after; and their guides a repercussive dread
Tooke from the horrid radiance of his refulgent head,
Which Pallas set on fire with grace. Thrice great Achilles
    spake,
And thrice (in heate of all the charge) the Troyans started
    backe.

XIX.374–408 [387–424] *Achilles arms himself and admonishes his steeds*

Then from his armoury he drew his lance, his father's
    speare,
Huge, weightie, firme, that not a Greeke but he himselfe
    alone
Knew how to shake; it grew upon the mountaine Pelion,
From whose height Chiron hew'd it for his Sire, and fatall
    twas
To great-soul'd men, of Pelion surnamed Pelias.
  Then from the stable their bright horse Automedon
    withdrawes
And Alcimus, put Poitrils on and cast upon their jawes
Their bridles, hurling backe the raines, and hung them on the
    seate.
The faire scourge then Automedon takes up, and up doth get
10 To guide the horse. The fight's seate last Achilles tooke
    behind,
Who lookt so arm'd as if the Sunne, there falne from heaven,
    had shin'd –

And terribly thus charg'd his steeds: *Achilles to his horse.*
   'Xanthus and Balius,
Seed of the Harpye, in the charge ye undertake of us,
Discharge it not as when Patroclus ye left dead in field.
But when with bloud, for this daye's fast observ'd, Revenge
   shall yeeld
Our heart satietie, bring us off.' Thus since Achilles spake
As if his aw'd steeds understood, twas Juno's will to make
Vocall the pallat of the one, who, shaking his faire head
(Which in his mane (let fall to earth) he almost buried),
20 Thus Xanthus spake: 'Ablest Achilles,   *Xanthus, the horse of*
   now (at least) our care   *Achilles, to Achilles.*
Shall bring thee off; but not farre hence the fatall minutes are
Of thy grave ruine. Nor shall we be then to be reprov'd,
But mightiest Fate and the great God. Nor was thy best
   belov'd
Spoil'd so of armes by our slow pace or courage's empaire.
The best of gods, Latona's sonne that weares the golden
   haire,
Gave him his death's wound through the grace he gave to
   Hector's hand.
We, like the spirit of the West that all spirits can command
For powre of wing, could runne him off. But thou thy selfe
   must go;
So Fate ordaines; God and a man must give thee overthrow.'
30   This said, the Furies stopt his voice. Achilles, farre in rage,
Thus answerd him: 'It fits not thee thus proudly   *Achilles' reply*
   to presage   *to Xanthus.*
My overthrow. I know my selfe it is my fate to fall
Thus farre from Phthia; yet that Fate shall faile to vent her
   gall
Till mine vent thousands.' These words usde, he fell to horrid
   deeds,
Gave dreadfull signall, and forthright made flie his one-hov'd
   steeds.

XXI.61–117 [64–119] _Achilles to Lycaon_

He was descried and flight was vaine, fearefull, he made
   more nie,
With purpose to embrace his knees, and now long'd much to
   flie
His blacke fate and abhorred death by coming in. His foe
Observ'd all this, and up he raisd his lance as he would
   throw.
And then Lycaon close ran in, fell on his breast and tooke
Achilles' knees, whose lance (on earth now staid) did
   overlooke
His still-turn'd backe, with thirst to glut his sharpe point with
   the blood
That lay so readie. But that thirst Lycaon's thirst withstood.
To save his blood, Achilles' knee in his one hand he knit,
10 His other held the long lance hard and would not part with it,
But thus besought: 'I kisse thy knees, divine   _Lycaon's ruthfull_
   Aecides.   _intercession to_
Respect me, and my fortunes rue. I now   _Achilles for_
   present th' accesse   _his life._
Of a poore suppliant for thy ruth: and I am one that is
Worthy thy ruth, O Jove's belov'd. First houre my miseries
Fell into any hand, twas thine. I tasted all my bread
By thy gift since – O since that houre that thy surprisall led
From forth the faire wood my sad feete, farre from my lov'd
   allies,
To famous Lemnos, where I found an hundred Oxen's prise
To make my ransome: for which now I thrise the worth will
   raise.
20 This day makes twelve since I arriv'd in Ilion, many daies
Being spent before in sufferance; and now a cruell fate
Thrusts me againe into thy hands. I should hant Jove with
   hate,

That with such set malignitie gives thee my life againe.
There were but two of us for whom Laothoe sufferd paine,
(Laothoe, old Altes' seed – Altes, whose pallace stood
In height of upper Pedasus, neare Satnius' silver flood,
And rulde the warre-like Lelegi). Whose seed (as many more)
King Priam married, and begot the godlike Polydor
And me acurst. Thou slaughterdst him, and now thy hand on
    me

30 Will prove as mortall. I did thinke, when here I met with
    thee,
    I could not not scape thee; yet give eare and adde thy mind
    to it.
    I told my birth to intimate, though one sire did beget
    Yet one wombe brought not into light Hector (that slue thy
    friend)
And me. O do not kill me then, but let the wretched end
Of Polydor excuse my life. For halfe our being bred
Brothers to Hector he (halfe) paid; no more is forfeited.'
    Thus su'd he humbly, but he heard with this austere replie:
'Foole, urge not ruth nor price to me, til that solemnitie
Resolv'd on for Patroclus' death pay all his rites to fate.

40 Till his death, I did grace to Troy, and many lives did rate
At price of ransome: but none now of all the brood of Troy
(Who ever Jove throwes to my hands) shall any breath enjoy
That death can beate out – specially that touch at Priam's
    race.
Die, die, my friend. What teares are these? What sad lookes
    spoile thy face?
Patroclus died, that farre past thee. Nay, seest thou not
    beside,
My selfe, even I, a faire yong man and rarely magnifide,
And (to my father, being a king) a mother have that sits
In ranke with goddesses; and yet, when thou hast spent thy
    spirits,
Death and as violent a fate must overtake even me –

50 By twilight, morne-light, day, high noone, when ever
    Destinie

Sets on her man to hurle a lance or knit out of his string
An arrow that must reach my life.' This said, alanguishing.
Lycaon's heart bent like his knees, yet left him strength
    t' advance
Both hands for mercie as he kneeld. His foe yet leaves his
    lance
And forth his sword flies, which he hid in furrow of a wound
Driven through the joynture of his necke; flat fell he on the
    ground,
Stretcht with death's pangs, and all the earth embrew'd with
    timelesse blood.

XXIV.532–54 [599–620] *Achilles consoles Priam*

               'Father, now thy wil's fit rites are paide,
Thy sonne is given up; in the morne thine eyes shall see him
    laid
Deckt in thy chariot on his bed: in meane space, let us eate.
The rich-hair'd Niobe found thoughts that made her take her
    meate,
Though twelve deare children she saw slaine – sixe daughters,
    sixe yong sons.
The sonnes incent Apollo slue; the maides' confusions
Diana wrought, since Niobe her merits durst compare
With great Latona's, arguing that she did onely beare
Two children and her selfe had twelve. For which those
    onely two
10 Slue all her twelve; nine dayes they lay steept in their blood;
    her woe
Found no friend to afford them fire; Saturnius had turnd
Humanes to stones. The tenth day yet the good celestials
    burnd
The trunkes themselves, and Niobe, when she was tyr'd with
    teares,
Fell to her foode; and now with rockes and wilde hils mixt
    she beares

(In Sipylus) the gods' wraths still – in that place where, 'tis said,
The Goddesse Fairies use to dance about the funerall bed
Of Achelous; where (though turn'd with cold griefe to a stone)
Heaven gives her heate enough to feele what plague comparison
With his powers (made by earth) deserves. Affect not then too farre
20 With griefe, like a god, being a man; but for a man's life care,
And take fit foode. Thou shalt have time, beside, to mourne thy sonne;
He shall be tearefull, thou being full; not here but Ilion
Shall finde thee weeping roomes enow.'   (1598-1611)

Chapman's *Odyssey* followed in two parts, printed in 1614 and 1615. It is cast in rhymed decasyllabic couplets, a change probably meant to smooth and urbanize, but which makes for obscurity. Chapman now emphasizes the allegoric and philosophic connotations of Odysseus' journey. What is very fine, nevertheless, is the rendition of the marine experience, of Odysseus the sailor and storm-racked survivor.

Homer's Odysses I.1–34 [1–21] *The incipit of the epic*

The Man, O Muse, informe, that many a way
Wound with his wisedome to his wished stay;
That wanderd wondrous farre when He the towne
Of sacred Troy had sackt and shiverd downe.

The information or fashion of an absolute man, and necessarie (or fatal) passage through many afflictions (according with the most sacred Letter) to his naturall haven and countrey, is the whole argument and scope of this inimitable and miraculous Poeme. And

The cities of a world of nations,
With all their manners, mindes and
    fashions,
He saw and knew; at Sea felt many
    woes,
Much care sustaind, to save from
    overthrowes
Himselfe and friends in their retreate for home.

10 But so their fates he could not overcome,
Though much he thirsted it. O men unwise,
They perish by their owne impieties,
That in their hunger's rapine would not shunne
The Oxen of the loftie-going Sunne,
Who therefore from their eyes the day bereft
Of safe returne. These acts, in some part left,
Tell us, as others, deified seed of Jove.

    Now all the rest that austere Death out-strove
At Troy's long siege at home safe anchor'd are,
20 Free from the malice both of sea and warre;
Onely Ulysses is denide accesse
To wife and home. The Grace of Goddesses,
The reverend Nymph Calypso, did detaine
Him in her Caves, past all the race of men
Enflam'd to make him her lov'd Lord and Spouse.
And when the Gods had destin'd that his house,
Which Ithaca on her rough bosome beares,
(The point of time wrought out by ambient yeares)
Should be his haven, Contention still extends
30 Her envie to him, even amongst his friends.
All Gods tooke pitie on him: onely he
That girds Earth in the cincture of the sea
Divine Ulysses ever did envie,
And made the fixt port of his birth to flie.

therefore is the epithete
πολύτροπον *given him in*
the first verse; πολύτροπος
signifying Homo cuius
ingenium velut per
multas, et varias vias,
vertitur in verum.

III.407-20 [293-302] *The homeward-bound Menelaus*

'There is a Rocke on which the Sea doth drive,
Bare and all broken, on the confines set
Of Gortys, that the darke seas likewise fret;
And hither sent the South a horrid drift
Of waves against the top, that was the left
Of that torne cliffe, as farre as Phaestus' Strand.
A litle stone the great sea's rage did stand.
The men here driven scapt hard the ships' sore shocks,
The ships themselves being wrackt against the rocks,
10 Save onely five, that blue fore-castles bore,
Which wind and water cast on Aegypt's shore –
When he (there victling well, and store of gold
Aboord his ships brought) his wilde way did hold,
And t'other languag'd men was forc't to rome.'

V.474-93 [365-79] *The tempest raised by Poseidon*

While this discourse emploid him, Neptune raisd
A huge, a high, and horrid sea, that seisd
Him and his ship and tost them through   Neptuni in Ulyssem
    the Lake.   inclementia.
As when the violent winds together take
Heapes of drie chaffe and hurle them every way,
So his long woodstacke Neptune strooke astray.
    Then did Ulysses mount on rib, perforce,
Like to a rider of a running horse,
To stay himselfe a time, while he might shift
10 His drenched weeds that were Calypso's gift.
When putting strait Leucothea's Amulet
About his necke, he all his forces set
To swim, and cast him prostrate to the seas.
When powrefull Neptune saw the ruthlesse prease

Of perils siege him thus, he mov'd his head,
And this betwixt him and his heart he said:
　'So, now feele ils enow, and struggle so,
Till to your Jove-lov'd Ilanders you row.
But my mind sayes you will not so avoid
20　This last taske too, but be with sufferance cloid.'

V.560–603 [424–50] *Odysseus survives*

　　　　　　　While this discourse he held,
A curst Surge gainst a cutting rocke impeld
His naked bodie, which it gasht and tore,
And had his bones broke, if but one sea more
Had cast him on it. But she prompted him　　　　　　　*Pallas.*
That never faild, and bad him no more swim
Still off and on, but boldly force the shore
And hug the rocke that him so rudely tore.
Which he with both hands sigh'd and claspt till past
10　The billowes' rage was; which scap't backe, so fast
The rocke repulst it, that it reft his hold,
Sucking him from it, and farre backe he rould.
And as the Polypus that (forc't from home
Amidst the soft sea, and neare rough land come
For shelter gainst the stormes that beate on her
At open sea, as she abroad doth erre)
A deale of gravill and sharpe little stones
Needfully gathers in her hollow bones:
So he forc't hither (by the sharper ill　　　　　Per asperiora vitare
20　Shunning the smoother), where he best hop't, still　　　laevia.
The worst succeeded: for the cruell friend,
To which he clingd for succour, off did rend
From his broad hands the soken flesh so sore
That off he fell and could sustaine no more.
Quite under water fell he, and, past Fate,
Haplesse Ulysses there had lost the state

He held in life, if (still the grey-eyd Maid
His wisedome prompting) he had not assaid
Another course and ceast t'attempt that shore,
30   Swimming, and casting round his eye, t'explore
Some other shelter. Then the mouth he found
Of faire Callicoe's flood, whose shores were crownd
With most apt succors – rocks so smooth they seemd
Polisht of purpose, land that quite redeemd
With breathlesse coverts th'other's blasted shores.
The flood he knew, and thus in heart implores:
'King of this River, heare! Whatever name
Makes thee invokt, to thee I humbly frame
My flight from Neptune's furies. Reverend is
40   To all the ever-living Deities
What erring man soever seekes their aid.
To thy both flood and knees a man dismaid
With varied sufferance sues. Yeeld then some rest
To him that is thy suppliant profest.'

VIII.90–127 [71–94] *Demodocus, the minstrel*

The rest then fell to feast, and when the fire
Of appetite was quencht, the Muse inflam'd
The sacred Singer. Of men highliest fam'd
He sung the glories, and a Poeme pend
That in applause did ample heaven ascend –
Whose subject was the sterne contention
Betwixt Ulysses and Great Thetis' Sonne,   *The contention of*
As at a banket sacred to the Gods   *Achilles and Ulysses.*
In dreadfull language they exprest their ods.
10   When Agamemnon sat rejoyc't in soule
To heare the Greeke Peeres jarre in termes so foule,
For Augur Phoebus in presage had told
The king of men (desirous to unfold

The war's perplexed end, and being therefore gone
In heavenly Pytho to the Porch of stone)
That then the end of all griefes should begin
Twixt Greece and Troy when Greece (with strife to winne
That wisht conclusion) in her kings should jarre,
And pleade if force or wit must end the warre.

20   This brave contention did the Poet sing,
Expressing so the spleene of either king
That his large purple weede Ulysses held
Before his face and eies, since thence   *Ulyssi movetur fletus.*
distilld
To let th'observing Presence note a teare.
But when his sacred song the meere Divine
Had given an end, a Goblet crownd with wine
Ulysses (drying his wet eies) did seise,
And sacrifisde to those Gods that would please
T'inspire the Poet with a song so fit   *The continued pietie of*
To do him honour and renowme his   *Ulysses through all places,*
    wit.   *times and occasions.*
30 Againe Ulysses could not chuse but yeeld
To that soft passion, which againe withheld
He kept so cunningly from sight that none
(Except Alcinous himselfe alone)
Discern'd him mov'd so much.

IX.483–508 [353–70] *Odysseus' ruse in the cave of the Cyclops*

'He tooke, and drunke, and vehemently joyd
To taste the sweet cup; and againe employd
My flagon's powre, entreating more, and said:
"Good Guest, againe affoord my taste thy aid,

And let me know thy name, and quickly now,
That in thy recompence I may bestow
A hospitable gift on thy desert,
And such a one as shall rejoyce thy heart.
For to the Cyclops too the gentle Earth
10   Beares generous wine, and Jove augments her birth
In store of such with showres. But this rich wine
Fell from the river that is meere divine,
Of Nectar and Ambrosia." This againe
I gave him, and againe; nor could the foole abstaine,
But drunke as often. When the noble Juyce
Had wrought upon his spirit, I then gave use
To fairer language, saying: "Cyclop! now
As thou demandest, I'le tell my name; do thou
Make good thy hospitable gift to me.
20   My name is No-Man; No-Man each degree
Of friends, as well as parents, call my name."
He answerd, as his cruell soule became:
"No-Man! I'le eate thee last of all thy friends;
And this is that in which so much amends
I vowd to thy deservings; thus shall be
My hospitable gift made good to thee."'

XI.642-66 [488-503] *Odysseus meets with Achilles in Hades*

'"Urge not my death to me, nor rub that wound.
I rather wish to live in earth a Swaine   *Achilles of the next life.*
Or serve a Swaine for hire, that scarce can gaine
Bread to sustaine him, than (that life once gone)
Of all the dead sway the Imperiall throne.
But say, and of my Sonne, some comfort yeeld,
If he goes on in first fights of the field,
Or lurks for safetie in the obscure Rere?
Or of my Father if thy royall care

10   Hath bene advertisde, that the Phthian Throne
     He still commands as greatest Myrmidon?
     Or that the Phthian and Thessalian rage
     (Now feete and hands are in the hold of Age)
     Despise his Empire? Under those bright rayes
     In which heaven's fervour hurles about the dayes
     Must I no more shine his revenger now,
     Such as of old the Ilian overthrow
     Witnest my anger, th'universall hoast
     Sending before me to this shadie Coast
20   In fight for Grecia. Could I now resort
     (But for some small time) to my Father's Court,
     In spirit and powre as then, those men should find
     My hands inaccessible, and of fire my mind,
     That durst with all the numbers they are strong
     Unseate his honour and suborne his wrong."'

XVII.386–442 [290–323] *The faithful dog, Argus*

Such speech they chang'd: when in the yeard there lay
A dogge call'd Argus, which, before his way   *Ulysses' dog,*
Assum'd for Ilion, Ulysses bred,   *called Argus.*
Yet stood his pleasure then in little sted
(As being too yong), but, growing to his grace,
Yong men made choise of him for every Chace,
Or of their wilde Goats, of their Hares, or Harts.
But, his King gone, and he now past his parts,
Lay all abjectly on the Stable's store,
10   Before the Oxe-stall and Mules' stable dore,
     To keepe the clothes cast from the Pessants' hands,
     While they laide compasse on Ulysses' Lands,
     The Dog with Tickes (unlook't to) over-growne.
     But by this Dog no sooner seene but knowne
     Was wise Ulysses, who (new enter'd there)
     Up went his Dog's laide eares, and (comming nere)

Up he himselfe rose, fawn'd, and wag'd his Sterne,
Coucht close his eares, and lay so – nor   *The Dog dyed as soone as*
    descerne   *hee had seen Ulysses.*
Could evermore his deere-lov'd Lord againe.
20 Ulysses saw it, nor had powre t'abstaine
From shedding tears – which (far-off seeing his Swain)
He dried from his sight cleane, to whom he thus
His griefe dissembled: ''Tis miraculous
That such a dog as this should have his laire
On such a dunghill, for his forme is faire.
And yet I know not if there were in him
Good pace or parts for all his goodly lim,
Or he liv'd empty of those inward things,
As are those trencher-Beagles tending Kings,
30 Whom for their pleasures or their glorie's sake,
Or fashion, they into their favours take.'
    'This Dog,' said he, 'was servant to one dead   *Eumaeus'*
A huge time since. But if he bore his head   *Description of*
(For forme and quality) of such a hight   *Ulysses' Dogge.*
As when Ulysses (bound for th'Ilian fight,
Or quickly after) left him, your rapt eyes
Would then admire to see him use his Thyes
In strength and swiftnes. He would nothing flye,
Nor any thing let scape. If once his eye
40 Seiz'd any wilde beast, he knew straight his scent:
Go where he would, away with him he went.
Nor was there ever any Savage stood
Amongst the thickets of the deepest wood
Long time before him, but he pull'd him downe –
As well by that true hunting to be showne
In such vaste coverts, as for speed of pace
In any open Lawne; for in deepe chace
He was a passing wise and well-nos'd Hound.
And yet is all this good in him uncroun'd
50 With any grace heere now, nor he more fed
Than any errant Curre. His King is dead

Farre from his country, and his servants are
So negligent, they lend his Hound no care.
Where Maysters rule not but let Men alone,
You never there see honest service done.
That Man's halfe vertue Jove takes quite away,
That once is Sun-burn'd with the servile day.'

XXI.520–77 [392–434] *Odysseus strings his bow*

Ulysses viewing, ere he tried to draw,
The famous Bow, which every way he mov'd,
Up and downe turning it – in which he prov'd
The plight it was in, fearing chiefly lest
The hornes were eate with wormes in so long rest.
But what his thoughts intended, turning so,
And keeping such a search about the Bow,
The wooers, little knowing, fell to jest,
And said: 'Past doubt, he is a man profest
10   In Bowyer's craft, and sees quite through the wood,
Or something (certaine) to be understood
There is in this his turning of it still.
A cunning Rogue he is at any ill.'
    Then spake another proud one: 'Would to heaven
I might (at will) get Gold, till he hath geven
That Bow his draught!' With these sharp jests did these
Delightsome woo'rs their fatall humors please.
But when the wise Ulysses once had laide
His fingers on it, and to proofe survaide
20   The stil sound plight it held, as one of skill
In song and of the Harpe doth at his will,
In tuning of his Instrument, extend
A string out with his pin, touch all, and lend
To every wel-wreath'd string his perfect sound,
Strooke all togither – with such ease drew round

The King the Bow. Then twang'd he up the string,
That as a Swallow in the aire doth sing
With no continu'd tune, but (pausing still)
Twinkes out her scatter'd voice in accents shrill –
30 So sharpe the string sung when he gave it touch,
Once having bent and drawne it. Which so much
Amaz'd the wooers, that their colours went
And came most grievously. And then Jove rent
The aire with thunder, which at heart did chere
The now–enough–sustaining Traveller,
That Jove againe would his attempt enable.
Then tooke he into hand from off the Table
The first drawne arrow – and a number more
Spent shortly on the wooers – but this one
40 He measur'd by his arme (as if not knowne
The length were to him), nockt it then, and drew,
And through the Axes, at the first hole, flew
The steele–chardg'd arrow – which when he had done,
He thus bespake the Prince: 'You have not wonne
Disgrace yet by your Guest, for I have strook
The marke I shot at, and no such toile tooke
In wearying the Bow with fat and fire
As did the wooers. Yet reserv'd entire
(Thanke heaven) my strength is, and my selfe am tried
50 No man to be so basely vilified
As these men pleas'd to thinke me. But free way
Take that, and all their pleasures: and while Day
Holds her Torch to you, and the howre of feast
Hath now full date, give banquet and the rest
(Poeme and Harpe) that grace a wel–fill'd boorde.'
   This saide, he beckn'd to his Sonne, whose sword
He straight girt to him, tooke to hand his Lance,
And, compleate arm'd, did to his Sire advance.

XXIII.388–430 [256–84] *The final voyage yet to come*

'The place of rest is ready,' she replyed,
'Your will at full serve, since the deified
Have brought you where your right is to command.
But since you know (God making understand
Your searching mind) informe me, what must be
Your last set labour? Since 'twill fall to me
(I hope) to heare it after, tell me now:
The greatest pleasure is before to know.'
'Unhappy!' said Ulysses, 'To what end
10   Importune you this labour? It will lend
Nor you nor me delight; but you shall know
I was commanded yet more to bestow
My yeares in travaile, many Cities more
By Sea to visit: and, when first for shore
I left my shipping, I was will'd to take
A navall Oare in hand, and with it make
My passage forth till such strange men I met
As knew no Sea, nor ever salt did eat
With any victles, who the purple beakes
20   Of Ships did never see, nor that which breakes
The waves in curles, which is a Fan-like Oare,
And serves as wings with which a ship doth soare.
To let me know, then, when I was arriv'd
On that strange earth where such a people liv'd,
He gave me this for an unfailing signe:
When any one that tooke that Oare of mine
Borne on my shoulder for a Corne-clense Fan
I met ashore, and shew'd to be a man
Of that Land's labour, there had I command
30   To fixe mine Oare, and offer on that strand
T'imperiall Neptune (whom I must implore)
A Lambe, a Bull, and Sow-ascending Bore –

And then turne home, where all the other Gods
That in the broad heaven made secure abods
I must solicite (all my curious heed
Given to the severall rites they have decreed)
With holy Hecatombes. And, then, at home
A gentle death should seize me, that would come
From out the Sea and take me to his rest
40   In full ripe age, about me living blest
My loving people – to which (he presag'd)
The sequell of my fortunes were engag'd.'   (1614–15)

Chapman's version of the *Lesser Homerica*, probably published in 1624, and intended to reach 'the End of all the Endless Works of Homer', is largely a failure. He simply did not understand the pseudo-Homeric Greek. Yet there is a touch of baroque magic in the birth of Hermes.

A Hymne to Hermes 15–51 [11–29]

The tenth moneth had in heaven confin'de the date
Of Maia's Labour, and into the sight
She brought, in one birth, Labours infinite:
For then she bore a sonne, that all tried waies
Could turne and winde to wisht events assaies,
A faire tongu'd, but false-hearted, Counsellor,
Rector of Ox-stealers, and for all stealths bore
A varied finger; Speeder of Night's spies
And guide of all her dreames' obscurities;
10   Guard of dore-Guardians; and was borne to be
Amongst th'Immortalls that wing'd Deitie
That in an instant should doe acts would aske
The Powres of others an Eternall Taske.
Borne in the Morne, he form'd his Lute at Noone,
At Night stole all the Oxen of the Sunne;

And all this in his Birth's first day was done,
Which was the fourth of the encreasing Moone.
Because Celestiall lims sustain'd his straines,
His sacred swath-bands must not be his chaines.
20   So (starting up) to Phoebus' Herde he stept,
Found strait the high-roof't Cave where they were kept,
And (th'entrie passing) he th'invention found
Of making Lutes; and did in wealth abound
By that Invention, since he first of all
Was author of that Engine Musicall,
By this meane mov'd to the ingenious worke:
Nere the Cave's inmost overture did lurke
A Tortois, tasting th'odoriferous grasse,
Leisurely moving; and this Object was
30   The motive to Jove's Sonne (who could convert
To profitablest uses all desert
That nature had in any worke convaid)
To forme the Lute; when (smiling) thus he said:
'Thou mov'st in me a note of excellent use,
Which thy ill forme shall never so seduce
T'evert the good to be inform'd by it,
In pliant force of my forme-forging wit.'   (1615)

THOMAS GRANTHAM (d. 1664)

'The first BOOKE of Homer's Iliads translated by Thomas
Grantham M.A. of Peter House in Cambridge, Professor of the
speedy way of teaching the Hebrew, Greek and Latine Tongues in
LONDON, in White-Bear-Court, Over against the Golden Ball
upon Aldine Hill LONDON Printed by L. Leek, for the author,
An. Dom. 1660'; the third book was printed in the same year, by a
different printer, and Mr Grantham has, by this time, changed his
London address, which was now 'in Mermaid-Court in Gutter-lane,
near Cheapside'. The translation is dedicated to King Charles. The
first few lines of the dedicatory poem read thus:

This Book that reach'd into a King before
Now scorns to beg at any Traitor's door:
In blood, in plunder, in a Trapaning fight
In Sequestrations it takes no delight.
Go meet King CHARLES, my Book, at Dover Clifs
For now his Foes are put unto their shifts,
Who caused our griefs [. . .]

At the end of the translation of the first book, Grantham gives a plain, yet touching description of the circumstances in which his translation was conceived:

In the Country (this last Summer) I tought a Gentleman's Son, and he being gone a hunting or coursing, I had great leisure, and began to translate Homer; at the first I translated sixteen verses, every time more or lesse, till I came almost to Nestor's speech: I read them to some scholars, and they pressed me to finish the first Booke, which (by God's assistance) I did, to whom be glory for ever.

The Iliads III [326–84] *Paris arms for battle*

Then all the Souldiers ranked in a round
Sate with their Horses, and their Arms on ground.
Then *Paris* arm'd himself for this same strife
Who fair-haired *Helen* had unto his wife.
First he put on his Boots, and these made fast
With silver Buttons which would strongly last.
Then he put on his breast-plate, this before
His brother *Lycaon* full oft has wore:
Then he put on his Damask sword in field
10 And after that his strong and mighty Shield:
His Helmet with a plume of Horses hair,
And as he daunced all the Armies stare:
And terribly he shewed in this advance,
For he did shake his huge and mighty Lance.

Then *Menelaus* in an angry mood,
With gallant Armor 'twixt the Armies stood;
Trojans and Grecians all abot did gaze,
For both the Armies were in great amaze
To see these men to come so strongly in,
20 And dare it out, for they came chin to chin.
Then *Paris* first did sling his Lance in field,
Which did reflect from *Menelaus* shield;
Then *Menelaus* did his Spear prepare
 · To sling, but first to *Jove* he made his prayer:
    Oh Jove! this *Paris* wrong'd me most of all;
Now grant that he under my hand may fall;
And every Guest in after-time shall fear
To wrong his Hoste, who was to him so dear:
This said, his Lance did pierce through *Paris* shield,
30 Stuck in his breast-plate, made it for the yield,
And cut the coat his bowels did contain;
But *Paris* stoopt, or *Paris* had been slain:
His helmet also with his sword he strake,
His sword in three or four pieces brake:
Then looking up to heaven, Oh *Jove!* said he,
There is no God so cruel unto me; ·
My Sword is brake, my Lance is flung in vain,
I durst have swore I should have *Paris* slain;
This said, he presently did catch his Guest
40 By th' Horse-hair-plume that dangled on his crest
And drew him to the Grecians all along,
Untill that *Venus* broke the Oxes thong
Which tied his Helmet to his throat, and then
He flung the Helmet to the Armed men.
Then *Menelaus* did his Lance advance;
But *Paris* was delivered from this chance
Of death, for *Venus* in a mist unknown
Kept him, and in his chamber set him down:
And *Helen* in a tower of great height,
50 Found with some Ladies there to see the fight.   (1660)

JOHN OGILBY (1600–1676)

Translator of Virgil, courtier to Charles II, whose restoration he
celebrates in these magnificently printed and illustrated folios, which
he himself printed, Ogilby is among the first of translators into
modern English. There is learned ostentation, sometimes self-taught,
in his copious notes. Pope sneered at and borrowed from him.
Homer's Iliads appeared in 1660. The *Homer's Odysses* followed in
1665.

Homer's Iliads XVII [543–604] *The combat around the fallen Patroclus*

Now round *Patroclus* they their Weapons dull
In cruel Fight, by *Pallas* spurr'd, whom *Jove*
(His Mind now chang'd) commanded from above
To chear the *Greeks*. Like the discolour'd Bow
The Thunderer bends, a Battell to foreshow,
Or bitter Tempests, which from Labour keep
Industrious Swains, and banefull are to Sheep:
She in such painted Robes concealed came,
The *Graecians* fainting Courage to inflame;
10 And first (like *Phoenix*) her Addresses made
To *Sparta*'s Prince, and thus to him she said;
  Atrides, since thou'lt have the deepest Share
In Grief and Shame, should Dogs *Patroclus* tear,
With a fresh Party charge the conquering Foe.
  Then he; Would *Pallas* Strength on me bestow,
And blunt their keener Weapons, undismay'd
With a fresh Charge the Body I would aid,
Who for his Death am ready to expire.
But routing *Hector* comes like raging Fire,
20 Mowing down Squadrons with his conquering Sword:
Celestiall Powers such Honour him afford.

Pleas'd that to her he first address'd his Praiers,
His wearie Limbs she with fresh Strength repairs.
As busie Flies, with biting Hunger keen,
Though oft repuls'd, fall on our tender Skin,
And piercing deep soon tast delicious Food,
Sweetly carowsing Draughts of humane Bloud:
Such Courage feeling *Menelaus* goes
Up to the Corps, and there his Javelin throws;

30 And *Podes*, *Eetion*'s Son, wealthie and great,
Whom *Hector* honouring at his Table set,
Pierc'd through his Belt, as he forsook his Ground.
Through's Arms and Breast the Point a Passage found.
Down falls the Hero: in *Atrides* leaps,
Dragging him thence, and his bright Armour strips.
Then *Phoebus* drawing near spurr'd *Hector* on,
Resembling stout *Phaenopus*, *Afius* Son,
His dearest Friend, who in *Abydos* dwelt;
And thus the Hero's Pulse *Apollo* felt:

40   What *Greek* will now renowned *Hector* fear,
Who daunted stands at *Menelaus* Spear?
He, whose weak Prowess all the Princes scoff,
Hath *Podes* slain, and dragg'd his Body off.
    This said, a Cloud of Grief his Brows involv'd,
And raging through the Van he breaks resolv'd.
Then *Jove*, his Golden Target shaking, shrowds
(Thundring and Lightning) *Ida* in black Clouds,
And, his bright *Aegis clashing*, Victory grants
The daring Foe, the worsted *Graecians* daunts.

50 First fled *Peneleus* on the Shoulder rac'd.
Polydamas him, as he him turning fac'd,
With his sharp Point (drawn up to him so near)
Hit on his Chin, wounding from Ear to Ear.
But *Hector* wounded *Leitus* on the Hand,
Alectryon's Son, and put him to a Stand.
Amaz'd he looking round no more could hope
To hold a Spear, nor with the *Trojans* cope.

XVIII [1–72] *Achilles is told of Patroclus' death and Thetis has been to comfort him*

THE ARGUMENT

Achilles hears *Hector his Friend had slain.*
Thetis *ascends with all her Virgin Train*
From Sea, her Son to comfort. Arms he wants,
Which at her Suit Vulcan *the Goddess grants:*
With Speed he anvills (sweating at his Forge)
A Cask, Greaves, Corslet, and a ponderous Targe.

Whilst thus both Parties fought like raging Flame,
Antilochus to renown'd *Achilles* came:
Whom at his Fleet he found, perplex'd with Fear,
10   Events presaging which effected were.
He to himself thus said; Ah! why again
In such Confusion fly they from the Plain?
I doubt the Gods have finish'd what of old
My Heav'n-inspired Mother me foretold,
That a stout *Myrmidon* (I yet alive)
The *Trojans* should of dearest Life deprive.
Patroclus much I fear. Him I desir'd,
When he had quench'd what hostile Flames had fir'd,
The Navie clear'd, and put the Foe to Flight,
20   Straight to retreat, nor valiant *Hector* fight.
To him surmising thus *Antilochus* made
This sad Addresse, and (Tears distilling) said;
   To thee, great Prince, I with sad Tidings come,
(Ah! would 'twere false, though I were ever dumb;)
Thy Friend is faln, his Corps in hot Dispute,
And *Hector* wears thy Arms in our Pursuit.
   A Cloud, this said, upon his Brows there hung,
Dust he on's manlie Face and Forehead flung;
Then, falling down, his Golden Tresses tore,
30   And with his Regal Habit swept the Floor.

The Virgins, his and dear *Patroclus* Prize,
At this so sad Alarm with hideous Cries
Surround the Prince, trembling with Grief and Fear,
Beat their fair Breasts, dishevelling their Hair.
    Antilochus the dolefull Musick fill'd
With as sad Notes, whilst he *Achilles* held,
Who sigh'd extremely, rack'd with torturing Fear
Lest they's Friend's Head should fix upon a Spear.
    His mother heard him 'midst her Virgin-Train,
40 In *Nereus* Palace, built beneath the Main.
Glauce, Thalia, and *Cymodoce* were,
Nesaea, Spio, Thoa, Halia there,
Cymothoe, Actaea, Limnoria,
Amphithoe, Agave, and *Melita,*
Iaera, Doto, Proto, Pherusa,
Dynamene, and *Callianira,*
Dexamene, Doris, and *Amphinome,*
Nemertes, Galatea, Panope,
Apseudes, Callianassa, Clymene,
50 *Oritbya, Innassa, Janire,*
Amathia, Maera, and more which haunt the Seas;
The Silver Cave was full of Goddesses:
All beat their Breasts, whilst thus their Queen complain'd:
    Draw near, my dearest Sisters, understand
How much (ah me!) I suffer, who brought forth
The valiant'st Hero ever trod the Earth,
And bred him like a Plant, where Seasons smile,
Where pleasant Fountains feed a fertil Soil;
Then sent him t' *Ilium* through the boisterous Main,
60 Against the *Trojans*; whom I ne'r again
Shall see return to *Peleus* royall Court:
Though a sad Life he lives, both sad and short,
Yet I, who am a Goddess, want the Power
His Life to ease, or adde to it one Hour.
But him I'll see, and hear what dire Event
Makes him thus loud and dolefully lament.

This said, she leaves the Cave, sad Nymphs attend:
And, breaking through divided Waves, th'ascend
To *Troy*'s fat Confines, where *Achilles* lay,
70   Whose drawn-up Vessels fring'd the trending Bay.   (1660)

Homer's Odysses XI [538–640] *As Achilles' ghost departs,*
Odysseus encounters other shades in the Underworld

Achilles Ghost, this said, thence marching goes
Proudly with Joy through flow'ry Meadows on,
Inform'd by me he had so brave a Son.
    Then other Shades drew near me, and relate
Their various Stories and unhappy Fate.
But *Ajax* woful Ghost far off alone
Still raging stood, vext I had him o'rethrown
When for *Achilles* Arms we pleaded so,
Which were jud'g mine by *Pallas* and the Fo.
10   Ah! would I had been conquer'd in that Strife,
Rather then such a Hero lose his Life,
Who next to great *Achilles* was the Flower
Of all the *Greeks*, their Champion and their Tower.
    To whom I mildly said; *Ajax*, 'tis fit
That after Death old Quarrels we forget,
Arms so destructive, forg'd by angry Fate
To ruine thee, and raise such dire Debate.
For thee the Camp did put on Mourning all,
And wept as at *Achilles* Funeral.
20   The Blame must lie on *Jove*, who us did hate,
And so impos'd on thee this heavy Fate.
Draw near, great Prince, and swelling Wrath allay,
And hear what I in my Defence can say.
    He answer'd not, but mix'd 'mongst other Souls,
Seeming to blow up yet revenging Coals.
But I more curious grew, my mind did drive
With others to discourse were not alive.

There I saw *Minos*, *Jove*'s illustrious Son,
With golden Scepter sitting on a Throne,
30   Where he heard Causes, and pale Spirits plead
Their Privilege and Customs of the Dead.
And next *Orion* hunting o're the Plain
Beasts which in desert Mountains he had slain,
Arm'd with a Club massy with Steel and strong.
  Tityus I saw lie there nine Acres long.
Stern Vultures on his mangled Bosom pearch
Tearing his Liver, and 's rent Bowels search:
Nor could he drive the Torturers from their Prey,
Because *Jove*'s Wife *Latona*, on her way
40   To *Pytho*, near sweet *Panopeus* he
Would once have forc'd. Next *Tantalus* I see
Suffering a horrid Torment, standing in
A pleasant River quite up to his Chin,
Who thirsty, still as he desir'd to drink,
Bare Ground appears, and the dry'd Waters shrink
Beneath his Feet, dry'd by some angry God.
About his Head Trees which rich Fruit did load,
Pears, Apples, Figs and Olives in a throng,
Their various kinds in dangling Clusters hung.
50   Still as th' old man strove one of them to catch,
A Wind straight came and blew it out of 's reach.
  There *Sisyphus* I cast my eye upon
In cruel Torture lugging a huge Stone,
Struggling with all his Strength, his Hands and Feet,
Up a steep Hill indeavouring it to get;
But soon as he attains the Mountain's Crown,
It with a Vengeance hurri'd tumbles down.
Then from the Plain his Task he doth repeat,
Dusty his Head, all over in a Sweat.
60   Next him I saw the great *Herculean* Shade,
But he himself in Heav'n *Jove*'s Daughter had,
Bright *Hebe*, and now feasts 'mongst Deities.
About him Ghosts did clamour, like the Cries

Of frighted Fowl. He like the Night march'd on,
His Bow bent, to the Head his Arrow drawn,
Frowning as if his Shafts he would have dealt:
Athwart his Shoulders hung his golden Belt,
Which Lions, Boars, Bears, Battels, Slaughter fill;
The like was never wrought, nor ever will.

70   He knew me straight, and having well survey'd,
The gentle Shadow pitying me thus said;
   Poor Prince *Ulysses*, thou like me wert born
The Mocking-stock of Fate, and Fortune's Scorn.
I, though *Jove*'s Son, much Misery indur'd,
By one much meaner then my self procur'd.
'Mongst many Toils which my strong Nerves did stretch,
He sent me hither *Cerberus* to fetch:
This was the greatest Task he put me too:
Yet from th' Infernal Gates the Dog I drew,
80   By *Hermes* and the bright *Minerva*'s Aid.
   Thus saying he retired to the Shade.
I firmly kept my Station to behold
Some ancient Hero's who had dy'd of old.
Theseus, *Pirithous*, Sons of Gods, I saw:
Near a vast Concourse with huge Clamour draw.
I sate surprised then with trembling Fear,
Suspecting that the *Gorgon*'s Head was there.
Thence straight my Friends call'd, we ourselves bestir'd;
We loose our Cables, and soon get aboard.
90   Plac'd on our Banks we down the River glide,
Fair Winds attending and a nimble Tide.   (1665)

THOMAS HOBBES (1588-1679)

Embittered, it is said, by the failure of his *Leviathan* to make a
greater impact, Hobbes turned to Homer. His *Travels of Ulysses*,
comprising Books IX–XII, appeared in 1673. A complete Homer

followed soon thereafter. It is the work of a philosopher in his mid-eighties, with no poetic talent, but a fierce insight into Homeric politics and homicidal war. The extensive preface 'Concerning the Virtues of an Heroic Poem' is still worth reading.

The Odyssey IX.385–436 [364–414] *The Cyclops*

Cyclops, since you my name desire to know,
    I'll tell it you, and on your word rely.
My name is Noman, all men call me so,
    My father, mother, and my company.
To which he soon and sadly made reply,
    Noman, I'll eat you last, none shall outlive you
Of all that are here of your company;
    And that's the gift I promised to give you.
And having said, he laid himself along
10   With bended neck, sleeping and vomiting
Gobbets of human flesh, and wine among,
    All he before had eaten uttering.
The bar with embers then I covered,
    Till, green as 'twas, with heat I made it shine,
And with few words my men encouraged,
    Lest any should have shrunk from the design.
The bar now hot, and ready to flame out,
    And, though green wood, yet glowing mightily,
To him my fellows carried now stout,
20   And set the point thereof upon his eye;
But I myself erecting, with my hand
    Twirled the bar about, with motion nimble,
As joiners with a string below do stand
    To give a piercing motion with a wimble,
So, whilst the brand was ent'ring, I it turn'd.
    The blood that down along it ran was hot,
And with his eye the lids and brows were burn'd,
    And all his eye-strings with the fire did strut,

As when a smith hath heat his axe or spade,
30   And quickly quenches it while hot it is,
To harden it, it makes a noise; so made
     His great moist eye the glowing brand to hiss.
He roared so as made the rocks resound,
     And from his eye he pull'd, with both his hands,
The burning brand, and threw it to the ground;
     And so awhile he there amazed stands,
And thence for more Cyclopses calls; and they,
     Who dwelt about in every hollow cave,
Came in, some one, and some another way;
40   And from without the den ask'd what he'd have.
What ails thee, Polyphemus, so to cry
     In dead of night, and make us break our sleep?
Goes any one about to make thee die,
     By force or fraud, or steal away thy sheep?
Then Polyphemus answered from his cave,
     Friends, Noman killeth me. Why then, said they,
We have no power from sickness you to save;
     You must unto your father Neptune pray.
This said, they parted each one to his own
50   Dark cavern; then within myself I laugh'd
To think how with my name the mighty clown
     I so deceived had, and gull'd by craft.   (1676)

XVII.465–502 [505–44] *Penelope calls for the Beggar*

While she thus and her women talking were,
     Ulysses supping sat upon the sill.
I fain, said she, would have the beggar here.
     Fetch him, Eumaeus, talk with him I will;
I'll ask him if Ulysses he has seen,
     For many men and cities knoweth he.
Eumaeus then made answer to the queen;
     If once the suitors would but silent be,

You would be pleas'd his history to hear.
10   Three days and nights he staid with me an end;
And of his suff'rings much he told me there,
    When new arriv'd; but came not to the end.
As when a man that knows the art of song,
    Sings lovely words, with sweet and well-tun'd voice,
The man that hears him thinks not the time long;
    So I, in his strange story did rejoice.
He said Ulysses was his father's guest,
    In th' isle of Crete, where reigneth Minos' race.
Himself, he said, with many woes oppress'd,
20   The fates, at last, him tumbled to this place.
And that he heard Ulysses is hard by,
    And that into Thesprotia he's come,
Alive and well; enriched mightily
    With treasure which he now is bringing home.
Then said Penelope: Go, call me hither
    The beggar. I myself will ask him all:
And meanwhile let the suitors chat together
    Where they think best, without or in the hall;
For merry they must be, since they feed here,
30   And their own corn and wine and cattle save,
And with our cattle make themselves good cheer,
    And on our corn and wine no mercy have;
For such as was Ulysses here is none,
    That should defend us from their injuries;
But were he hither come, he, and his son,
    Would bring destruction on these enemies.
This said, it chanced Telemachus to sneeze.
    She laugh'd, and for the beggar calls agen.   (1676)

JOHN DRYDEN (1631–1700)

The translations appeared (in *Fables Ancient and Modern*) shortly before Dryden's death and proved highly popular. They contain Book I of the *Iliad*. Dryden's programme for translation aims to transpose the source-text into a version 'such as would have been composed by the original author were he alive now and writing in English'.

In epic poetry, the 'authority of Homer' is beyond dispute. But at times, 'our master . . . is somewhat too talkative, and more than somewhat too digressive'. Homer's 'moral' is to urge concord among confederate states 'engaged in a war with a mighty monarch'.

In his preface to the *Fables*, the magisterial essay 'On Translating the Poets', Dryden expresses the hope of translating 'the whole *Ilias*'. The 'Grecian is more according to my genius than the Latin poet' (Virgil). Homer is 'violent, impetuous, and full of fire'. He is 'rapid in his thoughts', and yet 'copious' where the author of the *Aeneid*, which Dryden had translated, is 'confined'. The one is 'choleric and sanguine, the other phlegmatic and melancholic'. Thus 'I have translated the First Book with greater pleasure than any part of Virgil'.

But is this really so? Dryden's is a deeply incised Latinity. Virgil, Ovid, Horace were native to him as the Greek language is not. Observe the grotesque lapse in the closing line of the passage from Book I, with its endeavour to be 'epic' and 'primitive' at any cost. The fragment from Book VI, on the other hand, is magnificent, Hector's final parting from Andromache being so 'Virgilian' a motif.

The Iliad I.332–61 [223–47] *Achilles' renewed rage after Athena's visit*

> At her departure his disdain return'd:
> The fire she fann'd, with greater fury burn'd;
> Rumbling within, till thus it found a vent:
> Dastard, and drunkard, mean and insolent:

Tongue-valiant hero, vaunter of thy might,
In threats the foremost, but the lag in fight;
When didst thou thrust amid the mingled preace,
Content to bide the war aloof in peace?
Arms are the trade of each plebeian soul;
'Tis death to fight; but kingly to control.
Lord-like at ease, with arbitrary power,
To peel the chiefs, the people to devour.
These, traitor, are thy talents; safer far
Than to contend in fields, and toils of war.
Nor couldst thou thus have dar'd the common hate,
Were not their souls as abject as their state.
But, by this sceptre, solemnly I swear,
(Which never more green leaf or growing branch shall bear:
Torn from the tree, and given by Jove to those
Who laws dispense, and mighty wrongs oppose)
That when the Grecians want my wonted aid,
No gift shall bribe it, and no prayer persuade.
When Hector comes, the homicide, to wield
His conquering arms, with corpse to strow the field,
Then shalt thou mourn thy pride; and late confess
My wrong repented, when 'tis past redress.
He said: and with disdain, in open view,
Against the ground his golden sceptre threw;
Then sate: with boiling rage Atrides burn'd,
And foam betwixt his gnashing grinders churn'd.

VI.108–40 [444–65] *Hector's adieu*

Shall Hector, born to war, his birthright yield,
Belie his courage, and forsake the field?
Early in rugged arms I took delight,
And still have been the foremost in the fight:
With dangers dearly have I bought renown,
And am the champion of my father's crown,

And yet my mind forebodes, with sure presage,
That Troy shall perish by the Grecian rage.
The fatal day draws on, when I must fall,
10   And universal ruin cover all.
Not Troy itself, though built by hands divine,
Nor Priam, nor his people, nor his line,
My mother, nor my brothers of renown,
Whose valour yet defends the unhappy town;
Not these, nor all their fates which I foresee,
Are half of that concern I have for thee.
I see, I see thee, in that fatal hour,
Subjected to the victor's cruel power;
Led hence a slave to some insulting sword,
20   Forlorn, and trembling at a foreign lord;
A spectacle in Argos, at the loom,
Gracing with Trojan fights a Grecian room;
Or from deep wells the living stream to take,
And on thy weary shoulders bring it back.
While, groaning under this laborious life,
They insolently call thee Hector's wife;
Upbraid thy bondage with thy husband's name;
And from my glory propagate thy shame.
This when they say, thy sorrows will increase
30   With anxious thoughts of former happiness;
That he is dead who could thy wrongs redress.
But I, oppress'd with iron sleep before,
Shall hear thy unavailing cries no more.   (1700)

The 'Pope Constellation'. Translators (Congreve, Knightly Chetwood, Andrew Tooke, Arthur Mainwaring) immediately before Pope, as represented in the Twickenham edition of Pope's 'Homer'.

WILLIAM CONGREVE (1670–1729)

The Iliad XXIV, Appendix F, 121–73 [748–803]
Helen's lamentation

O *Hector*, thou wert rooted in my Heart,
No *Brother* there had half so large a part:
Scarce my own Lord, to whom such love I bore
That I forsook my Home; scarce he had more!
O would I ne're had seen that fatal day,
Would I had perish'd, when I came away.
Now, twenty Years are past, since that sad hour,
When first I landed on this ruin'd Shoar.
For Ruin (sure) and I, together came!
10 Yet all this time, from thee I ne're had blame,
Not one ungentle word, or look of Scorn,
Which I too often have from others born;
When you from their Reproach have set me free,
And kindly have reprov'd their Cruelty:
If by my Sisters, or the Queen revil'd,   ⎫
(For the good King, like you, was ever mild)   ⎬
Your kindness still, has all my grief beguil'd. ⎭
Ever in tears let me your loss bemoan,
Who had no Friend alive, but you alone:
20 All will reproach me now, where e're I pass,
And fly with Horrour from my hated Face.
This said; she wept, and the vast throng was mov'd,
And with a gen'ral *Sigh* her Grief approv'd

When *Priam* (who had heard the mourning Crowd)
Rose from his Seat, and thus he spake aloud.
Cease your Lamentings, Trojans, for a while,
And fell down Trees to build a Fun'ral Pile;
Fear not an Ambush by the Grecians *laid,*
For with Achilles, *twelve days Truce I made.*
30   He spake, and all obey'd as with one mind,
Chariots were brought, and Mules and Oxen joyn'd;
Forth from the City all the People went,
And nine days space was in that labour spent:
The tenth, a most stupendious *Pile* they made,
And on the top the Manly *Hector* laid,
Then gave it fire, while all, with weeping eyes
Beheld the rowling Flames and Smoak arise.
All night they wept, and all the night it burn'd,
But when the Rosie Morn with day return'd,
40   About the *Pile* the thronging People came,
And with black Wine quencht the remaining Flame.
His Brothers then, and Friends search'd ev'ry where,
And gath'ring up his Snowy Bones with care,
Wept o're 'em; when an Urn of Gold was brought,
Wrapt in soft purple *Palls*, and richly wrought,
In which the Sacred *Ashes* were inter'd;
Then o're his Grave a *Monument* they rear'd.
Mean time, strong Guards were plac'd, and careful Spies,
To watch the *Grecians*, and prevent surprize.
50   The Work once ended, all the vast resort
Of mourning People, went to *Priam*'s Court;
There, they refresh'd their weary Limbs with rest,
Ending the Fun'ral with a Solemn Feast.   (Date uncertain)

KNIGHTLY CHETWOOD
(1650–1720)

The Iliad VI.57–130 [490–565] Hector to Andromache

    Hector reply'd, *This you have said, and more,*
I have revolv'd in serious Thoughts before.
But I not half so much those Grecians *fear,*
As Carpet-Knights, State-Dames, and Flatterers here.
For they, if ever I decline the Fight,
Miscall wise Conduct Cowardise and Flight;
Others may methods chuse the most secure,
My Life no middle Courses can endure.
Urg'd by my own, and my great Father's Name,
10 *I must add something to our ancient Fame.*
Embarqu'd in Ilium's *Cause, I cannot fly,*
Will Conquer with it, or must for it die:
But still some boding Genius does portend
To all my Toils an unsuccessful end,
For how can Man with heavenly Powers contend?
The Day advances with the swiftest pace,
Which Troy, *and all her Glories, shall deface,*
Which Asia's *sacred Empire shall confound,*
And these proud Towers lay level with the ground:
20 *But all compar'd with you does scarce* appear,
When I presage your case, I learn to fear:
When you by some proud *Conqu'rour shall be led*
A mournful Captive *to a Master's Bed.*
Perhaps some haughty Dame your hands shall doom,
To Weave Troy's *Downfal, in a Grecian Loom.*
Or lower yet, you may be forc'd to bring
Water to Argos, *from* Hiperia's *Spring;*
And as you measure out the tedious way,
Some one shall, pointing to his Neighbour, say,

30   *See to what Fortune* Hector's *Wife is brought,*
That famous General, that for Ilium *fought.*
This will renew your sorrows without end,
Depriv'd in such a Day, of such a Friend.
But this is Fancy, or before it I
Low in the Dust will with my Country lie.

    Then to his Infant he his Arms addrest,
The Child clung, crying, to his Nurse's Breast,
Scar'd at the burnish'd Arms, and threat'ning Crest.
This made them smile, whilst *Hector* doth unbrace
40 His shining Helmet, and disclos'd his Face:
Then dancing the pleas'd Infant in the Air,
Kiss'd him, and to the Gods conceiv'd this Pray'r:

    Jove, *and you Heavenly Powers, whoever hear*
Hector'*s Request with a Propitious Ear,*
Grant, this my Child in Honour and Renown
May equal me, wear, and deserve the Crown;
And when from some great Action he shall come
Laden with Hostile Spoils in Triumph home,
May Trojans *say,* Hector *great things hath done,*
50 *But is surpass'd by his Illustrious Son.*
This will rejoyce his tender Mothers Heart,
And sense of Joy to my pale Ghost impart.

    Then in the Mothers Arms he puts the Child,
With *troubl'd* Joy, in flowing *Tears* she *smil'd.*
Beauty and *Grief* shew'd all their Pomp and Pride,
Whilst those soft Passions did her Looks divide.
This Scene even *Hector*'s Courage melted down,
But soon recovering, with a *Lover*'s Frown:

    Madam (says he) *these Fancies put away,*
60 *I cannot Die before my* fatal *Day.*
Heaven, when we first take in our vital Breath,
Decrees the way, *and* moment *of our Death.*
Women should fill their Heads with Womens Cares,
And leave to Men (unquestion'd) Mens affairs.

> *A Truncheon sutes not with a Ladies Hand,*
> *War is my Province that in chief Command.*
> The Beauteous Princess *silently* withdrew,
> Turns oft, and with *sad,* wishing Eyes, does her Lord's Steps
>   pursue.
> Pensive to her Apartment she returns,
70 And with *Prophetick* Tears approaching Evils mourns.
> Then tells all to her Maids, officious they
> His Funeral Rites to living *Hector* pay,
> Whilst forth he rushes through the *Scaean* Gate,
> Does his own part, and leaves the rest to *Fate.*   (1693)

ANDREW TOOKE (1673–1732)

The Iliad XIV.100–123 [312–36] *Jove's amorous lust*

> Then *Jove*; *This Journey* you may well delay,
> But *flitting Love* has Wings, and cannot stay:
> Here clasp'd in one another's Arms let's lie,
> And gather e'er it fade the blooming joy.
> Ne'er did Divine or Human Love inspire
> My Breast before with such an ardent fire:
> Not fair *Alcmena* charm'd with this delight,
> Nor all the pleasures of th' *extended* Night;
> Not *Semele,* whose vigorous Off-spring show'd
10 In what warm transports I begot the God;
> Not the fresh Beauties of *Latona*'s face,
> Nor comelier *Ceres* more Majestick Grace;
> Nor even *Thou thy self,* nor didst thou e'er
> Look so Divinely Bright, so charming Fair.
>   To him the Goddess thus repli'd, Great *Jove,*
> This place is not a proper Scene for Love:

He shuns the busy day, the prying Light,
And flies to the retreat of silent Night.
Caught by some God, I shall become their Jest
20   Both at the Council and the publick Feast;
When e'er I'm look'd on, I shall think they trace
The print of pleasure in my glowing face;
And by my Blushes and my Care reveal
That Secret which I labour to conceal.   (1701)

ARTHUR MAINWARING
(1668–1712)

The Iliad I.245–70 [223–46] *Achilles' rage*

  Achilles now in ruder Language rail'd,
His Rage encreasing as his Reason fail'd;
Thou Chief, more Heartless than a flying Deer,
Who dar'st not first in bloody Fields appear;
Nor doubtful Ambush for thy Foes design,
Vain empty Heroe, ever steep'd in Wine:
Fighting seems Death to thee, whose chief Delight
Is robbing Soldiers of their Legal Right.
Vile are the Slaves who thy dull Presence throng,
10   Thou hadst not else out-liv'd this brutal Wrong:
But by this awful Scepter now I swear,
(Which ne'er again will happy Branches bear,
Nor native Bark, nor growing Leaves will shoot,
But left on distant Hills the kindly Root;
And now with *Grecian* Judges must remain,
Who Right dispence, and Sacred Laws maintain)
Hear what I swear, When e'er the *Greeks* shall want
My needful Aid, Destruction to prevent,

And with Regret their lost *Achilles* mourn,
20   No Pray'rs, nor Gifts shall Bribe me to return;
Hector shall strow with slaughter'd Foes the Field,
And no Relief thy Impotence shall yield;
But, torn with deep Remorse, thy Heart shall break,
For wronging thus in Arms the bravest *Greek*.
  The Speech concluded, in Disdain he tost
His Scepter down, with Golden Studs Emboss'd . . .   (1704)

ALEXANDER POPE (1688–1744)

Pope's 'Homer' remains central. Proposals for this enterprise were issued in 1713. Books I–IV appeared in 1715 (followed two days later by Tickell's version of Book I). The years 1716–20 saw the completion of the work in six volumes. We now have the magisterial edition by Maynard Mack and his colleagues. Volumes VII–X of the *Twickenham Edition of the Poems of Alexander Pope* comprise both the *Iliad* and the *Odyssey*.

Pope's preoccupation with Homer dates back to his childhood. The project of a complete translation ripened after 1707. Pope drew richly if critically on his predecessors: on Chapman, on Ogilby and Hobbes, on Dryden's fragmentary version, on Houdart de La Motte's *Discours sur Homère* of 1714, and, above all, on Anne Lefevre Dacier's *Iliad* of 1711 and *Odyssey* of 1716.

But the vision which underlies this translation is profoundly that of Pope. Homer was for him the ultimate master of 'poetic Inventions'. His epics are at the same time 'histories' of events and mores in the ancient world. Historical verity is made undying art. To justify this estimate, Pope mitigates and elides what he judges to be gross or barbaric in Homer's theology and depiction of human conduct. In turn, he elaborates on the pictorial elements and the morally sententious. Where he can, Pope strives to render exemplary and typological what is individual in Homer's sense of persons and styles. The inevitable choice of heroic couplets organizes Pope's whole understanding. The great energies are 'rounded'; a paragraph-motion imposes itself. Yet, as Mack emphasizes, 'the glory of Pope's *Homer* is its variety'. Within the heroic-couplet determinations, we find an inspired wealth of local effects and tonal registers. Collaboration with Elijah Fenton and William Broome will weaken Pope's *Odyssey*. But taken together, these two 'Homers' constitute the principal 'epic act' after Milton in the language.

Pope's Preface calls for close attention. Strikingly, he finds in Homer 'a wild Paradise' (a tag which carries us from Milton to the Romantics and Blake). Homer's creativity is 'like a powerful Star, which in the Violence of its Course, drew all things within its *Vortex*'. There are comparisons to be drawn with the narrative 'simplicity of Scripture'. Like Matthew Arnold after him, Pope regards it as his main aim 'to keep alive that Spirit and Fire' which are Homer's distinctive glory. This prefatory *Essay on Homer* concludes with the verdict that the ancient poet was 'the Father of Learning, a Soul capable of ranging over the whole Creation with an intellectual View, shining alone in an Age of Obscurity'. The two Homeric epics 'shall always stand at the top of the sublime Character'.

Pope's main detractors have been those who have not read him.

The Iliad I.295–328 [223–47] *The rage of Achilles*

Nor yet the Rage his boiling Breast forsook,
Which thus redoubling on *Atrides* broke.
O Monster, mix'd of Insolence and Fear,
Thou Dog in Forehead, but in Heart a Deer!

---

2 Atrides] the Monarch *1715*.

4 *Thou Dog in Forehead*.] It has been one of the Objections against the Manners of *Homer*'s Heroes, that they are abusive. Mons. *de la Motte* affirms in his Discourse upon the *Iliad* ⟨II 32⟩, that great Men differ from the vulgar in their manner of expressing their Passion; but certainly in violent Passions

When wert thou known in ambush'd Fights to dare,
Or nobly face the horrid Front of War?
'Tis ours, the Chance of fighting Fields to try,
Thine to look on, and bid the Valiant dye.
So much 'tis safer thro' the Camp to go,
10   And rob a Subject, than despoil a Foe.
Scourge of thy People, violent and base!
Sent in *Jove*'s Anger on a slavish Race,
Who lost to Sense of gen'rous Freedom past
Are tam'd to Wrongs, or this had been thy last.
Now by this sacred Sceptre, hear me swear,

(such as those of *Achilles* and *Agamemnon*) the Great are as subject as any others to these Sallies; of which we have frequent Examples both from History and Experience. *Plutarch*, taking notice of this Line, gives it as a particular Commendation of *Homer*, that 'he constantly affords us a fine Lecture of Morality in his Reprehensions and Praises, by referring them not to the Goods of Fortune or the Body, but those of the Mind, which are in our Power, and for which we are blameable or praise-worthy. Thus, says he, *Agamemnon* is reproach'd for Impudence and Fear, *Ajax* for vain-bragging, *Idomeneus* for the Love of Contention, and *Ulysses* does not reprove even *Thersites* but as a Babbler, tho' he had so many personal Deformities to object to him. In like manner also the Appellations and Epithets with which they accost one another, are generally founded on some distinguishing Qualification of Merit, as *Wise* Ulysses, Hector *equal to* Jove *in Wisdom*, Achilles *chief Glory of* the Greeks,' and the like. Plutarch *of reading Poets* ⟨*De Aud. Poet.* 13 (35 A–C)⟩.

5 *In ambush'd Fights to dare.*] *Homer* has magnify'd the Ambush as the boldest manner of Fight. They went upon those Parties with a few Men only, and generally the most daring of the Army, on Occasions of the greatest Hazard, where they were therefore more expos'd than in a regular Battel. Thus *Idomeneus* in the thirteenth Book expressly tells *Meriones* that the greatest Courage appears in this way of Service, each Man being in a manner singled out to the Proof of it. *Eustathius.*

15 *Now by this sacred Sceptre.*] *Spondanus* ⟨*Iliad,* p. 13⟩ in this Place blames *Eustathius*, for saying that *Homer* makes *Achilles* in his Passion swear by the first thing he meets with; and then assigns (as from himself) two Causes which the other had mention'd so plainly before, that it is a wonder they could be overlook'd. The Substance of the whole Passage in *Eustathius* is, that if we consider the Sceptre simply as Wood, *Achilles* after the manner of the

Which never more shall Leaves or Blossoms bear,
Which sever'd from the Trunk (as I from thee)
On the bare Mountains left its Parent Tree;
This Sceptre, form'd by temper'd Steel to prove
20   An Ensign of the Delegates of *Jove*,
From whom the Pow'r of Laws and Justice springs:
(Tremendous Oath! inviolate to Kings)

Ancients takes in his Transport the first thing to swear by; but that *Homer* himself has in the Process of the Description assign'd Reasons why it is proper for the Occasion, which may be seen by considering it Symbolically. First, That as the Wood being cut from the Tree will never re-unite and flourish, so neither should their Amity ever flourish again, after they were divided by this Contention. Secondly, That a Sceptre being the mark of Power and Symbol of Justice, to swear by it might in effect be construed swearing by the God of Power, and by Justice itself; and accordingly it is spoken of by *Aristotle*, 3 *l. Polit.* ⟨III ix 7⟩ as a usual solemn Oath of Kings.

I cannot leave this Passage without showing in Opposition to some Moderns who have criticiz'd upon it as tedious, that it has been esteem'd a Beauty by the Ancients and engaged them in its Imitation. *Virgil* has almost transcrib'd it in his 12 *Aen.* for the Sceptre of *Latinus.*

Ut sceptrum hoc (sceptrum dextra nam forte gerebat)
Nunquam fronde levi fundet virgulta nec umbras;
Cum semel in silvis imo de stirpe recisum,
Matre caret, posuitque comas & bracchia ferro:
Olim arbos, nunc artificis manus aere decoro
Inclusit, Patribusque dedit gestare Latinis. ⟨206–11⟩

But I cannot think this comes up to the Spirit or Propriety of *Homer*, notwithstanding the Judgment of *Scaliger* who decides for *Virgil* upon a trivial comparison of the Wording in each, *l. 5. cap. 3. Poet* ⟨p. 225 a2⟩. It fails in a greater Point than any he has mention'd, which is that being there us'd on occasion of a Peace, it has no emblematical reference to Division, and yet describes the cutting of the Wood and its Incapacity to bloom and branch again, in as many Words as *Homer*. It is borrow'd by *Valerius Flaccus* in his third Book, where he makes *Jason* swear as a Warriour by his Spear,

Hanc ego magnanimi spolium Didymaonis hastam,
Ut semel est avulsa jugis a matre perempta,
Quae neque jam frondes virides neque proferet umbras,
Fida ministeria & duras obit horrida pugnas,
Testor. – ⟨III 707–11⟩

By this I swear, when bleeding *Greece* again
Shall call *Achilles*, she shall call in vain.
When flush'd with Slaughter, *Hector* comes, to spread
The purpled Shore with Mountains of the Dead,
Then shalt thou mourn th' Affront thy Madness gave,
Forc'd to deplore, when impotent to save:
Then rage in Bitterness of Soul, to know
30   This Act has made the bravest *Greek* thy Foe.
    He spoke; and furious, hurl'd against the Ground
His Sceptre starr'd with golden Studs around.
Then sternly silent sate: With like Disdain,
The raging King return'd his Frowns again.

VI.125–46 [102–18] *Hector enters the fray*

    Hector obedient heard; and, with a Bound,
Leap'd from his trembling Chariot to the Ground;
Thro' all his Host, inspiring Force he flies,
And bids the Thunder of the Battel rise.
With Rage recruited the bold *Trojans* glow,
And turn the Tyde of Conflict on the Foe:

And indeed, however he may here borrow some Expressions from *Virgil* or
fall below him in others, he has nevertheless kept to *Homer* in the Emblem,
by introducing the Oath upon *Jason*'s Grief for sailing to *Colchis* without
Hercules, when he had separated himself from the Body of the *Argonauts* to
search after *Hylas*. To render the Beauty of this Passage more manifest, the
Allusion is inserted (but with the fewest Words possible) in this Translation.
30 *Thy Rashness* ⟨sic⟩ *made the bravest* Greek *thy Foe.*] If self-praise had not
been agreeable to the haughty Nature of *Achilles*, yet *Plutarch* ⟨*De Laude
Ipsius* 6 (541 C–D)⟩ has mention'd a Case, and with respect to him, wherein it
is allowable. He says that *Achilles* has at other times ascrib'd his Success to
Jupiter, but it is permitted to a Man of Merit and Figure who is injuriously
dealt with, to speak frankly of himself to those who are forgetful and
unthankful.

Fierce in the Front he shakes two dazling Spears;
All *Greece* recedes, and 'midst her Triumph fears.
Some God, they thought, who rul'd the Fate of Wars,
10   Shot down avenging, from the Vault of Stars.
    Then thus, aloud. Ye dauntless *Dardans* hear!
And you whom distant Nations send to War!
Be mindful of the Strength your Fathers bore;
Be still your selves, and *Hector* asks no more.
One Hour demands me in the *Trojan* Wall,
To bid our Altars flame, and Victims fall:
Nor shall, I trust, the Matron's holy Train
And rev'rend Elders, seek the Gods in vain.
    This said, with ample Strides the Hero past;
20   The Shield's large Orb behind his Shoulder cast,
His Neck o'ershading, to his Ancle hung;
And as he march'd, the brazen Buckler rung.

VIII.685–708 [553–65] *The celebrated episode of the camp-fires, a crux for both admirers and critics of Pope*

    The Troops exulting sate in order round,
And beaming Fires illumin'd all the Ground.
As when the Moon, refulgent Lamp of Night!
O'er Heav'ns clear Azure spreads her sacred Light,

---

3 *As when the Moon,* &c.] This Comparison is inferior to none in *Homer*. It is the most beautiful Nightpiece that can be found in Poetry. He presents you with a Prospect of the Heavens, the Seas, and the Earth: The Stars shine, the Air is serene, the World enlighten'd, and the Moon mounted in Glory. *Eustathius* remarks that φαεινήν does not signify the Moon at full, for then the Light of the Stars is diminished or lost in the greater Brightness of the Moon. And others correct the word φαεινήν, to φάει νῆν, for φάει νέην, but this Criticism is forced, and I see no Necessity why the Moon may not be said to be bright, tho' it is not in the full. A Poet is not obliged to speak with the Exactness of Philosophy, but with the Liberty of Poetry.
4 spreads ⟨*first corrected to this in errata 1720*⟩] sheds *1716*.

When not a Breath disturbs the deep Serene;
And not a Cloud o'ercasts the solemn Scene;
Around her Throne the vivid Planets roll,
And Stars unnumber'd gild the glowing Pole,
O'er the dark Trees a yellower Verdure shed,
10   And tip with Silver ev'ry Mountain's Head;
Then shine the Vales, the Rocks in Prospect rise,
A Flood of Glory bursts from all the Skies:
The conscious Swains, rejoicing in the Sight,
Eye the blue Vault, and bless the useful Light.
So many Flames before proud *Ilion* blaze,
And lighten glimm'ring *Xanthus* with their Rays.
The long Reflections of the distant Fires
Gleam on the Walls, and tremble on the Spires.
A thousand Piles the dusky Horrors gild,
20   And shoot a shady Lustre o'er the Field.

---

19 *A thousand Piles.*] *Homer* in his Catalogue of the *Grecian* Ships, tho' he does not recount expresly the Number of the *Greeks*, has given some Hints from whence the Sum of their Army may be collected. But in the same Book where he gives an Account of the *Trojan* Army, and relates the Names of the Leaders and Nations of the Auxiliaries, he says nothing by which we may infer the Number of the Army of the besieged. To supply therefore that Omission, he has taken occasion by this Piece of Poetical Arithmetick, to inform his Reader, that the *Trojan* Army amounted to fifty thousand. That the Assistant Nations are to be included herein, appears from what *Dolon* says in *l.* 10. that the Auxiliaries were encamped that Night with the *Trojans.*

This Passage gives me occasion to animadvert upon a Mistake of a modern Writer, and another of my own. The *Abbé Terasson* in a late Treatise against *Homer* ⟨*Critical Dissertations on Homer's Iliad,* Engl. tr., London, 1745, I 46⟩, is under a grievous Error, in saying that all the Forces of *Troy* and the Auxiliaries cannot be reasonably suppos'd from *Homer* to be above ten thousand Men. He had entirely overlook'd this Place, which says there were a thousand Fires, and fifty Men at each of them. See my Observation on the second Book, where these Fires by a slip of my Memory are called Funeral Piles: I should be glad it were the greatest Error I have committed in these Notes. ⟨A sentiment I join in for myself. M.M.⟩

Full fifty Guards each flaming Pile attend,
Whose umber'd Arms, by fits, thick Flashes send.
Loud neigh the Coursers o'er their Heaps of Corn,
And ardent Warriors wait the rising Morn.

XI.654–81 [531–57] *Hector on the attack*

Thus having spoke, the Driver's Lash resounds;
Swift thro' the Ranks the rapid Chariot bounds;
Stung by the Stroke, the Coursers scour the Fields
O'er Heaps of Carcasses, and Hills of Shields.

---

23 *The Coursers o'er their Heaps of Corn.*] I durst not take the same Liberty
with M. *Dacier*, who has omitted this Circumstance, and does not mention
the Horses at all. In the following Line, the last of the Book, *Homer* has given
to the *Morning* the Epithet *fair-sphear'd*, or *bright-throned*, εὔθρονον ἠῶ. I have
already taken notice in the Preface of the Method of translating the Epithets
of *Homer*, and must add here, that it is often only the Uncertainty the
Moderns lie under, of the true genuine Signification of an ancient word,
which causes the many various Constructions of it. So that it is probable the
Author's own Words, at the time he used them, never meant half so many
things as we translate them into. Madam *Dacier* generally observes one
Practice as to these throughout her Version: She renders almost every such
Epithet in *Greek* by two or three in *French*, from a fear of losing the least part
of its Significance. This perhaps may be excusable in Prose; tho' at best it
makes the whole much more verbose and tedious, and is rather like writing a
Dictionary than rendring an Author: But in Verse, every Reader knows
such a Redoubling of Epithets would not be tolerable. A Poet has therefore
only to chuse that, which most agrees with the Tenor and main Intent of the
particular Passage, or with the Genius of Poetry itself.

It is plain that too scrupulous an Adherence to many of these, gives the
Translation an exotic, pedantic, and whimsical Air, which it is not to be
imagined the Original ever had. To call a Hero the *great Artificer of Flight*, the
swift of Foot, or the *Horse-tamer*, these give us Ideas of little Peculiarities, when
in the Author's Time they were Epithets used only in general to signify
Alacrity, Agility, and Vigor. A common Reader would imagine from these
servile Versions, that *Diomed* and *Achilles* were Foot-Racers, and *Hector* a
Horse-Courser, rather than that any of them were Heroes. A Man shall be
call'd a faithful Translator for rendring πόδας ὠκύς in *English*, *swift-footed*; but
laugh'd at if he should translate our *English* word *dext'rous* into any other
Language, *right-handed*.

The Horses Hoofs are bath'd in Heroes Gore,
And dashing purple all the Car before,
The groaning Axle sable Drops distills,
And mangled Carnage clogs the rapid Wheels.
Here *Hector* plunging thro' the thickest Fight
10 Broke the dark *Phalanx*, and let in the Light.
(By the long Lance, the Sword, or pondrous Stone,
The Ranks lie scatter'd, and the Troops o'erthrown)
Ajax he shuns, thro' all the dire Debate,
And fears that Arm whose Force he felt so late.
But partial *Jove*, espousing *Hector*'s Part,
Shot heav'n-bred Horror thro' the *Grecian*'s Heart;

---

15 *But partial* Jove, &c.] The Address of *Homer* in bringing off *Ajax* with
Decency is admirable: He makes *Hector* afraid to approach him: He brings
down *Jupiter* himself to terrify him; so that he retreats not from a Mortal, but
from a God.

This whole Passage is inimitably just and beautiful, we see *Ajax* drawn in
the most bold and strong Colours, and in a manner alive in the Description.
We see him slowly and sullenly retreat between two Armies, and even with a
Look repulse the one, and protect the other: There is not one Line but what
resembles *Ajax*; the Character of a stubborn but undaunted Warrior is
perfectly maintain'd, and must strike the Reader at the first view. He
compares him first to the Lion for his Undauntedness in Fighting, and then to
the Ass for his stubborn Slowness in retreating; tho' in the latter Comparison
there are many other Points of Likeness that enliven the Image: The Havock
he makes in the Field is represented by the tearing and trampling down the
Harvests; and we see the Bulk, Strength, and Obstinacy of the Hero, when
the *Trojans* in respect to him are compared but to Troops of Boys that
impotently endeavour to drive him away.

Eustathius is silent as to those Objections which have been rais'd against this
last Simile, for a pretended Want of Delicacy: This alone is Conviction to me
that they are all of a later Date: For else he would not have fail'd to have
vindicated his favourite Poet in a Passage that had been applauded many
hundreds of Years, and stood the Test of Ages.

But Monsieur *Dacier* has done it very well in his Remarks upon *Aristotle*
⟨*La Poétique d'Aristote . . . avec des Remarques*, Paris, 1692, p. 458⟩. 'In the
time of *Homer* (says that Author) an Ass was not in such Circumstances of
Contempt as in ours: The Name of that Animal was not then converted into
a Term of Reproach, but it was a Beast upon which Kings and Princes might
be seen with Dignity. And it will not be very discreet to ridicule this

Confus'd, unnerv'd in *Hector*'s Presence grown,
Amaz'd he stood, with Terrors not his own.
O'er his broad Back his moony Shield he threw,
20   And glaring round, by tardy Steps withdrew.

Comparison, which the holy Scripture has put into the Mouth of *Jacob*, who says in the Benediction of his Children, Issachar *shall be as a strong Ass.*' Monsieur *de la Motte* ⟨II 76–7⟩ allows this Point, and excuses *Homer* for his Choice of this Animal, but is unhappily disgusted at the Circumstance of the Boys, and the obstinate Gluttony of the Ass, which he says are Images too mean to represent the determin'd Valour of *Ajax*, and the Fury of his Enemies. It is answer'd by Madam *Dacier*, that what *Homer* here images is not the Gluttony; but the Patience, the Obstinacy, and Strength of the Ass (as *Eustathius* had before observ'd.) To judge rightly of Comparisons, we are not to examine if the Subject from whence they are deriv'd be great or little, noble or familiar; but we are principally to consider if the Image produc'd be clear and lively, if the Poet has the Skill to dignify it by poetical Words, and if it perfectly paints the thing it is intended to represent. A Company of Boys whipping a Top is very far from a great and noble Subject, yet *Virgil* has not scrupled to draw from it a Similitude which admirably expresses a Princess in the Violence of her Passion.

Ceu quondam torto volitans sub verbere turbo,
Quem pueri magno in gyro vacua atria circum
Intenti ludo exercent; ille actus habena
Curvatis fertur spatiis: stupet inscia supra
Impubesque manus, mirata volubile buxum:
Dant animos plagae – & c.   Aen. lib. 7. ⟨378–83⟩

However, upon the whole, a Translator owes so much to the Taste of the Age in which he lives, as not to make too great a Complement to a former; and this induced me to omit the mention of the word *Ass* in the Translation. I believe the Reader will pardon me, if on this Occasion I transcribe a Passage from Mr. *Boileau*'s Notes on *Longinus* ⟨'Ninth Reflection upon Longinus', *Works*, London, 1711, II 121–2; but the adaptation seems to be Pope's own.⟩.

'There is nothing (says he) that more disgraces a Composition than the Use of mean and vulgar Words; insomuch that (generally speaking) a mean Thought express'd in noble Terms, is more tolerable than a noble Thought express'd in mean ones. The Reason whereof is, that all the World are not capable to judge of the Justness and Force of a Thought; but there's scarce any Man who cannot, especially in a living Language, perceive the least Meanness of Words. Nevertheless very few Writers are free from this Vice: *Longinus* accuses *Herodotus*, the most polite of all the *Greek* Historians, of this Defect; and *Livy*, *Salust*, and *Virgil* have not escaped the same Censure. Is it

Thus the grim Lion his Retreat maintains,
Beset with watchful Dogs, and shouting Swains,
Repuls'd by Numbers from the nightly Stalls,
Tho' Rage impells him, and tho' Hunger calls,
Long stands the show'ring Darts, and missile Fires;
Then sow'rly slow th' indignant Beast retires.
So turn'd stern *Ajax*, by whole Hosts repell'd,
While his swoln Heart at ev'ry Step rebell'd.

XV.248–74 [221–42] *Jupiter's commandments to Apollo*

Behold! the God whose liquid Arms are hurl'd
Around the Globe, whose Earthquakes rock the World;
Desists at length his Rebel-war to wage,
Seeks his own Seas, and trembles at our Rage!

---

not then very surprizing, that no Reproach on this Account has been ever
cast upon *Homer*? tho' he has compos'd two Poems each more voluminous
than the *Aeneid*; and tho' no Author whatever has descended more frequently
than he into a Detail of little Particularities. Yet he never uses Terms which
are not noble, or if he uses humble Words or Phrases, it is with so much Art
that, as *Dionysius* observes, they become noble and harmonious. Undoubtedly
if there had been any Cause to charge him with this Fault, *Longinus* had
spared him no more than *Herodotus*. We may learn from hence the Ignorance
of those modern Criticks, who resolving to judge of the *Greek* without the
Knowledge of it, and never reading *Homer* but in low and inelegant Transla-
tions, impute the Meannesses of his Translators to the Poet himself; and
ridiculously blame a Man who spoke in one Language, for speaking what is
not elegant in another. They ought to know that the Words of different
Languages are not always exactly correspondent; and it may often happen
that a Word which is very noble in *Greek*, cannot be render'd in another
Tongue but by one which is very mean. Thus the word *Asinus* in *Latin*, and
Ass in *English*, are the vilest imaginable, but that which signifies the same
Animal in *Greek* and *Hebrew*, is of Dignity enough to be employed on the
most magnificent Occasions. In like manner the Terms of a *Hogherd* and
Cowkeeper in our Language are insufferable, but those which answer to them
in *Greek*, συβώτης and βουκόλος, are graceful and harmonious: and *Virgil* who
in his own Tongue entitled his Eclogs *Bucolica*, would have been ashamed to
have called them in ours, the *Dialogues of Cowkeepers*.'

Else had my Wrath, Heav'ns Thrones all shaking round,
Burn'd to the bottom of the Seas profound;
And all the Gods that round old *Saturn* dwell,
Had heard the Thunders to the Deeps of Hell.
Well was the Crime, and well the Vengeance spar'd;
10 Ev'n Pow'r immense had found such Battel hard.
Go thou my Son! the trembling *Greeks* alarm,
Shake my broad *Aegis* on thy active Arm,
Be godlike *Hector* thy peculiar Care,
Swell his bold Heart, and urge his Strength to War:
Let *Ilion* conquer, till th' *Achaian* Train
Fly to their Ships and *Hellespont* again:
Then *Greece* shall breathe from Toils – The Godhead said;
His Will divine the Son of *Jove* obey'd.
Not half so swift the sailing Falcon flies,
20 That drives a Turtle thro' the liquid Skies;
As *Phoebus* shooting from th' *Idaean* Brow,
Glides down the Mountain to the Plain below.
There *Hector* seated by the Stream he sees,
His Sense returning with the coming Breeze;

---

5 *Else had our* ⟨sic⟩ *Wrath*, & c.] This Representation of the Terrors which
must have attended the Conflict of two such mighty Powers as *Jupiter* and
Neptune, whereby the Elements had been mix'd in Confusion, and the whole
Frame of Nature endangered, is imaged in these few Lines with a Nobleness
suitable to the Occasion. *Milton* has a Thought very like it in his fourth Book,
where he represents what must have happen'd if *Satan* and *Gabriel* had
encounter'd.

> *– Not only* Paradise
> *In this Commotion, but the starry Cope*
> *Of Heav'n, perhaps, and all the Elements*
> *At least had gone to wrack, disturb'd and torn*
> *With Violence of this Conflict, had not soon*
> *Th' Almighty, to prevent such horrid Fray,* &c. ⟨991–6⟩

6 the] his *1718–32*.

Again his Pulses beat, his Spirits rise;
Again his lov'd Companions meet his Eyes;
Jove thinking of his Pains, they past away.

XVIII.637–64 [550–72] *One of the scenes depicted on Achilles' shield*

    Another Field rose high with waving Grain;
With bended Sickles stand the Reaper-Train:
Here stretch'd in Ranks the level'd Swarths are found,
Sheaves heap'd on Sheaves, here thicken up the Ground.
With sweeping Stroke the Mowers strow the Lands;
The Gath'rers follow, and collect in Bands;
And last the Children, in whose Arms are born
(Too short to gripe them) the brown Sheaves of Corn.
The rustic Monarch of the Field descries
10 With silent Glee, the Heapes around him rise.
A ready Banquet on the Turf is laid,
Beneath an ample Oak's expanded Shade.
The Victim-Ox the sturdy Youth prepare;
The Reaper's due Repast, the Women's Care.
    Next, ripe in yellow Gold, a Vineyard shines,
Bent with the pond'rous Harvest of its Vines;
A deeper Dye the dangling Clusters show,
And curl'd on silver Props, in order glow:

---

27 *Jove thinking of his Pains, they past away.*] *Eustathius* observes, that this is a very sublime Representation of the Power of *Jupiter*, to make *Hector*'s Pains cease from the Moment wherein *Jupiter* first turn'd his Thoughts towards him. *Apollo* finds him so far recover'd, as to be able to sit up, and know his Friends. Thus much was the Work of *Jupiter*; the God of Health perfects the Cure.
9 *The rustic Monarch of the Field.*] *Dacier* takes this to be a piece of Ground given to a Hero in reward of his Services. It was in no respect unworthy such a Person, in those Days, to see his Harvest got in, and to overlook his Reapers: It is very conformable to the Manners of the ancient Patriarchs, such as they are describ'd to us in the Holy Scriptures.

A darker Metal mixt, intrench'd the Place,
20 And Pales of glitt'ring Tin th' Enclosure grace.
To this, one Pathway gently winding leads,
Where march a Train with Baskets on their Heads,
(Fair Maids, and blooming Youths) that smiling bear
The purple Product of th' Autumnal Year.
To these a Youth awakes the warbling Strings,
Whose tender Lay the Fate of *Linus* sings;
In measur'd Dance behind him move the Train,
Tune soft the Voice, and answer to the Strain.

---

26 *The Fate of* Linus.] There are two Interpretations of this Verse in the Original: That which I have chosen is confirm'd by the Testimony of *Herodotus* lib. 2. ⟨79⟩ and *Pausanias, Boeoticis* ⟨IX xxix 6⟩. *Linus* was the most ancient Name in Poetry, the first upon Record who invented Verse and Measure among the *Grecians*: He past for the Son of *Apollo* or *Mercury*, and was Praeceptor to *Hercules, Thamyris,* and *Orpheus.* There was a solemn Custom among the *Greeks* of bewailing annually the Death of their first Poet: *Pausanias* informs us, that before the yearly Sacrifice to the Muses on Mount *Helicon,* the Obsequies of *Linus* were perform'd, who had a Statue and Altar erected to him, in that Place. *Homer* alludes to that Custom in this Passage, and was doubtless fond of paying this Respect to the old Father of Poetry. *Virgil* has done the same in that Fine Celebration of him, *Eclog.* 6.

Tum canit errantem Permessi ad flumina Gallum,
Utque viro Phoebi chorus assurrexerit omnis;
Ut Linus *haec illi, divino carmine, pastor*
(Floribus atque apio crines ornatus amaro)
Dixerit – &c. ⟨64, 66–9⟩

And again in the fourth *Eclog.*

Non me carminibus vincet nec Thracius Orpheus,
Nec Linus; *huic Mater quamvis, atque huic Pater adsit,*
Orphei Calliopea, Lino *formosus* Apollo ⟨55–7⟩.

XXIV.590–646 [480–512] *Priam enters Achilles' tent and makes supplication*

As when a Wretch, (who conscious of his Crime
Pursu'd for Murder, flies his native Clime)
Just gains some Frontier, breathless, pale! amaz'd!
All gaze, all wonder: Thus *Achilles* gaz'd:
Thus stood th' Attendants stupid with Surprize;
All mute, yet seem'd to question with their Eyes:
Each look'd on other, none the Silence broke,
Till thus at last the Kingly Suppliant spoke,
　　Ah think, thou favour'd of the Pow'rs Divine!
10　Think of thy Father's Age, and pity mine!
In me, that Father's rev'rend Image trace,
Those silver Hairs, that venerable Face;

---

9 *The Speech of* Priam *to* Achilles.] The Curiosity of the Reader must needs be awaken'd to know how *Achilles* would behave to this unfortunate King; it requires all the Art of the Poet to sustain the violent Character of *Achilles*, and yet at the same time to soften him into Compassion. To this end the Poet uses no Preamble, but breaks directly into that Circumstance which is most likely to mollify him, and the two first Words he utters are, μνῆσαι Πατρός, *see thy Father*, O Achilles, *in me!* Nothing could be more happily imagin'd than this Entrance into his Speech; *Achilles* has every where been describ'd as bearing a great Affection to his Father, and by two Words the Poet recalls all the Tenderness that Love and Duty can suggest to an affectionate Son.

Priam tells *Achilles* that *Hector* fell in the Defence of his Country: I am far from thinking that this was inserted accidentally; it could not fail of having a very good Effect upon *Achilles*, not only as one brave Man naturally loves another, but as it implies that *Hector* had no particular Enmity against *Achilles*, but that tho' he fought against him it was in Defence of his Country.

The Reader will observe that *Priam* repeats the Beginning of his Speech, and recalls his Father to his Memory in the Conclusion of it. This is done with great Judgment; the Poet takes care to enforce his Petition with the strongest Motive, and leaves it fresh upon his Memory; and possibly *Priam* might perceive that the mention of his Father had made a deeper Impression upon *Achilles* than any other part of his Petition, therefore while the Mind of *Achilles* dwells upon it, he again sets him before his Imagination by this Repetition, and softens him into Compassion.

His trembling Limbs, his helpless Person, see!
In all my Equal, but in Misery!
Yet now perhaps, some Turn of human Fate
Expells him helpless from his peaceful State;
Think from some pow'rful Foe thou see'st him fly,
And beg Protection with a feeble Cry,
Yet still one Comfort in his Soul may rise;
20   He hears his Son still lives to glad his Eyes;
And hearing still may hope, a better Day
May send him thee to chase that Foe away.
No Comfort to my Griefs, no Hopes remain,
The best, the bravest of my Sons are slain!
Yet what a Race? e'er *Greece* to *Ilion* came,
The Pledge of many a lov'd, and loving Dame;
Nineteen one Mother bore – Dead, all are dead!
How oft, alas! has wretched *Priam* bled?
Still One was left, their Loss to recompense;
30   His Father's Hope, his Country's last Defence.
Him too thy Rage has slain! beneath thy Steel
Unhappy, in his Country's Cause he fell!
    For him, thro' hostile Camps I bent my way,
For him thus prostrate at thy Feet I lay;
Large Gifts, proportion'd to thy Wrath, I bear;
Oh hear the Wretched, and the Gods revere!
    Think of thy Father, and this Face behold!
See him in me, as helpless and as old!
Tho' not so wretched: There he yields to me,
40   The First of Men in sov'reign Misery.
Thus forc'd to kneel, thus grov'ling to embrace
The Scourge and Ruin of my Realm and Race;
Suppliant my Childrens Murd'rer to implore,
And kiss those Hands yet reeking with their Gore!
    These Words soft Pity in the Chief inspire,

---

45 *These Words soft Pity,* &c.] We are now come almost to the end of the
Poem, and consequently to the end of the Anger of *Achilles*: And *Homer* has

Touch'd with the dear Remembrance of his Sire.
Then with his Hand (as prostrate still he lay)
The Old Man's Cheek he gently turn'd away.
Now each by turns indulg'd the Gush of Woe;
50 And now the mingled Tides together flow:
This low on Earth, that gently bending o'er,
A Father one, and one a Son, deplore:
But great *Achilles* diff'rent Passions rend,
And now his Sire he mourns, and now his Friend.
Th' infectious Softness thro' the Heroes ran;
One universal, solemn Show'r began;
They bore as Heroes, but they felt as Man.   (1715-20)

ALEXANDER POPE *et al.*

The following selections illustrate the work of Pope's collaborators.

Homer's Odyssey, IV.683-740 [512-47] (ELIJAH
FENTON, 1683-1730) *Agamemnon's fatal homecoming as told
to Menelaus*

By *Juno's* guardian aid, the wat'ry Vast
Secure of storms, your royal brother past:
'Till coasting nigh the Cape, where *Malea* shrouds
Her spiry cliffs amid surrounding clouds;

---

describ'd the Abatement of it with excellent Judgment. We may here observe
how necessary the Conduct of *Homer* was, in sending *Thetis* to prepare her
Son to use *Priam* with Civility: It would have ill suited with the violent
Temper of *Achilles* to have used *Priam* with Tenderness without such Pre-
admonition; nay, the unexpected Sight of his Enemy might probably have
carry'd him into Violence and Rage: But *Homer* has avoided these Absurdities;
for *Achilles* being already prepared for a Reconciliation, the Misery of this
venerable Prince naturally melts him into Compassion.

A whirling gust tumultuous from the shore,
Across the deep his lab'ring vessel bore.
In an ill-fated hour the coast he gain'd,
Where late in regal pomp *Thyestes* reign'd;
But when his hoary honours bow'd to fate,
10   *Aegisthus* govern'd in paternal state.
The surges now subside, the tempest ends;
From his tall ship the King of men descends:
There fondly thinks the Gods conclude his toil!
Far from his own domain salutes the soil;
With rapture oft the verge of *Greece* reviews,
And the dear turf with tears of joy bedews.
Him thus exulting on the distant strand,
A Spy distinguish'd from his airy stand;
To bribe whose vigilance, *Aegisthus* told
20   A mighty sum of ill-persuading gold:
There watch'd this guardian of his guilty fear,
'Till the twelfth moon had wheel'd her pale career;
And now admonish'd by his eye, to court
With terror wing'd conveys the dread report.
Of deathful arts expert, his Lord employs
The ministers of blood in dark surprize:
And twenty youths in radiant mail incas'd,
Close ambush'd nigh the spacious hall he plac'd.
Then bids prepare the hospitable treat:
30   Vain shews of love to veil his felon hate!
To grace the victor's welcome from the wars,
A train of coursers, and triumphal cars
Magnificent he leads: the royal guest
Thoughtless of ill, accepts the fraudful feast.
The troop forth issuing from the dark recess,
With homicidal rage the King oppress!
So, whilst he feeds luxurious in the stall,
The sov'reign of the herd is doom'd to fall.

---

37 *So, whilst he feeds luxurious in the stall*, &c.] Dacier translates βοῦν, by
taureau a bull; and misunderstands *Eustathius* who directly says, that in the 2d

The partners of his fame and toils at *Troy*,
40 Around their Lord, a mighty ruin! lye:
Mix'd with the brave, the base invaders bleed;
Aegisthus sole survives to boast the deed.

He said; chill horrors shook my shiv'ring soul,
Rack'd with convulsive pangs in dust I roul;
And hate, in madness of extreme despair,
To view the sun, or breathe the vital air.
But when superior to the rage of woe,
I stood restor'd, and tears had ceas'd to flow;
Lenient of grief, the pitying God began. –
50 Forget the brother, and resume the man:
To fate's supreme dispose the dead resign,
That care be fate's, a speedy passage thine.
Still lives the wretch who wrought the death deplor'd,
But lives a victim for thy vengeful sword;
Unless with filial rage *Orestes* glow,
And swift prevent the meditated blow:
You timely will return a welcome guest,
With him to share the sad funereal feast.

V.343–60 [269–81] (ALEXANDER POPE) *Ulysses under way after leaving Calypso*

And now, rejoycing in the prosp'rous gales,
With beating heart *Ulysses* spreads his sails;
Plac'd at the helm he sate, and mark'd the skies,
Nor clos'd in sleep his ever-watchful eyes.

Iliad the Poet compares *Agamemnon* to a bull, in this place to an oxe, ταύρῳ
εἴκασεν, νῦν δὲ βοῒ αὐτὸν ὡμοίωσεν. The one was undoubtedly design'd to
describe the courage and majestic port of a warrior, the other to give us an
image of a Prince falling in full peace and plenty, ὡς βοῦν ἐπὶ φάτνῃ.
2 Ulysses *spreads his sails*.] It is observable that the Poet passes over the
parting of *Calypso* and *Ulysses* in silence; he leaves it to be imagin'd by the
Reader, and prosecutes his main action. Nothing but a cold compliment
could have proceeded from *Ulysses*, he being overjoy'd at the prospect of

There view'd the *Pleiads*, and the northern Team,
And great *Orion*'s more refulgent beam,
To which, around the axle of the sky
The Bear revolving, points his golden eye;
Who shines exalted on th' etherial plain,
Nor bathes his blazing forehead in the main.
Far on the left those radiant fires to keep
The Nymph directed, as he sail'd the deep.
Full sev'nteen nights he cut the foamy way;
The distant land appear'd the following day:
Then swell'd to sight *Phaeacia*'s dusky coast,
And woody mountains, half in vapours lost;

10

---

returning to his country: it was therefore judicious in *Homer* to omit the relation; and not draw *Calypso* in tears, and *Ulysses* in a transport of joy. Besides, it was necessary to shorten the Episode: the commands of *Jupiter* were immediately to be obey'd; and the story being now turn'd to *Ulysses*, it was requisite to put him immediately upon action, and describe him endeavouring to re-establish his own affairs, which is the whole design of the *Odyssey*.

13 *Full sev'nteen nights he cut the foamy way.*] It may seem incredible that one person should be able to manage a vessel seventeen days without any assistance; but *Eustathius* vindicates *Homer* by an instance, that very much resembles this of *Ulysses*. A certain *Pamphylian* being taken prisoner, and carried to *Tamiathis* (afterwards *Damietta*) in *Aegypt*, continued there several years; but being continually desirous to return to his country, he pretends a skill in sea affairs; this succeeds, and he is immediately employ'd in Maritime business, and permitted the liberty to follow it according to his own inclination, without any inspection. He made use of this opportunity, and furnishing himself with a sail, and provisions for a long voyage, committed himself to the sea all alone; he cross'd that vast extent of waters that lies between *Aegypt* and *Pamphylia*, and arriv'd safely in his own country: In memory of this prodigious event he chang'd his name, and was called μονοναύτης, or the *sole-sailor*; and the family was not extinct in the days of *Eustathius*.

It may not be improper to observe, that this description of *Ulysses* sailing alone is a demonstration of the smallness of his vessel; for it is impossible that a large one could be managed by a single person. It is indeed said that twenty trees were taken down for the vessel, but this does not imply that all the trees were made use of, but only so much of them as was necessary to his purpose.

That lay before him, indistinct and vast,
Like a broad shield amid the watry waste.

IX.248–67 [213–27] (ALEXANDER POPE) *Ulysses' foreboding in the land of the Cyclops*

My soul foreboded I should find the bow'r
Of some fell monster, fierce with barb'rous pow'r,
Some rustic wretch, who liv'd in heav'n's despight,
Contemning laws, and trampling on the right.
The cave we found, but vacant all within,
(His flock the Giant tended on the green)
But round the grott we gaze, and all we view
In order rang'd, our admiration drew:
The bending shelves with loads of cheeses prest,
10   The folded flocks each sep'rate from the rest,
(The larger here, and there the lesser lambs,
The new-fall'n young here bleating for their dams;
The kid distinguish'd from the lambkin lies:)
The cavern ecchoes with responsive cries.
Capacious chargers all around were lay'd,
Full pails, and vessels of the milking trade.
With fresh provision hence our fleet to store
My friends advise me, and to quit the shore;
Or drive a flock of sheep and goats away,
20   Consult our safety, and put off to sea.

---

18 *Like a broad shield amid the watry waste.*] This expression gives a very lively idea of an Island of small extent, that is, of a form more long than large: *Aristarchus* ⟨Dindorf, p. 272⟩, instead of ῥινόν, writes ἐρινόν, or resembling a *Fig*; others tell us, that ῥινόν is used by the *Illyrians* to signify ἀχλύς, or a *Mist*; this likewise very well represents the first appearance of land to those that sail at a distance: it appears indistinct and confus'd, or as it is here express'd, like a Mist. *Eustathius.*

3 *Some rustic wretch, who liv'd, &c.*] This whole passage must be consider'd as told by a person long after the adventure was past, otherwise how should

XI.741–74 [601–27] (WILLIAM BROOME, 1689–1745)
The shade of Hercules in Hades

Now I the strength of *Hercules* behold,
A tow'ring spectre of gigantic mold,
A shadowy form! for high in heav'n's abodes
Himself resides, a God among the Gods;
There in the bright assemblies of the skies,
He Nectar quaffs, and *Hebe* crowns his joys.
Here hovering ghosts, like fowl, his shade surround,
And clang their pinions with terrific sound;
Gloomy as night he stands, in act to throw
10   Th' aerial arrow from the twanging bow.
Around his breast a wond'rous Zone is rowl'd,
Where woodland monsters grin in fretted gold,
There sullen Lions sternly seem to roar,
The bear to growl, to foam the tusky boar:
There war and havoc and destruction stood,
And vengeful murther red with human blood.

Ulysses know that this cave was the habitation of a savage monster before he had seen him? and when he tells us that himself and twelve companions went to search, what people were inhabitants of this Island? *Eustathius* and *Dacier* seem both to have overlook'd this observation : for in a following note she condemns *Ulysses* for not flying from the Island, as he was advis'd by his companions. But if, on the other hand, we suppose that *Ulysses* was under apprehensions from the savageness of the place, of finding a savage race of people; it will be natural enough that his mind should forebode as much; and it appears from other passages, that this sort of instinctive presage was a favourite opinion of *Homer's*.

1 – Hercules, ⟨. . .⟩ *A shadowy form.*] This is the passage formerly referr'd to in these annotations, to prove that *Hercules* was in Heaven, while his shade was in the infernal regions; a full evidence of the partition of the human composition into three parts: The body is buried in the earth; the image or εἴδωλον descends into the regions of the departed; and the soul, or the divine part of man, is receiv'd into Heaven: Thus the body of *Hercules* was consumed in the flames, his image is in Hell, and his soul in Heaven. There is

Thus terribly adorn'd the figures shine,
Inimitably wrought with skill divine.
The mighty ghost advanc'd with awful look,
20   And turning his grim visage, sternly spoke.
    O exercis'd in grief! by arts refin'd!
O taught to bear the wrongs of base mankind!
Such, such was I! still tost from care to care,
While in your world I drew the vital air;
Ev'n I who from the Lord of thunders rose,
Bore toils and dangers, and a weight of woes;

---

a beautiful moral couch'd in the fable of his being married to *Hebe*, or *youth*,
after death: to imply, that a perpetual youth or a reputation which never
grows old, is the reward of those Heroes, who like *Hercules* employ their
courage for the good of humankind.

18 *Inimitably wrought with skill divine.*] This verse is not without obscurity;
Eustathius gives us several interpretations of it.

Μὴ τεχνησάμενος, μηδ᾽ ἄλλο τι τεχνήσαιτο

The negative *μή*, by being repeated, seems to be redundant; and this in a
great measure occasions the difficulty; but in the *Greek* language two negatives
more strongly deny; this being premis'd, we may read the verse as if the
former *μὴ* were absent, and then the meaning will be, 'He that made this
zone, never made any thing equal to it:' as if we should say that *Phidias* who
made the statue of *Jupiter* never made any other statue like it; that is, he
employ'd the whole power of his skill upon it. Others understand the verse as
an execration: *Oh, never, never may the hand that made it, make any thing again
so terrible as this Zone!* And this will give some reason for the repetition of the
negative particles. *Dacier* approves of this latter explanation, and moralizes
upon it: It proceeds (says she) from a tender sentiment of humanity in *Ulysses*,
who wishes that there may never more be occasion for such a design, as the
artist executed in this belt of *Hercules*; that there may be no more giants to
conquer, no more monsters to tame, or no more human blood be shed. I
wish that such a pious and well-natured explication were to be drawn from
the passage! But how is it possible that the artist who made this Zone should
ever make another, when he had been in his grave some Centuries? (for such
a distance there was between the days of *Hercules* and *Ulysses*;) and conse-
quently it would be impertinent to wish it. I have therefore follow'd the
former interpretation. I will only add, that this belt of *Hercules* is the reverse
of the girdle of *Venus*; in that, there is a collection of every thing that is
amiable, in this a variety of horrors; but both are master-pieces in their kind.

To a base Monarch still a slave confin'd,
(The hardest bondage to a gen'rous mind!)
Down to these worlds I trod the dismal way,
30   And drag'd the three-mouth'd dog to upper day;
Ev'n hell I conquer'd, thro' the friendly aid
Of *Maia*'s off-spring and the martial Maid.
    Thus he, nor deign'd for our reply to stay,
But turning stalk'd with giant strides away.

XIX.544-74 [467-90] (ELIJAH FENTON)
Eurycleia identifies Ulysses by his scar

Deep o'er his knee inseam'd, remain'd the scar:
Which noted token of the woodland war
When *Euryclea* found, th' ablution ceas'd;
Down dropp'd the leg, from her slack hand releas'd!
The mingled fluids from the vase redound;
The vase reclining floats the floor around!
Smiles dew'd with tears the pleasing strife exprest
Of grief, and joy, alternate in her breast.
Her flutt'ring words in melting murmurs dy'd;
10   At length abrupt – my son! – my King! – she cry'd.

---

10 – *abrupt – my son! – my King! – she cry'd.*] It may seem incredible that this dialogue between *Ulysses* and *Eurycleia* could be held in the presence of *Penelope* and she not hear it: How is this to be reconcil'd to probability? I will answer in the words of *Eustathius*: The Poet, says he, has admirably guarded against this objection; it is for this reason that he mentions the falling of *Ulysses*'s leg into the water, the sound of the vessel from that accident, the overturning of it, and the effusion of the water: all these different sounds may easily be suppos'd to drown the voice of *Eurycleia*, so as it might not be heard by *Penelope*; it is true, she could not but observe this confusion that happen'd while *Eurycleia* washes; but the age of *Eurycleia* might naturally make her believe that all this happen'd by accident thro' her feebleness, and *Penelope* might be persuaded that it was thus occasioned, having no reason to suspect the truth: besides, what is more frequent on the Theatre than to speak to the audience, while the persons on the stage are suppos'd not to hear? In reality, it is evident that *Ulysses* and *Eurycleia* were at a proper distance from *Penelope*,

His neck with fond embrace infolding fast,
Full on the Queen her raptur'd eyes she cast,
Ardent to speak the Monarch safe restor'd:
But studious to conceal her royal Lord,
Minerva fix'd her mind on views remote,
And from the present bliss abstracts her thought.
His hand to *Euryclea*'s mouth apply'd,
Art thou foredoom'd my pest? the Heroe cry'd:
Thy milky founts my infant lips have drain'd;
20 And have the Fates thy babling age ordain'd
To violate the life thy youth sustain'd?
An exile have I told, with weeping eyes,
Full twenty annual suns in distant skies:
At length return'd, some God inspires thy breast
To know thy King, and here I stand confest.
This heav'n-discover'd truth to thee consign'd,
Reserve, the treasure of thy inmost mind:
Else if the Gods my vengeful arm sustain,
And prostrate to my sword the Suitor-train;
30 With their lewd mates, thy undistinguish'd age
Shall bleed a victim to vindictive rage.

XXI.438–64 [404–23] (ALEXANDER POPE)
Ulysses bends his bow

Heedless he heard them; but disdain'd reply;
The bow perusing with exactest eye.
Then, as some heav'nly minstrel, taught to sing
High notes responsive to the trembling string,

---

probably out of decency while the feet were washing; for as soon as that
office is over, *Homer* tells us that *Ulysses* drew nearer to the fire where
Penelope sate, that he might resume the conference.

Αὖτις ἄρ ἀσσοτέρω πυρὸς ἕλκετο δίφρον Ὀδυσσεύς.

3 *Then, as some heav'nly minstrel, &c.*] *Eustathius* confesses himself to be

To some new strain when he adapts the lyre,
Or the dumb lute refits with vocal wire,
Relaxes, strains, and draws them to and fro;
So the great Master drew the mighty bow:
And drew with ease. One hand aloft display'd
10   The bending horns, and one the string essay'd.
From his essaying hand the string let fly
Twang'd short and sharp, like the shrill swallow's cry.
A gen'ral horror ran thro' all the race,
Sunk was each heart, and pale was ev'ry face.
Signs from above ensu'd: th' unfolding sky
In lightning burst; *Jove* thunder'd from on high.

---

greatly pleas'd with this comparison; it is very just, and well suited to the
purpose; the strings of the lyre represent the bow-string, and the ease with
which the Lyrist stretches them, admirably paints the facility with which
Ulysses draws the bow. When similitudes are borrow'd from an object
entirely different from the subject which they are brought to illustrate, they
give us a double satisfaction, as they surprize us by shewing an agreement
between such things in which there seems to be the greatest disagreement.

11   – *the string let fly*
Twang'd short and sharp, like the shrill swallow's cry.]

The comparison is not intended to represent the sweetness of the sound, but
only the quality and nature of it; and means a harsh or jarring sound, or
somewhat rough, ὑπότραχυ, as *Eustathius* interprets it; such a sound as the
swallow makes when she sings by starts, and not in one even tenour. The
swallow is inharmonious, and *Aristophanes* uses χελιδόνων μουσεῖα in his Frogs
⟨93⟩ to signify those who are enemies to the Muses; and here the Poet uses
it to denote a shrill, harsh, or jarring sound.
15 *Signs from above ensu'd* –] The signal of battle is here given in thunder by
Jupiter, as in the eleventh book of the *Iliad* ⟨52–4⟩.

Ev'n Jove, *whose thunder spoke his wrath, distill'd*
Red drops of blood o'er all the fatal field. ⟨69–70⟩

And again ⟨XI 45–6⟩,

That instant Juno *and the martial maid*
In happy thunders promis'd Greece *their aid.* ⟨57–8⟩

This prepares us for the greatness of the following action, which is usher'd in
with thunder from heaven: And we are not surpriz'd to see *Ulysses* defeat his

Fir'd at the call of Heav'n's almighty Lord,
He snatch'd the shaft that glitter'd on the board:
(Fast by, the rest lay sleeping in the sheath,
20   But soon to fly the messengers of death)
     Now sitting as he was, the chord he drew,
Thro' ev'ry ringlet levelling his view;
Then notch'd the shaft, release, and gave it wing;
The whizzing arrow vanish'd from the string,
Sung on direct, and thredded ev'ry ring.
The solid gate its fury scarcely bounds;
Pierc'd thro' and thro', the solid gate resounds.

XXIII.321–70 [300–343] (WILLIAM BROOME,
1689–1745) *Ulysses recounts his adventures to Penelope*

But in discourse the King and Consort lay,
While the soft hours stole unperceiv'd away;
Intent he hears *Penelope* disclose
A mournful story of domestic woes,

---

enemies, when *Jupiter* declares himself in his favour. *Homer* calls this thunder
a sign and a prodigy: It is a sign because it predicts the event; and a prodigy,
because the thunder proceeds from a serene sky. *Eustathius*.

4 *A mournful story of domestic woes.*] It is with great judgment that the Poet
passes thus briefly over the story of *Penelope*; he makes her impatience to hear
the history of *Ulysses* the pretended occasion of her conciseness; the true
reason is, he is unwilling to tire his Reader by repeating what he already
knows: It is likewise remarkable, that *Ulysses* does not begin his own adven-
tures by a detail of his sufferings during the war of *Troy*; for this would have
been foreign to the design of the *Odyssey*; but with his sailing from *Troy* to
the *Cicons*, and enters directly into the subject of it. He likewise concludes an
Epitome of the whole *Odyssey* in the compass of one and thirty lines; and pur-
posely contracts it, because we are already acquainted with the whole relation.

   Lycophron ⟨648–819⟩ has given us a summary of the wandrings of *Ulysses*;
which if any one is desirous to compare with this of *Homer*, he will see the
difference between a clear, and an obscure Writer. *Tibullus* in his *Panegyric* on
Messala has been more successful than *Lycophron*, he follows the order of
Homer, and treads directly in his footstep ⟨III vii 54–9⟩.

His servants insults, his invaded bed,
How his whole flocks and herds exhausted bled,
His generous wines dishonour'd shed in vain,
And the wild riots of the Suitor-train.
The King alternate a dire tale relates,
10 Of wars, of triumphs, and disastrous fates;
All he unfolds: His list'ning spouse turns pale
With pleasing horror at the dreadful tale,
Sleepless devours each word; and hears, how slain
Cicons on *Cicons* swell th' ensanguin'd plain;
How to the land of *Lote* unblest he sails;
And images the rills, and flowry vales:
How dash'd like dogs, his friends the *Cyclops* tore,
(Not unreveng'd) and quaff'd the spouting gore;

Nam Ciconumque manus adversis reppulit armis,
Non valuit lotos captos avertere cursus;
Cessit & Aetnaeae Neptunius incola rupis,
Victa Maronaeo foedatus lumina baccho.
Vexit & Aeolios placidum per Nerea ventos;
Incultos adiit Laestrygonas, &c.

Dacier is of opinion, that this recapitulation in *Homer* has a very good effect. I will translate her observation. We learn from it, that the subject of the *Odyssey* is not alone the return of *Ulysses* to his country, and his re-establishment in it; but that it comprehends all his wandrings and all his voyages; all that he saw, or suffer'd in his return to it; in a word, all that he underwent after he set sail from the shores of *Troy*: Another advantage we reap from it is, that we see the order and train of the adventures of his Heroe, as they really happen'd, naturally and historically: for in his relation of them in his Poem, he uses an artificial order; that is, he begins at the latter end, and finds an opportunity to insert all that precedes the opening of his Poem by way of narration to the *Phaeacians*: Here he sets every event in its natural order, so that with a glance of the eye we may distinguish what gives continuity to the action, and what is comprehended in it. By this method we are able to separate the time of the duration of the Poem, from the time of the duration of the Action; for in reality the Poem begins many years before the return of *Ulysses*; but *Homer* begins his action but thirty five days before he lands in his own country. In the course, therefore of the *Odyssey*, *Homer* gave us the artificial, here the natural order; which is an ease and assistance to the memory of the Reader.

How, the loud storms in prison bound, he sails
20   From friendly *Aeolus* with prosp'rous gales;
Yet Fate withstands! a sudden tempest roars
And whirls him groaning from his native shores:
How on the barb'rous *Laestrigonian* coast,
By savage hands his fleet and friends he lost;
How scarce himself surviv'd: He paints the bow'r,
The spells of *Circe*, and her magic pow'r;
His dreadful journey to the realms beneath,
To seek *Tiresias* in the vales of death
How in the doleful mansions he survey'd
30   His royal mother, pale *Anticlea*'s shade;
And friends in battle slain, heroic ghosts!
Then how unharm'd he past the *Siren*-coasts,
The justling rocks where fierce *Charybdis* raves,
And howling *Scylla* whirls her thund'rous waves,
The cave of death! How his companions slay
The oxen sacred to the God of day,

---

35   *– How his companions slay*
The oxen sacred to the God of day.]

The story of these oxen is fully related, *lib.* 12. I refer to the Annotations ⟨161n⟩. The crime of the companions of *Ulysses* was sacrilege, they having destroy'd the herds sacred to a God. These herds were said to be immortal: I have there given the reason of it, but too concisely, and will therefore add a supplement from the *Polyhymnia* of *Herodotus* ⟨vii 83⟩; I ought to have mention'd, that the body of soldiers call'd Immortal, was a select number of men in the army of *Xerxes*: so nam'd, because upon the death of any one of their number, whether by war or sickness, another was immediately substituted into his room, so that they never amounted to more or less than ten thousand. If we apply this piece of History to the herds of *Apollo*, it excellently explains *Homer*'s Poetry: they are call'd Immortal, because upon the death of any one of the whole herd, another was brought into its place; they are said neither to increase nor decay, because they were always of a fix'd number, and continually supply'd upon any vacancy.

   The Reader will be appriz'd of the heinousness of the crime in killing these oxen, from an observation of *Bochart*, *p.* 314 ⟨Pt II: 1 xxvii (p. 570)⟩. The *Phoenicians* and *Aegyptians* so superstitiously abstain'd from the flesh of the ox, that, as *Porphyry* affirms ⟨*De Abstinentia*, II 11⟩, they would sooner feed upon

'Till *Jove* in wrath the ratling Tempest guides,
And whelms th' offenders in the roaring tydes:
How struggling thro' the surge, he reach'd the shores
40   Of fair *Ogygia*, and *Calypso*'s bow'rs;
Where the gay blooming Nymph constrain'd his stay,
With sweet reluctant amorous delay;

---

human flesh than that of such beasts. *Aelian* ⟨*V.H.* v. 14, (but Aelian says nothing of the Phrygians)⟩ tells us, that it was death amongst the *Phrygians* to kill a labouring ox; and *Varro, Rust. lib.* 2. cap. 5. ⟨11 v 4⟩ thus writes; *ab hoc antiqui manus ita abstinere voluerunt, ut capite sanxerint, si quis occidisset.* Thus also *Columella*, in praefat. *lib.* 7 ⟨vi Preface 7⟩. *Cujus tanta fuit apud antiquos veneratio, ut tam capitale esset bovem necasse, quam civem.*

I have been the more full upon this head, to shew that *Homer*'s fiction is built upon a foundation of truth, and that he writes according to the religion of the Ancients: *Rapin* ⟨Comparaison xv, 1 157⟩ is very severe upon him for ascribing the death of the companions of *Ulysses*, to the violation of these herds of *Apollo*. 'The reason (says he) why they are destroy'd is very ridiculous, because, *lib.* 1.

              – *they dar'd to prey*
On herds devoted to the God of day. ⟨9–10⟩

This is certainly a far-fetch'd destruction: The Heroe, or the Poet was willing to be freed from them.' But from this observation, they will be found to be guilty of sacrilege, and a violation of what was regarded by the world with the utmost veneration; and consequently the crime is adequate to the punishment. Besides, *Horace Epist.* 6. *lib.* 1 ⟨62–4⟩ gives sentence against these companions of *Ulysses*.

              – *Caerite cera*
Digni, remigium vitiosum Ithacensis Ulixei
Cui potior patria fuit interdicta voluptas.

41 *Where the gay blooming Nymph constrain'd his stay*]. This is a circumstance (observes Madam *Dacier*) that *Ulysses* ought by no means to forget; for it gives him an opportunity to pay an high compliment to his wife, by letting her know he preferr'd her person to that of *Calypso* a Goddess: this is the reason why he enlarges upon it in five verses; whereas he concludes most of the other adventures in little more than one. But (adds that Lady) we may easily believe that he was silent about the nature of his conversation with that Nymph; and indeed it would have lessen'd the compliment, and perhaps his welcome home, if he had not been able to keep a secret; he is very cautious in this respect; he enlarges upon the fondness of *Calypso* for his person, but suppresses, for a very obvious reason, the kind returns he made for her civilities.

And promis'd, vainly promis'd, to bestow
Immortal life exempt from age and woe:
How sav'd from storms *Phaeacia*'s coast he trod,
By great *Alcinous* honour'd as a God,
Who gave him last his country to behold,
With change of rayment, brass, and heaps of gold.
    He ended, sinking into sleep, and shares
50 A sweet forgetfulness of all his cares.

THOMAS TICKELL (1686–1740)

A disciple of Addison, a composer of love-ballads and pastorale,
Tickell is remembered for the bitter quarrel which his Homer-
project occasioned between Addison and Pope. This 'specimen' is
not, however, altogether a failure.

A specimen of an *Iliad* translation I [1–16]

Achilles' fatal Wrath, whence Discord rose,
That brought the Sons of *Greece* unnumber'd Woes,
O Goddess sing. Full many a Hero's Ghost
Was driv'n untimely to th' Infernal Coast,
While in promiscuous Heaps their Bodies lay,
A Feast for Dogs, ans ev'ry Bird of Prey.
So did the Sire of Gods and Men fulfill
His steadfast Purpose, and Almighty Will;
What time the haughty Chiefs their Jars begun,
10 *Atrides* King of Men, and *Peleus'* godlike Son?
What God in Strife the Princes did engage?
Apollo burning with vindictive rage.
Against the scornful King, whose impious Pride
His Priest dishonour'd, and his Pow'r defy'd.
Hence swift Contagion, by God's commands
Swept through the Camp, and thinn'd the *Graecian* Bands.

For Wealth immense the holy Chryses bore,
(His Daughter's Ransom), to the Tended Shore:
His Sceptre strethching forth, the golden Rod,
20 Hung round with hallow'd Garlands of his God
Of all the Host, of evr'y Princely Chief,
But first of Atreus' Sons he begg'd Relief.   (1715)

JAMES MACPHERSON (1736–96)

An *Iliad* by the immensely celebrated and suspect begetter of
Ossian. Severely received on publication, it has lapsed into oblivion.
None the less, the cadenced, monumental prose, with its scriptural
touches, is not without a certain aura. And it anticipates not only
Victorian tactics of 'archaic nobility' but also Doughty and T. E.
Lawrence.

The Iliad of Homer VIII [335–80] *Watched by the rival Olympians, the Trojans rush the ditch*

The thunderer again comes forth. He rouzes the souls of the
Trojans to arms. To the deep trench they repell the Greeks. In the
front moves the furious Hector, rolling fiercely his eyes around. As
when some generous hound in the chace, pursues a lion or
mountain-boar. Trusting to his speed he flies, and, assails the fierce
savage behind: His side or his haunch he attacks, marking well,
when he turns him around. So Hector the Argives subdued, slaying
the last, as they fled amain.

When o'er the ditch, o'er the rampire they passed; when many fell,
subdued by the foe. Near the ships, on the shore, they stood. Each other
they encouraged to fight. To all the gods they exalted their hands. Each
his voice raised, in prayer, aloud. Hector, mean time, to every
side, o'er all drove his long-maned steeds; rolling round his Gorgon
eyes. In looks like destroyer Mars. Juno beheld him from high. The

white-armed goddess pitied her Argives. Straight to the blue-eyed Pallas, she thus her winged words addressed.

'Alas! warlike daughter of Aegis-bearing Jove! Shall we not, in this last extream, aid the Argives now falling in war? Or, compleating their disastrous fate, must they perish by the wrath of one chief? Unbounded is the fury of Hector. The son of Priam rages amain. Many are the dire deeds of his hand!'

To her blue-eyed Pallas replied. 'Long this Hector his fury had lost; long his soul had been poured on the winds, beneath the deadly hands of the Argives; transfixed in his native land. But that my Sire still rages in soul; cruel, unjust, and opposed to my will! Things past have escaped from his mind. He remembers not my service of old. When I, often, saved his son beloved, pressed with toils, which Eurystheus imposed. To broad heaven looked the chief in his tears. To aid him I descended from Jove, by command. But had I this divined in my soul; when he sent him to the strong-gated chambers of death, to bring from Erebus profound, the fierce dog of relentless Pluto: He should not have returned to the light, from the hoarse, deep-rushing streams of the dreadful Styx. But, now, his once-loved daughter he hates: He only silver-footed Thetis regards; Thetis, who kissed his sacred knees; who seized his beard with her suppliant hand; to honour her wrathful son; Achilles, the destroyer of towns! But hereafter, the time will come, when Jove will call me his blue-eyed maid. Hasten thou, and bear us hence. Join thy fleet steeds to the car of gold. Whilst I enter the halls, the house of Aegis-bearing Jove! To arm for tremendous war. Soon shall the trial be made, whether Hector, so great in arms, whether this illustrious son of Priam, shall rejoice, when we both shall appear, rolling death, through the lanes of war. Some Trojan shall feast with his fat, shall glut the dogs and birds of prey; laid low, at the ships of Achaia.'

XII [141–61] *In the thick of the mêlée*

... The two chiefs rouzed the Argives to fight, to save their hollow ships, from fire. Still within the wall were the troops, but, when they saw the Trojans rushing amain; flight and clamour arose around. The Argives fled back from the wall. Issuing forth, the two heroes, alone, before the gate, sustain the war.

As when two mountain-boars, in the wild paths of their hilly groves, wait the rushing tumult of men, the shrill clamour of all their hounds. Side-long they rush on the foe. Around, they break the lofty wood. Sheer from the roots, fall the trees. Dreadful swells the crash of their teeth, till some hunter the javelin shall launch, and lay them, breathless, along the ground. Thus sounded the bright steel, on their breasts, as o'er their mails, redouble the blows. Bold above mankind, they fought, trusting to their friends, on the wall, but more to the strength of their arms. The Argives stood, aloft, in the well-built towers. Huge stones fly, in showers, from their hands, for themselves, for tents they fought; for the ships, which should bear them away.

As falls the snow, on the ground, borne along, by the boisterous winds; when the blast bursts the laden clouds, and pours the thick-flying flakes, on the world. So thick flew the darts, from each side: from the hands of the Argives, from the Trojans renowned in arms. Hoarsely sound the struck helms to the sky, the breast-plates, the bossy-shields, as pour, on all, the flying stones.

XVII [516–32] *The fight around the fallen Patroclus*

He spoke: And, vibrating, hurled his long lance. He struck the broad shield of the godlike Arëtus. The bright orb sustained not the point. Through and through rushed the eager steel. Through the belt it swiftly passed; and, fixed in his nether belly, remained. As when a youth, with his hand robust, rears aloft the gleaming ax, in the air: Down falls the forceful weapon, with speed, behind the horns of a savage bull. The whole sinew is divided in twain. He bounds and tumbles, in death, on the ground. Thus bounding, the youth fell supine. In his entrails shook the sharp-pointed spear; and his limbs were unbraced, as he lay.

Hector hurled his bright lance, through the air, at the breast of

the great Automedon. He saw the gleaming steel, as it came, and,
stooping forward, avoided its point. Behind him, it stood fixed in
the ground. The staff quivered, as the head sunk in earth. But soon
the strong spear remitted its force as it shook. Then, hand to hand,
had the heroes closed; then had they urged, with their swords the
fight; but the Ajaces rushed in between. They parted the chiefs, as
they glowed. Through the deep ranks had the warriors come, at the
well-known voice of their friend.   (1773)

WILLIAM COWPER (1731–1800)

'I have omitted nothing; I have invented nothing.' A version contra
Pope, founded on a 'similarity of manner' between Homer and
Milton. Cowper aims 'neither to creep nor to bluster'. His Homer
'writes always to the eye' and 'with all his sublimity and grandeur,
has the minuteness of a Flemish painter'. Cowper takes advice from
Fuseli.

The Iliad XIII [95–124] *Neptune exhorts the Greek warriors*

   Oh shame, ye Greecians! vigorous as ye are
And in life's prime, to your exertions most
I trusted for the safety of our ships.
If *ye* renounce the labours of the field,
Then hath the day arisen of our defeat
And final ruin by the powers of Troy.
Oh! I behold a prodigy, a sight
Tremendous, deem'd impossible by me,
The Trojans at our ships! the dastard race
10 Fled once like fleetest hinds the destined prey
Of lynxes, leopards, wolves; feeble and slight
And of a nature indisposed to war
They rove uncertain; so the Trojans erst

Stood not, nor to Achaian prowess dared
The hindrance of a moment's strife oppose.
But now, Troy left afar, even at our ships
They give us battle, through our leader's fault
And through the people's negligence, who fill'd
With fierce displeasure against *him*, prefer
20   Death at their ships, to war in their defence.
But if the son of Atreus, our supreme,
If Agamemnon, have indeed transgress'd
Past all excuse, dishonouring the swift
Achilles, ye at least the fight decline
Blame-worthy, and with no sufficient plea.
But heal we speedily the breach; brave minds
Easily coalesce. It is not well
That thus your fury slumbers, for the host
Hath none illustrious as yourselves in arms.
30   I can excuse the timid if he shrink,
But am incensed at *you*. My friends, beware!
Your tardiness will prove ere long the cause
Of some worse evil. Let the dread of shame
Affect your hearts; oh tremble at the thought
Of infamy! Fierce conflict hath arisen,
Loud-shouting Hector combats at the ships
Nobly, hath forced the gates and burst the bar.

XVI [364–83] *The Trojans flee before Patroclus*

As when the Thunderer spreads a sable storm
O'er ether, late serene, the cloud that wrapp'd
Olympus' head escapes into the skies,
So fled the Trojans from the fleet of Greece
Clamouring in their flight, nor pass'd the trench
In fair array; the coursers fleet indeed
Of Hector, him bore safe with all his arms
Right through, but in the foss entangled foul
He left his host, and struggling to escape.

10   Then many a chariot-whirling steed, the pole
     Broken at its extremity, forsook
     His driver, while Patroclus with the shout
     Of battle calling his Achaians on,
     Destruction purposed to the powers of Troy.
     They, once dispersed, with clamour and with flight
     Fill'd all the ways, the dust beneath the clouds
     Hung like a tempest, and the steeds firm-hoof'd
     Whirl'd off at stretch the chariots to the town.
     He, wheresoe'er most troubled he perceived
20   The routed host, loud-threatening thither drove,
     While under his own axle many a chief
     Fell prone, and the o'ertumbled chariots rang.
     Right o'er the hollow foss the coursers leap'd
     Immortal, by the gods to Peleus given,
     Impatient for the plain, nor less desire
     Felt he who drove to smite the Trojan chief,
     But him his fiery steeds caught swift away.

XXI [240–72] *The river Scamander turns on Achilles*

     Terrible all around Achilles stood
     The curling wave, then, falling on his shield
     Dash'd him, nor found his footsteps where to rest.
     An elm of massy trunk he seized and branch
     Luxuriant, but it fell torn from the root
     And drew the whole bank after it; immersed
     It damm'd the current with its ample boughs,
     And join'd as with a bridge the distant shores.
     Upsprang Achilles from the gulf and turn'd
10   His feet, now wing'd for flight, into the plain
     Astonish'd; but the god not so appeased,
     Arose against him with a darker curl,
     That he might quell him and deliver Troy.
     Back flew Achilles with a bound, the length
     Of a spear's cast, for such a spring he own'd

As bears the black-plumed eagle on her prey
Strongest and swiftest of the fowls of air.
Like her he sprang, and dreadful on his chest
Clang'd his bright armour. Then, with course oblique
20   He fled his fierce pursuer, but the flood,
Fly where he might, came thundering in his rear.
As when the peasant with his spade a rill
Conducts from some pure fountain through his grove
Or garden, clearing the obstructed course,
The pebbles, as it runs, all ring beneath,
And, as the slope still deepens, swifter still
It runs, and, murmuring, outstrips the guide,
So him, though swift, the river always reach'd
Still swifter; who can cope with power divine!
30   Oft as the noble chief, turning, essay'd
Resistance, and to learn if all the gods
Alike rush'd after him, so oft the flood,
Jove's offspring, laved his shoulders. Upward then
He sprang distress'd, but with a sidelong sweep
Assailing him, and from beneath his steps
Wasting the soil, the stream his force subdued.
Then, looking to the skies, aloud he mourn'd.   (1791)

Cowper's *Odyssey* is closer to his natural sentiments, but the translation shows fatigue and betrays the mental stress under which the poet laboured.

The *Odyssey* V [203–24] *The exchange between Calypso and Ulysses*

    Laertes' noble son, for wisdom famed
And artifice! oh canst thou thus resolve
To seek, incontinent, thy native shores!

I pardon thee. Farewell! but could'st thou guess
The woes which fate ordains thee to endure
Ere yet thou reach thy country, well-content
Here to inhabit, thou would'st keep my grot
And be immortal, howsoe'er thy wife
Engage thy every wish day after day.
10   Yet can I not in stature or in form
Myself suspect inferior aught to her,
Since competition cannot be between
Mere mortal beauties and a form divine.
    To whom Ulysses, ever-wise, replied.
Aweful divinity ! be not incensed.
I know that my Penelope in form
And stature altogether yields to thee,
For she is mortal, and immortal thou,
From age exempt; yet not the less I wish
20   My home, and languish daily to return.
But should some god amid the sable deep
Dash me again into a wreck, my soul
Shall bear *that* also; for, by practice taught,
I have learn'd patience, having much endured
By tempest and in battle both. Come then
This evil also! I am well prepared.

VI [161–77] *Ulysses to Nausicaa on the shore*

Wonder-rapt I gaze.
Such erst, in Delos, I beheld a palm
Beside the altar of Apollo, tall,
And growing still; (for thither too I sail'd,
And numerous were my followers in a voyage
Ordain'd my ruin) and as I then view'd
That palm long time amazed, for never grew
So straight a shaft, so lovely from the ground,
So, princess! thee with wonder I behold,

10   Charm'd into fixt astonishment, by awe
      Alone forbidden to embrace thy knees,
      For I am one on whom much woe hath fallen.
      Yesterday I escaped (the twentieth day
      Of my distress by sea) the dreary deep;
      For, all those days, the waves and rapid storms
      Bore me along, impetuous, from the isle
      Ogygia; till at length the will of heaven
      Cast me, that I might also here sustain
      Affliction, on your shore; for rest, I think,
20   Is not for me. No. The immortal gods
      Have much to accomplish ere that day arrive.
      But, oh queen, pity me! who after long
      Calamities endured, of all who live
      Thee first approach, nor mortal know beside
      Of the inhabitants of all the land.

XVII [290–310] *The Argus episode*

    Thus they discoursing stood; Argus the while,
      Ulysses' dog, uplifted where he lay
      His head and ears erect. Ulysses him
      Had bred long since himself, but rarely used,
      Departing first to Ilium. Him the youths
      In other days led frequent to the chase
      Of wild goat, hart, and hare; but now he lodged
      A poor old cast-off, of his lord forlorn,
      Where mules and oxen had before the gate
10   Much ordure left, with which Ulysses' hinds
      Should, in due time, manure his spacious fields.
      There lay, with dog-devouring vermin foul
      All over, Argus; soon as he perceived
      Long-lost Ulysses nigh, down fell his ears
      Clapp'd close, and with his tail glad sign he gave
      Of gratulation, impotent to rise

And to approach his master as of old.
Ulysses, noting him, wiped off a tear
Unmark'd, and of Eumaeus quick enquired.
20   I can but wonder seeing such a dog
Thus lodged, Eumaeus! beautiful in form
He is, past doubt, but whether he hath been
As fleet as fair I know not; rather such
Perchance as masters sometimes keep to grace
Their tables, nourish'd more for show than use.

XXIV [321–50] *Ulysses to his father, Laertes*

My father! I am he. Thou seest thy son
Absent these twenty years at last return'd.
But bid thy sorrows cease; suspend henceforth
All lamentation; for I tell thee true,
(And the occasion bids me briefly tell thee)
I have slain all the suitors at my home,
And all their taunts and injuries avenged.
    Then answer thus Laertes quick return'd.
If thou hast come again, and art indeed
10 My son Ulysses, give me then the proof
Indubitable, that I may believe.
    To whom Ulysses, ever wise, replied.
View, first, the scar which with his ivory tusk
A wild boar gave me, when at thy command
And at my mother's, to Autolycus
Her father, on Parnassus, I repair'd
Seeking the gifts which, while a guest of yours,
He promised should be mine. Accept beside
This proof. I will enumerate all the trees
20 Which, walking with thee in this cultured spot
(Boy then) I begg'd, and thou confirm'dst my own.
We paced between them, and thou madest me learn
The name of each. Thou gavest me thirteen pears,

Ten apples, thirty figs, and fifty ranks
Didst promise me of vines, their alleys all
Corn-cropp'd between. There oft as sent from Jove
The influences of the year descend,
Grapes of all hues and flavours clustering hang.
   He said; Laertes conscious of the proofs
30   Indubitable by Ulysses given,
With faultering knees and faultering heart both arms
Around him threw. The hero toil-inured
Drew to his bosom close his fainting sire,
Who, breath recovering, and his scatter'd powers
Of intellect, at length thus spake aloud.   (1791)

ANON.

Homeric parodies, travesties, caricatures abound from antiquity to
Daumier, Offenbach and Durrell. In a sense, Joyce offers the pre-
eminent example.

   But a full-length travesty, such as this burlesque *Iliad* in two
tomes, is, so far as we are aware, rare. According to an insertion in
our copy, the author (one T. Bridges ?) was 'disowned by his father'
for having perpetrated this voluminous jape.

A Burlesque Translation of Homer The Iliad VI [186–
95] *Bellerophon vanquishes the Amazons and obtains the hand of
the daughter of the Lycian king*

To them the Amazons succeed,
A strange hermaphroditish breed:
No mortal man these jades could match,
'Cause they could scold, and bite, and scratch;
But, by the help of cod and oysters,
He quickly tam'd this crew of roysters:

Soon as they felt his strokes and thwacks,
The brims all fell upon their backs.
Tho' here his troubles did not cease,
10   Nor was he yet to live in peace.
Under a farmer's old pigsty
A dozen rogues conceal'd did lie;
But, when he got them in his clutches,
He qualify'd 'em all for crutches,
Left 'em so bruis'd upon the plain,
Not one could limp it home again.
    Zooks! said the king, I'll lay a groat,
There's more in this than first I thought:
This man can be no earth-born clod,
20   But bastard to some whoring god.
A fellow that can make such slaughter,
And would have trimm'd my other daughter,
Since he by some strange chance has mist her,
I think I'll let him trim her sister;
And, that the youth the girl may keep,
I'll take him into partnership.
My trade he'll learn, I do not fear,
In far less time than half a year;
'Tis but to kick, and cuff, and swear.
30   I knew a good old monarch that,
When angry, only kick'd his hat:
Now, when I'm vex'd, both friends and foes
Have felt the force of my square toes.
Favours once got, they come none near you;
But kick 'em, and they always fear you:
And this I ever will maintain
The best and easiest way to reign.
    No sooner was it said than done,
He made him partner of his throne;
40   I mean the very morning after
He'd done his best to please his daughter:
For she, when ask'd of his behaviour,
Had spoken greatly in his favour;

And swore, like royal F——'s wife,
She ne'er was thrum'd so in her life;
On which the Lycians gave him stone
And ground to build a house upon,
With a good orchard full of fruit,
And a brave field of wheat to boot.

XI *The Argument*

The Grecian chief his jacket put on,
Tho' there was not a single button,
Either of horn, or metal cast,
Remain'd upon't, to make it fast.
Yet as they could not do without him,
He tied it with a cord about him;
Not a grand swashy green or red cord,
But an old rotten piece of bed-cord;
Then don'd a pair of piss-burnt brogues on,
10   And went to lead his ragged rogues on; –
Whilst Hector, ever bold and steady,
Soon got his trusty Trojans ready.
For signal, two celestial strumpets
Employ their tongues instead of trumpets.
Jove thunder'd too, but all the sound
In their superior noise was drown'd;
For such a din they made at starting,
His thunder sounded just like farting.
And now, whilst Agamemnon mauls 'em,
20   And with his crab-tree cudgel galls 'em,
Jove call'd for Iris, to direct her
To go and caution bully Hector
To let this Grecian bruiser roam
Till some chance knock should send him home.   (1797)

CHARLES LAMB (1775–1834)

Hoping to prolong the success of the *Tales from Shakespeare* of 1807, Lamb produced this prose 'retelling', closely dependent on Chapman's *Odyssey*. The little book was rapidly forgotten.

The Adventures of Ulysses pp. 37–8 [from Book X]
Circe restores human shape to Odysseus' companions

. . . She called her handmaids, four that served her in chief, who were daughters to her silver fountains, to her sacred rivers, and to her consecrated woods, to deck her apartments, to spread rich carpets, and set out her silver tables with dishes of the purest gold, and meat as precious as that which the gods eat, to entertain her guest. One brought water to wash his feet, and one brought wine to chase away, with a refreshing sweetness, the sorrows that had come of late so thick upon him, and hurt his noble mind. They strewed perfumes on his head, and after he had bathed in a bath of the choicest aromatics they brought him rich and costly apparel to put on. Then he was conducted to a throne of massy silver, and a regale, fit for Jove when he banquets, was placed before him. But the feast which Ulysses desired was to see his friends (the partners of his voyage) once more in the shapes of men; and the food which could give him nourishment must be taken in at his eyes. Because he missed this sight, he sat melancholy and thoughtful, and would taste of none of the rich delicacies placed before him. Which when Circe noted, she easily divined the cause of his sadness, and leaving the seat in which she sat throned, went to her sty, and let abroad his men, who came in like swine, and filled the ample hall, where Ulysses sat, with gruntings. Hardly had he time to let his sad eye run over their altered forms and brutal metamorphosis, when with an ointment which she smeared over them, suddenly their bristles fell off, and they started up in their own shapes men as before. They knew their leader again, and clung about him, with joy of their late restoration, and some shame for their late change; and wept so loud, blubbering out their joy in broken accents, that the palace was filled with a sound of pleasing mourning, and the witch herself, great Circe, was not unmoved at the sight. To make her atonement complete, she sent for the remnant of Ulysses's men who staid behind at the ship, giving up their great commander for lost; who when they came, and saw him again alive, circled with their fellows, no expression can tell what joy they felt; they even cried out with rapture, and to have seen their frantic expressions of mirth, a man might have supposed that they were just in sight of their country earth, the cliffs of rocky Ithaca. Only Eurylochus would hardly be persuaded to enter that palace of wonders, for he remembered with a kind of horror how his companions had vanished from his sight.

Then great Circe spake, and gave order, that there should be no more sadness among them, nor remembering of past sufferings. For as yet they fared like men that are exiles from their country, and if a gleam of mirth shot among them, it was suddenly quenched with the thought of their helpless and homeless condition. Her kind persuasions wrought upon Ulysses and the rest, that they spent twelve months in all manner of delight with her in her palace. For Circe was a powerful magician, and could command the moon from her sphere, or unroot the solid oak from its place to make it dance for their diversion, and by the help of her illusions she could vary the taste of pleasures, and contrive delights, recreations, and jolly pastimes, to 'fetch the day about from sun to sun, and rock the tedious year as in a delightful dream.'

pp. 131–3 [from Book XIII] *Odysseus comes to Ithaca and meets with Athene*

Ulysses was joyed enough to find himself in his own country, but so prudently he carried his joy, that dissembling his true name and quality, he pretended to the shepherd that he was only some foreigner who by stress of weather had put into that port; and framed on the sudden a story to make it plausible, how he had come from Crete in a ship of Phaeacia; when the young shepherd laughing, and taking Ulysses's hand in both his, said to him: 'He must be cunning, I find, who thinks to over-reach you. What, cannot you quit your wiles and your subtleties, now that you are in a state of security? must the first word with which you salute your native earth be an untruth? and think you that you are unknown?'

Ulysses looked again; and he saw, not a shepherd, but a beautiful woman, whom he immediately knew to be the goddess Minerva, that in the wars of Troy had frequently vouchsafed her sight to him; and had been with him since in perils, saving him unseen.

'Let not my ignorance offend thee, great Minerva,' he cried, 'or move thy displeasure, that in that shape I knew thee not; since the skill of discerning of deities is not attainable by wit or study, but hard to be hit by the wisest of mortals. To know thee truly through all thy changes is only given to those whom thou art pleased to grace. To all men thou takest all likenesses. All men in their wits think that they know thee, and that they have thee. Thou art wisdom itself. But a semblance of thee, which is false wisdom, often is taken for thee: so thy counterfeit view appears to many, but thy true presence to few: those are they which, loving thee above all, are inspired with light from thee to know thee. But this I surely know, that all the time the sons of Greece waged war against Troy, I was sundry times graced with thy appearance; but since, I have never been able to set eyes upon thee till now: but have wandered at my own discretion, to myself a blind guide, erring up and down the world, wanting thee.'

Then Minerva cleared his eyes, and he knew the ground on which he stood to be Ithaca, and that cave to be the same which the people of Ithaca had in former times made sacred to the sea-nymphs, and where he himself had done sacrifices to them a thousand times; and full in his view stood Mount Nerytus with all his woods: so that now he knew for a certainty that he was arrived in his own country, and with the delight which he felt he could not forbear stooping down and kissing the soil.   (1808)

T. S. BRANDRETH (1788–1873)

An attempt 'to let Homer speak for himself', and, 'as far as possible word for word'. In 'drumming decasyllables'.

The Iliad of Homer VI.119–90 [119–90] *The encounter of Glaucus and Diomedes*

Then Glaucus, of Hippolochus the son,
And Diomedes in the middle met.
And when they near against each other came,
Him valiant Diomedes first address'd;
Who art thou, chief of mortal men? for ne'er
I thee have seen in man-ennobling fight
Before; and now thou far excellest all
In courage, since thou waitest my long spear.
The sons of the unhappy meet my force.
10 But if from heaven thou some Immortal come,
I would not with Olympian Gods contend.
Not long did Dryas' son, Lycurgus, live,
When he contended with Olympian Gods.
He erst the nurses of mad Bacchus drove
Down goodly Nysa; they at once their rods
Threw on the ground, by fell Lycurgus struck
With an ox-goad; and Bacchus fled dismay'd
Beneath the sea, where Thetis him received;
For dreadful terror seized him from his threats.
20 With him the Gods, who live at ease, were grieved,
And Jove with blindness struck him; and not long
He lived, since he was hated by the Gods.
So with blest Gods I seek not to contend.
But if thou art of those, who eat earth's fruit,
Come near, that quickly thou death's term mayst reach.
Him then Hippolochus' brave son address'd;

Why, great Tydides, dost thou ask my race?
Alike the races are of leaves and men;
The wind the leaves disperses, and the wood
30   Produces others in the hour of spring;
So flourishes and fades each race of men.
If thou would'st these things learn, that thou mayst know
Our lineage, which to many men is known,
There is a city, Ephyra, in Greece,
Where Sisyphus, the son of Aeolus,
Of men most skilful, lived; he Glaucus got,
And Glaucus good Bellerophontes got;
To him the Gods gave beauty and fair grace;
But Proetus 'gainst him evil thoughts conceived,
40   And drove him from the land; for he all Greeks
Excell'd; and them Jove 'neath his sceptre tamed.
With him Antëa, Proetus' wife, desired
To join in friendship; but she nought prevail'd,
Nor chaste Bellerophontes could persuade.
She then king Proetus with deceit address'd;
'Die, Proetus, or Bellerophontes slay,
Who me unwilling would in friendship know.'
When this he heard, resentment seized the king;
Yet him he slew not, for he this revered,
50   But writing many soul-destroying things
In folded tablets, him to Lycia sent,
And bade him shew them to his consort's sire;
He then to Lycia with Gods' guidance went.
But when he Lycia and fair Xanthus reach'd,
With honour him wide Lycia's king received;
Nine days he feasted, and nine oxen slew;
But when the tenth rose-finger'd Morn appear'd,
He question'd him, and ask'd to see the sign,
Which he from his son Proetus to him bore.
60   But when the king the evil sign received,
He bade him first the dire Chimaera slay,
Which of divine, not mortal, race was sprung,

With lion's head, goat's body, and snake's tail,
Breathing the dreadful force of burning fire;
And her he slew, relying on Gods' signs.
Next 'gainst the noble Solymans he fought;
The strongest battle this of men, he said.
Thirdly the manly Amazons he slew.
Then he another secret snare contrived;
70   Choosing the best men of wide Lycia's realm,
He placed an ambush; but none home return'd;
For good Bellerophontes slew them all.   (1816)

JOHN KEATS (1795–1821)

The first of these famous sonnets appears in the 1817 *Poems*. The second, written in the spring of 1818, was published posthumously. They remain among the stellar 'Homer experiences' in the language.

Two Sonnets on Homer

On First Looking into Chapman's Homer

Much have I travell'd in the realms of gold,
    And many goodly states and kingdoms seen;
    Round many western islands have I been
Which bards in fealty to Apollo hold.
Oft of one wide expanse had I been told
    That deep-brow'd Homer ruled as his demesne;
    Yet did I never breathe its pure serene
Till I heard Chapman speak out loud and bold:
Then felt I like some watcher of the skies
10   When a new planet swims into his ken;
Or like stout Cortez when with eagle eyes

He star'd at the Pacific – and all his men
Look'd at each other with a wild surmise –
   Silent, upon a peak in Darien.   (1817)

To Homer

Standing aloof in giant ignorance,
   Of thee I hear and of the Cyclades,
As one who sits ashore and longs perchance
   To visit dolphin-coral in deep seas.
So wast thou blind; – but then the veil was rent,
   For Jove uncurtain'd heaven to let thee live,
And Neptune made for thee a spumy tent,
   And Pan made sing for thee his forest-hive;
Aye on the shores of darkness there is light,
10   And precipices show untrodden green,
There is a budding morrow in midnight,
   There is a triple sight in blindness keen;
Such seeing hadst thou, as it once befel
To Dian, Queen of Earth, and Heaven, and Hell.   (1818)

PERCY BYSSHE SHELLEY
(1792–1822)

Written in 1818, these versions of the so-called *Homeric Hymns* are
the work not only of one of the great English poets, but of a
learned and sensitive student of ancient Greek. Certain touches take
us back to the Neoplatonic flavour of Renaissance and baroque
interpretations of Homer 'the sage'.

Homeric Hymns

Hymn 33 Homer's Hymn to Castor and Pollux

Ye wild-eyed Muses, sing the Twins of Jove,
Whom the fair-ankled Leda, mixed in love
With mighty Saturn's Heaven-obscuring Child,
On Taygetus, that lofty mountain wild,
Brought forth in joy: mild Pollux, void of blame,
And steed-subduing Castor, heirs of fame.
These are the Powers who earth-born mortals save
And ships, whose flight is swift along the wave.
When wintry tempests o'er the savage sea
Are raging, and the sailors tremblingly
Call on the Twins of Jove with prayer and vow,
Gathered in fear upon the lofty prow,
And sacrifice with snow-white lambs, – the wind
And the huge billow bursting close behind,
Even then beneath the weltering waters bear
The staggering ship – they suddenly appear,
On yellow wings rushing athwart the sky,
And lull the blasts in mute tranquillity,
And strew the waves on the white Ocean's bed,
Fair omen of the voyage; from toil and dread
The sailors rest, rejoicing in the sight,
And plough the quiet sea in safe delight.   (1818)

Hymn 32 Homer's Hymn to the Moon

Daughters of Jove, whose voice is melody,
Muses, who know and rule all minstrelsy,
Sing the wide-wingèd Moon! Around the earth,
From her immortal head in Heaven shot forth,

Far light is scattered – boundless glory springs;
Where'er she spreads her many-beaming wings
The lampless air glows round her golden crown.

But when the Moon divine from Heaven is gone
Under the sea, her beams within abide,
Till, bathing her bright limbs in Ocean's tide,
Clothing her form in garments glittering far,
And having yoked to her immortal car
The beam-invested steeds whose necks on high
Curve back, she drives to a remoter sky
A western Crescent, borne impetuously.
Then is made full the circle of her light,
And as she grows, her beams more bright and bright
Are poured from Heaven, where she is hovering then,
A wonder and a sign to mortal men.

The Son of Saturn with this glorious Power
Mingled in love and sleep – to whom she bore
Pandeia, a bright maid of beauty rare
Among the Gods, whose lives eternal are.

Hail Queen, great Moon, white-armed Divinity,
Fair-haired and favourable! thus with thee
My song beginning, by its music sweet
Shall make immortal many a glorious feat
Of demigods, with lovely lips, so well
Which minstrels, servants of the Muses, tell.   (1818)

Hymn 30 Homer's Hymn to the Earth: Mother of All

O universal Mother, who dost keep
From everlasting thy foundations deep,
Eldest of things, Great Earth, I sing of thee!
All shapes that have their dwelling in the sea,

All things that fly, or on the ground divine
Live, move, and there are nourished – these are thine;
These from thy wealth thou dost sustain; from thee
Fair babes are born, and fruits on every tree
Hang ripe and large, revered Divinity!

10   The life of mortal men beneath thy sway
Is held; thy power both gives and takes away!
Happy are they whom thy mild favours nourish;
All things unstinted round them grow and flourish.
For them, endures the life-sustaining field
Its load of harvest, and their cattle yield
Large increase, and their house with wealth is filled.
Such honoured dwell in cities fair and free,
The homes of lovely women, prosperously;
Their sons exult in youth's new budding gladness,
20   And their fresh daughters free from care or sadness,
With bloom-inwoven dance and happy song,
On the soft flowers the meadow-grass among,
Leap round them sporting – such delights by thee
Are given, rich Power, revered Divinity.

    Mother of gods, thou Wife of starry Heaven,
Farewell! be thou propitious, and be given
A happy life for this brief melody,
Nor thou nor other songs shall unremembered be.   (1818)

Hymn 28 *Homer's Hymn to Minerva*

I sing the glorious Power with azure eyes,
Athenian Pallas! tameless, chaste, and wise,
Tritogenia, town-preserving Maid,
Revered and mighty; from his awful head
Whom Jove brought forth, in warlike armour dressed,
Golden, all radiant ! wonder strange possessed
The everlasting Gods that Shape to see,

Shaking a javelin keen, impetuously
Rush from the crest of Aegis-bearing Jove;
10   Fearfully Heaven was shaken, and did move
Beneath the might of the Cerulean-eyed;
Earth dreadfully resounded, far and wide;
And, lifted from its depths, the sea swelled high
In purple billows, the tide suddenly
Stood still, and great Hyperion's son long time
Checked his swift steeds, till, where she stood sublime,
Pallas from her immortal shoulders threw
The arms divine; wise Jove rejoiced to view.
 Child of the Aegis-bearer, hail to thee,
20   Nor thine nor others' praise shall unremembered be.   (1818)

ANON.

Anonymous versions of Homeric fragments are numerous. Much rarer is an anonymous rendition of a whole epic, such as that of *The Iliad of Homer Translated into English Prose* (1821). Its author, who seeks to translate 'as literally as the different idioms of the Greek and English languages will allow', seems to have had connections with Harrow and describes himself as an Oxford graduate. He translates in prose paragraphs. He footnotes, sometimes pedantically.

The Iliad of Homer Translated into English Prose XXI, pp. 288–9 [394–422] *Mars battles with Athena*

'Why thus, O most impudent, possessing boundless confidence, joinest thou the Gods in battle? Hath thy mighty soul incited thee? Rememberest thou not when thou didst impel Diomede, the son of Tydeus, to strike me? And, thyself taking the spear, didst guide it right against me, and lacerate my fair flesh. Now, therefore, I think that I will chastise thee for all that thou hast wrought against me.'

So saying, he struck against the aegis, shaggy and horrible, which not even the bolt of Jove will subdue; then blood-polluted Mars smote her with his long spear. But she, retiring back, seized in her strong hand a stone lying in the plain, black, rugged, and huge; which men of former days had placed to be the boundary of a field. With this she struck the fierce Mars upon the neck, and loosened his knees. Seven acres he covered, falling, and defiled his hair with dust; and his armour rang round him. But Pallas Minerva laughed, and, boasting over him, addressed to him these winged words:

'Fool, hast thou not yet perceived how much I boast myself to be superior *to thee*, that thou opposest thy strength to me? Thus indeed shalt thou suffer the vengeance of thy mother's fury,* who meditates mischiefs to thee, enraged because thou hast deserted the Greeks, and dost assist the truce-breaking Trojans.'

Thus having spoken, she turned away her shining eyes. But Venus, the daughter of Jove, taking him by the hand, led him away, groaning very heavily; whilst with difficulty he collected his spirit. Whom, as soon as Juno, the white-armed Goddess, perceived, she immediately addressed to Minerva these winged words:

'Alas! unconquered child of the Aegis-bearing Jove, see how, most impudent, she leads Mars, the destroyer of men, through the throng, from the glowing battle. But follow.'   (1821)

ALFRED, LORD TENNYSON
(1809–92)

Published in the 1832 collection of his poems, this diptych and internal dialogue, 'The Lotos-eaters' and 'Ulysses', are among the pre-eminent 'Homer-experiences' in our literature. They are made the more powerful by the studied interference of Virgil and Dante's 'Homers' between Tennyson and his Greek source.

---

* Thus shalt thou wash out the furies of thy mother.

'Achilles over the Trench' seems to be Tennyson's only stab at a direct translation.

The Lotos-eaters

'Courage!' he said, and pointed toward the land,
'This mounting wave will roll us shoreward soon.'
In the afternoon they came unto a land
In which it seemed always afternoon.
All round the coast the languid air did swoon,
Breathing like one that hath a weary dream.
Full-faced above the valley stood the moon;
And like a downward smoke, the slender stream
Along the cliff to fall and pause and fall did seem.

10   A land of streams! some, like a downward smoke,
Slow-dropping veils of thinnest lawn, did go;
And some thro' wavering lights and shadows broke,
Rolling a slumbrous sheet of foam below.
They saw the gleaming river seaward flow
From the inner land: far off, three mountain-tops,
Three silent pinnacles of aged snow,
Stood sunset-flush'd: and, dew'd with showery drops,
Up-clomb the shadowy pine above the woven copse.

The charmed sunset linger'd low adown
20   In the red West: thro' mountain clefts the dale
Was seen far inland, and the yellow down
Border'd with palm, and many a winding vale
And meadow, set with slender galingale:
A land where all things always seem'd the same!
And round about the keel with faces pale,
Dark faces pale against that rosy flame,
The mild-eyed melancholy Lotos-eaters came.

Branches they bore of that enchanted stem,
Laden with flower and fruit, whereof they gave
30 To each, but whoso did receive of them,
And taste, to him the gushing of the wave
Far far away did seem to mourn and rave
On alien shores; and if his fellow spake,
His voice was thin, as voices from the grave;
And deep-asleep he seem'd, yet all awake,
And music in his ears his beating heart did make.

They sat them down upon the yellow sand,
Between the sun and moon upon the shore;
And sweet it was to dream of Fatherland,
40 Of child, and wife, and slave; but evermore
Most weary seem'd the sea, weary the oar,
Weary the wandering fields of barren foam.
Then some one said, 'We will return no more;'
And all at once they sang, 'Our island home
Is far beyond the wave; we will no longer roam.'

CHORIC SONG

I
There is sweet music here that softer falls
Than petals from blown roses on the grass,
Or night-dews on still waters between walls
Of shadowy granite, in a gleaming pass;
50 Music that gentlier on the spirit lies,
Than tir'd eyelids upon tir'd eyes;
Music that brings sweet sleep down from the blissful skies.
Here are cool mosses deep,
And thro' the moss the ivies creep,
And in the stream the long-leaved flowers weep,
And from the craggy ledge the poppy hangs in sleep.

II

Why are we weigh'd upon with heaviness
And utterly consumed with sharp distress,
While all things else have rest from weariness?
60 All things have rest: why should we toil alone,
We only toil, who are the first of things,
And make perpetual moan,
Still from one sorrow to another thrown:
Not ever fold our wings,
And cease from wanderings,
Nor steep our brows in slumber's holy balm;
Nor harken what the inner spirit sings,
'There is no joy but calm!'
Why should we only toil, the roof and crown of things?

III

70 Lo! in the middle of the wood,
The folded leaf is woo'd from out the bud
With winds upon the branch, and there
Grows green and broad, and takes no care,
Sun-steep'd at noon, and in the moon
Nightly dew-fed; and turning yellow
Falls, and floats adown the air.
Lo! sweeten'd with the summer light,
The full-juiced apple, waxing over-mellow,
Drops in a silent autumn night.
80 All its allotted length of days,
The flower ripens in its place,
Ripens and fades, and falls, and hath no toil,
Fast-rooted in the fruitful soil.

IV

Hateful is the dark-blue sky,
Vaulted o'er the dark-blue sea.
Death is the end of life; ah, why
Should life all labour be?

Let us alone. Time driveth onward fast,
And in a little while our lips are dumb.
90   Let us alone. What is it that will last?
All things are taken from us, and become
Portions and parcels of the dreadful Past.
Let us alone. What pleasure can we have
To war with evil? Is there any peace
In ever climbing up the climbing wave?
All things have rest, and ripen toward the grave
In silence; ripen, fall and cease:
Give us long rest or death, dark death, or dreamful ease.

V

How sweet it were, hearing the downward stream,
100   With half-shut eyes ever to seem
Falling asleep in a half-dream!
To dream and dream, like yonder amber light,
Which will not leave the myrrh-bush on the height;
To hear each other's whisper'd speech;
Eating the Lotos day by day,
To watch the crisping ripples on the beach,
And tender curving lines of creamy spray;
To lend our hearts and spirits wholly
To the influence of mild-minded melancholy;
110   To muse and brood and live again in memory,
With those old faces of our infancy
Heap'd over with a mound of grass,
Two handfuls of white dust, shut in an urn of brass!

VI

Dear is the memory of our wedded lives,
And dear the last embraces of our wives
And their warm tears: but all hath suffer'd change:
For surely now our household hearths are cold:
Our sons inherit us: our looks are strange:
And we should come like ghosts to trouble joy.
120   Or else the island princes over-bold

Have eat our substance, and the minstrel sings
Before them of the ten years' war in Troy,
And our great deeds, as half-forgotten things.
Is there confusion in the little isle?
Let what is broken so remain.
The Gods are hard to reconcile:
'Tis hard to settle order once again.
There *is* confusion worse than death,
Trouble on trouble, pain on pain,
130   Long labour unto aged breath,
Sore task to hearts worn out by many wars
And eyes grown dim with gazing on the pilot-stars.

VII

But, propt on beds of amaranth and moly,
How sweet (while warm airs lull us, blowing lowly)
With half-dropt eyelid still,
Beneath a heaven dark and holy,
To watch the long bright river drawing slowly
His waters from the purple hill –
To hear the dewy echoes calling
140   From cave to cave thro' the thick-twined vine –
To watch the emerald-colour'd water falling
Thro' many a wov'n acanthus-wreath divine!
Only to hear and see the far-off sparkling brine,
Only to hear were sweet, stretch'd out beneath the pine.

VIII

The Lotos blooms below the barren peak:
The Lotos blows by every winding creek:
All day the wind breathes low with mellower tone:
Thro' every hollow cave and alley lone
Round and round the spicy downs the yellow Lotos-dust is
     blown.
150   We have had enough of action, and of motion we,
Roll'd to starboard, roll'd to larboard, when the surge was
     seething free,

Where the wallowing monster spouted his foam-fountains in
    the sea.
Let us swear an oath, and keep it with an equal mind,
In the hollow Lotos-land to live and lie reclined
On the hills like Gods together, careless of mankind.
For they lie beside their nectar, and the bolts are hurl'd
Far below them in the valleys, and the clouds are lightly
    curl'd
Round their golden houses, girdled with the gleaming world:
Where they smile in secret, looking over wasted lands,
160   Blight and famine, plague and earthquake, roaring deeps and
    fiery sands,
Clanging fights, and flaming towns, and sinking ships, and
    praying hands.
But they smile, they find a music centred in a doleful song
Steaming up, a lamentation and an ancient tale of wrong,
Like a tale of little meaning tho' the words are strong;
Chanted from an ill-used race of men that cleave the soil,
Sow the seed, and reap the harvest with enduring toil,
Storing yearly little dues of wheat, and wine and oil;
Till they perish and they suffer – some, 'tis whisper'd down
    in hell
Suffer endless anguish, others in Elysian valleys dwell,
170   Resting weary limbs at last on beds of asphodel.
Surely, surely, slumber is more sweet than toil, the shore
Than labour in the deep mid-ocean, wind and wave and oar;
Oh rest ye, brother mariners, we will not wander
    more.   (1832)

Ulysses

It little profits that an idle king,
By this still hearth, among these barren crags,
Match'd with an aged wife, I mete and dole
Unequal laws unto a savage race,

That hoard, and sleep, and feed, and know not me.
I cannot rest from travel: I will drink
Life to the lees: all times I have enjoy'd
Greatly, have suffer'd greatly, both with those
That loved me, and alone; on shore, and when
10   Thro' scudding drifts the rainy Hyades
Vext the dim sea: I am become a name;
For always roaming with a hungry heart
Much have I seen and known; cities of men
And manners, climates, councils, governments,
Myself not least, but honour'd of them all;
And drunk delight of battle with my peers,
Far on the ringing plains of windy Troy.
I am a part of all that I have met;
Yet all experience is an arch wherethro'
20   Gleams that untravell'd world, whose margin fades
For ever and for ever when I move.
How dull it is to pause, to make an end,
To rust unburnish'd, not to shine in use!
As tho' to breathe were life. Life piled on life
Were all too little, and of one to me
Little remains: but every hour is saved
From that eternal silence, something more,
A bringer of new things; and vile it were
For some three suns to store and hoard myself,
30   And this gray spirit yearning in desire
To follow knowledge like a sinking star,
Beyond the utmost bound of human thought.

    This is my son, mine own Telemachus,
To whom I leave the sceptre and the isle –
Well-loved of me, discerning to fulfil
This labour, by slow prudence to make mild
A rugged people, and thro' soft degrees
Subdue them to the useful and the good.
Most blameless is he, centred in the sphere
40   Of common duties, decent not to fail

In offices of tenderness, and pay
Meet adoration to my household gods,
When I am gone. He works his work, I mine.
   There lies the port; the vessel puffs her sail:
There gloom the dark broad seas. My mariners,
Souls that have toil'd, and wrought, and thought with me
That ever with a frolic welcome took
The thunder and the sunshine, and opposed
Free hearts, free foreheads – you and I are old;
50 Old age hath yet his honour and his toil;
Death closes all: but something ere the end,
Some work of noble note, may yet be done,
Not unbecoming men that strove with Gods.
The lights begin to twinkle from the rocks:
The long day wanes: the slow moon climbs: the deep
Moans round with many voices. Come, my friends,
'Tis not too late to seek a newer world.
Push off, and sitting well in order smite
The sounding furrows; for my purpose holds
60 To sail beyond the sunset, and the baths
Of all the western stars, until I die.
It may be that the gulfs will wash us down:
It may be we shall touch the Happy Isles,
And see the great Achilles, whom we knew.
Tho' much is taken, much abides; and tho'
We are not now that strength which in old days
Moved earth and heaven; that which we are, we are;
One equal temper of heroic hearts,
Made weak by time and fate, but strong in will
70 To strive, to seek, to find, and not to yield.   (1832)

Iliad XVIII [202–31] *Achilles over the Trench*

So saying, light-foot Iris pass'd away.
Then rose Achilles dear to Zeus; and round
The warrior's puissant shoulders Pallas flung
Her fringed aegis, and around his head
The glorious goddess wreath'd a golden cloud,
And from it lighted an all-shining flame.
As when a smoke from a city goes to heaven
Far off from out an island girt by foes,
All day the men contend in grievous war
10 From their own city, but with set of sun
Their fires flame thickly, and aloft the glare
Flies streaming, if perchance the neighbours round
May see, and sail to help them in the war;
So from his head the splendour went to heaven.
From wall to dyke he stept, he stood, nor join'd
The Achaeans – honouring his wise mother's word –
There standing, shouted, and Pallas far away
Call'd; and a boundless panic shook the foe.
For like the clear voice when a trumpet shrills,
20 Blown by the fierce beleaguerers of a town,
So rang the clear voice of Aeakidês;
And when the brazen cry of Aeakidês
Was heard among the Trojans, all their hearts
Were troubled, and the full-maned horses whirl'd
The chariots backward, knowing griefs at hand;
And sheer-astounded were the charioteers
To see the dread, unweariable fire
That always o'er the great Peleion's head
Burn'd, for the bright-eyed goddess made it burn.
30 Thrice from the dyke he sent his mighty shout,
Thrice backward reel'd the Trojans and allies;
And there and then twelve of their nobles died
Among their spears and chariots.   (1832)

WILLIAM SOTHEBY (1757–1833)

A prolific translator (Wieland, Virgil) and tragedian, Sotheby takes us to the threshold of Victorian readings of Homer. This urbane version had considerable success.

The Odyssey of Homer X [302–44] *The Moly flower saves Ulysses from Circe's spell*

'He spake, and gave me, pluck'd from earth, the root,
And taught the nature of that hallow'd shoot.
Black was the root, but white as milk its flower,
And Moly call'd by each celestial power:
Arduous for mortal to uproot from earth,
But all is easy to immortal birth.

   'Then Hermes passing, sought his heavenly home,
And I went onward to the Enchantress' dome.
And my heart burnt within me as I stood
10   Lone on her threshold, 'mid the magic wood.
I call'd aloud: the Goddess heard my call,
Came forth, and open'd wide her palace hall,
And woo'd me in: her footstep I pursued,
Tho' grief and fear my spirit half subdued.
She led me on, and to repose me, placed
A throne of silver with a footstool graced.
Then in a golden bowl the beverage pour'd
That I might gladly drink it thus allured;
And inly cast her drugs: then gave the bowl:
20   I took, and drank, nor felt unmann'd my soul,
When, as she struck me, thus I heard her cry, –
Go to thy friends, and wallow in their sty. –

'I drew my sword, and swift with fell intent
Sprung on her as in act of murder bent.
She, loudly shrieking, rush'd beneath my sword,
And clasp'd my knees, and weeping, spake the word: –

'Who art thou? what thy parents? city? whence?
How drink these drugs with unenchanted sense?
None whoe'er drank them tasted unsubdued
30   When once their magic had the lip embued.
Thou in thy mortal body bear'st enshrined
An iron and indomitable mind –
Thou art the wise Ulysses, oft foretold
By Hermes, bearer of the rod of gold,
Who here should sail from Troy: but, sheathe thy blade,
And let us on the couch of pleasure laid,
The fore-past scene in sweet oblivion close,
And on each other's faith in love repose.

'How bid me, I replied, to thee incline,
40   Thou, who hast thus transform'd my friends to swine?
And here detain'st, and woo'st me to thy bed
To heap thy frauds, Enchantress! on my head,
And leave me vile, unmann'd. Not thus betray'd,
E'er shall Ulysses on thy couch be laid,
Till sworn the oath, that binds the gods above,
Thou wilt not injure whom thou lurest to love.'   (1834)

J. G. LOCKHART (1794–1854)

Lockhart's hexameter version of the *Iliad*, XXIV, appeared in *Blackwood's Magazine* for March 1846. It was unsigned, in accord with the conventions of the journal. This experiment will exercise considerable influence. Lockhart translates from various European literatures and, as befits Sir Walter Scott's biographer, is drawn to archaic and heroic ballads.

The Iliad XXIV [677–759] *Priam's return to Troy*

All then of Gods upon high, ever-living, and warrior
    horsemen,
Slept through the livelong night in the gentle dominion of
    slumber;
But never slumber approach'd to the eyes of beneficent
    Hermes,
As in his mind he revolv'd how best to retire from the
    galleys
Priam the king, unobserv'd of the sentinels sworn for the
    night-watch.
Over his head, as he slept, stood the Argicide now, and
    address'd him:
'Old man, bodings of evil disturb not thy spirit, who
    slumber'st
Here among numberless foes, because noble Peleides has
    spared thee.
True that thy son has been ransom'd, and costly the worth of
    the head-gifts;
10 Yet would the sons that are left thee have three times more
    to surrender,
Wert thou but seen by the host, and the warning convey'd to
    Atreides.'
    Thus did he speak, but the king was in terror, and waken'd
    the herald.
Then, when beneficent Hermes had harness'd the mules and
    the horses,
Swiftly he drove through the camp, nor did any observe the
    departure.
So did they pass to the ford of the river of beautiful waters,
Xanthus the gulfy, begotten of thunder-delighting Kronion;
Then from the chariot he rose and ascended to lofty
    Olympus.

But now wide over earth spread morning mantled in
    saffron,
As amid groaning and weeping they drew to the city; the
    mule-wain
20 Bearing behind them the dead: Nor did any in Ilion see
    them,
Either of men, as they came, or the well-girt women of
    Troia:
Only Cassandra, that imaged in grace Aphrodité the golden,
Had to the Pergamus clomb, and from thence she discover'd
    her father
Standing afoot on the car, and beside him the summoning
    herald;
And in the waggon behind them the wrapt corse laid on the
    death-bier.
Then did she shriek, and her cry to the ends of the city resounded:
    'Come forth, woman and man, and behold the returning
        of Hector!
Come, if ye e'er in his life, at his home-coming safe from the
    battle
Joyfully troop'd; and with joy might it fill both the town
    and the people.'
30   So did she cry; nor anon was there one soul left in the city,
Woman or man, for at hand and afar was the yearning
    awaken'd.
Near to the gate was the king when they met him conducting
    the death-wain.
First rush'd, rending their hair, to behold him the wife and
    the mother,
And as they handled the head, all weeping the multitude
    stood near: –
And they had all day long till the sun went down into
    darkness
There on the field by the rampart lamented with tears over
    Hector,

But that the father arose in the car and entreated the people:
'Yield me to pass, good friends, make way for the mules –
and hereafter
All shall have weeping enow when the dead has been borne
to the dwelling.'
40   So did he speak, and they, parting asunder, made way for the
mule-wain.
But when they brought him at last to the famous abode of
the princes,
He on a fair-carv'd bed was compos'd, and the singers around
him
Rang'd, who begin the lament; and they, lifting their
sorrowful voices,
Chanted the wail for the dead, and the women bemoan'd at
its pausings.
But in the burst of her woe was the beauteous Andromache
foremost,
Holding the head in her hands as she mourn'd for the slayer
of heroes: –
    'Husband! in youth hast thou parted from life, and a
desolate widow
Here am I left in our home; and the child is a stammering
infant
Whom thou and I unhappy begat, nor will he, to my
thinking,
50   Reach to the blossom of youth; ere then, from the roof to
the basement
Down shall the city be hurl'd – since her only protector has
perish'd,
And without succour are now chaste mother and stammering
infant.
Soon shall their destiny be to depart in the ships of the
stranger,
I in the midst of them bound; and, my child, thou go with
them also,
Doom'd for the far-off shore and the tarnishing toil of the
bondman,

Slaving for lord unkind. Or perchance some remorseless Achaian
Hurl from the gripe of his hand, from the battlement down to perdition,
Raging revenge for some brother perchance that was slaughter'd of Hector,
Father, it may be, or son; for not few of the race of Achaia
60   Seiz'd broad earth with their teeth, when they sank from the handling of Hector;
For not mild was thy father, O babe, in the blackness of battle –
Wherefore, now he is gone, through the city the people bewail him.
But the unspeakable anguish of misery bides with thy parents,
Hector! with me above all the distress that has no consolation:
For never, dying, to me didst thou stretch forth hand from the pillow,
Nor didst thou whisper, departing, one secret word to be hoarded
Ever by day and by night in the tears of eternal remembrance.'
   Weeping Andromache ceased, and the women bemoan'd at her pausing;
Then in her measureless grief spake Hecuba, next of the mourners:
70   'Hector! of all that I bore ever dearest by far to my heart-strings!
Dear above all wert thou also in life to the gods everlasting;
Wherefore they care for thee now, though in death's dark destiny humbled!
Others enow of my sons did the terrible runner Achilles
Sell, whomsoever he took, far over the waste of the waters,
Either to Samos or Imber, or rock-bound harbourless Lemnos;
But with the long-headed spear did he rifle the life from thy bosom,

And in the dust did he drag thee, oft times, by the tomb of
    his comrade,
Him thou hadst slain; though not so out of death could he
    rescue Patroclus.
Yet now, ransom'd at last, and restored to the home of thy
    parents,
80   Dewy and fresh liest thou, like one that has easily parted,
Under a pangless shaft from the silvern bow of
        Apollo.'   (1846)

WILLIAM MAGINN (1794–1842)

There is a method behind the 'madness' and unintended comedy of
this adaptation. Maginn conceives of Homer as a blind singer of
ballads (Irish in style) whose audience would, surely, not have
tolerated the long sections taken over by previous translators. Sup-
pose he was right . . .

The *Odyssey* XVII [290–327] *The Dog Argus*

Then as they spake, upraised his head,
    Pricked up his listening ear,
The dog, whom erst Odysseus bred,
    Old Argus lying near.

2
He bred him, but his fostering skill
    To himself had naught availed;
For Argus joined not the chase, until
    The king had to Ilion sailed.

3

To hunt the wild-goat, hart, and hare,
10   Him once young huntsmen sped;
But now he lay an outcast there,
Absent his lord, to none a care,
    Upon a dunghill bed,

4

Where store of dung, profusely flung
    By mules and oxen, lay;
Before the gates it was spread along
    For the hinds to bear away,

5

As rich manure for the lands they tilled
    Of their prince beyond the sea;
20 There was Argus stretched, his flesh all filled
    With the dog-worrying flea.

6

But when by the hound his king was known,
    Wagged was the fawning tail,
Backward his close-clapped ears were thrown,
And up to his master's side had he flown;
    But his limbs he felt to fail.

7

Odysseus saw, and turned aside
    To wipe away the tear;
From Eumaeus he chose his grief to hide,
30 And 'Strange, passing strange, is the sight,' he cried,
    'Of such a dog laid here!

8

'Noble his shape, but I cannot tell
  If his worth with that shape may suit;
If a hound he be in the chase to excel,
  For fleetness of his foot:

9

'Or worthless as a household hound,
  Whom men by their boards will place,
For no merit of strength or speed renowned,
  But admired for shapely grace.'

10

40 'He is the dog of one now dead,
  In a far land away;
But if you had seen,' the swineherd said,
  'This dog in his better day,
When Odysseus hence his warriors led
  To join in the Trojan fray,

11

'His strength, his plight, his speed so light,
  You had with wonder viewed;
No beast that once had crossed his sight,
  In the depths of the darkest wood,
50 'Scaped him, as, tracking sure and right,
  He on its trace pursued.

12

'But now all o'er in sorrows sore
  He pines in piteous wise;
The king upon some distant shore
  In death has closed his eyes;
And the careless women here no more
  Tend Argus as he lies.

13

'For slaves who find their former lord
　No longer holds the sway
60 No fitting service will afford,
　Or just obedience pay.

14

'Far-seeing Jove's resistless power
　Takes half away the soul
From him, who of one servile hour
　Has felt the dire control.'

15

This said, the swineherd passed the gate,
　And entered the dwelling tall,
Where proud in state the suitors sate
　Within the palace hall.

16

70 And darksome death checked Argus' breath
　When he saw his master dear;
For he died his master's eye beneath,
　All in that twentieth year.   (1850)

F. W. NEWMAN (1805–97)

Newman's translation is remembered, if at all, as the target of
Matthew Arnold's devastating critique. This is to miss Newman's
point and the (no doubt unfortunate) translation strategy. He adopts
'a more or less antiquated' idiom, with echoes from Anglo-Saxon
poetry and alliterative verse, in order to communicate Homer's
'strangeness' and remoteness. Newman seeks to echo the peculiarity
of the original *the more foreign it may happen to be*'. This is a valid
insight, and it will have later imitators.

The Iliad XI [1-55] *The Greeks and Agamemnon prepare for battle*

The Queen of Morning from the bed of glorious Tithonus
Uprose, to carry light to men   and eke to gods immortal.
But to the sharp Achaian ships   from Jove came Quarrel darting,
Noisome, who bare within her hands battle's portentous ensign:
And on Ulysses' galley black   she stood; which midmost couched,
Huge like to some leviathan,   to shout both ways adapted,
Alike toward the tented camp   of Telamonian Ajax
And to Achilles' bands, which haul'd their evenbalanc'd galleys
Last on the strand, on bravery   and stubborn strength reliant.
There did the goddess station her   and shouted sharp and dreadful
With voice highlifted, and infus'd   to each Achaian bosom
Vigour immense, unceasingly   to toil in war and combat.
And sweeter suddenly became   the battle, than the voyage
Unto their native land belov'd   on smoothly-hollow galleys.
    The son of Atreus, shouting, bade the Argive host to gird them
For battle: mid them he himself   in dazzling brass equipp'd him.
First on his shins the dapper greaves, with silver anklets clever,
He fasten'd; next, to guard his chest, enwrapt him in a corslet,
Which erst from Cinyras he gat   as hospitable token,
What time the mighty rumour reach'd to Cyprus, that the Argives
Would shortly on their galleys sail   against the land of Troas.
Therefore on him bestow'd he it,   to gratify the monarch.
Ten stripes of blue and dusky steel   ran o'er its polish'd surface;
Its stripes of gold were six and six,   but these of tin were twenty
On either side toward the neck   three blue resplendent serpents
Did arch their throats; to rainbows like, which on the cloudy heaven
Saturnius may plant, a sign   to voice-dividing mortals.
Then slung he round his neck the sword, with golden studs all-brilliant,
And guarded in a silver sheath,   which hung on golden braces.
Above, he took his muchwrought shield, man-hiding, fit for sally,
Round which ten brazen circles ran. On the fair front in centre,
Mid twenty bosses of white tin,   one of blue steel protruded.

Upon it Gorgon horrid-ey'd   was carv'd along the border,
With dreadful glances; and around sat Flight and Consternation.
The strap with silver was encas'd: o'er it an azure serpent
Was twin'd with three out-gazing heads, forth from one neck proceeding.
But on his head a four-plum'd casque with double ridge he settled,
Bushy with horsetail: dreadfully   the crest above it nodded.
A pair of valiant spears he grasp'd,   with copper tipp'd and sharpen'd,
And from them shone the yellow gleam afar into the heaven,
From Juno and Athene then   a thunder-clap forth rumbled,
In honor to the stately king   of gold-endow'd Mycenae.
    So to his proper charioteer   each chief gave urgent bidding,
There on the moat in order due   to bridle-in the horses:
But they themselves on foot, with arms and panoply accoutred,
Stream'd wildly; and from early dawn incessant rose the clamour.
Before the charioteers they reach'd the moat, all fitly marshall'd.
Nor long the charioteers behind   were left: but Saturn's offspring
Amid them evil tumult rous'd,   and from the lofty heaven
Sent mistiness of gory dew;   sith that he now was minded,
Forward to fling to Aïdes   full many a gallant spirit.

XXIV [486–506] *Priam to Achilles*

    'Achilles, image of the gods!   thy proper sire remember,
Who on the deadly steps of Eld   far on, like me, is carried.
And haply him the dwellers-round   with many an outrage harry,
Nor standeth any by his side   to ward annoy and ruin.
Yet doth he verily, I wis,   while thee alive he learneth,
Joy in his soul, and every day   the hope within him cherish,
His loved offspring to behold,   return'd from land of Troas.
Mine is a direr fate; for I   the noblest sons had gotten
Of all in wide-spread Troy: of whom not one, I say, remaineth.
Fifty I had, when first arriv'd   the children of Achaia:
Of these a score complete, save one, came from a single mother,
My proper queen: the rest were born from women in my chambers.
Beneath fierce Ares, most of them with knees unstrung are fallen;

But him who was my only guard   to kin and folk and city,
Him, fighting for his native land,   thyself hast lately vanquish'd, –
Hector. And therefore now I seek   the galleys of Achaia,
From thee his body to redeem,   and brilliant ransom bear thee.
But, Achileus! revere the gods,   and for my years have pity,
Thy proper sire remembering: but sadder far my portion,
Who have endur'd, what none beside of men on earth would venture,
Unto my lips to raise the hand   which hath my children slaughter'd.'

(1856)

W. E. GLADSTONE (1809–98)

Gladstone's interest in matters Homeric led to a number of important essays.

These were gathered into the three-volume *Studies on Homer and the Homeric Age* (1858). These studies contain fragments of translation.

The *Iliad* IV [422–43]

As when the billow gathers fast
   With slow and sullen roar
Beneath the keen northwestern blast
   Against the sounding shore:
First far at sea it rears its crest,
   Then bursts upon the beach.
Or with proud arch and swelling breast,
   Where headlands outward reach,
It smites their strength, and bellowing flings
10   Its silver foam afar;
So, stern and thick, the Danaan kings
   And soldiers marched to war.

Each leader gave his men the word;
Each warrior deep in silence heard.
So mute they march'd, thou could'st not ken
They were a mass of speaking men:
And as they strode in martial might,
Their flickering arms shot back the light.
But as at even the folded sheep
20   Of some rich master stand,
Ten thousand thick their place they keep,
       And bide the milkman's hand,
And more and more they bleat, the more
       They hear their lamblings cry;
So, from the Trojan host, uproar
       And din rose loud and high.
They were a many-voicèd throng:
       Discordant accents there,
That sound from many a differing tongue,
30   Their differing race declare.
These, Mars had kindled for the fight;
Those, starry-ey'd Athenè's might,
And savage Terror and Affright,
And Strife, insatiate of wars,
The sister and the mate of Mars:
Strife, that, a pigmy at her birth,
       By gathering rumour fed,
Soon plants her feet upon the earth,
       And in the heav'n her head.

XIX [404–18]

Xanthus, hark! a voice hath found,
Xanthus of the flashing feet:
Whitearm'd Herè gave the sound.
   'Lord Achilles, strong and fleet!

Trust us, we will bear thee home:
Yet cometh nigh thy day of doom:
No doom of ours, but doom that stands
By God and mighty Fate's commands.
'Twas not that we were slow or slack
10   Patroclus lay a corpse, his back
All stript of arms by Trojan hands.
The prince of gods, whom Leto bare,
Leto with the flowing hair,
He forward fighting did the deed,
And gave to Hector glory's meed.
In toil for thee, we will not shun
Against e'en Zephyr's breath to run,
Swiftest of winds: but all in vain:
By God and man shalt thou be slain.'
20   He spake: and here, his words among,
Erinnys bound his faltering tongue   (1858)

P. S. WORSLEY (1835–66)

A translation in Spenserian metre and stanzas which 'strives to see vividly what Homer sees'. Worsley is persuaded that 'no metre in the English language can bear comparison with the Spenserian' for narrative pace and suppleness. He garners praise from Matthew Arnold.

The Odyssey IV [219–64] *Helena to Menelaus*

32

Then Helena the child of Zeus strange things
Devised, and mixed a philter in their wine,
Which so cures heartache and the inward stings,

That men forget all sorrow wherein they pine.
He who hath tasted of the draught divine
Weeps not that day, although his mother die
And father, or cut off before his eyen
Brother or child beloved fall miserably,
Hewn by the pitiless sword, he sitting silent by,

33

10   Drugs of such virtue did she keep in store,
Given her by Polydamna, wife of Thôn,
In Egypt, where the rich glebe evermore
Yields herbs in foison, some for virtue known,
Some baneful. In that climate each doth own
Leech-craft beyond what mortal minds attain;
Since of Paeonian stock their race hath grown.
She the good philter mixed to charm their pain,
And bade the wine outpour, and answering spake again:

34

'O Atreus' son, and ye that boast your blood
20   From loins heroic, what if Zeus to all
Deal as he listeth evil things and good –
Who all things can? Feast freely in the hall
And charm you with the tale I now recal.
Yet can I not unfold, nor even name,
Half that the brave Odysseus did befal.
Yet this one work he wrought of glorious fame,
When woe by Troia's walls on you the Achaians came.

35

'For self-disfigured with unseemly scars,
And clothed in many a vile habiliment,
30   In menial aspect past the foeman's bars
His course into the wide-wayed town he bent,
In beggar's weeds disguising his intent,

Who was far other by the Achaian fleet.
So masked among the silent crowd he went.
I only knew him, and did oft repeat
My questionings, which he with sleights did still defeat.

36

'But when I washed his limbs and rubbed with oil,
And robed him, and a mighty oath had sworn
By no discovery his design to foil,
40   Nor of Odysseus' name the Trojans warn,
Till that he safely from the foe were borne
Unto the swift ships and the huts, lo! then
He showed me all the Achaian mind in turn,
And having with his sword slain many men
Back to the Argive camp with tidings came again.

37

'Then all the other Trojan dames wept sore,
But o'er my breast a gladdening change there lay.
Already had my heart gone back before
Homeward; already I bewailed the day
50·   When Aphrodite did my steps convey
From Sparta and my fatherland so dear,
Leaving my child an orphan far away,
And couch, and husband who had known no peer,
First in all grace of soul, and beauty shining clear.'

XIV [462–533] *Odysseus to Eumaeus*

59

'Hear now, Eumaeus, and thy comrades all!
I speak for glory, since by wine made bold
Often to singing even the wise will fall,
Light laughter and the dance, nor can withhold
Words that in sooth were better far untold –
Yet, fairly launched, I swerve not. Would to-night
Such were my strength as in the days of old,
When, mid the sufferings of the ten years' fight,
Once we lay crouched in ambush under Troia's height!

60

10   'Atrides Menelaus held command,
Odysseus, and I third; such was their will.
Close to the city's walls we ranged our band,
Armed, in the marsh-reeds cowering, mute and still.
Down came the bad Night, and cut piercing chill
With ice-winds from the north. The snow like rime
Glazed on the shields, which the keen frost did frill.
There, couched beneath their shields, in that fell clime
Wrapt in warm cloaks the rest slept soundly all the time.

61

'I, like a fool, had left my cloak behind,
20   Not dreaming it would freeze. Doublet and shield
Alone now fenced me from the wintry wind.
But in the third watch, when the stars had wheeled,
I nudged Odysseus, and his sleep unsealed,
And spake: "Odysseus, wise Laértiades,
Guile of some god hath lured me to this field
Cloakless; remaineth nor escape nor ease;
Soon shall I leave the living, so direly doth it freeze."

62

    'Thus spake I: soon did his shrewd sense appear:
    Such was he ever both to scheme and fight.
30   Softly he whispered: "Hush, lest some one hear!"
    And, on his elbow leaning to the right,
    Spake to his fellows: "Hark, my friends! this night
    A dream from heaven hath sought me in my sleep.
    Far lie the ships. Go some one, and incite
    Atrides Agamemnon, who doth keep
Our host, to send more soldiers inland from the deep."

63

    'He spake; and quickly rose Andraemon's son,
    Thoas, and leaving there his purple cloak
    Swift in the chill night to the ships did run.
40   I in his garment slumbered warm, till broke
    The golden-thronèd morning; then I woke.
    O were my strength firm as in years of old,
    One of the swineherds would soon lend a cloak
    For friendship, reverencing a warrior bold!
Now am I scorned, because vile rags my form enfold.'

64

    Swineherd Eumaeus, thou didst answer make:
    'Old man, well said! thy words have all been good;
    And thou shalt fairly of our robes partake,
    Yea find all comfort that a suppliant should,
50   Now – in the morning thine own raiment rude
    Must serve thy turn: few changes keep we here:
    Each hath his own one suit, not oft renewed.
    But, when my lord's son comes, robes and good cheer
He will vouchsafe, and send thee whither thou list to fare.'

65

This said, he rose up, and beside the fire
Spread forth a couch with skins of goats and sheep.
There lay Odysseus, wrapt in warm attire,
Which the good swineherd for a change did keep,
Whenso from heaven a furious storm might sweep.
There lay Odysseus, and beside him slept
The young men; but the swineherd would not sleep
Far from his swine, but from the doors forth stept,
Armed and accoutred well, such faithful charge he kept.

66

Glad was Odysseus that so much he cared
His master to serve well, though far away.
With sword flung o'er his shoulders forth he fared,
Adjusting the good cloak which round him lay,
Proof to all winds, a very warm array;
Then took the hide of a great goat well fed,
And spear, both dogs and men to keep at bay.
So mid the swine, where arched rocks overhead
Fenced off the Boreal blast, the swineherd sought his bed.

(1861–2)

MATTHEW ARNOLD (1822–88)

Three famous lectures form one of the 'hinges' in our anthology.
Written in riposte to the Homer-translations of Sotheby, Wright
and Newman, they postulate four criteria for just translation:
eminent rapidity; eminent plainness and directness both in vocab-
ulary and syntax; eminent plainness in 'matter and ideas'; eminent
nobility. Pope is held to have violated formal plainness. Newman
replies and Arnold returns to the fray in his 'Last Words' (1862)
with their praise for Worsley's Spenserian *Odyssey*. Versions by

Maginn, Wright, Sotheby, Hawtrey (in *English Hexameter Transla-tions* of 1847), Brandreth and Worsley can be seen to form a cluster around Arnold's argument.

Arnold says clearly that he does not regard himself as poetically qualified to produce the necessary hexameter version. But he does illustrate his critique by translating a few passages.

On Translating Homer. The Iliad VI [441–65] *Hector's farewell to Andromache*

Woman, I too take thought for this; but then I bethink me
What the Trojan men and Trojan women might murmur,
If like a coward I skulked behind, apart from the battle.
Nor would my own heart let me; my heart, which has bid
    me be valiant
Always, and always fighting among the first of the Trojans,
Busy for Priam's fame and my own, in spite of the future.
For that day will come, my soul is assured of its coming,
It will come, when sacred Troy shall go to destruction,
Troy, and warlike Priam too, and the people of Priam.
10 And yet not that grief, which then will be, of the Trojans,
Moves me so much – not Hecuba's grief, nor Priam my
    father's,
Nor my brethren's, many and brave, who then will be lying
In the bloody dust, beneath the feet of their foemen –
As thy grief, when, in tears, some brazen-coated Achaian
Shall transport thee away, and the day of thy freedom be
    ended.
Then, perhaps, thou shalt work at the loom of another, in
    Argos,
Or bear pails to the well of Messeïs, or Hypereia,
Sorely against thy will, by strong Necessity's order.
And some man may say, as he looks and sees thy tears falling:
20 *See, the wife of Hector, that great pre-eminent captain*
Of the horsemen of Troy, in the day they fought for their city.

So some man will say; and then thy grief will redouble
At thy want of a man like me, to save thee from bondage.
But let me be dead, and the earth be mounded above me,
Ere I hear thy cries, and thy captivity told of.

The Iliad XIX [400–424] *Achilles to his steeds*

'Xanthus and Balius both, ye far-famed seed of Podarga!
See that ye bring your master home to the host of the
    Argives
In some other sort than your last, when the battle is ended;
And not leave him behind, a corpse on the plain, like
    Patroclus.'
  Then, from beneath the yoke, the fleet horse Xanthus
    addressed him:
Sudden he bowed his head, and all his mane, as he bowed it,
Streamed to the ground by the yoke, escaping from under
    the collar;
And he was given a voice by the white-armed Goddess Hera.
  'Truly, yet this time will we save thee, mighty Achilles!
10 But thy day of death is at hand; nor shall *we* be the reason –
No, but the will of heaven, and Fate's invincible power.
For by no slow pace or want of swiftness of ours
Did the Trojans obtain to strip the arms from Patroclus;
But that prince among Gods, the son of the lovely-haired
    Leto,
Slew him fighting in front of the fray, and glorified Hector.
But, for us, we vie in speed with the breath of the West-
    Wind,
Which, men say, is the fleetest of winds; 'tis thou who art fated
To lie low in death, by the hand of a God and a Mortal.'
  Thus far he; and here his voice was stopped by the Furies.
20 Then, with a troubled heart, the swift Achilles addressed him:
  'Why dost thou prophesy so my death to me, Xanthus?
    It needs not.

I of myself know well, that here I am destined to perish,
Far from my father and mother dear: for all that I will not
Stay this hand from fight, till the Trojans are utterly routed.'

So he spake, and drove with a cry his steeds into battle. (1861)

THOMAS STARLING NORGATE (1807–93)

No prior version has given 'to the English reader anything like an adequate version of what Homer is – whether in his matter, or in his manner . . .' Dramatic blank verse, such as is used by Shakespeare and Milton's *Comus* 'seems to me the best vehicle for Homeric translation'. An indiscriminate archaism soon defeats Norgate's high intentions.

The Iliad IX [376–416] *Achilles' bitter reply to the lords who come from Agamemnon pleading for help*

Be it enough: away with him in peace!
For Zeus the lord of Counsel has bereft him
Of all his wits. To me his gifts too are hateful:
And Him I value – at a snip of hair.
Nor if he gave me ten and twenty times
As much as all is now his own, and if
From any quarter yet were added more;
Nor all the wealth that comes to Orchomenos,
Nor to Aegyptian Thebes, where lie vast treasures
In chambers, – that rich Town of a hundred gates,
Wherethrough at each come warriors forth two hundred
With horse and chariot; neither if he gave me
Gifts countless as the dust and sand, – yet so,
Never should Agamemnon move my heart,
Until at least he has giv'n me back full quittance

For this heart-grieving outrage. And not marry
Will I Atreidès Agamemnon's daughter.
Not e'en if might she vie in comeliness
With golden Aphrodîtè, and might e'en equal
20   Bright-eyed Athênè in handiwork, — yet so,
I would not marry her: but of the Achaians
Some other Let him catch, — one that may suit him,
And has more kingship. For now should the gods
Preserve me safe, and I reach home, sure Then
A wife for me Pêleus himself will find.
Achaian ladies, daughters of high chiefs,
Defenders of their Towns, there are in Hellas,
And also in Phthia, many a one; of Them,
Her may I take to wife, e'en whom I would:
30   And fain has been my gallant heart full oft
To woo and wed a wife, a consort meet,
And cheer me in the wealth, which the old man Pêleus
Has gotten him in possession. For with me
Not to be weighed 'gainst *Life* is all the wealth,
How great soe'er they say it was, that Ilion
This fair-built City did possess, before,
In time of peace, ere came the sons of Argives;
Nor all the treasures that in rocky Pytho
Are shut up safe within, by the stone threshold
40   Of the Archer, bright Apollo. For both beeves
And goodly flocks are to be won for booty;
And chesnut horses, many a head, and tripods
Sure *may* be gained: but the Life-breath of man,
To come again, is neither to be won,
Nor may be caught, when once it shall have passed
Its fence of teeth. And silver-footed Thetis
My goddess mother says, how Destinies
Twofold are bearing me to the term of Death.
If would I here indeed remain besieging
50   The Trojans' Town, then home-return for me
Is Lost, — but undecaying shall be my Glory:

But if I home again should rather go
To my dear fatherland, then my fair Glory
Is at an end, but lengthened unto me
For long shall be my Life, nor should the term
Of Death soon overtake me.'   (1864)

DERBY, THE FOURTEENTH
EARL OF (1799–1869)

Among prime ministers, two at least have taken an active interest in
Homer, Gladstone and the Earl of Derby. The latter's blank-verse
Iliad was issued privately in 1862 and published in 1864. A 'trans-
lation and not a paraphrase', this version proved eminently success-
ful. A fifth edition was in print by 1865.

Homer's Iliad V.568–608 [497–532] *The Trojan counter-attack*

The tide was turned; again they faced the Greeks:
In serried ranks the Greeks, undaunted, stood.
As when the wind from off a threshing-floor,
Where men are winnowing, blows the chaff away;
When yellow Ceres with the breeze divides
The corn and chaff, which lies in whitening heaps;
So thick the Greeks were whitened o'er with dust,
Which to the brazen vault of Heaven arose
Beneath the horses' feet, that with the crowd
10   Were mingled, by their drivers turned to flight.
Unwearied still, they bore the brunt; but Mars
The Trojans succouring, the battle-field
Veiled in thick clouds, from every quarter brought.
Thus he of Phoebus of the golden sword

Obeyed the injunction, bidding him arouse
The courage of the Trojans, when he saw
Pallas approaching to support the Greeks.
    Then from the wealthy shrine Apollo's self
Aeneas brought, and vigour fresh infused:
20 Amid his comrades once again he stood;
They joyed to see him yet alive, and sound,
And full of vigour; yet no question asked:
No time for question then, amid the toils
Imposed by Phoebus of the silver bow,
And blood-stained Mars, and Discord unappeased.
    Meanwhile Ulysses, and the Ajaces both,
And Diomed, with courage for the fight
The Grecian force inspired; they undismayed
Shrank not before the Trojan's rush and charge;
30 In masses firm they stood, as when the clouds
Are gathered round the misty mountain top
By Saturn's son, in breathless calm, while sleep
The force of Boreas and the stormy winds,
That with their breath the shadowy clouds disperse;
So stood the Greeks, nor shunned the Trojans' charge.
Through all the army Agamemnon passed,
And cried, 'Brave comrades, quit ye now like men;
Bear a stout heart; and in the stubborn fight,
Let each to other mutual succour give;
40 By mutual succour more are saved than fall;
In timid flight nor fame nor safety lies.'

XXII.107–55 [90–130] *Hector reflects on his fate as he awaits
the onrush of Achilles*

    Thus they, with tears and earnest prayers imploring,
Addressed their son; yet Hector firm remained,
Waiting the approach of Peleus' godlike son.
As when a snake upon the mountain side,

With deadly venom charged, beside his hole
Awaits the traveller, and filled with rage,
Coiled round his hole, his baleful glances darts;
So filled with dauntless courage Hector stood,
Scorning retreat, his gleaming buckler propped
Against the jutting tower; then, deeply moved,
Thus with his warlike soul communion held:
  'Oh woe is me! if I should enter now
The city gates, I should the just reproach
Encounter of Polydamas, who first
His counsel gave within the walls to lead
The Trojan forces, on that fatal night
When great Achilles in the field appeared.
I heeded not his counsel; would I had!
Now, since my folly hath the people slain,
I well might blush to meet the Trojan men,
And long-robes dames of Troy, lest some might say,
To me inferior far, "This woful loss
To Hector's blind self-confidence we owe."
Thus shall they say; for me, 'twere better far,
Or from Achilles, slain in open fight,
Back to return in triumph, or myself
To perish nobly in my country's cause.
What if my bossy shield I lay aside,
And stubborn helmet, and my ponderous spear
Propping against the wall, go forth to meet
The unmatched Achilles? What if I engage
That Helen's self, and with her all the spoil,
And all that Paris in his hollow ships
Brought here to Troy, whence first this war arose,
Should be restored; and to the Greeks be paid
An ample tribute from the city's stores,
Her secret treasures; and hereafter bind
The Trojans by their Elders' solemn oaths
Nought to withhold, but fairly to divide
Whate'er of wealth our much-loved city holds?

40   But wherefore entertain such thoughts, my soul?
      Should I so meet him, what if he should show
      Nor pity nor remorse, but slay me there,
      Defenceless as a woman, and unarmed?
      Not this the time, nor he the man, with whom
      By forest oak or rock, like youth and maid,
      To hold light talk, as youth and maid might hold.
      Better to dare the fight, and know at once
      To whom the victory is decreed by Heaven.'   (1864)

J. HENRY DART (1817–87)

A version in English hexameters, clearly influenced by Matthew Arnold's criteria. There is a certain dramatic motion.

The Iliad XVIII [239–83] *Polydamas addresses the Trojans*

Now, the unwearied Sun, at the bidding of beautiful Herè,
Slow and reluctant, sank from the Earth to the streams of the
    Ocean.
Slowly the orb went down; and the godlike sons of Achaia
Paused from the levelling fight, and the furious shout of the
    onset.
And, on the side of the foes, Troy's armies, retreating from
    combat,
And from the hard-fought field, from the cars unloosen'd the
    war-steeds.
And, ere thinking of food, they assembled together in
    council.
Standing erect, they assembled; for no man dared to be
    seated;

Such was the nervous dread that was fallen on all; since, Achilleus,

10 Now had appear'd once more; after dreary cessation from battle.

First, and with anxious heart, did Polydamas rise and address them:

Panthus' son; who presaged of the future by aid of the past time.

Hector's chosen friend; they were both of them born in the same night.

Excellent one in speech, and the other was great with his weapon.

Now, much moved for the weal of the people, he rose and address'd them.

'Ponder it, deeply, my friends! – for myself let me earnestly urge you,

Back, to the walls of the city; nor tarry for morning to find us

Here, on the open plain, by the fleet, far away from the ramparts!

While yon man was at feud with the godlike chief Agamemnon,

20 It was an easier war, that we waged with the sons of Achaia.

Even myself felt keenly the pleasure of camping at nightfall,

Close by the well-bench'd ships, which we eyed as the prize of the morrow.

But I am, now – and I own it – in mortal dread of Pelides.

Such is his pride of soul, that I fear he will not be restricted

More, to the open plain, where the armies of Troy and Achaia

Long, with alternate fortune, engaged in the struggle of Ares.

Battle is now to be done for the town itself, and our consorts.

Therefore, retreat at once, to the city, I pray: – and for this cause: –

Night – ambrosial night – now fetters the mighty Pelides;
30   But on the morrow's dawn, if, arising in armor, he find us
Here – where we now are camp'd – there are many among
        us, will know him,
Unto the bitter cost – and will long to re-enter the town-
        wall,
If they, perchance, may attain it. – I trow that the vultures
        and wild-dogs
Will have a feast on Trojans. – I pray that I never may know
        it! –
But if we do, as I say – though grievous, I own, is
        compliance –
Let us, throughout this night, hold council of means: – let the
        bulwarks,
Gates of towering height, and the great panels fitted upon
        them,
Polish'd, and sturdily barr'd, be arranged as the city's
        defences.
Let us, at dawn of day, all arm'd and resplendent in armor,
40   Stand, and man our walls. – He will find, if he drives from
        the galleys,
It is a difficult task to compel us, perforce, to engage him.
Backward and forward, in vain, he may guide the high necks
        of his war-steeds
Under the strong town-walls, till he drive them, in weariness,
        homewards.
But, he will never attempt to advance to the storm of the
        rampart;
Nor, if he do, will he storm it: – the wild-dogs sooner will
        tear him.'   (1865)

EDWIN W. SIMCOX

Yet another 'Homer' from a year replete with translations (in response to Arnold). A line-for-line hexameter text promising to convey to the reader what Homer *really* says. There are, in fact, attractive moments in this forgotten labour.

Homer's Iliad XVIII.96–137 [97–137] *Achilles and his mother*

Then, deeply groaning, thus spoke swift-footed Achilleus:
'Instantly I should have died when I could not aid my
    companion
While he was being slain; he far, far away from his country,
Perished has, while longing for me to defend him in battle.
Now, since I shall not return to the much-loved land of my
    country,
Nor did aid to Patroclos bring, nor my other companions,
Many of whom have slaughtered been by Hector the noble;
And by the ships I sit, a useless weight on the sea-shore,
Being in battle unequalled quite by the brass-mailed
    Achaians,

10 Though full many a chief, than I, is wiser in council;
Would that strife were abolished all from the gods and from
    mortals,
And wrath too, which prompteth oft e'en a wise man to
    fury;
Sweeter it seems by far than the luscious down-dropping
    honey,
And, in the bosoms of men, it still, like a vapour, increaseth;
Thus did me, but now, provoke the king Agamemnon.
But let us leave the past alone, howsoe'er we may sorrow,
And the wrath, our breasts within, let necessity vanquish.
Now will I go, of that dear head, to find the destroyer,

Hector; and then will I receive what fortune soever

20   Zeus may will to send, and the rest of the deities deathless.

Death might not avoided be by the strength of Heracles,

Who was most dear to Zeus the king, the offspring of
     Kronos;

But fate o'ercame him, and the heavy anger of Herè.

So shall I soon lie dead, if, like his, my fate is determined;

But yet, ere I die, I will win some excellent glory,

And I shall make some one of the Trojan deep-bosomed
     matrons

With both hands to wipe away the tears from her soft cheeks,

While she her moan incessantly pours for the loss of her
     husband;

And they shall know that I have long abstained from the
     battle.

30   Do not then, dear, forbid me to war, for thou canst not
     persuade me.'

   To him thus did Thetis reply, the silvery-footed:

'What thou sayest, my son, is true, nor is it unworthy

Thee to ward off bitter death from thy hard-pressed
     companions;

But thy beautiful arms are now retained by the Trojans,

Brazen and glistening all; them, brilliant-helmeted Hector,

Having upon his shoulders, is glad; but I do not consider

That he will long in them exult, for death is upon him.

But do not thou, as yet, engage in the labour of Ares,

Ere thou me, with thine eyes shalt behold, to this place
     returning;

40   For I will, with the morning, return, when the sun shall be
     rising,

Bringing thee new and beautiful arms from the monarch
     Hephaistos.'   (1865)

G. MUSGRAVE (1798–1883)

Did London booksellers show anything but new 'Homers' in 1865?
Musgrave is convinced that the Homeric epics resemble Holy Writ (he
is neither the first nor the last to believe this). Homer, he opines, must
have seen the Old Testament and derived from it 'sublime precepts'.

Homer's Odyssey XII.96–168 [66–114] *Circe foretells the
menace of the 'Wandering Rocks'*

'"But, from this rock no ship's crew yet hath 'scap'd
That e'er drew nigh it: for, the ocean wave
And hurricanes and storms whose lightning flash
Destruction deals, the timbers of the ships
And dead men's corses in one ruin plunge.
That one and only Ship that o'er the main
Its prosp'rous course was destin'd to pursue,
ARGO, alone, this rock hath pass'd – that bark
Of world-wide int'rest, which this course to shape
10 Aeetes left; and, haply, might the surge
With sudden shock against the fearful steep
Her hull have driven, had not Juno's self
Who Jason fondly tender'd, brought it off.
But, as to these two rocks, the fine sharp peak
Of one upsoars to sky, and a dark cloud
Around it hangs and never shifts; nor doth
The over-arching vault of heav'n serene
In sultry Summer or in Autumn-tide
That summit ever brighten. Mortal man
20 With twice ten hands and feet that rock in vain
Might strive to climb, or from its height descend;
So smooth its surface, even as a cone
In every part high polish'd. At its base
And in site central, to the West oppos'd

And Erebus, a darkling cavern yawns –
And thither, great Ulysses! steer thy bark.
A youth that on its deck from bended bow
An arrow should discharge, that deep recess
In vain might strive to reach. Here Scylla dwells!

30   In screams most fearful wailing: – Though her voice
Doth but the cry resemble of some whelp
But newly born, she is, herself, in shape
A monster foul; and ill would any one,
E'en though a god her presence should confront,
The sight of her endure. Twelve feet she hath,
And all deform'd; – six necks, extremely long –
On each of which is a most dreadful head,
Three rows of teeth containing, thickly set
And numerous; – of deadly venom full.

40   Deep in the centre of that yawning cave
Is she immerg'd; and from that horrid depth
Her sev'ral heads protrude; and on the watch
For dolphins and sea-dogs she angles there:
And many another monster fish would fain
Thus make her prey, such as in countless shoals
The hollow-roaring Amphitrite tends.
No mariners have yet the vaunt made good
That in their ship they ever alongside
The cavern of this rock have rush'd unscath'd:

50   For, she with each of her six heads a man
From the dark hull down tearing drags him in.

'"The other rock, Ulysses, thou wilt see
Not from the other distant, but less steep;
And this thou mightest with an arrow reach.
Hereon is a large fig-tree of wild growth
In foliage abundant, under which
Mystic Charybdis the dark stream imbibes:
For, thrice in the same day she casts it forth
And thrice with horrid suction draws it in.

60 While she is thus engorging, may'st thou ne'er
    This rock approach; for, not ev'n Neptune's aid
    Could from disaster shield thee. With all heed
    While thou to Scylla's rock thy vessel's course
    Art steering, with the swiftest impulse urge
    Thy passage onward: for, 'twere better far
    That six companions' loss thou should'st deplore
    From thy ship's crew, than that the whole be lost!"

    'She ended; and, in answer, thus I spake: –
    "Well! – but, of this, O goddess, make me sure –
70 If, haply, from Charybdis' deadly pow'r
    I should succeed in fleeing, could I then
    My vengeance wreak upon her, and the fate
    Of my lost friends redress?"'   (1865)

CHARLES STUART
CALVERLEY (1831–84)

Wholly representative of the 'Etonian' school of verse-translations by
both masters and pupils from the Victorian to the Georgian period.

Homer's Iliad II [1–47] *The deceiving dream is sent to Agamemnon*

So all else – gods, and charioted chiefs –
Slept the night through. But sweet sleep bound not Zeus;
Pondering what way Achilles to exalt,
And by the Achaian ships make many fall.

This to his soul the fairest counsel seemed;
To send to Atreus' son an evil Dream:
And to the Dream he spake with wingèd words.

'Go, evil Dream, to yon Greek war-ships; seek
The tent of Agamemnon, Atreus' son;
10 And tell him, truly, all I tell to thee.
Say, "Arm right speedily thy unshorn Greeks;
This hour is Ilion and her broad streets thine.
For lo! no longer are the immortals – they
Whose home is heaven – divided. Herè's prayer
Hath bent them all; and woes are nigh to Troy."'

He spake. The Dream, obedient, went his way;
Came swiftly to the war-ships of the Greeks,
And sought out Atreus' son: – (at rest he lay,
Divine sleep floating o'er him, in his tent:) –
20 And stood above his head; in form most like
To Nestor, Neleus' son: of all who sat
In council Agamemnon ranked him first.
In such shape spake to him the heaven-sent Dream.

'Sleep'st thou, O son of Atreus? son of one
At heart a warrior, tamer of the steed?
Not all night long a counsellor should sleep,
A people's guard, whose cares are manifold.
Now hear me. Zeus's messenger am I;
Who, though far off, yet cares, yet grieves for thee.
30 He bids thee arm in haste the unshorn Greeks;
Saying, "Now is Ilion and her broad streets thine.
For lo! no longer are the immortals – they
Whose home is heaven – divided. Herè's prayer
Hath bent them all; and woes are nigh to Troy,"
Woes which Zeus sends. This ponder in thy mind:
Nor be the captive of forgetfulness,
So soon as thou shalt wake from honeyed sleep.'

    He spake: and parting left him there, to muse
In secret on the thing that might not be.
40 For in that day he thought to scale Priam's walls,
And knew not, simple one, the wiles of Zeus;
How he would bring more woes, more groanings yet,
On Trojan and on Greek in hard-fought fields.
He woke: and sate erect – the heavenly voice
Still floating o'er him: donned his tunic soft
And fair and new: flung o'er him his great robe,
Harnessed fair sandals to his shining feet,
And o'er his shoulder swung his silver-studded sword.
And took his fathers' sceptre in his hand,
50 Imperishable aye: and sought therewith
The vessel of the brazen-coated Greeks.   (1866)

JAMES INGLIS COCHRANE

A translator of Goethe, Cochrane responds to Arnold's call for
hexameters. There is in this posthumously and privately printed
version something of the awkward music of Longfellow.

Homer's Iliad XIX.341-74 [364-403] *Achilles readies for combat*

Full in the midst of the host stood godlike Achilles accoutred,
Gnashing his teeth, and his eyes were as fire-balls vividly
    burning.
Wrung his enraged soul anguish terrific, and fury 'gainst
    Troia,
While in the armour Hephaistos with great skill forged he
    begirt him.

Foremost the greaves, well-polish'd and bright, on his thighs
  he adjusted,
Fasten'd with silvery clasps, on his breast thereafter the
  corslet,
Then on his shoulders he slung his immense sword, studded
  with silver.
Lifted the huge shield last, like the moon far shining
  resplendent.
E'en as the blaze of a fire bright-burning for mariner toiling,
10 Kindled on some lone spot, high up on the top of a mountain
(Still from their friends on the deep sea far they are driven
  reluctant):
So from the beautiful, fine-form'd shield of Achilles the lustre
Heavenward shone, as the brass-wrought helmet he placed on
  his temples,
Where with its horse-hair crest like a star it effulgently
  shimmer'd;
While on the cone shook, nodding, the gold tufts wrought
  by Hephaistos.
Girded, he now tried whether the bright arms fitted his
  stature,
Moving his light-form'd limbs to essay if they carried him
  freely:
Wings they to him proved, full scope giving the guide of the
  people.
Then from its rest he uplifted his sires' long-shadowèd war-
  spear,
20 Sturdy and stout, which in sooth no son of Achaia could
  brandish,
Saving Achilles alone, who could hurl it; of Pelion's famous
Ash it was form'd, from the top of the mount, for his father
  by Chiron
Whilom hewn, a destruction to prove long after to heroes.
Alcimos now, and Automedon brave, having harness'd the
  horses,
Yoked, with precision adjusting the beautiful collars: the bridles

Next put into their mouths, and the reins drew back to the
    carriage:
Whereon Automedon, seizing the glittering lash with a firm
    hand,
Into the seat now leapt, and Achilles, accoutred for battle,
Mounted behind, like the orient sun all dazzling in armour;
30   Giving in accents terrific the word to the steeds of his father:
'Xanthos and Balios, both of the far-famed breed of
    Podarges,
See that ye fail not, as whilom, your charioteer to the
    Argives
Safe to restore, when his soul he has satiate fully with battle:
Dead on the field him leave not, as erst my companion
    Patroclus.'

                        (1867)

G. W. EDGINGTON

The Odyssey II.152–83 [146–76] *Halitherses foretells the
doom of the suitors*

    Wide-seeing Jove two eagles then to him
Sent forth to fly from lofty mountain top;
In the winds breezes these flew round some time
With outstretch'd wings, by one anothers side;
But when they o'er that clamorous council came,
They round in circles flapp'd their pow'rful wings;
And look'd on all their heads, presaging death;
With their claws, mangling their own cheeks and necks;
They then flew off both through the house, and town.
10   All wonder'd at the birds, beholding them,
And ponder'd what deeds were to come to pass.
Then aged Halitherses spoke to them;

E'en Mestor's son; for he surpass'd them all
In judging auguries and fate's decrees;
He then with kindly thought thus spoke to them;
    'Hear now my words, ye men of Ithaca,
But to you suitors most of all I speak;
For dangers great hang o'er you: not long now
Ulysses will be absent: but somewhere
20 At hand, devises death to all of you!
And many others too will ills befall,
Of us who dwell in westward Ithaca,
Let us much ponder, how to curb these men,
But, *far best*, let them cease of their own selves:
Not blind, but knowing well, I prophesy,
For I declare that all has been fulfill'd
To him, as I foretold him when the Greeks
Went up to Troy, Ulysses too with them;
I said he having borne much ills, and all
30 His comrades lost, would in the twentieth year
Return home, quite unknown to all his friends,
And now these things have surely come to pass!'   (1869)

W. CULLEN BRYANT (1794–1878)

The first American version in this book. By a Boston brahmin,
poet, scholar and man of letters. This is a thoroughly readable
'Homer'. Quite often, it is more than that.

The Odyssey XI.67–101 [54–80] *Elpenor and Odysseus in
Hades*

'I said these winged words: "How camest thou,
Elpenor, hither into these abodes
Of night and darkness? Thou hast made more speed,

Although on foot, than I in my good ship."
    'I spake; the phantom sobbed and answered me: –
"Son of Laertes, nobly born and wise,
Ulysses! 't was the evil doom decreed
By some divinity, and too much wine,
That wrought my death. I laid myself to sleep

10 In Circè's palace, and, remembering not
The way to the long stairs that led below,
Fell from the roof, and by the fall my neck
Was broken at the spine; my soul went down
To Hades. I conjure thee now, by those
Whom thou hast left behind and far away,
Thy consort and thy father, – him by whom
Thou when a boy wert reared, – and by thy son
Telemachus, who in thy palace-halls
Is left alone, – for well I know that thou,

20 In going hence from Pluto's realm, wilt moor
Thy gallant vessel in the Aeaean isle, –
That there, O king, thou wilt remember me,
And leave me not when thou departest thence
Unwept, unburied, lest I bring on thee
The anger of the gods. But burn me there
With all the armor that I wore, and pile,
Close to the hoary deep, a mound for me, –
A hapless man of whom posterity
Shall hear. Do this for me, and plant upright

30 Upon my tomb the oar with which I rowed,
While yet a living man, among thy friends."
    'He spake and I replied: "Unhappy youth,
All this I duly will perform for thee."'

XX.70–108 *Penelope prays to Diana*

The glorious lady prayed to Dian thus: –
    'Goddess august! Diana, child of Jove!
I would that thou wouldst send into my heart

A shaft to take my life, or that a storm
Would seize and hurl me through the paths of air,
And cast me into ocean's restless streams,
As once a storm, descending, swept away
The daughters born to Pandarus. The gods
Had slain their parents, and they dwelt alone
10   As orphans in their palace, nourished there
By blessed Venus with the curds of milk,
And honey, and sweet wine, while Juno gave
Beauty and wit beyond all womankind,
And chaste Diana dignity of form,
And Pallas every art that graces life.
Then, as the blessed Venus went to ask
For them, of Jove the Thunderer, on the heights
Of his Olympian mount, the crowning gift
Of happy marriage, – for to Jove is known
20   Whatever comes to pass, and what shall be
The fortune, good or ill, of mortal men, –
The Harpies came meantime, bore off the maids,
And gave them to the hateful sisterhood
Of Furies as their servants. So may those
Who dwell upon Olympus make an end
Of me, or fair-haired Dian strike me down,
That, with the image of Ulysses still
Before my mind, I may not seek to please
One of less worth. This evil might be borne
30   By one who weeps all day, and feels at heart
A settled sorrow, yet can sleep at night.
For sleep, when once it weighs the eyelids down,
Makes men unmindful both of good and ill,
And all things else. But me some deity
Visits with fearful dreams. There lay by me,
This very night, one like him, as he was
When with his armed men he sailed for Troy;
And I was glad, for certainly I deemed
It was a real presence, and no dream.'

(1873)

THOMAS A. BUCKLEY (1825–56)

A scholarly translation in prose. Yet the underlying metrical pattern is that of verse. The volume appeared posthumously.

The Odyssey of Homer VI [85–141] *The Phaeacian maidens come down to the strand*

When they had now reached the most beautiful stream of the river, where were continual places for washing, and much beautiful water flowed out, [enough] even to cleanse very filthy things: there they loosed the mules from under the chariot and drove them close to the eddying river, that they might eat the sweet grass; but they took the garments out of the chariot with their hands, and put them into the black water and they trod them in the cisterns, quickly showing rivalry. But when they had washed and cleared all the filth, they spread them in order on the shore of the sea, where the wave most washed the stones to the beach. And having washed and anointed themselves with the smooth oil, they then took their meal near the banks of the river: but they waited for their garments to be dried by the beams of the sun. But when her handmaidens and herself were satiated with food, they played at ball, having thrown off their head-dresses; and white-armed Nausicaa began the song for them. Such as Diana who rejoices in the bow, traverses over the mountain, either lofty Täygetus or Erimanthus, delighting herself with boars and fleet stags, and with her the rural nymphs, daughters of Aegis-bearing Jove, sport; and Latona rejoices in her mind; and she is [eminent] above all by her head and her forehead, for she is easily known, but all of them are fair: so this chaste virgin excelled among her handmaidens. But when they were now about to return home again, having yoked the mules, and folded the beautiful garments, then the blue-eyed goddess Minerva meditated other things, that Ulysses should be roused, and behold the beautiful damsel, who might lead him to the city of the Phaeacians. Then the queen threw the ball to a handmaiden: it missed the handmaiden, and fell into a deep eddy. But they cried out loudly; and divine Ulysses was aroused; and sitting up, he deliberated in his soul and in his mind.

'Woe is me, into the land of what mortals am I now come? Are they violent and wild, and not just? Or are they hospitable, and have they a holy mind? Since a female voice of damsel nymphs, who possess the lofty summits of the mountains, and the fountains of the rivers, and the grassy marshes, has come around me; or am I by chance near men who possess the power of speech? But come, I myself will try, and see.'

Thus having spoken, divine Ulysses went from under the thickets; and with his strong hand he broke a branch of leaves from the thick wood, that he might cover the unseemly parts of a man around his body. And he hastened, like as a lion nourished in the mountains, trusting in his might, that goes rained and blown upon; and his eyes burn; and he comes after oxen, or sheep, or the wild stags; for hunger commands him to enter even a close abode to make an attempt upon the flocks: thus Ulysses, although naked, was about to mingle with the fair-haired damsels; for necessity came upon him. But he appeared dreadful to them, being defiled by the brine; and they fled in terror each in different ways through the projecting shores. But the daughter of Alcinous alone remained; for Minerva put confidence in her mind, and took fear from her limbs; and she stood keeping herself before him.   (1874)

JOHN BENSON ROSE

A translation by 'a public servant of tried values'. Rose seems to have been typical of the 'amateur classics' in the Victorian civil service.

Homer's Iliad I [26–56] *The dismissal and prayer of the seer, Chrysa*

'Away, old man, nor let me find you here
Hanging about our hosts, and hollow barks,
Lest that thy golden sceptre and the wreath,
The emblems of thy god, protect thee not.
Thy daughter is my captive – until she
In Argos shall grow old, my fatherland;
There at the loom, and partner of my bed
To bide whilst me it please. Now, hence, away.'
He spoke, and the old man withdrew in dread
10 And trod the shores of the unquiet sea,
And there the old man loosed his words in prayer
Unto his lord Apollo, son of Leto:
'Lord of the silver bow, whom Chrysa's shores,
And Cilla the divine, and Tenedos,
Own for their god, O Smintheus! if I e'er
Graced with my off'ring thy holy fane
And on thy shrine shed fat of bulls and goats,
Hear now my prayer, and on the Danaan host
Launch forth thy shaft, revengeful of my tears.'
20 He prayed and he was heard. From high Olympus
Phoebus Apollo with resounding bow
And quiver full, descended, in his might
And anger there, rattled the pent-up shafts
As he approached with brow as black as night;
And when he saw the ships he loosed the string
And the dart parted from the silver bow.
He smote the wards and sentries, nor ceased from man
Until the pyres of death blazed far and wide.
Nine days the tempest rained upon the camp,
30 But on the tenth Achilles called the hosts
To meet in council – so the bright-armed Hera
Touched at the sight of dying Danaans
Inspired his soul to do.

(1874)

JEMIMAH MAKEPIECE STURT (1843(?)-81)

This amateurish lyric is to be found in a diary for October 1875. The unpublished document is on deposit at the Municipal Library and Athenaeum in Centersville, Ohio.

Penelope's Musings

I know thee not, yet know thee well,
Thine eyes have seen the deeps of Hell.
Thy limbs have lain in witches' arms,
I know the cunning of thy charms.
Why have you come to claim my heart,
When we so long have dwellt a'part?
When I can hear within your blood
The changing dalliance of the flood?
Stay with me, if you must, a'while,
10   The stars shine cold in your soft smile,
The desert winds sing in your breath,
I know I'll be alone at death.   (1875)

S. H. BUTCHER (1850–1910) and A. LANG (1844–1912)

This prose-translation became one of the most successful and influential of all. It is very much in the spirit of the suggestion made by Arnold in his third lecture: Homer translators should look to the Authorized Version. Butcher and Lang feel that biblical English 'seems as nearly analogous to the Epic Greek, as anything our tongue can offer'. This *Odyssey* is, therefore, a fulfilment of the *Homerus hebraizon* argued for by the Cambridge divine, Zachary Bogan, in 1658, and soon to be 'trumped' by Joyce's Leopold Bloom.

Our selections are followed by two sonnets, one by A. Lang, one by E. Myers, who joined in translating the *Iliad*. They are not 'Keats', but touching none the less.

The Odyssey of Homer XIX [386–490] *The Nurse recognizes Odysseus*

Thereupon the crone took the shining cauldron, which she used for the washing of feet, and poured in much cold water and next mingled therewith the warm. Now Odysseus sat aloof from the hearth, and of a sudden he turned his face to the darkness, for anon he had a misgiving of heart lest when she handled him she might know the scar again, and all should be revealed. Now she drew near her lord to wash him, and straightway she knew the scar of the wound, that the boar had dealt him with his white tusk long ago, when Odysseus went to Parnassus to see Autolycus, and the sons of Autolycus, his mother's noble father, who outdid all men in thievery and skill in swearing. This skill was the gift of the god himself, even Hermes, for that he burned to him the well-pleasing sacrifice of the thighs of lambs and kids; wherefore Hermes abetted him gladly. Now Autolycus once had gone to the rich land of Ithaca, and found his daughter's son a child new-born, and when he was making an end of supper, behold, Eurycleia set the babe on his knees, and spake and hailed him: 'Autolycus find now a name thyself to give thy child's own son; for lo, he is a child of many prayers.'

Then Autolycus made answer and spake: 'My daughter and my daughter's lord, give ye him whatsoever name I tell you. For, behold, I am come hither in great wrath against many a one, both man and woman, over the fruitful earth, wherefore let the child's name be "a man of wrath," Odysseus. But when the child reaches his full growth, and comes to the great house of his mother's kin at Parnassus, whereby are my possessions, I will give him a gift out of these and send him on his way rejoicing.'

Therefore it was that Odysseus went to receive the splendid gifts. And Autolycus and the sons of Autolycus grasped his hands and greeted him with gentle words, and Amphithea, his mother's mother, cast her arms about him and kissed his face and his beautiful eyes. Then Autolycus called to his renowned sons to get ready the meal, and they hearkened to the call. So presently they led in a five-year-old bull, which they flayed and busily prepared, and cut up all the limbs and deftly chopped them small, and pierced them with spits and roasted them cunningly, dividing the messes. So for that livelong day they feasted till the going down of the sun, and their soul lacked not ought of the equal banquet. But when the sun sank and darkness came on, then they laid them to rest and took the boon of sleep.

Now so soon as early Dawn shone forth, the rosy-fingered, they all went forth to the chase, the hounds and the sons of Autolycus, and with them went the goodly Odysseus. So they fared up the steep hill of wood-clad Parnassus, and quickly they came to the windy hollows. Now the sun was but just striking on the fields, and was come forth from the soft flowing stream of deep Oceanus. Then the beaters reached a glade of the woodland, and before them went the hounds tracking a scent, but behind came the sons of Autolycus, and among them goodly Odysseus followed close on the hounds, swaying a long spear. Thereby in a thick lair was a great boar lying, and through the coppice the force of the wet winds blew never, neither did the bright sun light on it with his rays, nor could the rain pierce through, so thick it was, and of fallen leaves there was great plenty therein. Then the noise of the men's feet and the dogs' came upon the boar, as they pressed on in the chase, and forth from his lair he sprang towards them with his back bristled up and fire shining in his eyes, and stood at bay before them all. Then Odysseus was the first to rush in, holding his spear aloft in his strong hand, most keen to smite; but the boar was too quick for him and struck him above the knee, ripping through much flesh with his tusk as he charged sideways, but he reached not to the bone of the man. Then Odysseus aimed well and smote him on his right shoulder, so that the point of the bright spear went clean through, and the boar fell in the dust with a cry, and his life passed from him. Then the dear sons of Autolycus began to busy them with the carcase, and as for the wound of the noble godlike Odysseus, they bound it up skilfully, and stayed the black blood with a song of healing, and straightway returned to the house of their dear father. Then Autolycus and the sons of Autolycus got him well healed of his wound, and gave him splendid gifts, and quickly sent him with all love to Ithaca, gladly speeding a glad guest. There his father and lady mother were glad of his returning, and asked him of all his adventures, and of his wound how he came by it, and duly he told them all, namely, how the boar gashed him with his white tusk in the chase, when he had gone to Parnassus with the sons of Autolycus.

Now the old woman took the scarred limb and passed her hands down it, and knew it by the touch and let the foot drop suddenly, so that the knee fell into the bath, and the brazen vessel rang, being turned over on the other side, and behold, the water was spilled on the ground. Then grief and joy came on her in one moment, and both her eyes filled up with tears, and the voice of her utterance was stayed, and touching the chin of Odysseus she spake to him, saying:

'Yea verily, thou art Odysseus, my dear child, and I knew thee not before, till I had handled all the body of my lord.'

Therewithal she looked towards Penelope, as minded to make a sign that her husband was now home. But Penelope could not meet her eyes nor take note of her, for Athene had bent her thoughts to other things. But Odysseus feeling for the old woman's throat seized it with his right hand and with the other drew her closer to him and spake saying:

'Woman, why wouldest thou indeed destroy me? It was thou that didst nurse me there at thine own breast, and now after travail and much pain I am come in the twentieth year to mine own country. But since thou art ware of me, and the god has put this in thy heart, be silent, lest another learn the matter in the halls. For on this wise I will declare it, and it shall surely be accomplished: – if the gods subdue the lordly wooers unto me, I will not hold my hand from thee, my nurse though thou art, when I slay the other handmaids in my halls.'   (1879)

*

The sacred soil of Ilios is rent
 With shaft and pit; foiled waters wander slow
Through plains where Simois and Scamander went
 To war with gods and heroes long ago.
Not yet to dark Cassandra lying low
 In rich Mycenae do the Fates relent;
The bones of Agamemnon are a show,
 And ruined is his royal monument.
The dust and awful treasures of the dead
10 Hath learning scattered wide: but vainly thee,
Homer, she meteth with her Lesbian lead,
 And strives to rend thy songs, too blind is she
To know the crown on thine immortal head
 Of indivisible supremacy.   A. L. (1879)

*

Athwart the sunrise of our western day
 The form of great Achilles, high and clear,
Stands forth in arms, wielding the Pelian spear.
The sanguine tides of that immortal fray,
Swept on by gods, around him surge and sway,
 Wherethrough the helms of many a warrior peer,
Strong men and swift, their tossing plumes uprear.
But stronger, swifter, goodlier he than they,
More awful, more divine. Yet mark anigh;
10 Some fiery pang hath rent his soul within,
  Some hovering shade his brows encompasseth.
What gifts hath Fate for all his chivalry?
 Even such as hearts heroic oftenest win;
  Honour, a friend, anguish, untimely death.   E. M. (1879)

HENRY DUNBAR (d. 1883)

This work of scholarship is still in use today. To its first edition, Dunbar appended his own attempt at Homeric translation. The curious metre varies between Chapman's fourteener and alexandrines.

The Iliad I.1–65 [1–52] *The start of the epic*

A Few Lines of an Attempt to Translate (as Nearly Literally as Possible) the First Book of the 'Iliad,' in Long Metre

The baneful wrath of Peleus' son, Achilles, goddess sing,
Which numberless distresses upon the Greeks did bring;
And many noble souls to Pluto down did send
Of heroes, and themselves a prey, corporeally consigned
To dogs and birds carnivorous, that range the earth and air,
From that time when, contending first, then disunited were
The king of men Atrides, and Achilles far above
His compeers all, whilst being was, fulfilled the will of Jove.
Which now of the gods, these two engaged, in strife, to war
    between?
10 Apollo, Jove's and Leto's son, for, incensed against the king,
He caused to spread, throughout the camp, a dire and fatal
    pest,
By which the host was perishing, and their warfare set at rest,
Because Atrides, on a priest, indignity had brought,
Chryses by name, for he had come, with earnest purpose
    fraught,
Unto the Greeks' fast sailing ships, his loved and loving
    daughter
To free by ransom, if he might, and bringing 'cross the water

All costly and unstinted gifts, and bearing in his hands,
Entwined upon his golden staff, Apollo's fillet bands;
The whole Greek host, and both the sons, of Atreus, much
    the more
20   The army's marshallers, then did he, most earnestly implore.
'By you, ye sons of Atreus, and ye other Greeks well
    greaved,
May the overthrow of Priam's towers be speedily achieved;
The Olympian dwelling deities now granting ye this boon,
Whereby ye homeward may return, full safely, and full soon.
But, oh to me, deliver up, my daughter well beloved,
Receive these ransoms, and by them, may all your hearts be
    moved,
The while all duly holding, in dread, the son of Jove
Far darter called, oh then, do not, despise a parent's love.'

Then, thereupon, the whole Greek host, respectful assent
    gave,
30   In due regard, to hold the priest, and the splendid gifts
    receive;
But this resolve, Atrides' mind, and temper, sorely tried;
Perversely he dismissed the priest, and harshly thus replied.
'Thee, aged man, let me not find, passing thy time away,
Beside our barks, that hollow are, delaying day by day;
Or, once away, thy mind resolved, a second time, this shore
To visit, on such errand bent, take heed, for never more
Will the sceptre, or the fillet, of the god, thee guard or aid,
No, on her sooner, come old age, ere I release the maid;
Far distant from her native land, at Argos, in my home,
40   My bed she'll make and share with me, and work too at the
    loom.
But, as for thee, depart in peace, no more my temper chafe,
That thy return may speedier be, and for thy sake, more
    safe.'

Thus spoke Atrides, and the priest obeyed the marked
    command;
Impressed with awe, in silence wrapt, he strode along the
    strand
Of ocean much resounding, then apart he took his way,
And to fair Leto's kingly son, the old man much did pray.

'Apollo of the silver bow, oh hear this prayer of mine,
Thou who throwest thy shield o'er Chrysè, and Cilla the
    divine;
O Smintheus, thou who Tenedos, dost rule with might and
    power.
50 If ever I, thy graceful fane, with a roof did'st cover over,
Or if moreo'er, at any time, to thee I've set to burn
Fat thighs of bulls, or those of goats, for me make this return,
Fulfil my earnest wish, I pray, that by thy darts, the Greeks
May make atone, for all the tears, that course now down my
    cheeks.'

Imploringly, thus spake he, and Apollo him did hear,
Enraged at heart, from the Olympian heights, down he
    descended sheer,
With bow and quiver on his back, close covered all around,
And forward as he movèd on, in wrath, a rattling sound
The arrows, on his shoulders, did emit, and like to night,
60 Proceeded forward on his way, Apollo, God of light.
Then from the ships, apart he sat, and an arrow them among
He sent, and from the silver bow, fear-inspiring was the
    clang.
The mules he first attacked, and then, the dogs of nimble
    foot;
Discharging next a pointed shaft, against themselves, he
    smote
The Greeks, and in successive course, thick were the funeral
    pyres
Of men untimely slaughtered, burnt, continually in the
    fires.   (1880)

A. LANG (1844–1912), W. LEAF (1852–1927) and E. MYERS (1844–1921)

For generations of schoolboys, university undergraduates and general readers, 'Lang, Leaf & Myers' became synonymous with 'Homer'. Leaf took on Books I–IX; Lang, X–XVI; Myers, XVII–XXIV. They achieved an astonishing uniformity of style and interpretation. Even today, verse-translations and twentieth-century prose have not altogether superseded this fine battle-horse.

The Iliad of Homer XI [531–96] *Aias [Ajax] in fierce combat*

So spake he, and smote the fair-maned horses with the shrill sounding whip, and they felt the lash, and fleetly bore the swift chariot among the Trojans and Achaians, treading on the dead, and the shields, and with blood was sprinkled all the axle-tree beneath, and the rims round the car with the drops from the hooves of the horses, and with drops from the tires about the wheels. And Hector was eager to enter the press of men, and to leap in and break through, and evil din of battle he brought among the Danaans, and brief space rested he from smiting with the spear. Nay, but he ranged among the ranks of other men, with spear, and sword, and with great stones, but he avoided the battle of Aias son of Telamon, [for Zeus would have been wroth with him, if he fought with a better man than himself].

Now father Zeus, throned in the highest, roused dread in Aias, and he stood in amaze, and cast behind him his sevenfold shield of bull's hide, and gazed round in fear upon the throng, like a wild beast, turning this way and that, and slowly retreating step by step. And as when hounds and country folk drive a tawny lion from the mid-fold of the kine, and suffer him not to carry away the fattest of the herd; all night they watch, and he in great desire for the flesh maketh his onset, but takes nothing thereby, for thick the darts fly from strong hands against him, and the burning brands, and these he dreads for all his fury, and in the dawn he departeth with vexed heart; even so at that time departed Aias, vexed at heart, from among the Trojans, right unwillingly, for he feared sore for the ships of the Achaians. And as when a lazy ass going past a field hath the better of the boys with him, an ass that hath had many a cudgel broken about his sides, and he fareth into the deep crop, and wasteth it, while the boys smite him with cudgels, and feeble is the force of them, but yet with might and main they drive him forth, when he hath had his fill of fodder, even so did the high-hearted Trojans and allies, called from many lands, smite great Aias, son of Telamon, with darts on the centre of his shield, and ever followed after him. And Aias would now be mindful of his impetuous valour, and turn again, and hold at bay the battalions of the horse-taming Trojans, and once more he would turn him again to flee. Yet he hindered them all from making their way to the fleet ships, and himself stood and smote between the Trojans and the Achaians, and the spears from strong hands stuck some of them in his great shield, fain to win further, and many or ever they reached his white body stood fast halfway in the earth, right eager to sate themselves with his flesh.

But when Eurypylos, the glorious son of Euaimon, beheld him oppressed by showers of darts, he went and took his stand by him, and cast with his shining spear, and smote Apisaon, son of Phausios, shepherd of the host, in the liver, below the midriff, and straightway loosened his knees; and Eurypylos sprang on him, and stripped the harness from his shoulders.

But when godlike Alexandros beheld him stripping the harness from Apisaon, straightway he drew his bow against Eurypylos, and smote him with a shaft on the right thigh, and the reed of the shaft brake, and weighed down the thigh. Then Eurypylos withdrew back into the host of his comrades, avoiding fate, and with a piercing voice he shouted to the Danaans: 'O friends, leaders and counsellors of the Argives, turn and stand and ward off the pitiless day from Aias, that is oppressed with darts, nor methinks will he escape out of the evil din of battle. Nay, stand ye the rather at bay round great Aias, son of Telamon.'

So spake Eurypylos being wounded, and they stood close together beside him, sloping the shields on their shoulders, and holding up their spears, and Aias came to meet them, and turned and stood when he reached the host of his comrades.

So they fought like unto burning fire.   (1882)

WILLIAM MORRIS (1834–96)

William Morris had planned a cycle of poems on the fall of Troy. He composed a number of epic poems, treating classical and medieval themes. He translated the *Aeneid* (1876). His *Odyssey* appears in 1887, at the heart of his Ruskinian-socialist period. It is composed in rhyming verse of varying syllabic lengths, and in verse-paragraphs interconnected by varying rhyme-schemes. The Spenserian stanza inhabits, as it were, Morris's technique of narrative rhyme. The idiom is often characteristic of Victorian medievalism. The influence of Tennyson's Arthurian narrative is patent. In this text we learn far more of Morris than we do of Homer.

The Odyssey of Homer I.XII [73–100] *Circe tells Odysseus of the den of Scylla*

'"Now the other way two rocks are: one goeth to the
        heavens wide,
Sharp-peaked, and the dark-blue cloud-rack besets it every
        side,
And neither in the summer, nor on any harvest day,
Its head 'gainst the clear sky showeth, nor draweth the rack
        away;
And no man on earth that dieth may climb it up or down,
Nay, not had he twenty hands or twenty feet of his own.

For smooth is the rock and polished as though by the hands
    of men.
Now there amidst that rockwall is a hollow darkling den,
Turned toward the west and the nightland; and thereby shall
    ye steer
10   Your hollow ship beneath you, O Odysseus lief and dear.
Nor could one from thy ship a-shooting in the prime of the
    life of men
Send an arrow by a bowshot to the inmost of the den.
And therein Scylla dwelleth, and fearfully doth yelp;
And forsooth the voice comes from her as the voice of a
    new-born whelp.
But an ill most monstrous is she, nor fain would any be
As he went his ways to behold her, not e'en if a God were
    he.
Twelve feet there are to her body, misshapen things ill-
    grown,
And six necks exceeding long, and a head on every one,
Most fearful; and within them are threefold rows of teeth
20   Thick-thronging, close together, fulfilled with dusky death.
In the hollow den is she sunken right up to her midmost
    there,
But aloft her heads she holdeth from out of that gulf of fear.
There she fisheth, peering around the rocks in every way
For seadogs or for dolphins, or for whales as a greater prey,
Of the myriads Amphitrite loud-wailing feeds at sea.
Her never yet might shipmen boast them unscathed to flee,
For with each head she snatcheth and beareth off with her
One man of every ship black-bowed that passeth there." '

II.XVII [328-47] *Odysseus enters the Hall*
with Eumaeus

But Telemachus the godlike, the first of all men there,
Saw the swineherd come through the house, and he nodded
    to him straightway,

And called him; who looked around him and took a bench
    that lay
Near-hand, and thereon the carver was wont to sit withal,
Dealing much flesh to the Wooers as they feasted in the hall.
This then to Telemachus' table as now Eumaeus drew,
And thereon sat over against him, and the henchman came
    thereto,
And took and dealt him his share, and bread from the basket
    withal.

But hard on his heels was Odysseus, and he entered his house
    and his hall
10 Most like to a wretched beggar, and a staff-carle bent and
    old,
And woeful was the raiment that his body did enfold.
There he sat on the ashen threshold within the feast-hall's
    door,
Leaned against a cypress pillar, which the wright in days of yore
Had smoothed by dint of cunning and straightened by the line.

Then Telemachus called to Eumaeus, and spake to the herder
    of swine
When a whole loaf he had taken from out the basket fair,
And of the flesh moreover as much as his hands might bear:
'Go take and give to the stranger, and bid him now to wend
From Wooer unto Wooer, and beg from end to end,
20 For nothing good, meseemeth, to a needy man is
    shame.'   (1887)

THOMAS CLARK

Re-edited as recently as 1952, this interlinear belongs to the great
family of cribs, 'trots' and school editions used by generations of
pupils. But also by adults with scant Greek or imperfect memories.

The Hamiltonian system simplifies Homer's syntax. Sydney Smith speaks of the way in which such interlinears replace 'the dull solitude of the dictionary'. Walter Benjamin sees in them the final ideal of *all* translations; for it is between their lines that emerge the lineaments of the lost Adamic tongue which underlies all others.

The Iliad of Homer I [1–5]

Ἄειδε   Θεὰ,   οὐλομένην[(2a. part. m.)]   μῆνιν
Sing, O-||Goddess (*Muse*), (the) ||destroying [pernicious] anger

Ἀχιλῆος   Πηληϊάδεω,   ἣ   ἔθηκε[(1a.)]   μυρία   ἄλγεα
of-Achilles, son-of-Peleus, which ||placed (*caused*) innumerable woes

Ἀχαιοῖς,   δὲ   προΐαψεν[(1a.)] πολλὰς   ἰφθίμους
to (the) 'Achæans, ||but (*and*) prematurely-sent many   brave

ψυχὰς   ἡρώων   Ἄϊδι,   δὲ   τεῦχε[(imp.)] αὐτοὺς   ἑλώρια
souls   of-heroes   to-Orcus,   and   made   them   preys

κύνεσσιν, τε   πᾶσι   οἰωνοῖσί   δὲ   βουλή   Διὸς
to-dogs, and   to-all   birds-of-prey: but   (the)   will   of-Jove

5] ἐτελείετο·[(imp.)]   ἐξ   οὗ   δὴ τὰ πρῶτα
    was-being-fulfilled: ||out-of (*from*)   what (time)   indeed – first

τε   Ἀτρείδης,   ἄναξ ἀνδρῶν, χαί δίος Ἀχιλλεύς
both (the) son-of-Atreus, the king of-men, and divine Achilles

ἐρίσαντε[(1a.part.)]   διαστήτην.[(2 a.)]
having-contended ||stood-apart (*separated*).

V [280–95]

280] Ἦ   ῥα,   καὶ ἀμπεταλὼν   προΐει   δολι-
      He-said indeed, and brandishing (it) he-hurled (his) long

χόσχιον   ἔγχος,   καὶ   βάλε   κατ᾽ ἀσπίδα
shadowing   spear,   and   struck (the) – shield   of   (the)

   Τυδείδαο,   δέ   χαλκείη   αἰχμὴ   πταμένη
[1]son-of-Tydeus, and   (the)   brazen   spear   having-[1]winged

            διαπρὸ   τῆς   πελάσθη   θώρηκι.   Δ᾽
(its) [1]way entirely-through this was-brought-near (the) corselet. And

            ἀγλαὸς   υἱός Λυκάονος   ἄϋσε   μακρὸν ἐπὶ τῷ.
(then· the) illustrious son of-Lycaon shouted loudly over him:

  "Βέβληαι   κενεῶνα   διαμπερὲς,   οὐδε
  "Thou-art-wounded [1]in (the) [1]flank through-and-through, nor

ὀίω   σ᾽ ἀνσχήσεσθαι   ἔτι δηρὸν· δὲ ἐμοὶ
do-I-think (that) you will-endure   (it) now long; but to-me

ἔδωκας   μέγ᾽ εὖχος."
you-have-given great glory."   [285

  Δὲ   τὸν   κρατερὸς Διομήδης οὐ ταρβήσας προσέφη·
  But him (the) powerful Diomede not alarmed   addressed:

""Ἥμβοτες,   οὐδ᾽ ἔτυχες·   ἀτὰρ   γ᾽ ὀίω
"You-have-missed, nor have-you-hit (me); but [1]I at-least [1]think

μὲν   οὐ πρίν γ᾽ ἀποπαύσεσθαι, πρίν   γ᾽ ἢ
indeed (that you) [1]will not before – cease, before – that (the)

ἕτερον   γε   πεσόντα   ἆσαι   αἵματος Ἄρηα,
one-of-you at-least having-fallen will-satiate (with his) blood Mars,

    πολεμιστήν   ταλαύρινον."
(the) warrior   (having the) tough bull's hide-shield."

  Ὥς   φάμενος   προέηχε·   δ᾽   Ἀθήνη
  Thus having-spoken he-hurled (his) lance); and Minerva   [290

ἴθυνεν   βέλος   ῥῖνα παρ᾽   ὀφθαλμόν,   δ᾽
guided (the) missile (to his) nose near (the) eye,   and

ἐπέρησεν   λευκοὺς ὀδόντας·   δὲ   μὲν
it-passed-through (his) white   teeth;   and indeed (the)

ἀτειρὴς   χαλκὸς τάμε   πρυμνὴν   γλῶσσαν
indomitable brass   cut   (the) root (of the) tongue

ἀπὸ τοῦ, δ'   αἰχμὴ ἐξεχύθη   παρὰ νείατον
from him, and (the) point was-driven-forth at (the) bottom

                ἀνθερεῶνα. Δ' ἤριπε ἐξ   ὀχέων,   δὲ
¹of (his) ¹chin. And he-fell from (his) chariot, and (his)

παμφανόωντα,   αἰόλα,   ἐπ' αὐτῷ τεύχε' ἀράβησε·
all-resplendent, easily-wielded, on   him   arms   resounded;

295] δὲ οἱ ὠκύποδες ἵπποι   παρέτρεσσαν·   δ'
      but the swift-footed horses started-aside-from-fear; and

αὖθι ψυχή τοῦ   λύθη   τέ,   τε
there (the) soul of-him was-dissolved indeed, (as) likewise (his)

μένος.
strength.   (1888)

ROBERT BROWNING (1812–89)

In this delightful autobiographical monologue from *Development*,
Browning tells of the 'Homer experience' of his childhood. In this
passage, he takes issue, not altogether seriously, with the inroads
made on any innocent view of the *Iliad* and *Odyssey* by German
'higher textual criticism' (Friedrich August Wolf, Christian Gottlob
Heyne, Philip Karl Buttmann).

Homer

It happened, two or three years afterward,
That – I and playmates playing at Troy's Siege –

My father came upon our make-believe.
'How would you like to read yourself the tale
Properly told, of which I gave you first
Merely such notion as a boy could bear?
Pope, now, would give you the precise account
Of what, some day, by dint of scholarship,
You'll hear – who knows? – from Homer's very mouth.
Learn Greek by all means, read the "Blind Old Man,
Sweetest of Singers" – *tuphlos* which means "blind",
Hedistos which means "sweetest". Time enough!
Try, anyhow, to master him some day;
Until when, take what serves for substitute,
Read Pope, by all means!'
                                    So I ran through Pope.
Enjoyed the tale – what history so true?
Also attacked my Primer, duly drudged,
Grew fitter thus for what was promised next –
The very thing itself, the actual words,
When I could turn – say, Buttmann to account.

Time passed, I ripened somewhat: one fine day,
'Quite ready for the *Iliad*, nothing less?
There's Heine, where the big books block the shelf:
Don't skip a word, thumb well the Lexicon!'

I thumbed well and skipped nowise till I learned
Who was who, what was what, from Homer's tongue,
And there was an end of learning. Had you asked
The all-accomplished scholar, twelve years old,
'Who was it wrote the *Iliad*?' – what a laugh!
'Why, Homer, all the world knows: of his life
Doubtless some facts exist: it's everywhere:
We have not settled, though, his place of birth:
He begged, for certain, and was blind beside:

Seven cities claimed him – Scio, with best right,
Thinks Byron. What he wrote? Those Hymns we have.
Then there's the "Battle of the Frogs and Mice,"
That's all – unless they dig "Margites" up
(I'd like that) nothing more remains to know.'
Thus did youth spend a comfortable time;

40   Until – 'What's this the Germans say is fact
That Wolf found out first? It's unpleasant work
Their chop and change, unsettling one's belief:
All the same, while we live, we learn, that's sure.'
So, I bent brow o'er *Prolegomena*.

And, after Wolf, a dozen of his like
Proved there was never any Troy at all.
Neither Beseigers nor Beseiged, – nay, worse, –
No actual Homer, no authentic text,
No warrant for the fiction I, as fact,

50   Had treasured in my heart and soul so long –
Ay, mark you! and as fact held still, still hold,
Spite of new knowledge, in my heart of hearts
And soul of souls, fact's essence freed and fixed
From accidental fancy's guardian sheath.

Assuredly thenceforward – thank my stars! –
However it got there, deprive who could –
Wring from the shrine my precious tenantry,
Helen, Ulysses, Hector and his Spouse,
Achilles and his Friend? – though Wolf – ah, Wolf!

60   Why must he needs come doubting, spoil a dream?

But then 'No dream's worth waking' – Browning says:
And here's the reason why I tell thus much.
I, now mature man, you anticipate,
May blame my Father justifiably
For letting me dream out my nonage thus,
And only by such slow and sure degrees

Permitting me to sift the grain from the chaff,
Get truth and falsehood known and named as such.
Why did he ever let me dream at all,
70   Nor bid me taste the story in its strength?

Suppose my childhood was scarce qualified
To rightly understand mythology,
Silence at least was in his power to keep:
I might have – somehow – correspondingly –
Well, who knows by what method, gained my gains,
Been taught, by forthrights not meanderings,
My aim should be to loathe, like Peleus' son,
A lie as Hell's Gate, love my wedded wife,
Like Hector, and so on with all the rest.
80   Could I not have excogitated this
Without believing such men really were?   (1888–9)

GEORGE HERBERT PALMER
(1846–1926)

A version which looks to Ossian, Blake and Whitman. Which aims
at a '*tertium quid*' between speech and verse. For its melodic criteria,
Palmer's idiom draws on 'church chant or Wagner's recitative'.
This text proved highly popular and served T. E. Lawrence as his
main crib. The passages chosen here are the same as those from
Lawrence. The comparison is instructive.

The Odyssey V [228–81] *Odysseus builds his raft*

Soon as the early rosy-fingered dawn appeared, quickly Odysseus
dressed in coat and tunic; and the nymph dressed herself in a long
silvery robe, finespun and graceful, she bound a beautiful golden

girdle round her waist, and put a veil upon her head. Then she prepared to send forth brave Odysseus. She gave him a great axe, which fitted well his hands; it was an axe of bronze, sharp on both sides, and had a beautiful olive handle, strongly fastened; she gave him too a polished adze. And now she led the way to the island's farther shore where trees grew tall, alder and poplar and sky-stretching pine, long-seasoned, very dry, that would float lightly. When she had shown him where the trees grew tall, homeward Calypso went, the heavenly goddess, while he began to cut the logs. Quickly the work was done. Twenty in all he felled, and trimmed them with the axe, smoothed them with skill, and leveled them to the line. Meanwhile, Calypso, the heavenly goddess, brought him augers, with which he bored each piece and fitted all, and then with pins and crossbeams fastened the whole together. As when a man skillful in carpentry lays out the deck of a broad freight-ship, of such a size Odysseus built his broad-beamed raft. He raised a bulwark, set with many ribs, and finished with long timbers on the top. He made a mast and sail-yard fitted to it; he made a rudder, too, with which to steer. And then he caulked the raft from end to end with willow withes, to guard against the water, and much material he used. Meanwhile, Calypso, the heavenly goddess, brought him cloth to make a sail, and well did he contrive this too. Braces and halyards and sheet-ropes he set up in her and then with levers heaved her into the sacred sea.

The fourth day came, and he had finished all. So on the fifth divine Calypso sent him from the island, putting upon him fragrant clothes and giving him a bath. A skin the goddess gave him, filled with dark wine, a second large one full of water, and provisions in a sack. She put upon the raft whatever dainties pleased him and sent along his course a fair and gentle breeze. Joyfully to the breeze royal Odysseus spread his sail, and with his rudder skillfully he steered from where he sat. No sleep fell on his eyelids as he gazed upon the Pleiads, on Boötes which sets late, and on the Bear which men call Wagon too, which turns around one spot, watching Orion, and alone does not dip in the Ocean-stream; for Calypso, the heavenly goddess, bade him to cross the sea with the Bear upon his left. So seventeen days he sailed across the sea, on the eighteenth there came in sight the dim heights of Phaeacia, where nearest him it lay. It seemed a shield laid on the misty sea.

XVIII [66–107] *Odysseus vanquishes the boastful Iris*

. . . Meanwhile Odysseus gathered his rags around his waist and showed his thighs, so fair and large, and his broad shoulders came in sight, his breast and sinewy arms. Athene, drawing nigh, filled out the limbs of the shepherd of the people, that all the suitors greatly wondered. And glancing at his neighbor one would say:

'Irus will soon be no more Irus, but catch a plague of his own bringing; so big a thigh the old man shows under his rags.'

So they spoke, and Irus' heart was sorely shaken; nevertheless, the serving-men girt him and led him out, forcing him on in spite of fears. The muscles quivered on his limbs. But Antinoüs rebuked him and spoke to him and said:

'Better you were not living, loud-mouthed bully, and never had been born, if you quake and are so mightily afraid at meeting this old man, one broken by the troubles he has had. Nay, this I tell you and it shall be done: if he shall win and prove the better man, I will toss you into a black ship and send you to the mainland, off to king Echetus, the bane of all mankind; and he will cut your nose and ears off with his ruthless sword, and tearing out your bowels give them raw to dogs to eat.'

So he spoke, and a trembling greater still fell on the limbs of Irus. But into the ring they led him, and both men raised their fists. Then long-tried royal Odysseus doubted whether to strike him so that life might leave him as he fell, or to strike lightly and but stretch him on the ground. Reflecting thus, it seemed the better way lightly to strike, for fear the Achaeans might discover it was he. So when they raised their fists, Irus struck the right shoulder of Odysseus; but he struck Irus on the neck below the ear and crushed the bones within. Forthwith from out his mouth the red blood ran, and down in the dust he fell with a moan, gnashing his teeth and kicking on the ground. The lordly suitors raised their hands and almost died with laughter. But Odysseus caught Irus by the foot and dragged him through the door-way, until he reached the courtyard and the opening of the porch. Against the courtyard wall he set him up aslant, then thrust a staff into his hand, and speaking in winged words he said:

'Sit there awhile, and scare off dogs and swine; and do not try to be the lord of strangers and of beggars, while pitiful yourself, or haply some worse fate may fall upon you.'   (1891)

SAMUEL BUTLER (1835–1902)

A passion for Handel had inspired Butler to compose an oratorio-text on the *Odyssey*. A visit to Asia Minor persuaded Butler that a Greek from the Troad, secretly in favour of the Trojans, had written the *Iliad*. The *Odyssey*, on the other hand, had been composed by a woman (Nausicaa?) at Trapani in Sicily (cf. Butler's *The Authoress of the Odyssey*, published in 1897). A 'Tottenham Court Rd. English' version of the *Iliad* appeared in 1898. Lang, Leaf and Myers are drawn upon throughout. Butler deems the 'sanguinary parts' of the epic to be ill-suited to an English public. But like Bérard, Joyce's source, Butler is among the first to try to situate the Homeric epics in their Mediterranean locale. There are, moreover, episodes in which we recognize the author of an 1892 lecture on 'The Humour of Homer'.

The Iliad of Homer XI [472–514] *Ajax rescues Ulysses*

He led the way and mighty Ajax went with him. The Trojans had gathered round Ulysses like ravenous mountain jackals round the carcase of some horned stag that has been hit with an arrow – the stag has fled at full speed so long as his blood was warm and his strength has lasted, but when the arrow has overcome him, the savage jackals devour him in the shady glades of the forest. Then heaven sends a fierce lion thither, whereon the jackals fly in terror and the lion robs them of their prey – even so did Trojans many and brave gather round crafty Ulysses, but the hero stood at bay and kept them off with his spear. Ajax then came up with his shield before him like a wall, and stood hard by, whereon the Trojans fled in all directions. Menelaus took Ulysses by the hand, and led him out of the press while his squire brought up his chariot, but Ajax rushed furiously on the Trojans and killed Doryclus, a bastard son of Priam; then he wounded Pandocus, Lysandrus, Pyrasus, and Pylartes; as some swollen torrent comes rushing in full flood from the mountains on to the plain, big with the rain of heaven – many a dry oak and many a pine does it engulf, and much mud does it bring down and cast into the sea – even so did brave Ajax chase the foe furiously over the plain, slaying both men and horses.

Hector did not yet know what Ajax was doing, for he was fighting on the extreme left of the battle by the banks of the river Scamander, where the carnage was thickest and the war-cry loudest round Nestor and brave Idomeneus. Among these Hector was making great slaughter with his spear and furious driving, and was destroying the ranks that were opposed to him; still the Achaeans would have given no ground, had not Alexandrus husband of lovely Helen stayed the prowess of Machaon shepherd of his people, by wounding him in the right shoulder with a triple-barbed arrow. The Achaeans were in great fear that as the fight had turned against them the Trojans might take him prisoner, and Idomeneus said to Nestor, 'Nestor son of Neleus, honour to the Achaean name, mount your chariot at once; take Machaon with you and drive your horses to the ships as fast as you can. A physician is worth more than several other men put together, for he can cut out arrows and spread healing herbs.'   (1898)

This 'poem was written entirely by a very young woman' (Goethe had toyed with this notion) 'who lived at the place now called Trapani, and introduced herself into her work under the name of Nausicaa'. Her text is, naturally enough, 'over-saturated' with borrowings from the *Iliad*.

The Odyssey of Homer VI [149–210] *Ulysses and Nausicaa on the shore*

'Oh queen,' he said, 'I implore your aid – but tell me, are you a goddess or are you a mortal woman? If you are a goddess and dwell in heaven, I can only conjecture that you are Jove's daughter Diana, for your face and figure resemble none but hers; if on the other hand you are a mortal and live on earth, thrice happy are your father and mother – thrice happy, too, are your brothers and sisters; how proud and delighted they must feel when they see so fair a scion as yourself going out to a dance; most happy, however, of all will he be whose wedding gifts have been the richest, and who takes you to his own home. I never yet saw any one so beautiful, neither man nor woman, and am lost in admiration as I behold you. I can only compare you to a young palm tree which I saw when I was at Delos growing near the altar of Apollo – for I was there, too, with much people after me, when I was on that journey which has been the source of all my troubles. Never yet did such a young plant shoot out of the ground as that was, and I admired and wondered at it exactly as I now admire and wonder at yourself. I dare not clasp your knees, but I am in great distress; yesterday made the twentieth day that I have been tossing about upon the sea. The winds and waves have taken me all the way from the Ogygian island, and now fate has flung me upon this coast that I may endure still further suffering; for I do not think that I have yet come to the end of it, but rather that, heaven has still much evil in store for me.

'And now, oh queen, have pity upon me, for you are the first person I have met, and I know no one else in this country. Show me the way to your town, and let me have anything that you may have brought hither to wrap your clothes in. May heaven grant you in all things your heart's desire – husband, house, and a happy, peaceful home; for there is nothing better in this world than that man and wife should be of one mind in a house. It discomfits their enemies, makes the hearts of their friends glad, and they themselves know more about it than any one.'

To this Nausicaa answered, 'Stranger, you appear to be a sensible well-disposed person. There is no accounting for luck; Jove gives prosperity to rich and poor just as he chooses, so you must take what he has seen fit to send you, and make the best of it. Now, however, that you have come to this our country, you shall not want for clothes nor for anything else that a foreigner in distress may reasonably look for. I will show you the way to the town, and will tell you the name of our people; we are called Phaeacians, and I am daughter to Alcinous, in whom the whole power of the state is vested.'

Then she called her maids and said, 'Stay where you are, you girls. Can you not see a man without running away from him? Do you take him for a robber or a murderer? Neither he nor any one else can come here to do us Phaeacians any harm, for we are dear to the gods, and live apart on a land's end that juts into the sounding sea, and have nothing to do with any other people. This is only some poor man who has lost his way, and we must be kind to him, for strangers and foreigners in distress are under Jove's protection, and will take what they can get and be thankful; so, girls, give the poor fellow something to eat and drink, and wash him in the stream at some place that is sheltered from the wind.'   (1900)

J. W. MacKAIL (1859–1945)

Greatly admired at the time, this version in quatrains remains an oddity.

The Odyssey XI [51–80] *Elpenor to Odysseus in Hades*

'Then came Elpenor's ghost the first of all,
Our comrade, who not yet had burial
Under the wide-wayed earth: for we had left
Unburied and unwept in Circe's hall

'His body, since another labour pressed:
And him I wept to see, and thus addressed,
And spake to him in winged words of ruth:
Elpenor, how beneath the misty West

'Came you to this dark land across the sea?
For quicker you have come afoot than we
With our black ship might compass. Thus I said:
And he replied and sighing spake to me:

'High-born Odysseus of the subtle soul,
Son of Laertes, this thing wrought my dole,
Ill fate heaven-destined and excess of wine:
In Circe's house I lay in sleep's control,

'And waking, quite forgot aback to go
By the long ladder to the ground, and so
Fell headlong from the roof and brake my neck,
And my soul fled to the Dark House below.

'I pray you now by those whom you desire
In absence, by your wife and by the sire
That reared your childhood, and Telemachus,
The only child you left beside your fire:

'For passing hence from the Dark House I know
Back to the isle Aeaean you shall go
On your well-fashioned ship: remember me,
Prince, I beseech you, there, nor leave me so,

'Unwept, unburied, when your way you take,
Lest the Gods hold you guilty for my sake:
But burn me with the armour that I wore,
And heap my grave-mound where the grey waves break;

'A sign for generations yet to be
Of my unhappy fate: do this for me,
And plant on it the oar I rowed with once,
While yet I lived, among your company.

'So said he: and I made reply thereto:
This, O ill-starred, will I perform and do.'   (1903–10)

H. B. COTTERILL

A sustained argument for the use of hexameters. Cotterill appeals to examples of this metre in Tennyson and to Lockhart's hexameter-version of the *Iliad*, Book XXIV, in *Blackwood's Magazine* for 1846.

Homer's Odyssey III [103–47] *Nestor's narration to Telemachus of the tragic aftermath to the fall of Troy*

'Ah, dear friend, thou recallest the sorrows that once in the
          distant
Trojan land we endured, the invincible sons of Achaea –
All those toils that we suffered in ships on the mist-bound
          ocean,
Seeking for spoil wherever Achilles was wishful to lead us.
How too fighting in front of the strong-built city of Priam
Battle we waged. Here fell of Achaeans the best and the
          bravest;
Here lies Ajax, the equal of Ares; here is Achilles,
Here Patroclus, in counsel a peer of the gods everlasting;
Here too lieth my son, my belovéd, the strong and the noble
10   Antilochus, who with fleetness excelled in the race and the
          battle:
Ay and besides all this, what travail unending we suffered –

Where is the mortal on earth to be found that can fully relate
    it?
Even for five whole years, or for six, 'twere vain to abide
    here
Asking to hear of the woes once borne by the noble
    Achaeans;
Ere it was told, outwearied, I ween, thou'dst sail for thy
    homeland.
Nine years warring at Troy did we busily scheme for its
    downfall,
Weaving a tissue of wiles, which Zeus scarce granted
    fulfilment.
There might never another with him in devices of wisdom
Dare to compete, since far he surpassed all others in cunning,
20   Godlike Odysseus I mean, ay even thy father – if truly
He was thy sire; and amazement possesseth me while I behold
    thee,
Seeing that verily even in speech thou art like him, nor
    would one
Say that a man so young could speak so like to an elder.
All these years have never myself and the godlike Odysseus
Spoken diversely at meetings of men or the councils of
    chieftains;
Ever we held one mind, and with counsels of prudence and
    wisdom
Planned for the Greeks that it all might turn to the highest
    advantage.
Yet, when at last we had wasted the high-built city of Priam,
After from thence we had sailed and a god had dispersed the
    Achaeans,
30   Then in his heart did the Father a terrible homeward
    returning
Plot for them, seeing that neither with wisdom at all nor
    with justice
Most of them acted; and many encountered a doom right
    doleful,

Whelmed by the wrath of the grey-eyed daughter of Zeus
    the Almighty;
Yea, it was she that the quarrel excited between the Atridae;
These then called to the place of assembly the host of
    Achaeans
Hurriedly, all in disorderly haste, when the sun was a-
    sinking.
Heavy with wine they collected together, the sons of Achaea.
Both then spake of the reason for which they had summoned
    the people;
First Menelaus addressed him to all the Achaeans and bade
    them
40 Think of the homeward return o'er broad expanses of ocean;
Nor pleased this Agamemnon at all, for he ordered the
    people
Still to remain and sacred oblations of cattle to offer,
Thus to appease by atonement the terrible wrath of Athene,
Fool that he was, not knowing she ne'er would list to
    persuasion,
Seeing that lightly is turned not the mind of the gods
    everlasting.

XXII [391–418] *Odysseus' rebuke to Eurycleia after the slaughter of the suitors*

'Telemachus, go call me the old nurse Eurycleia,
So that I tell her a thing that is stirring my spirit within me.'
Thus did he speak, and the youth, as his well-loved father
    commanded,
Rattled the door of the chamber and called nurse Eurycleia:
'Hither in haste, old dame, who over the women attendants
Keepest an eye and hast charge of them all in the palace as
    matron.
Haste! for my father is bidding thee come. He has something
    to tell thee.'

Thus did he speak, and the word that he uttered abode with
    her wingless.
Opening quickly the door of the fair-built women's
    apartment,
10 Over the threshold she stept; and the youth went onward
    before her,
Till to Odysseus she came. In the midst of the dead he was
    standing,
Smeared all over with blood and filthy with gore. As a lion,
Leaving the place in the which he has eaten an ox of the
    farmstead,
Goes on his way, and the whole of the chest and the cheeks
    of the monster
Drip with the gore – and a terror befalleth the man who
    beholds him –
So all smeared with the blood on his hands and his feet was
    Odysseus.

Now when the slain she beheld and the terrible blood, and in
    triumph
Fain had exulted aloud (for she saw that the deed was
    accomplished),
Then did Odysseus, perceiving her longing, restrain and
    rebuke her,
20 While upraising his voice these swift-winged words he
    addressed her:
'Woman, exult in thy heart, but in silence, subduing thy
    triumph.
Triumphing over the slain is a deed unseemly, unholy.
These hath the doom of the gods in the midst of their
    wickedness smitten,
Seeing they treated alike all earth-born men with dishonour,
Good no less than the bad – yea every one that approached
    them.
So hath a terrible doom o'erwhelmed them because of their
    madness.

> Come now, tell me of all concerning the maids in the palace,
> Which of them honour me not and which are guiltless
>   among them.'   (1911)

A. T. MURRAY (1866–1940)

This is the famous Loeb Classical Library Homer, still in use. Aimed at a wide audience with little or no Greek, Murray's style is mildly archaic and seeks to preserve the 'recurrent lines and phrases' in the original.

The Odyssey III [253–312] *Nestor tells of dread homecomings*

Then the horseman, Nestor of Gerenia, answered him: 'Then verily, my child, will I tell thee all the truth. Lo, of thine own self thou dost guess how this matter would have fallen out, if the son of Atreus, fair-haired Menelaus, on his return from Troy had found Aegisthus in his halls alive. Then for him not even in death would they have piled the up-piled earth, but the dogs and birds would have torn him as he lay on the plain far from the city, nor would any of the Achaean women have bewailed him; for monstrous was the deed he devised. We on our part abode there in Troy fulfilling our many toils; but he, at ease in a nook of horse-pasturing Argos, ever sought to beguile with words the wife of Agamemnon. Now at the first she put from her the unseemly deed, the beautiful Clytemnestra, for she had an understanding heart; and with her was furthermore a minstrel whom the son of Atreus straitly charged, when he set forth for the land of Troy, to guard his wife. But when at length the doom of the gods bound her that she should be overcome, then verily Aegisthus took the minstrel to a desert isle and left him to be the prey and spoil of birds; and her, willing as he was willing, he led to his own house. And many thigh-pieces he burned upon the holy altars of the gods, and many offerings he hung up, woven stuffs and gold, since he had accomplished a mighty deed beyond all his heart had hoped.

'Now we were sailing together on our way from Troy, the son of Atreus and I, in all friendship; but when we came to holy Sunium, the cape of Athens, there Phoebus Apollo assailed with his gentle shafts and slew the helmsman of Menelaus, as he held in his hands the steering-oar of the speeding ship, even Phrontis, son of Onetor, who excelled the tribes of men in piloting a ship when the storm winds blow strong. So Menelaus tarried there, though eager for his journey, that he might bury his comrade and over him pay funeral rites. But when he in his turn, as he passed over the wine-dark sea in the hollow ships, reached in swift course the steep height of Malea, then verily Zeus, whose voice is borne afar, planned for him a hateful path and poured upon him the blasts of shrill winds, and the waves were swollen to huge size, like unto mountains. Then, parting his ships in twain, he brought some to Crete, where the Cydonians dwelt about the streams of Iardanus. Now there is a smooth cliff, sheer towards the sea, on the border of Gortyn in the misty deep, where the South-west Wind drives the great wave against the head-land on the left toward Phaestus, and a little rock holds back a great wave. Thither came some of his ships, and the men with much ado escaped destruction, howbeit the ships the waves dashed to pieces against the reef. But the five other dark-prowed ships the wind, as it bore them, and the wave brought to Egypt. So he was wandering there with his ships among men of strange speech, gathering much livelihood and gold; but meanwhile Aegisthus devised this woeful work at home. Seven years he reigned over Mycenae, rich in gold, after slaying the son of Atreus, and the people were subdued under him; but in the eighth came as his bane the goodly Orestes back from Athens, and slew his father's murderer, the guileful Aegisthus, for that he had slain his glorious father. Now when he had slain him, he made a funeral feast for the Argives over his hateful mother and the craven Aegisthus; and on the self-same day there came to him Menelaus, good at the war-cry, bringing much treasure, even all the burden that his ships could bear.'   (1919)

GEORGE ERNLE

The sumptuously printed extracts from the *Iliad* that appeared in Ernle's *Wrath of Achilles* (1922) carry to near-absurdity the project of a translation in quantitative hexameters. They were published in the same year as Joyce's *Ulysses*.

> *The Wrath of Achilles* I.378–96 [318–44] *The heralds come to take Briseis from Achilles*

While Achileus sat amongst the vessels, Agamemnon
    Atrides
Held the threat in memory which he erst had spoken against
    him,
And summoning the heralds, that were his trusted attendants,
Eurybates and Talthybios, thus gave them his orders.
'Go to the Myrmidones' encampment. Enter Achilleus'
Tent there. Seize fair-cheeked Briseis. Bring me the maiden.
Say, if he will not let you, that I with an army behind me
Shall come apace and take her, – a way less likely to please
    him.'
   So he address'd the heralds and laid stern order upon them;
10   And the men, unwilling as they were, went over the shingle
Unto the Myrmidones, to the ships and tents of Achilleus.
There the son of Peleus was seated, close to his own ship,
And when he saw the heralds was nowise greatly delighted.
Trembling in reverence and fear of royal Achilleus
They stood afar and did not accost him, neither approach
    him.
He, guessing at the errand they came on, gave them a
    greeting.
  'Hail, reverend and holy heralds! I pray you approach me
Nearer. It is nowise your fault, your master Atrides
Sends you to take the woman Briseis wrongfully from me.

20   Come, bring her out, I pray you, Patroclos. Render the
        maiden
     Up to the King's Summoners. Ye twain, bear witness against
        him
     Truly before perishing mankind and blissful Immortals
     And this accursed Ruler, if e'er hereafter Atrides
     Comes to require Achileus to avert some deadly disaster
     From the Achaean people! He now raves, wild as a madman,
     And as a fool looks neither before him, neither behind him,
     Reckless of imperilling both ships and people of
        Argos.'   (1922)

JAMES JOYCE (1882–1941)

In one sense, Homer is everywhere present in Joyce's *Ulysses*. His
'actual' appearances are, however, rare. The most poignant occurs at
the close of the episode of the 'Sirens', as Bloom hears the tap, tap
of the cane of the blind beggar (Homer). Note Joyce's choice of a
young Homer.

Ulysses, 1223–94

Tap. Tap. Tap. Tap. Tap. Tap. Tap. Tap.
    Bloom went by Barry's. Wish I could. Wait. That wonderworker
if I had. Twentyfour solicitors in that one house. Counted them.
Litigation. Love one another. Piles of parchment. Messrs Pick and
Pocket have power of attorney. Goulding, Collis, Ward.
    But for example the chap that wallops the big drum. His vocation:
Mickey Rooney's band. Wonder how it first struck him. Sitting at
home after pig's cheek and cabbage nursing it in the armchair.
Rehearsing his band part. Pom. Pompedy. Jolly for the wife. Asses'
skins. Welt them through life, then wallop after death. Pom.
Wallop. Seems to be what you call yashmak or I mean kismet. Fate.

Tap. Tap. A stripling, blind, with a tapping cane came taptaptap-ping by Daly's window where a mermaid hair all streaming (but he couldn't see) blew whiffs of a mermaid (blind couldn't), mermaid, coolest whiff of all.

Instruments. A blade of grass, shell of her hands, then blow. Even comb and tissuepaper you can knock a tune out of. Molly in her shift in Lombard street west, hair down. I suppose each kind of trade made its own, don't you see? Hunter with a horn. Haw. Have you the? *Cloche. Sonnez la.* Shepherd his pipe. Pwee little wee. Policeman a whistle. Locks and keys! Sweep! Four o'clock's all's well! Sleep! All is lost now. Drum? Pompedy. Wait. I know. Towncrier, bumbailiff. Long John. Waken the dead. Pom. Dignam. Poor little *nominedomine.* Pom. It is music. I mean of course it's all pom pom pom very much what they call *da capo.* Still you can hear. As we march, we march along, march along. Pom.

I must really. Fff. Now if I did that at a banquet. Just a question of custom shah of Persia. Breathe a prayer, drop a tear. All the same he must have been a bit of a natural not to see it was a yeoman cap. Muffled up. Wonder who was that chap at the grave in the brown macin. O, the whore of the lane!

A frowsy whore with black straw sailor hat askew came glazily in the day along the quay towards Mr Bloom. When first he saw that form endearing? Yes, it is. I feel so lonely. Wet night in the lane. Horn. Who had the? Heehaw shesaw. Off her beat here. What is she? Hope she. Psst! Any chance of your wash. Knew Molly. Had me decked. Stout lady does be with you in the brown costume. Put you off your stroke, that. Appointment we made knowing we'd never, well hardly ever. Too dear too near to home sweet home. Sees me, does she? Looks a fright in the day. Face like dip. Damn her. O, well, she has to live like the rest. Look in here.

In Lionel Marks's antique saleshop window haughty Henry Lionel Leopold dear Henry Flower earnestly Mr Leopold Bloom envisaged battered candlesticks melodeon oozing maggoty blowbags. Bargain: six bob. Might learn to play. Cheap. Let her pass. Course everything is dear if you don't want it. That's what good salesman is. Make you buy what he wants to sell. Chap sold me the Swedish razor he shaved me with. Wanted to charge me for the edge he gave it. She's passing now. Six bob.

Must be the cider or perhaps the burgund.

Near bronze from anear near gold from afar they chinked their clinking glasses all, brighteyed and gallant, before bronze Lydia's tempting last rose of summer, rose of Castile. First Lid, De, Cow, Ker, Doll, a fifth: Lidwell, Si Dedalus, Bob Cowley, Kernan and big Ben Dollard.

Tap. A youth entered a lonely Ormond hall.

Bloom viewed a gallant pictured hero in Lionel Marks's window. Robert Emmet's last words. Seven last words. Of Meyerbeer that is.

– True men like you men.

– Ay, ay, Ben.

– Will lift your glass with us.

They lifted.

Tschink. Tschunk.

Tip. An unseeing stripling stood in the door. He saw not bronze. He saw not gold. Nor Ben nor Bob nor Tom nor Si nor George nor tanks nor Richie nor Pat. Hee hee hee hee. He did not see.

Seabloom, greaseabloom viewed last words. Softly. *When my country takes her place among.*

Prrprr.

Must be the bur.

Fff! Oo. Rrpr.

Nations of the earth. No-one behind. She's passed. *Then and not till then.* Tram kran kran kran. Good oppor. Coming. Krandlkrankran. I'm sure it's the burgund. Yes. One, two. *Let my epitaph be.* Kraaaaaa. *Written. I have.*

Pprrpffrrppffff.

Done.   (1922)

FRANCIS CAULFIELD (b. 1907)

Translated for the Bohn Library, this version is cast 'in the original metre'. Though aimed at a general reader, it exhibits considerable learning and reflection on Homer.

The Odyssey IV [235–89] *Helen and Meneläus tell of Odysseus' cunning and self-control at the fall of Troy*

'O Meneläus Atreides, Zeus-nurtured, and all our friends
    here,
Sons of gallant men: God gives, to one and another,
Evil and good as He wills: for He has power o'er all things.
Sit now and feast in our hall, and hear what tales I can tell
    you,
For I will speak of things that will pleasantly suit the occasion.
Though, by no means, am I able to tell or even to mention
All of the gallant deeds of the much-enduring Odysseus,
Yet I will tell what was done and dared by that valiant hero
Right in the heart of Troy to succour the hard-pressed
    Achæans
10 Bruising himself with degrading blows, and over his
    shoulders
Throwing unseemly rags like some poor drudge of the
    household
Into the fine broad streets of the foemen's city he entered,
In his disguise appearing a different man, a beggar,
He who was far from such when commanding the ships of
    Achæans.
So did he enter the city: and, who he was, no one suspected:
But I could see at a glance that the man was no commonplace
    beggar,
And I put questions to him, which he by his cunning evaded.
But, when I washed him, and then, with oil of olive
    anointed,

Clothed him in seemly garments, and swore with great
    imprecations
20 Not to betray him or let the Trojans know of his presence
Till he had safely reached the tents and the line of the galleys
Then did he tell me at length the whole design of the
    Grecians.
And, after men not a few before his long weapon had fallen,
Safe he arrived at his camp and brought back much
    information.
Then did the rest of the women begin to wail: but my own
    heart
Bounded with joy, for already, with longing and hope it was
    turning
Back to my home: and I mourned for the wrong which fair
    Aphrodité
Wrought when she lured me to Troy, so far from the land of
    my fathers,
Leaving in folly my daughter, my bed and my own dear
    husband,
30 Who, in his mind and appearance, is just what a husband
    should be.'
    And, unto her in reply, thus spoke fair-haired Meneläus:
'Yes, my wife, you have told these things most wisely and
    truly:
For I have learnt, ere now, how great was many a hero
Both to perceive and to plan, and much have I seen in my
    travels:
But, never yet, have I seen any man to compare with
    Odysseus,
Steadfast heart, who did and dared what now I will tell you
Where, in the polished horse, we chosen chiefs of the Argives
Then were sitting concealed, to bring slaughter and death to
    the Trojans.
You, at that time, came there, urged on no doubt by the
    Power
40 Always at hand to confer success on the Trojans: and with you

Followed Deïphobus, godlike to see: and thrice did you walk
    round
Feeling the den where we lurked, and calling by name on the
    chieftains
Of the Achæans, and feigning the sound of their dear wives'
    voices.
But Diomedés and I and godlike Odysseus were seated
Crammed in the midst of the others, and heard you when
    you were calling.
We two wanted at once to jump from our seats and to rush
    out
Or to reply from within: but the wise Odysseus restrained us.
Then all the other Achæans were silent: while Anticlus only
Wanted to shout a reply: but Odysseus pressed his hands
    firmly
50 Over his mouth, and held it, and thus saved all the Achæans:
Nor did he loose his hold till Athené from thence had
    withdrawn you.'   (1923)

A. T. MURRAY

The second instalment of the Loeb Homer.

The Iliad II [441–83] *Agamemnon leads his host*

So spake he, and the king of men, Agamemnon, failed not to
hearken. Straightway he bade the clear-voiced heralds summon to
battle the long-haired Achaeans. And they made summons, and the
host gathered full quickly. The kings, nurtured of Zeus, that were
about Atreus' son, sped swiftly, marshalling the host, and in their
midst was the flashing-eyed Athene, bearing the priceless aegis, that
knoweth neither age nor death, wherefrom are hung an hundred
tassels all of gold, all of them cunningly woven, and each one of the

worth of an hundred oxen. Therewith she sped dazzling throughout the host of the Achaeans, urging them to go forth; and in the heart of each man she roused strength to war and to battle without ceasing. And to them forthwith war became sweeter than to return in their hollow ships to their dear native land.

Even as a consuming fire maketh a boundless forest to blaze on the peaks of a mountain, and from afar is the glare thereof to be seen, even so from their innumerable bronze, as they marched forth, went the dazzling gleam up through the sky unto the heavens.

And as the many tribes of winged fowl, wild geese or cranes or long-necked swans on the Asian mead by the streams of Caÿstrius, fly this way and that, glorying in their strength of wing, and with loud cries settle ever onwards, and the mead resoundeth; even so their many tribes poured forth from ships and huts into the plain of Scamander, and the earth echoed wondrously beneath the tread of men and horses. So they took their stand in the flowery mead of Scamander, numberless, as are the leaves and the flowers in their season.

Even as the many tribes of swarming flies that buzz to and fro throughout the herdsman's farmstead in the season of spring, when the milk drenches the pails, even in such numbers stood the long-haired Achaeans upon the plain in the face of the men of Troy, eager to rend them asunder.

And even as goatherds separate easily the wide-scattered flocks of goats, when they mingle in the pasture, so did their leaders marshal them on this side and on that to enter into the battle, and among them lord Agamemnon, his eyes and head like unto Zeus that hurleth the thunderbolt, his waist like unto Ares, and his breast unto Poseidon. Even as a bull among the herd stands forth far the chiefest over all, for that he is pre-eminent among the gathering kine, even such did Zeus make Agamemnon on that day, pre-eminent among many, and chiefest amid warriors.

XX [41–75] *The gods join the fray*

Now as long as the gods were afar from the mortal men, even for so long triumphed the Achaeans mightily, seeing Achilles was come forth, albeit he had long kept him aloof from grievous battle; but upon the Trojans came dread trembling on the limbs of every man in their terror, when they beheld the swift-footed son of Peleus, flaming in his harness, the peer of Ares, the bane of men. But when the Olympians were come into the midst of the throng of men, then up leapt mighty Strife, the rouser of hosts, and Athene cried aloud, – now would she stand beside the digged trench without the wall, and now upon the loud-sounding shores would she utter her loud cry. And over against her shouted Ares, dread as a dark whirlwind, calling with shrill tones to the Trojans from the topmost citadel, and now again as he sped by the shore of Simoïs over Callicolone.

Thus did the blessed gods urge on the two hosts to clash in battle, and amid them made grievous strife to burst forth. Then terribly thundered the father of gods and men from on high; and from beneath did Poseidon cause the vast earth to quake, and the steep crests of the mountains. All the roots of many-fountained Ida were shaken, and all her peaks, and the city of the Trojans, and the ships of the Achaeans. And seized with fear in the world below was Aïdoneus, lord of the shades, and in fear leapt he from his throne and cried aloud, lest above him the earth be cloven by Poseidon, the Shaker of Earth, and his abode be made plain to view for mortals and immortals – the dread and dank abode, wherefor the very gods have loathing: so great was the din that arose when the gods clashed in strife. For against king Poseidon stood Phoebus Apollo with his winged arrows, and against Enyalius the goddess, flashing-eyed Athene; against Hera stood forth the huntress of the golden arrows, and the echoing chase, even the archer Artemis, sister of the god that smiteth afar; against Leto stood forth the strong helper, Hermes, and against Hephaestus the great, deep-eddying river, that gods call Xanthus, and men Scamander.

Thus gods went forth to meet with gods.   (1924-5)

ANNETTE MEAKIN (d. 1959)

World-traveller and journalist, Meakin aptly chose Book VI of the *Odyssey* for translation into hexameters, in *Nausikaa* (1926). Her text builds a bridge, as it were, between Samuel Butler's thesis on the authorship of the epic and future women-translators.

The *Odyssey* VI [224–331] *Odysseus and Nausikaa on the strand*

Meanwhile the hero, Odysseus, was washing himself in the river.
Washing away the brine and mire from his back and broad shoulders,
Freeing his head from the muddy foam which the waves had collected.
When he had bathed himself, and his limbs with oil had anointed,
He put on the clothes, which Nausikaa had provided,
And as he did so, Athene, daughter of Zeus, the all-powerful,
Filled out his form and made him look taller, and far more handsome,
Gave him a head of curly hair, like the hyacinth flower; –
Just as a goldsmith spreadeth the liquid gold around silver,
10   Taught by Hephaistos himself; and, trained by Pallas Athene
In the secrets of art, he fashioneth exquisite objects. –
Thus poured Athene grace round the hero's head and his shoulders.
Walking along by the water, he seated himself on the sea shore,
Beaming with beauty and grace. Nausikaa saw him and marvelled.
And to her curly-tressed maids she spoke in the following manner:

'Hearken, my white-armed maidens, to what I am going
   to tell ye!
Not in defiance of all the gods who dwell in Olympus,
Came this man to the land of the godlike Phaakan people.
When I beheld him first, he appeared so needy and wretched!
20   Now he is like the gods, who have in the heavens their
      dwelling!
Ah! should it fall to my lot – if for me such a husband were
   chosen
From our country's best – and if it should please him to stay
   here!
But food and drink, my maidens, I pray ye give to the
   stranger.'
   Such were her words; and the maidens readily heard and
      obeyed her,
Placing food and drink in front of the hero, Odysseus.
Heartily ate and drank the sore-tried and famished Odysseus,
For it was many a day since a good meal had been set before
   him.
   Meanwhile Nausikaa, the white-armed, remembered her
      errand.
Now she folded the garments, and placed them all in the
   wagon;
30   Harnessed the strong-hoofed mules, took her seat: and then
      to Odysseus –
   'Stranger,' she cried, 'bestir thyself! Thou must walk to the
      city.
Follow me to the halls of the king, my valiant father.
There thou wilt meet the bravest and best of the Phaakan nobles.
But this is what thou must do – and I see that thou lackest
   not prudence, –
Walk with my maids by the wagon and mules so long as we
   pass through
Fields and furrowed land, at a brisk pace; I will conduct thee,
But when we come to the city, with towering bulwarks
   surrounded,

And, on either side, a fine, but narrow-mouthed harbour.
(For they are crowded with swaying vessels; and each has its
    own dock.)

40   There thou wilt see the market, encircling the fane of
    Poseidon,
Paved all round with large hewn stones; it is there that the
    tackle,
And the shipping-gear, are stored for our sea-going vessels.
There we keep the sails, the ropes, and the well-polished oars,
    too.
For the Phaakan men never bend the bow, nor use quivers.
Masts they need, and oars; and go down to the sea in their
    vessels.
These are the joy of their heart as they cut through the dark,
    surging water.
Passing there, I wish to avoid raising talk, lest some idler,
Seeing thee with me, should say: "What a handsome young
    fellow
Nausikaa has caught! He is following after her chariot!

50   Where did she find him, I wonder? She surely will make him
    her husband!
Is he some roaming stranger, whom she has rescued from
    ship-wreck,
Hailing from distant lands? For the Phaakans have no close
    neighbours.
Or have her prayers brought down some god from the
    heavens to wed her,
Whom she will keep on earth by her side as long as she
    liveth?
Ah, it was best she should find a husband among foreign
    peoples,
Seeing that she despises the men of the Phaakan country,
Who are courting her; though they be many and worthy." –
Thus, indeed, they will talk; and much it would pain me to
    hear them.
I should blame her myself, if another maid acted in that way.

60   If 'gainst the will of her friends, her father and her fond
          mother,
     She were openly seen with men before her betrothal.
     Stranger, I beg thee, give heed to my words, if thou'd'st have
          from my father
     Safe conduct home and a speedy return. Thou wilt find on
          the roadside,
     Sacred to Pallas Athene, a grove of beautiful poplars;
     In their midst there rises a spring, that waters the meadows.
     There my father has his estate, fruitful gardens and vineyard.
     Only so far from the town as a voice will easily carry.
     Sit down there, and wait, till we, going on to the city,
     Reach my father's palace; and, when thou thinkest we are
          there,
70   Coming into the town of the Phaakans, ask for the palace.
     Where my father dwells, – wise Alkinoos, the greathearted.
     Easy it is to find; and any child could direct thee,
     For there is no other palace so fine in the Phaakan city,
     As the home of my father, the mighty warrior, Alkinoos.
     When thou hast come to the inner court, and reachest the
          threshold,
     Then pass swiftly through the hall till thou findest my
          mother,
     Seated upon the hearth, and in the glow of the firelight;
     Turning the wheel and spinning the sea-purple yarn; 'tis a
          fine sight! –
     Leaning against a pillar she sits, and her maidens behind her.
80   Placed by her side, is a stately chair, the chair of my father.
     There he sits and sips his wine, as the gods might themselves
          do.
     Pass him by, and throw thy arms round the knees of my
          mother.
     Thou may'st hope to return with joy to thy home, and thy
          country,
     And thy ancestral halls, although they should be far distant,
     If my mother's heart thou canst win, and thy cause she espouses.'

So saying, she, with resounding whip, smote the mules and
    they started.
Brisk was the trot of the mules, and they soon left the sea
    shore behind them.
But she held them in check with the reins, for the sake of the
    walkers;
Skilfully using the whip, for the sake of her maids and
    Odysseus.

90 And the sun had set when they came to the grove and the
    poplars;
Beautiful trees were they, and sacred to Pallas Athene.
Sitting down, Odysseus prayed to the great Zeus's daughter:
  'Hear me! daughter of Aegis-bearing Zeus, the
    unconquered!
Hear me now! I entreat thee! though hitherto deaf to my
    pleading, –
When ship-wrecked by the earth-shaking god of the waves,
    and an outcast, –
Grant that the Phaakan people receive me with kindness and
    pity!' –
  Thus did he pray. And his prayer was heard by Pallas
    Athene.
Yet, on account of her father's brother, Poseidon, she came
    not;
Whose unceasing vengeance pursued the godlike Odysseus,

100 Till he reached, at length, his home and the land of his
    fathers.

                                         (1926)

MAURICE HEWLETT (1861–1923)

Aims to 'get something of Homer's effect of a river-flood, of
unstaying, streaming, irresistible flow . . .' Homer was 'a *jongleur* of
his time and place'. A translator must capture his 'idiom' and 'racy
language'.

The Iliad X [349–457] *Odysseus and Diomedes ambush Dolon*

So saying, they left
The track and hid themselves among the dead;
And Dolon went by heedless, and had gone
About the length of a furrow made by mules,
Which better far than oxen hale the plow
Through fallow land, when they were after him,
And he stood still to listen, in his heart
Deeming his friends were come to turn him back,
By Hektor's countermand; but when they were
10 A spear's cast off or less he knew them foes
And stretcht his legs to run; and they flew fast
Behind him. As two sharp-fang'd hunting dogs
Press on a doe or hare in woodland glade,
Who screaming flies, so press'd on him those two,
Diomede and Odysseus, and cut him off
His friends; and then, speeding towards the ships,
Just when he stood to reach the guard, great might
Athené put in Diomede, for fear
Some Greek might vaunt to have smitten him the first
20 And Diomede come second: on he dasht
With spear uplift, and 'Stand, or feel my spear,'
Said he, 'nor think longer to save thyself.'
Thereon he cast, and mist him purposely;
O'er his right shoulder flew the spear, and stuck
Into the ground. But Dolon stood in fear,
Shuddering, with teeth that clatter'd in his mouth,
And sickly-hued. Quick-breathing came the pair
And seized his hands, whereat he fell to weep,
Saying, 'Take me alive, and let me pay
30 A ransom – lo, great store of bronze we have,
And gold and hammer'd iron, whereof great store
Should be my father's grace-gift to you both:
Ransom untold, if he might know me alive

Upon your ships.'
                    The wise Odysseus said,
'Courage, think not on death; but tell me now
And truly wherefore goest thou thus alone
Away from the host towards the ships, in the night,
When others sleep? Com'st thou to strip the dead?
Or was it Hektor sent thee spying about
40   The hollow ships? Or was it daring of thine?'
Shaking in every limb, said Dolon, 'Lo,
'Twas Hektor that with many a fond conceit
Beguil'd my wits, promising me the steeds
And chariot of Achilles. I must go
Thro' the swift dark of night, and drawing near
The enemy, learn whether you watch your ships
As once you did, or whether in defeat
You are debating flight and care not watch
The night thro', overcome by sore fatigue.'
50   Smiling, Odysseus said, 'There was thy heart
Fixt on a mighty gift. Achilles' horses!
Hard manège they are for the sons of men;
Too hard for any man to drive but him,
Born of a deathless mother. Tell me now,
And truly, where was Hektor when thy course
Thou shapedst hither? Where his arms, and where
His chariot and horses? How are set
The Trojan watch, and whereabouts their beds?
What plans have they? Have they a mind to stand
60   Out here beside the ships, or to draw off
Into the town, having defeated us?'
    Dolon, son of Eumedes, said, 'I tell
You all, and truly: Hektor with them who make
His Council holdeth conference by the tomb
Of holy Ilos, apart from all the strife;
As for the watch whereof thou askest, Sir,
There is no chosen watch upon the host,
Nor sentry; but the Trojans have their fires,

As needs they must, and men look after those
70 And keep each other to work; but the allies
From many lands are sleeping, with the charge
To watch laid on the Trojans – for of theirs
No wife or child is near.' Odysseus said,
'Tell me now where sleep those – whether among
The Trojans, or apart, that I may know it.'
And Dolon, 'I will tell you all the truth.
The Karians lie towards the sea; there too
And Kaukones, and proud Pelasgians.
The Paionian bowmen, and the Leleges,
80 The Lykians are by Thymbre, and thereby
The Mysians, Phrygian horsemen, and the knights
Of the Maionians – but wherefore know all this?
If you would seek an entry to our host
There are the Thrakians, newcomers, apart
From all the rest, and with them is their king,
Rhesos, the son of Eïoneus.
He has the finest horses and the best
I ever saw; whiter than snow they are,
Swifter than any wind. His car is wrought
90 In gold and silver; the harness is of gold,
Astounding, and a wonder to behold.
All this he brought with him, unfit for men
To wear, fit only the immortal Gods.
Now take me to the ships, or leave me here
Bound rigidly in bonds till you return
With proofs of me, whether I lie or not.'
  But Diomede lookt grimly, and he said,
'Let no thought of escape be in thy mind,
Dolon, whatso good news thou givest us.
100 Once in our hands, to set thee free again
Or let thee go, would bring thee back again
Later, to spy upon our ships or fight
In the open. Nay, but if under my hand
Thou drop thy life, no bane to us art thou

Hereafter.' Then, as Dolon made to touch
His chin with the hand, imploring him, he hew'd
Full in his neck, with the sword heavy on him,
And cut both sinews thro', so that his head,
Still wailing, met the dust.   (1928)

HERBERT BATES (1905–74)

This version in iambic tetrameter blank verse (dactylic hexameters
are 'unsuited to the spirit of the English language') aims at 'a light,
rapid, lyric narrative form that lets the story show through'. The
original is abridged in the interest of swift narrative progress. The
intended audience is one of teachers and students. Thoroughly
neglected, Bates's rendition is actually full of freshness and pathos.

The Odyssey XX [92–121] *Odysseus, home in disguise,*
receives a happy omen

                    It chanced
That as his wife thus wept, Odysseus
Heard her voice plainly. In his breast
He pondered deeply, for it seemed
That she must know him and must now
Be standing by his bed. So quickly
He gathered up the robe and fleeces
Whereon he slept, and laid them all
Upon a chair within, and bore
10   The oxhide, then, forth through the door
And spread it on the earth. And thus
With hands upraised he prayed:
                    'O Zeus,
Great Father, if you gods once more

Have brought me home to my own land
Over the firm earth and the waters
Of the wide sea, though you have given
My fill of evil too – now grant,
If still your hearts look on me kindly,
That some one in the house may speak
20   A word of lucky omen! Grant me
Without the house, a second sign
From mighty Zeus himself.'

                          So prayed he.
And all-wise Zeus hearkened his prayer.
Straightway he sent his thunder pealing
Down from his shining home, Olympus,
Out of the clouds on high. Odysseus
Heard it with joy.

                   And now there came
A word of lucky omen spoken
By one within, a woman grinding
30   The corn within the house, where stood
The millstones of that folk's good shepherd.
For here twelve women toiled to grind
The meal and flour that give men strength,
And all but one now slept, their meal
Being ground already, but she still,
Since she was weakest of them all,
Ceased not her task. But now she stayed
Her busy mill and spoke these words
Of fortune for her lord:

                        'O Zeus,
40   Father wide-ruling over gods
And men alike, loudly thou now
Hast thundered forth from starry heaven
Though not a cloud was seen. And surely
Thou showest in this a sign. So grant
Even for my poor sake, that this
Which I now say may be accomplished:

Grant that this feast the wooers hold
To-day here in Odysseus' hall
Shall be their last, their utmost! Aye,
50   Let those men who have worn my knees
To weakness with heart-breaking labor,
The while I ground their grain, now feast them
For the last time!'
                    So spoke the woman,
And great Odysseus then was glad
To hear her words of lucky omen
And Zeus' loud thunder.   (1929)

EZRA POUND (1885–1972)

Clearly one of the very high moments in any anthology of the
'Homeric' in the language. And an indication of the extent to
which the *Cantos*, at their outset and in the light of Joyce, were
themselves conceived as an *Odyssey* by one of the manifold and
storm-tossed spirits of our age.

Odyssey XI [1ff] Canto I *The departure from Circe*

And then went down to the ship,
Set keel to breakers, forth on the godly sea, and
We set up mast and sail on that swart ship,
Bore sheep aboard her, and our bodies also
Heavy with weeping, and winds from sternward
Bore us out onward with bellying canvas,
Circe's this craft, the trim-coifed goddess.
Then sat we amidships, wind jamming the tiller,
Thus with stretched sail, we went over sea till day's end.
10   Sun to his slumber, shadows o'er all the ocean,

Came we then to the bounds of deepest water,
To the Kimmerian lands, and peopled cities
Covered with close-webbed mist, unpierced ever
With glitter of sun-rays
Nor with stars stretched, nor looking back from heaven
Swartest night stretched over wretched men there.
The ocean flowing backward, came we then to the place
Aforesaid by Circe.
Here did they rites, Perimedes and Eurylochus,
20   And drawing sword from my hip
I dug the ell-square pitkin;
Poured we libations unto each the dead,
First mead and then sweet wine, water mixed with white
        flour.
Then prayed I many a prayer to the sickly death's-heads;
As set in Ithaca, sterile bulls of the best
For sacrifice, heaping the pyre with goods,
A sheep to Tiresias only, black and a bell-sheep.
Dark blood flowed in the fosse,
Souls out of Erebus, cadaverous dead, of brides
30   Of youths and of the old who had borne much;
Souls stained with recent tears, girls tender,
Men many, mauled with bronze lance heads,
Battle spoil, bearing yet dreory arms,
These many crowded about me; with shouting,
Pallor upon me, cried to my men for more beasts;
Slaughtered the herds, sheep slain of bronze;
Poured ointment, cried to the gods,
To Pluto the strong, and praised Proserpine;
Unsheathed the narrow sword,
40   I sat to keep off the impetuous impotent dead,
Till I should hear Tiresias.
But first Elpenor came, our friend Elpenor,
Unburied, cast on the wide earth,
Limbs that we left in the house of Circe,
Unwept, unwrapped in sepulchre, since toils urged other.

Pitiful spirit. And I cried in hurried speech:
'Elpenor, how art thou come to this dark coast?
'Cam'st thou afoot, outstripping seamen?'
　　　And he in heavy speech:
50　'Ill fate and abundant wine. I slept in Circe's ingle.
'Going down the long ladder unguarded,
'I fell against the buttress,
'Shattered the nape-nerve, the soul sought Avernus.
'But thou, O King, I bid remember me, unwept, unburied,
'Heap up mine arms, be tomb by sea-bord, and inscribed:
'*A man of no fortune, and with a name to come.*
'And set my oar up, that I swung mid fellows.'

And Anticlea came, whom I beat off, and then Tiresias
　　　Theban,
Holding his golden wand, knew me, and spoke first:
60　'A second time? why? man of ill star,
'Facing the sunless dead and this joyless region?
'Stand from the fosse, leave me my bloody bever
'For soothsay.'
　　　And I stepped back,
And he strong with the blood, said then: 'Odysseus
'Shalt return through spiteful Neptune, over dark seas,
'Lose all companions.' And then Anticlea came.
Lie quiet Divus. I mean, that is Andreas Divus,
In officina Wecheli, 1538, out of Homer.
70　And he sailed, by Sirens and thence outward and away
And unto Circe.
　　　Venerandam,
In the Cretan's phrase, with the golden crown, Aphrodite,
Cypri munimenta sortita est, mirthful, orichalchi, with
　　　golden
Girdles and breast bands, thou with dark eyelids
Bearing the golden bough of Argicida.　　　(1930, 1934)

W. H. D. ROUSE (1863–1950)

Rouse exercised wide influence as a schoolmaster impassioned by the classics and as a translator. This retelling of the *Odyssey* 'into plain English' (Rouse also published an *Iliad*), anticipates E. V. Rieu's popular version. Paradoxically, Rouse speaks of 'Mr. Ezra Pound the onlie begetter' of these 'Homers'. There are fascinating letters on Homer and translation between the two men.

The Story of Odysseus XIX [100–163] *Penelope questions the stranger*

The housewife hurried off and brought the chair and the rug, and Odysseus patiently seated himself. Then Penelopeia spoke:

'Stranger,' she said, 'I will begin myself by asking you this question: Who are you? What is your country and your family?'

Odysseus must have all his wits about him now. He began as follows:

'My lady, no one in this wide world could find fault with you. Your name resounds to the heavens, like the fame of a noble king, a god-fearing man who rules over a mighty nation and upholds justice, while the black soil yields him barley and wheat, his trees are heavy with fruit, the sheep yean their young unfailing, the sea provides fish; for he is a good ruler, and the people prosper under him. Then ask me anything else you will, now I am in your house; but do not ask my family and my country, and fill my heart yet more with sorrow when I remember. I am a man of many sorrows, but I must not sit grieving and lamenting in another man's house; eternal lacrimation is a sorry occupation. The servants might not like it, nor you perhaps yourself. They might think me a drunken man all afloat in tears.'

'Ah no!' said Penelopeia. 'All my comeliness and my good looks are gone; the immortals took them from me when the army embarked for the war, and my husband with them. If that man would return and care for me, my name and fame would be better for it.

'But now I am in distress; see what trouble fate has poured upon me! All the chief men of the islands, from Dulichion and Samê and woody Zacynthos, and all my neighbours in Ithaca, want to take me for a wife against my will, and they are wasting my house. So I take no heed of strangers or suppliants, or public heralds with their messages, but I pine away with longing for my husband.

'These men are in a great hurry, but I wind my schemes on my distaff. First there was the shroud. Some kind spirit put it into my head to set up a web on my loom, a great web of my finest thread. Then I said to them, "My good young men, you want me for a wife now Odysseus is dead, and you are in a hurry: but wait until I finish this cloth, for I don't want to waste the thread I have made for it. This is to be a shroud for my lord Laërtês, when the fate of dolorous death shall take him off. I should be sorry to have a scandal among our women if he should lack a shroud, when he had all those great possessions."

'After that I used to weave the web in the daytime, but in the night I unravelled it by torchlight. For three years I kept up the pretence, and they believed it: but when the fourth year came round, the maids let out the secret, shameless things who cared nothing! and they came and caught me, and there was a great to-do. So I had to finish that, because I must, not because I would.

'And now I cannot avoid marriage, I cannot think of anything else to try. My parents urge me to marry and have done with it, my son chafes because they are eating everything up; he notices things now, and he is already quite man enough to manage a house with some credit in the world. But never mind, tell me who you are and where you come from. Your father was not a tree or a stone, as they say.'   (1932)

D. H. LAWRENCE (1885–1930)

A moving salute to the classical-Homeric experience by one not given to facile sentiments. The close could serve as motto for any collection such as this book.

The Argonauts

They are not dead, they are not dead!
Now that the sun, like a lion, licks his paws
and goes slowly down the hill:
now that the moon, who remembers, and only cares
that we should be lovely in the flesh, with bright, crescent
     feet,
pauses near the crest of the hill, climbing slowly, like a queen
looking down on the lion as he retreats.

Now the sea is the Argonaut's sea, and in the dawn
Odysseus calls the commands, as he steers past those foamy
     islands

10   wait, wait, don't bring the coffee yet, nor the *pain grillé*.
The dawn is not off the sea, and Odysseus' ships
have not yet passed the islands. I must watch them still.   (1933)

C. DAY-LEWIS (1904–72)

One of the innumerable evocations in English literatures of the Sirens. They range from Shakespeare and Milton to a cartoon in the *Spectator* for May 1994. Three buxom Sirens watch Odysseus, chained to his mast, sailing by: 'Has no one told him that we're not into bonding?'

Nearing Again the Legendary Isle

Nearing again the legendary isle
Where sirens sang and mariners were skinned,
We wonder now what was there to beguile
That such stout fellows left their bones behind.

Those chorus-girls are surely past their prime,
Voices grow shrill and paint is wearing thin,
Lips that sealed up the sense from gnawing time
Now beg the favor with a graveyard grin.

We have no flesh to spare and they can't bite,
10   Hunger and sweat have stripped us to the bone;
A skeleton crew we toil upon the tide
And mock the theme-song meant to lure us on:

No need to stop the ears, avert the eyes
From purple rhetoric of evening skies.   (1933)

A. S. WAY

A strangely archaizing solution (for *The Homeric Hymns*), in rhyming
couplets, by a classical scholar.

Hymn 8 – To Ares

Ares the mighty one, Chariot-lord of the helmet of gold,
Shield-bearer and fortress-saver, bronze-harnessed,
        impetuous-souled,
Strong-handed spear-wielder, untiring, Heaven's battle-stay,

Father of fair-fought victory, Justice's champion aye,
Queller of rebels, captain of men who the right revere,
Sceptre-bearer of valour, who whirlest thy fiery-flashing
     sphere
Mid the planet's sevenfold course through the sky, where thy
     steeds of flame
Bear thee for ever above the high Third Firmament's frame –
Hear, Helper of mortals, giver of youth's undaunted might!
10   Shed thou a gracious splendour down on my life from thine
     height
And prowess in battle, that I may be able to chase away
From mine head that bitter panic that blenches from the fray,
And may wrestle down each impulse that would misguide
     my soul,
And may rein my passionate spirit from speeding me past
     control
To tread in the paths of strife. O blessèd One, grant unto me
Boldness to bide by the laws unaggressive of peace, and to
     flee
From contention of hate, from the Fates that slay men
     violently.   (1934)

T. E. SHAW (1888–1935)

Under a somewhat transparent pseudonym, T. E. Lawrence pro-
duced his version of 'the first novel of Europe'. The prose idiom is a
hybrid of biblical, argot, military and archaizing elements. Lawrence
says of Homer: 'He is all adrift when it comes to fighting, and had
not seen death in battle . . . Very bookish, this house-bred man.' As
to Odysseus' family: 'the sly cattish wife . . . and the priggish son'.

A version 'definitely made for non-scholars' (to B. Liddell-Hart
on 18 August 1934). But Lawrence feels himself to be 'in a strong
position vis-à-vis Homer' and other translators. 'For years we were

digging up a city of roughly the Odysseus period. I have handled the weapons, armour, utensils of those times, explored their houses, planned their cities. I have hunted wild boars and watched wild lions, sailed the Aegean (and sailed ships), bent bows, lived with pastoral peoples, woven textiles, built boats and killed many men' (to Bruce Rogers on 31 January 1931).

These two passages show something of Lawrence's uses of G. H. Palmer.

The *Odyssey* V [234–61] *The building of the raft*

First she gave him a great axe of cutting copper, well-suited to his reach. It was ground on both edges and into the socketed head was firmly wedged the well-rounded handle of olive-wood. Then she gave him a finished smoothing-adze and led the way to the end of the island where the trees grew tall, the alders and the poplars with heaven-scaling pines, withered long since and sapless and very dry, which would float high for him. She showed him where the loftiest trees had grown, did Calypso that fair goddess: then she returned to her cavern while he busily cut out his beams, working with despatch. Twenty trees in all he threw and axed into shape with the sharp copper, trimming them adeptly and trueing them against his straight-edge.

Then his lovely goddess brought to him augers with which he bored the logs for lashing together: firmly he fastened them with pegs and ties. As broad as a skilled shipwright would design and lay down the floor of a roomy merchant-ship, just so full in beam did Odysseus make his raft. To carry his upper deck he set up many ribs, closely kneed and fitted, and he united the heads of these with long rubbing-strakes, for gunwales. He put a mast into his craft, with a yard in proportion: also a stern sweep with which to steer her. To defend himself from breaching seas he fenced in the sides of the raft with wicker work, wattling it cunningly all of osiers like a basket and adding a lavish reinforcement of stanchions. Calypso came again with a bolt of cloth for sails, which he stitched strongly.

Then he set up stays and sheets and halyards, and at last with levers he worked the raft down into the sacred sea.

XVIII [66–107] *The bout with Irus*

. . . Odysseus kilted up his rags like a loin-cloth, baring his massive, shapely thighs, his arching shoulders, chest and brawny arms. Attendant Athene magnified the limbs of the shepherd of the people. The suitors were startled out of their wits and stared at each other, saying, 'Such hams has the old fellow brought out from his rags that soon our tout will be outed by an evil of his own procuring.' Their boding shook Irus to the core. The workmen had to truss him forcibly: they brought him on with the flesh of his limbs quaking in panic. Antinous spoke to him sharply: 'Now, bully, you were better dead or not born, maybe, if you will start so in terror of an old man crippled with suffering. Let me tell you this, for certain. Should he best you and win, I shall thrust you into a black ship for export to the continent; to King Echetus, bane of the earth, who will hack off your nose and ears with his cruel knives and tear away your privy parts for throwing all raw to his dogs as food.' These words gave the trembling a deeper hold upon his limbs.

However they haled him into the open, and there the two squared off. Royal Odysseus was puzzling himself if it were better to smite the other so starkly that life would leave him where he fell, or to tap him gently and just stretch him out. On the whole the gentle way seemed right, to save himself from too close notice by the Achaeans. So when they put up their hands and Irus hit at his right shoulder Odysseus only hooked him to the neck under the ear and crushed the bones inward, so that blood gushed purple from his lips and with a shriek he fell in the dust, biting the ground and drumming with his feet. The suitor lords flung up their hands and died of laughing; but Odysseus took him by the leg and dragged him through the entrance, across the yard and to the outer-gate, where he propped him with his back against the precinct-fence and his beggar's crutch between his hands, remarking bitterly, 'Sit there

and play bogy to the dogs and pigs: but unless you want a worse
beating never again set up your silly self as beggar-king.'   (1932)

WILLIAM BENJAMIN SMITH
(1850–1934) and WALTER MILLER
(1864–1949)

This claims to be the first complete and line-for-line translation into
dactylic hexameters. Its approach is close to that of American
fundamentalists when they treat of the Bible. It accepts 'the tradi-
tional date of 1184 BC for the fall of Troy'. This in 1945! Yet there
are undeniably 'epic' moments.

The Iliad XIII [769–809] *Paris replies to Hector's chiding*

   'Shame-Paris! fairest in form, thou woman-demented
        seducer!
   Where is Deïphobus? Where are Helenus, royal and mighty,
   Adamas, Asius' son, and the son of Hyrtacus, Asius?
   Where is Othryoneus, pray thee? For lo! all Ilium hath fallen
   Down from her pinnacle high; sheer ruin and certain
        impendeth.'
      Then, in his turn, made answer to him Alexander, the
        godlike:
      'Hector, since thou art minded to cast the blame on the
        blameless,
   Haply tomorrow but never today I might shrink from the
        warfare,
   Since our mother hath borne even me not wholly a coward.
10 Ever since thou hast arrayed by the ships thy comrades to
        battle,

Since then here we abide, with the Danaans striving in
 combat
Unintermitted; but slain are those comrades for whom thou
 inquirest!
Only Deïphobus, only Helenus, royal and mighty,
Two have withdrawn; for indeed long lances wounded them
 sorely
Both in the arm; but Cronion the doom of death hath
 averted.
Lead on now, where'er thy mind and thy spirit command
 thee.
Eagerly we will follow along, and, methinketh, in no way
Shall we be lacking in valor, whatever of strength may be
 ours.
Passing his strength, however, not e'en the most eager can
 battle.'
20 These words spoken, the hero persuaded the mind of his
 brother.
Forth then hurried the twain where the war-din had raged
 and the direst
Strife round Cebriones bold and Pulydamas, hero undaunted,
Phalces, and peer of the gods, Polyphetes, round good
 Orthaeus,
Palmys, Ascanius, too, and a son of Hippotion, Morys –
These had come as reliefs from the deep-loamed land of
 Ascania
Only the morning before, and now Zeus spurred them to
 battle.
On they went, like the blast of violent winds in their going,
When it descends upon earth 'mid the thunder of Zeus, the
 All-Father;
Then in the salt-sea spume with astounding roar it commingles,
30 Wave upon wave high-swelling, the sea's loud-thundering
 surges,
Arching and crested with foam, some vanward, others behind
 them:

So were the Trojans arrayed, some forward, some to the
    rearmost;
Coated in harness of bronze bright-gleaming, they followed
    their leaders.
Hector, Priam's son, the equal of man's bane Ares,
Led them; he held his shield, all evenly rounded, before him,
Thick with hides, and bronze was heavily welded upon it;
Over his temples the while kept swaying his radiant helmet.
Striding along, he was testing at all points whether the
    squadrons
Haply would yield, as he charged behind his broad-rimmed
    buckler.
40 Yet noway he confounded the heart in the breast of th'
    Achaeans.
First in his challenge was Ajax, with long strides stalking
    before them . . .
                                (1945)

E. V. RIEU (1887–1972)

Intended to make Homer 'easy reading for those who are unfamiliar
with the Greek world', Rieu's prose version proved immensely
successful. Customs officials stopped Rieu on a trip to the Continent
to thank him for the wonders of a sea-story of which they took him
to be the author. Denounced by some as 'the Agatha Christie
version of Homer', Rieu's rendition has become dated, by its very
contemporaneity. But it marks the new era of the pocket-book
classic, obtainable at airports or railway news-stands. Revised, the
Rieu *Odyssey* continues its active life.

The Odyssey XII [153–200] *Odysseus passes the Sirens*

'I was much perturbed in spirit and before long took my men
into my confidence. "My friends," I said, "it is not right that only

one or two of us should know the prophecies that Circe, in her divine wisdom, has made to me, and I am going to pass them on to you, so that we may all be forewarned, whether we die or escape the worst and save our lives. Her first warning concerned the mysterious Sirens. We must beware of their song and give their flowery meadow a wide berth. I alone, she suggested, might listen to their voices; but you must bind me hard and fast, so that I cannot stir from the spot where you will stand me, by the step of the mast, with the rope's ends lashed round the mast itself. And if I beg you to release me, you must tighten and add to my bonds."

'I thus explained every detail to my men. In the meantime our good ship, with that perfect wind to drive her, fast approached the Sirens' Isle. But now the breeze dropped, some power lulled the waves, and a breathless calm set in. Rising from their seats my men drew in the sail and threw it into the hold, then sat down at the oars and churned the water white with their blades of polished pine. Meanwhile I took a large round of wax, cut it up small with my sword, and kneaded the pieces with all the strength of my fingers. The wax soon yielded to my vigorous treatment and grew warm, for I had the rays of my Lord the Sun to help me. I took each of my men in turn and plugged their ears with it. They then made me a prisoner on my ship by binding me hand and foot, standing me up by the step of the mast and tying the rope's ends to the mast itself. This done, they sat down once more and struck the grey water with their oars.

'We made good progress and had just come within call of the shore when the Sirens became aware that a ship was swiftly bearing down upon them, and broke into their liquid song.

'"Draw near," they sang, "illustrious Odysseus, flower of Achaean chivalry, and bring your ship to rest so that you may hear our voices. No seaman ever sailed his black ship past this spot without listening to the sweet tones that flow from our lips, and none that listened has not been delighted and gone on a wiser man. For we know all that the Argives and Trojans suffered on the broad plain of Troy by the will of the gods, and we have foreknowledge of all that is going to happen on this fruitful earth."

'The lovely voices came to me across the water, and my heart was filled with such a longing to listen that with nod and frown I signed to my men to set me free. But they swung forward to their oars and rowed ahead, while Perimedes and Eurylochus jumped up, tightened my bonds and added more. However, when they had rowed past the Sirens and we could no longer hear their voices and the burden of their song, my good companions were quick to clear their ears of the wax I had used to stop them, and to free me from my shackles.' (1946)

Rieu's *Iliad* followed in 1950. It proved somewhat less of a revelation for the 'common reader'.

The Iliad IV [422–72] *A battle scene*

And now battalion on battalion of Danaans swept relentlessly into battle, like the great waves that come hurtling onto an echoing beach, one on top of the other, under a westerly gale. Far out at sea their crests begin to rise, then in they come and crash down on the shingle with a mighty roar, or arch themselves to break on a cliff and send the sea foam flying. Each of the captains shouted his orders to his own command, but the men moved quietly. They obeyed their officers without a sound, and came on behind them like an army of the dumb. The metalled armour that they marched in glittered on every man.

It was otherwise with the Trojans. They were like the sheep that stand in their thousands in a rich farmer's yard yielding their white milk and bleating incessantly because they hear their lambs. Such was the babel that went up from the great Trojan army, which hailed from many parts, and being without a common language used many different cries and calls.

Ares, the god of War, spurred on the Trojan forces; Athene of the Flashing Eyes, the Achaeans. Terror and Panic were at hand.

And so was Strife, the War-god's Sister, who helps him in his bloody work. Once she begins, she cannot stop. At first she seems a little thing, but before long, though her feet are still on the ground, she has struck high heaven with her head. She swept in now among the Trojans and Achaeans, filling them with hatred of each other. It was the groans of dying men she wished to hear.

At last the armies met, with a clash of bucklers, spears and bronze-clad fighting men. The bosses of their shields collided and a great roar went up. The screams of the dying were mingled with the vaunts of their destroyers, and the earth ran with blood. So, in winter, two mountain rivers flowing in spate from the great springs higher up mingle their torrents at a watersmeet in some deep ravine, and far off in the hills a shepherd hears their thunder. Such was the tumult and turmoil as the two armies came to grips.

Antilochus was the first to kill his man, Echepolus son of Thalysius, who was fighting in full armour in the Trojan front. With the first cast he struck this man on the ridge of his crested helmet. The spear-point, landing in his forehead, pierced the bone; darkness came down on his eyes, and he crashed in the mêlée like a falling tower. He was scarcely down when Prince Elephenor son of Chalcodon and leader of the fiery Abantes seized him by the feet and tried to drag him quickly out of range to spoil him of his armour – an enterprise he did not carry far, for the valiant Agenor saw him dragging the corpse away. With his bronze-headed shaft Agenor caught him on the flank, which the shield had left exposed as Elephenor stooped. The man collapsed, and over his lifeless body a grim struggle ensued between Trojans and Achaeans. They leapt at each other like wolves, and men tossed men about.   (1950)

S. O. ANDREW (1868–1952)

Having, under Quiller-Couch's aegis, translated the *Iliad* and also *Sir Gawain and the Green Knight*, Andrew proceeded to the *Odyssey*. He uses a flexible line with five basic stresses. The metre can be regarded as primarily dactylic. The reiterative, formulaic structure of the original is respected. Longfellow seems to hover in the background.

Homer's Odyssey IX [62–104] *The Lotus-eaters*

'Thence fared we onward again, sore stricken at heart,
Glad of our lives, though griev'd for the loss of our friends,
And yet no sail did we set in our swift-going ships
Ere each of our hapless companions thrice we had hail'd,
The comrades that died on the plain at the Cicones' hands,
And Zeus that gathers the clouds a North-wind awoke
With terrible tempest, and shrouded with storm-driven
    wrack
Both earth and the deep, and down rush'd night from the
    heav'n.
Headlong our vessels were driv'n o'er the welter of waves,
10 And our sails were torn into shreds by the force of the wind;
And we furl'd them, in terror of death, and stow'd them
    away
And row'd, with such speed as we might, our ships to the
    land.
And so for two days and nights continuously
We lay there, in sorrow and weariness eating our hearts;
But when fair-tress'd Dawn had the third day lighted on
    earth,
We set up the masts and the white sails hoisted again,
And wind and helmsman together guided the ships.
And then, unscath'd, had I reach'd my own native land,
But current and wind, as I rounded Malea's cape,
20 Far south of the isle of Cythéra swept me away.
    'Nine long days was I driv'n by the ruinous winds
O'er the fish-teeming deep; on the tenth we arriv'd at the
    land
Of the Lotus-eaters, who live on a flowery food;

And we stepp'd ashore to draw fresh water and then
My comrades quickly prepar'd us a meal by the ships.
But when to our hearts' content we had eaten and drunk,
Some of my crew I commanded to go and explore
What manner of men here liv'd by bread upon earth –
Two did I choose, and a third as a herald I sent.

30 To the Lotus-eaters they came and had converse with them,
And the strange people thought not of death in their hearts
But gave my comrades to taste of the lotus and eat.
Now whoso partook of that honey-sweet fruit with his lips
No more bethought him to bring back tidings to us,
But there with the Lotus-eaters was fain to abide
Eating the flowery food, and forgot to return.
These therefore I brought back weeping, constraining their
    will,
And, thrusting them under the benches, bound them with
    cords,
And the rest of my well-lov'd comrades I instantly bade
40 Make speed to depart from that land on the swift-going
    ships,
Lest any should eat and their homeward journey forget;
And they straightway embark'd and their places took on the
    thwarts
Where, sitting in order, the grey salt water they smote. (1948)

F. L. LUCAS (1894–1967)

F. L. Lucas, the classicist and man of letters. Homer's supremacy
rests 'also on the simple fact that he was a finer person – more
vigorous and vital than Virgil, more merciful than Dante, more
generous than Milton'. The *Odyssey* surpasses the *Iliad* in 'mastery
of construction'.

The Odyssey V.118–53 [118–70] *Calypso complains to the gods, but tells Odysseus that she will let him go*

'Ye are harsh, ye are passing jealous, ye Gods! – if to her bed
A Goddess takes a mortal man, and hides it not,
But makes him her own dear husband, ye grudge her happy
        lot.
When Dawn the rosy-fingered to Orion gave her love,
Ye grudged that too, ye Gods, at your ease in Heaven
        above –
Him Artemis the maiden, Queen of the Golden Throne,
Slew in Ortygia's island, by her painless shafts o'erthrown.
And when fair-tressed Demeter obeyed her passionate heart
And lay in love with Iásion, in a thrice-ploughed field apart,
10   Like fate was hers – ere long the tidings of it came
        To Zeus, and He smote her lover with the lightning's white-
                hot flame.
Now me in my turn ye envy, ye Gods, that I should keep
A mortal man, though I saved him, alone, from out the deep
Astride the keel of his galley that Zeus had split in twain
With the white flame of His lightning amid the wine-dark
        main.
All of his noble comrades had died, with none to save,
And alone he drifted hither, the sport of wind and wave.
I loved him, and I cherished – I dreamed that it might be
I should make him ageless and deathless for evermore with
        me.
20   But since what Aegis-wielding Zeus shall once ordain,
No other God may avoid it, no other God make vain,
Hence with him – if Zeus sends him, and hath commanded
        so –
Across the barren breakers! I cannot make him go –
I have no well-oared galleys, no mariners are mine
To bear him on his journey o'er the long backs of the brine;
Yet I will counsel him kindly, and hide the truth no more,

That so he may come, at last, safe to his native shore.'
Then the Herald, the Argus-slayer, replied – 'Send him away,
And tempt not Zeus to anger, lest He turn on *thee* one day.'
30 So the mighty Argus-slayer departed, with that word;
But the queenly Nymph, Calypso, now that she had heard
The will of Zeus, went forth and found beside the sea
The noble Odysseus, sitting with eyes that ceaselessly
O'erflowed with tears – such longing to see his native shore
Wasted for him life's sweetness; for the Nymph pleased him
      no more.
Each night, indeed, beside her in her hollow cave he slept
Perforce – by *her* will, not by his – but daylong wept;
Sitting among the boulders on the borders of the deep.
Staring across the waters that never man may reap,
40 He wrung his soul with sighing and tears in anguish shed.
Beside him the noble Goddess came now and stood and said:
'Unhappy man, I pray thee, weep not for ever apart,
Wasting thy life. For homeward I will send thee with all my
      heart.
Come now, rise up and hew thee tall timber, and prepare
With the edge of the bronze a broad-beamed raft, and fasten
      there
A deck above, to take thee across the misty tide.
Water, and bread, and good red wine I will provide,
To cheer thee and stay thy hunger; and bring thee too, with
      these,
Raiment to wear; and send thee, astern, a favouring breeze.
50 So shalt thou come, unscathed, back to thy home again,
If so the Gods that hold the boundless Heaven ordain –
For mightier They than I am, alike to know and do.'   (1948)

The selections from the *Iliad* appeared in 1950, again with the Folio Society (London).

The Iliad VIII [542–59]/IX [1–8] *The Trojans encamp before the Greek wall*

So Hector; and loud the Trojans acclaimed the words he
    spoke,
And loosed their horses, steaming, from underneath the yoke,
And haltered them by their chariots, and brought in haste
Kine and fat sheep and wine, honey-sweet to the taste,
And corn from their homes in the city, and piled the faggots
    high;
Then fat the smoke of their feasting blew rolling up the sky.
On the bridges of the battle, with spirits high upraised,
All night they sat; and thickly their leaguer's campfires
    blazed.
As when, high up in Heaven, the stars shine sharp and bright
10 All round the moon in her splendour, while windless lies the
    night;
Each glen, each hill, each mountain-peak shows clear its face,
And far above bursts open the Heaven's infinite space
With all its stars; and the heart of the shepherd fills with joy;
So thick flamed through the darkness the fires of the hosts of
    Troy
Between the ships and Xanthus, before the Trojan wall.
There in the plain a thousand burned; and fifty men by all
Sat in the blaze, with their horses by the chariots champing
    rye
And barley white, as they waited for Morning throned on
    high.
So waited and watched the Trojans. But on the Achaean part
20 Lay deadly Fear, the comrade of Flight that chills the heart.
Even their bravest spirits were numbed with utter woe.
As when o'er the teeming surges, all of a sudden, blow

From Thrace two winds together, Zephyr and Boreas –
Dark swell the crested rollers and high on shore they mass
The wild sea-wrack. So troubled the hearts of Achaea grew.

XVI [5-35] *Patroclus pleads with Achilles*

Then seeing him the noble Achilles, the swift of foot, was
    moved;
And the words came winging from him, and he said to the
    friend he loved:
'Why all in tears, Patroclus? – as a little maid will cry,
Plucking her mother's dress, to be lifted up on high –
Running beside and clinging, as her mother hurries past,
And looking up all tearful, till she wins her way at last.
Like such a child, Patroclus, thou weepest piteously.
Hast thou some news for the Myrmidons? Some tale for me?
Come tidings out of Phthīa, that are unknown to us?
10 And yet they say that Actor's son, Menoetius,
Is living – and Pēleus lives, among the Myrmidons –
Whose death were bitter hearing for us that are their sons.
Or are thy tears for the Argives, as they perish in their need
There by the hollow galleys, for their own evil deed?
Speak out. Hide not thy feeling. Best that we both should
    know.'
    Then saidst thou, knightly Patroclus, with voice of utter
    woe:
'O Achilles, son of Pēleus, Achaea's goodliest,
Do not be vexed – so sorely the Argives now are pressed.
For all the chiefs that aforetime they counted first in might,
20 Now by the ships are lying, wounded or maimed in fight.
For the gallant son of Tydeus, Diomed, is wounded sore.
Wounded lies Agamemnon, and Odysseus famed in war;
Eurýpylus is smitten – in his thigh a shaft;
And round them, with all their simples, the leeches ply their
    craft,

Healing their hurts. O Achilles, what man may deal with
    thee!
Never may *I* nurse anger so implacably,
Thou dreadful heart of valour! Wilt thou serve some race
    unborn,
When in shame and ruin the Argives have perished by thy
    scorn?
Ah pitiless! – no Thĕtis bare *thee* beneath her heart,
30 No knightly Pēleus fathered *thee*. The child thou art
Of the grey sea and its footless crags, inexorable
    one! . . .'
                                     (1950)

I. A. RICHARDS (1893–1979)

In a fascinating preface to *The Wrath of Achilles, The Iliad of Homer
Shortened and in a New Translation*, Richards aims to present a piece
of 'world literature' in what is now 'the world language'. Every-
thing which can 'impede communication' is to be eliminated.
Adduces modern diagrams of semantic transfer from 'information
source' to 'message destination'. 'Noises' – the purely decorative,
the extraneous – are to be jettisoned. In actual fact, this prose-
version is charged with I. A. Richards's characteristic sinewy
power and wit.

The Iliad XII [251–328] *The struggle around the Greek walls*

So saying, he went on, and Zeus, the thunderbolt thrower, sent
down from Ida a storm wind that blew the dust thick over the
Greek ships. So he blinded the Greeks and gave glory to the
Trojans and Hector. And they went to work now to pull down the
wall, dragging at its supports, hoping to open a way through it. But

the Greeks did not give way and threw everything they had at the Trojans as they came up under the wall.

The two Ajaxes went everywhere on the walls urging on the Greeks, saying honeyed words to some and hard words to others when they saw anyone fall back. 'O friends,' they cried, 'good fighters or bad or in between, for men cannot all be equal in battle, there is work enough here for us all; you know it yourselves. Let there be no turning back to the ships now; keep one another in heart. It may be that Zeus, Lord of the lightning, will help us now to throw them back and drive them toward the city.'

So these lifted up the Greeks' spirits. As flakes of snow fall thick on a winter day, when Zeus, the counselor, is moved to snowing, and sends these arrows of his among men; and he quiets the winds and snows on, hour after hour, till he has covered the tops of the mountains and the high headlands and the rich fields of men; and over the harbors and the edges of the gray sea the snow lies deep, but the wave as it rolls keeps it off; all other things were weighted down by the storm of Zeus; even so from both sides stones flew thick from Trojans and from Greeks as they threw at one another.

But the Trojans and glorious Hector would not have broken down the gates if Zeus had not turned his son Sarpedon against the Greeks, like a lion against cattle. With his gold-threaded shield before him, and waving his two spears in the air, he went at the Greeks as a mountain lion, who has had no meat for days, will break into a well-built sheepfold to attack the sheep. He may find the shepherds with their dogs and spears are keeping watch over them, but he is in no mind to be driven away till he has either taken one or himself been hit by a spear from some swift hand; so did his soul urge on Sarpedon. And he said to Glaucus, son of Hippolochus: 'Why are we two held in honor, given the first places, and the best meat and full cups in Lycia, while men look up to us as gods? And wide fields are ours, too, by the banks of Xanthus, and fair apple trees and far-stretching plowland. For this we must now take our stand at the head of the Lycians and face the Greeks before them, so that one may say to another: "Truly these men who rule in Lycia are not inglorious. They eat fat sheep and drink the best of wine; but they are strong, for they fight among the first in battle." Ah, friend, if when we were through this fight we could live on getting no older forever, I would neither fight myself nor send you into the battle. But death in a thousand shapes hangs over us always. So let us go forward, to win glory or give it to another.'

XXII [437–515] *The close, as Andromache learns of Hector's fate*

Andromache, Hector's wife, knew nothing of these things. No one had come to tell her that her husband was still outside the gates. She was working on a great purple cloth in the innermost part of her house, threading into it flowers of many colors. And she told her fair-haired handmaids to put a great vessel, a tripod, on the fire, for a hot bath to be ready for Hector when he came back from the fighting. She did not know that far from all baths Athene had overthrown him by the hand of Achilles. Then she heard loud cries and moans from the wall and she was shaken and the needle fell from her hand. And to her handmaids she said: 'Two of you, come with me and let us see what it is. It was Hecuba's voice I heard. I am afraid Achilles may have cut off Hector from the city.'

So saying she went quickly out and onto the wall. There she stopped and looked, and saw him as he was dragged before the city. The swift horses were dragging him toward the Greek ships. Then dark night came down on her and she fell backward breathing out her spirit. From her head fell her headdress and the veil that golden Aphrodite had given her on the day that Hector took her as his bride from Eëtion's house after bringing bride gifts unnumbered. Her husband's sisters and his brothers' wives came round her and supported her, for she was near to death in her trouble. Then she breathed again. And she came to herself and lifted up her voice in sorrow among the women of Troy, saying: 'Ah, Hector, to one fate we were born, you in Troy in the house of Priam and I in Thebe under wooded Placus in the house of Eëtion, ill-fated father of a cruel-fated child! Would that he had never begotten me. You go now into the house of Hades under earth and you leave me, in bitter sorrow, a widow in your house. And our son is a child. You can do nothing now for him, Hector, nor he for you. If he escapes from this war, still trouble and sorrow will be his, for other men will take your lands. A child is cut off from his friends on the day his father dies; his head is bent low and his face is wet with tears. In his need he goes to his father's friends; he takes one by the coat and pulls at the shirt of another. And of those who are moved with pity, one holds out a small cup to his mouth for a little; his lips he wets but his mouth is not made wet. And some child with a living father and mother pushes him away from the feast with blows saying: "Out with you! No father of yours is at our table." Then he goes back in tears to his mother – Astyanax, who ate only marrow and the rich fat of sheep on his father's knee; and when he had played till he was tired, he would sleep in his nurse's arms in a soft bed; but now that he has no father, evil days come on him, my poor Astyanax. The Trojans gave him that name because only you guarded their gates and their long walls. But now by the ships, far from your parents, worms will eat you when the dogs have ended. Naked you will lie, though here in your house are stores of linen, delicate, fair, made by the hands of women. But I will burn all this – no profit to you who will not lie in it – to be honor to you from the men and the women of Troy.'

So she said in her sorrowing, and the women joined their cry.   (1950)

H. D. F. KITTO (1897–1982)

This sample, by a very influential scholar and popularizer of ancient Greek literature and civilization, follows closely on Rieu. But seeks a middle way between the ideal of a popular narrative and of a scholarly interpretation.

The Iliad I [1–34]

Divine Muse, sing of the ruinous wrath of Achilles, Peleus' son, which brought ten thousand sorrows to the Greeks, sent the souls of many brave heroes down to the world of the dead, and left their bodies to be eaten by dogs and birds: and the will of Zeus was fulfilled. Begin where they first quarrelled, Agamemnon the King of Men, and great Achilles.

Which god was it who made them enemies? Apollo, son of Zeus and Leto. He was enraged with the King, and sent an evil pestilence on the host, and men began to die, because his priest had been treated with scorn by Atreus' son Agamemnon. He had come to the swift ships of the Achaeans to ransom his daughter; he had brought untold money to buy her back. In his hands, on his golden staff, he carried Apollo's garland: and he besought all the Achaeans, and above all their commanders, the two sons of Atreus:

'Sons of Atreus, and you other well-armed Achaeans, may the gods who live in Olympus grant it to you to sack Priam's city and to return home in triumph: only release for me my own daughter. Take this as the price, and show your respect for the son of Zeus, Apollo the far-shooter.'

Then all the Achaeans cried, 'Yes: respect the priest, and accept his splendid gifts'. – But not Agamemnon: this did not please him, but he sent Chryses away with contempt, and said roughly: 'Sir, let me not find you loitering by our hollow ships, now or at any other time, or no protection will you find in your holy sceptre and garland. I will not set free your daughter. Sooner than that, old age shall come upon her, in my house in Argos, a long way from her own country: she shall walk to and fro at the loom, and she shall come to my bed. Begone! and do not answer back, or you will not go safe and sound.'

So he spoke: and the old man was frightened, and obeyed. He walked away in grief along the shore of the splashing sea.

I [43–83]

So he prayed, and Phoebus Apollo heard him. He came down from the summits of Olympus, angry at heart, with his bow hung from his shoulder, and with his close-covered quiver: and as he moved, the arrows rattled at his shoulder, so angry was he. He came like night. Then he sat, far from the ships, and let fly an arrow, and terrible was the noise that came from his silver bow. First he assailed the pack animals and the swift dogs; then he aimed his painful darts against the men themselves, and he kept on shooting. Many a pyre was lit to burn the dead.

For nine days the god's shafts fell upon the army. On the tenth, great Achilles summoned the people to council; the white-armed goddess Hera had put it into his mind, for she was anxious for the Greeks, as she saw them dying.

When they were assembled there and were all together, swift-footed Achilles arose and spoke to them. 'Son of Atreus, now I think we shall be driven – if we escape death – to return home again, since we Achaeans are beset at the same time both by war and by pestilence. Come, let us ask some seer, or priest, or maybe a reader of dreams – for it is Zeus who sends dreams – who may tell us why Phoebus Apollo is so angry: whether he sees fault in us for some vow or sacrifice neglected. Perhaps in return for the smoke of lambs and sacrificial goats, he will save us from the pestilence.'

So Achilles spoke, and sat down. From among them Calchas arose, most excellent of seers, who knew what was, what would be, and what had been before. By the secret knowledge that Phoebus Apollo had given him he had guided the Achaean ships to Ilion. He then, with good intent, spoke, and said to them:

'Achilles, beloved of Zeus, you bid me expound the wrath of Lord Apollo who shoots from afar; therefore I tell you. But you must make a compact: you must swear on oath that you will be quick to help me in word and deed; for I think that someone will be angry, someone who has great sway over all the Argives, and the Achaeans obey him too: for when a King is angry with a poor man,

he is too strong for him. Even if he does swallow his rage for that
day, yet he keeps his resentment in his heart, to satisfy it another
time. Tell me if you will protect me.'   (1951)

RICHMOND LATTIMORE (b. 1906)

The Iliad of Homer is the translation of a distinguished scholar,
drawing on the latest Homeric scholarship. Formulae are preserved
wherever possible, but the idiom is that of the American English of
Lattimore's own day. The lines run to six beats but are much freer
and more various than would be any strict English hexameter.
Lattimore's *Iliad* exercised great influence via its use in schools and
universities.

The Iliad I [1-16] *The beginning of the epic*

    Sing, goddess, the anger of Peleus' son Achilleus
and its devastation, which put pains thousandfold upon the
    Achaians,
hurled in their multitudes to the house of Hades strong souls
of heroes, but gave their bodies to be the delicate feasting
of dogs, of all birds, and the will of Zeus was accomplished
since that time when first there stood in division of conflict
Atreus' son the lord of men and brilliant Achilleus.
    What god was it then set them together in bitter collision?
Zeus' son and Leto's, Apollo, who in anger at the king drove
10   the foul pestilence along the host, and the people perished,
since Atreus' son had dishonoured Chryses, priest of Apollo,
when he came beside the fast ships of the Achaians to ransom
back his daughter, carrying gifts beyond count and holding
in his hands wound on a staff of gold the ribbons of Apollo
who strikes from afar, and supplicated all the Achaians,
but above all Atreus' two sons, the marshals of the people . . .

V [1–75], *Diomedes and other Greek champions in the thick of combat*

There to Tydeus' son Diomedes Pallas Athene
granted strength and daring, that he might be conspicuous
among all the Argives and win the glory of valour.
She made weariless fire blaze from his shield and helmet
like that star of the waning summer who beyond all stars
rises bathed in the ocean stream to glitter in brilliance.
Such was the fire she made blaze from his head and his shoulders
and urged him into the middle fighting, where most were
  struggling.
  There was a man of the Trojans, Dares, blameless and
  bountiful,
10 priest consecrated to Hephaistos, and he had two sons,
Phegeus and Idaios, well skilled both in all fighting.
These two breaking from the ranks of the others charged
  against him,
riding their chariot as Diomedes came on, dismounted.
Now as in their advance these had come close to each other
first of the two Phegeus let go his spear far-shadowing.
Over the left shoulder of Tydeus' son passed the pointed
spear, nor struck his body, and Diomedes thereafter
threw with the bronze, and the weapon cast from his hand
  flew not vain
but struck the chest between the nipples and hurled him from
  behind
20 his horses. And Idaios leaping left the fair-wrought chariot
nor had he the courage to stand over his stricken brother.
Even so he could not have escaped the black death-spirit
but Hephaistos caught him away and rescued him, shrouded
  in darkness,
that the aged man might not be left altogether desolate.
But the son of high-hearted Tydeus drove off the horses

and gave them to his company to lead back to the hollow
    vessels.
Now as the high-hearted Trojans watched the two sons of
    Dares,
one running away, and one cut down by the side of his
    chariot,
the anger in all of them was stirred. But grey-eyed Athene
30 took violent Ares by the hand, and in words she spoke to
    him:
'Ares, Ares, manslaughtering, blood-stained, stormer of strong
    walls,
shall we not leave the Trojans and Achaians to struggle
after whatever way Zeus father grants glory to either,
while we two give ground together and avoid Zeus' anger?'
    So she spoke, and led violent Ares out of the fighting
and afterwards caused him to sit down by the sands of
    Skamandros
while the Danaans bent the Trojans back, and each of the
    princes
killed his man. And first the lord of men Agamemnon
hurled tall Odios, lord of the Halizones, from his chariot.
40 For in his back even as he was turning the spear fixed
between the shoulders and was driven on through the chest
    beyond it.
He fell, thunderously, and his armour clattered upon him.
    Idomeneus killed Phaistos the son of Maionian Boros,
who had come out of Tarne with the deep soil. Idomeneus
the spear-renowned stabbed this man just as he was
    mounting
behind his horses, with the long spear driven in the right
    shoulder.
He dropped from the chariot, and the hateful darkness took
    hold of him.
    The henchmen of Idomeneus stripped the armour from
    Phaistos,

while Menelaos son of Atreus killed with the sharp spear
50   Strophios' son, a man of wisdom in the chase, Skamandrios,
the fine huntsman of beasts. Artemis herself had taught him
to strike down every wild thing that grows in the mountain
            forest.
Yet Artemis of the showering arrows could not now help
            him,
no, nor the long spearcasts in which he had been pre-
            eminent,
but Menelaos the spear-famed, son of Atreus, stabbed him,
as he fled away before him, in the back with a spear thrust
between the shoulders and driven through to the chest beyond
            it.
He dropped forward on his face and his armour clattered
            upon him.
    Meriones in turn killed Phereklos, son of Harmonides,
60   the smith, who understood how to make with his hand all
            intricate
things, since above all others Pallas Athene had loved him.
He it was who had built for Alexandros the balanced
ships, the beginning of the evil, fatal to the other
Trojans, and to him, since he knew nothing of the gods'
            plans.
This man Meriones pursued and overtaking him
struck in the right buttock, and the spearhead drove straight
on and passing under the bone went into the bladder.
He dropped, screaming, to his knees, and death was a mist
            about him.
    Meges in turn killed Pedaios, the son of Antenor,
70   who, bastard though he was, was nursed by lovely Theano
with close care, as for her own children, to pleasure her
            husband.
Now the son of Phyleus, the spear-famed, closing upon him
struck him with the sharp spear behind the head at the tendon,

and straight on through the teeth and under the tongue cut
  the bronze blade,
and he dropped in the dust gripping in his teeth the cold
  bronze.   (1951)

The Odyssey of Homer (1965) can be seen to be far less convincing.
This was not Lattimore's world. It is as if Fitzgerald's rival version
(see page 286) has lamed his confidence.

The Odyssey XII [420–53] *The storm-tossed Odysseus reaches Kalypso's island*

'But I went on my way through the vessel, to where the
    high seas
had worked the keel free out of the hull, and the bare keel
    floated
on the swell, which had broken the mast off at the keel; yet
still there was a backstay made out of oxhide fastened
to it. With this I lashed together both keel and mast, then
rode the two of them, while the deadly stormwinds carried
    me.
  'After this the West Wind ceased from its stormy blowing,
and the South Wind came swiftly on, bringing to my spirit
grief that I must measure the whole way back to Charybdis.
All that night I was carried along, and with the sun rising
I came to the sea rock of Skylla, and dreaded Charybdis.
At this time Charybdis sucked down the sea's salt water,
but I reached high in the air above me, to where the tall fig
    tree
grew, and caught hold of it and clung like a bat; there was no
place where I could firmly brace my feet, or climb up it,
for the roots of it were far from me, and the branches hung
    out

far, big and long branches that overshadowed Charybdis.
Inexorably I hung on, waiting for her to vomit
the keel and mast back up again. I longed for them, and they
    came
20 late, at the time when a man leaves the law court, for dinner,
after judging the many disputes brought him by litigious
    young men;
that was the time it took the timbers to appear from
    Charybdis.
Then I let go my hold with hands and feet, and dropped off,
and came crashing down between and missing the two long
    timbers,
but I mounted these, and with both hands I paddled my way
    out.
But the Father of Gods and men did not let Skylla see me
again, or I could not have escaped from sheer destruction.
    'From there I was carried along nine days, and on the tenth
    night
the gods brought me to the island Ogygia, home of Kalypso
30 with the lovely hair, a dreaded goddess who talks with
    mortals.
She befriended me and took care of me. Why tell the rest of
this story again, since yesterday in your house I told it
to you and your majestic wife? It is hateful to me
to tell a story over again, when it has been well told.'   (1965)

W. H. AUDEN (1907–73)

This poem is, together with texts by Keats, Tennyson, Browning
and Pound, one of the finest 'Homer-experiences' in the language.
Note the arch echoes of Keats's 'Grecian Urn'.

The Shield of Achilles

> She looked over his shoulder
>   For vines and olive trees.
> Marble well-governed cities
>   And ships upon untamed seas.
> But there on the shining metal
>   His hands had put instead
> An artificial wilderness
>   And a sky like lead.

A plain without a feature, bare and brown,
10   No blade of grass, no sign of neighborhood.
Nothing to eat and nowhere to sit down.
    Yet, congregated on its blankness, stood
    An unintelligible multitude.
A million eyes, a million boots in line,
Without expression, waiting for a sign.

Out of the air a voice without a face
    Proved by statistics that some cause was just
In tones as dry and level as the place:
    No one was cheered and nothing was discussed:
20   Column by column in a cloud of dust
They marched away enduring a belief
Whose logic brought them, somewhere else, to grief.

> She looked over his shoulder
>   For ritual pieties.
> White flower-garlanded heifers,
>   Libation and sacrifice.
> But there on the shining metal
>   Where the altar should have been,
> She saw by his flickering forge-light
30   Quite another scene.

Barbed wire enclosed an arbitrary spot
   Where bored officials lounged (one cracked a joke)
And sentries sweated for the day was hot:
   A crowd of ordinary decent folk
   Watched from without and neither moved nor spoke
As three pale figures were led forth and bound
To three posts driven upright in the ground.

The mass and majesty of this world, all
   That carries weight and always weighs the same
40 Lay in the hands of others; they were small
   And could not hope for help and no help came:
   What their foes liked to do was done, their shame
Was all the worst could wish; they lost their pride
And died as men before their bodies died.

      She looked over his shoulder
        For athletes at their games,
     Men and women in a dance
        Moving their sweet limbs
     Quick, quick, to music.
50   But there on the shining shield
     His hands had set no dancing-floor
        But a weed-choked field.

A ragged urchin, aimless and alone,
   Loitered about that vacancy; a bird
Flew up to safety from his well-aimed stone:
   That girls are raped, that two boys knife a third,
   Were axioms to him, who'd never heard
Of any world where promises were kept.
Or one could weep because another wept.

60   The thin-lipped armorer,
        Hephaestos, hobbled away.
      Thetis of the shining breasts

Cried out in dismay
At what the god had wrought
To please her son, the strong
Iron-hearted man-slaying Achilles
Who would not live long.   (1952)

BARBARA LEONIE PICARD
(d. 1917)

A 'retelling of the entire story of the poem for young people'.
'Homers' for the young form a lively class of their own. Together
with Charles Lamb's, the Picard version is among the most
attractive.

The Odyssey IX [437–90] Polyphemus and the Cyclops

By that time it was dawn, and the rams were eager to be grazing
in the rich pastures. Bleating, they moved together to the entrance
of the cave, where Polyphemus felt across the back of each one as it
came to him, before passing it through into the courtyard. But he
never thought to feel beneath the animals, so the six men went
safely out. Last of all to come was the leader of the flock, walking
slowly under the weight of Odysseus, clinging to its fleece.

As Polyphemus felt its back he spoke to it. 'My good ram, you
are ever the foremost of the flock, leading the others to their
grazing ground. Why are you last today? Are you grieved for your
master, blinded by wicked No-one, and would stay to comfort
him? I would that you could speak and tell me where he hides, that
wretch who took away my sight. But go, dear ram, join your
companions in the fields.' And Polyphemus moved his hand aside
and the ram stepped through the opening into the sunlight, bearing
Odysseus.

Once outside the courtyard, Odysseus freed himself from his

hiding-place and went to release his companions. Then hastily they drove the sheep down to the ship and their comrades waiting on the shore. With no delay they stowed the flock on board and set out to row back to the island where the fleet was moored.

A little way from the shore Odysseus stood up in the ship and shouted with all his might, 'Now indeed, wicked Cyclops, do you know what ills your cruelty to helpless strangers has brought to you.'

Polyphemus heard him and came out from his cave in fury, and breaking off a huge piece of rock he flung it into the sea in the direction of Odysseus' voice. It fell in the water by the bows and the great waves made by its fall washed the ship back towards the shore; but Odysseus seized a long pole and pushed off again, and his men fell to rowing hard once more.   (1952)

ROBERT GRAVES (1895–1986)

A 'life-tragedy salted with humour'. To 'become entertainment once more'. The similes derive from 'authentic festival songs' of Ionian provenance. A more popular corpus of prose tales continues to challenge the immense prestige given to the 'Homeric' epics by the mid-sixth-century-BC Peisistratian recension (the editorial grouping of the more ancient and probably oral material). Homer's wit can be 'merciless': particularly in reference to Agamemnon in Books II, IV, and IX. The view of the Olympian gods is 'utterly cynical'. This is acceptable precisely at a time when the Greeks 'were already practising free philosophic speculation'. Achilles is 'the real villain of the piece'. His love of Patroclus 'proves to be pure self-love which grudges his comrade pre-eminence in battle'. The battles are never realistic. No common soldier ever kills a nobleman; the heavy-chariot tactics are already wholly unfamiliar to Homer. But Troy and the burning of it are historical (c.1230 BC). The similarities with the Irish *War of the Bulls* suggest a shared Indo-European fount – perhaps the *Mahabharata*. There are links to

Gilgamesh. Imitating the ancient Irish and Welsh bards, Graves will 'sing' only where prose does not suffice. This will restore the truth of the *Iliad* as 'mixed entertainment'.

The Anger of Achilles, Homer's Iliad II [182–234]
Odysseus restores order

Odysseus knew Athene's voice and, casting away his cloak – which Eurybates, the Ithacan herald, retrieved – ran through the camp, found Agamemnon, borrowed the aforesaid imperishable sceptre and, thus armed, walked around carrying out the goddess' instructions. Whenever he met an officer in command of a ship, he would say politely: 'My lord, it ill becomes you to catch this panic. Sit down, keep calm, and force your crew to do the same. You have entirely missed the drift of Agamemnon's speech: he was just testing the army's courage. And you had better take care that he does not punish you for this morning's rebellion. The foster-sons of Omniscient Zeus are proud of the divine honours bestowed on them; and he jealously protects them from affront.'

But whenever Odysseus met a rowdy man-at-arms, he shook the sceptre at him. 'Sit down,' he would shout, 'and await orders! You count for nothing, either as a soldier or a thinker. All Greeks cannot be kings. It is a bad army in which each soldier claims freedom of action: we need a united command, and our leader is Agamemnon, High King and representative of Zeus, Son of Cronus. Father Zeus, in his inscrutable wisdom, has conferred this sceptre on him, with the right to exact obedience from you.'

Odysseus made his authority felt everywhere; and the men hurried back to their benches on the Assembly Ground, raising as much noise as when:

> A western wave rolls growling up the reach
> And thunderously breaks on the long beach . . .

There they took their places again and everyone sat quiet – except a certain Thersites, who had no control over his tongue, and poured out an endless stream of abuse against his superiors, saying whatever came into his head that might raise a laugh. Thersites was by far the ugliest man in the Greek army: bandy-legged, lame, hump-backed, crook-necked and almost bald. His main butts were Achilles and Odysseus, who both detested him. On this occasion, careless of the annoyance his words might cause, he taunted Agamemnon. 'Son of Atreus,' he cried, 'what more can you want of us? We have surely by now filled your huts with enough bronze vessels and slave-girls to satisfy your greed? When a city is sacked, you are always voted the pick of the loot. I daresay you hope to do even better soon: by squeezing the father of some Trojan prisoner whom I or my comrades may take, for a gold ransom. Or shall we capture yet another pretty little concubine to warm your bed? No commander-in-chief should treat his men so meanly!'

IV [411–38] *The joining of battle*

Diomedes looked sternly at Sthenelus. 'Brother,' he said, 'I forbid you to utter another word! Our High King may exhort the troops in whatever way he pleases. After all, who stands to win the greatest glory if we defeat the Trojans and take their city? And who stands to suffer the worst disgrace if we abandon the siege ...? Come, we too must show our fighting spirit!' Then Diomedes leaped from the tail-board of his chariot with a clang of bronze that might have scared even a hero.

> The west wind blustering out at sea
>   Provokes a wave to lift its head,
> To travel shoreward menacingly
>   Compact and huge, a sight to dread;
> Arching, it breaks with an uproarious boom
> Against the headland, scattering clouds of spume.

The Greek army moved forward in the same relentless style, wave upon wave, bright sunlight glittering on arms and decorated armour. As soon as the commanders had given their orders, you would have thought them all dumb, so silently they advanced!

> Listen to the ewes complaining
>   In our wide courtyard;
> They can hear the lambs, I fear,
>   From their udders barred.
>
> What loud bleating and entreating!
>   Patience, pretty dams:
> Half the milk is for my master,
>   Half is for your lambs.

Just such a clamour was raised by the Trojan troops, who came from many distant regions and spoke no common language.

VI [440-66] Hector to Andromache

Hector answered: 'Your forebodings weigh heavily on my heart, yet I should lose my self-respect if the Trojan nobles and their womenfolk caught me malingering. I could not bring myself to do so, in any case; I have always fought courageously with the vanguard for my father's glory and my own. But let me tell you this: it is my conviction that our holy city must soon fall, and that every man in Troy must die around King Priam. What agony awaits my mother, my father, my brothers, and the many hundreds of brave Trojans doomed to lie in the dust at our enemies' feet! I confess, though, that all this troubles me little when I brood on the agony that awaits you – led weeping into slavery by some mail-clad conqueror! In Greece you will have to work the loom under the eye of a harsh mistress, and draw water at her orders from the spring of Messeis or of Hypereia, suffering ill-treatment and perpetual restraint. As your tears flow, fingers will point, and it will be said: "Look, she was once the wife of Hector, the Trojan Commander-in-Chief during the recent war!" Then fresh grief will stab your heart for the loss of a husband who so long postponed the dreadful hour of your captivity. May I lie deep beneath a barrow before you are rudely carried off – may I be spared the sound of your heart-broken shrieks!'

XIV [313-53] *Zeus to Hera*

'Darling Hera,' said Zeus, 'surely another day will do as well? Let us make love at once! Never in my entire life have I felt such intense longing for goddess or nymph as I feel for you this afternoon! Why, my interest in Ixion's wife Dia, on whom I begot the wise Peirithous, was nothing by comparison; and this also applies to Danaë, daughter of Acrisius, the girl with the beautiful ankles, on whom I begot the hero Perseus; and to the celebrated Europa, daughter of Phoenix, on whom I begot King Minos and his brother Rhadamanthus. Indeed, it applies to Semele, on whom I begot the universally adored Dionysus; and to Alcmene the Theban, on whom I begot bold Heracles; and to our sister Demeter, the goddess with the beautiful hair, on whom I begot Persephone; and to the famous Leto, on whom I begot Apollo and Artemis. Why, I would venture to say, dearest wife, that I have never yet conceived so delirious a passion even for you yourself!'

Hera's answer was as sly as before: 'Revered Son of Cronus, what a shocking idea! Do you actually mean us to make love up here, in full sight of Olympus? Suppose some god were to play spy, and tell the other Immortals all he had seen? I should not have the face to go home after that; it certainly would give me a pardonable grievance against you. But if I must humour you in this inconvenient fashion, pray escort me to your Olympian bed-chamber, with its stout doors hinged to pillars, built by our son Hephaestus. We can be private there.'

'No, no, Hera,' replied Zeus. 'You need not fear that any god or man will witness our marital sport! I shall spread an immense golden cloud over you, which the brightest eye in existence, the Sun's, would fail to pierce.'

Zeus then caught hold of Hera, laid her down masterfully, and took his pleasure of her. The earth beneath them was divinely induced to sprout a soft, thick, vigorous crop of fresh grass, tender clover, crocuses and hyacinth flowers, that raised the lovers a hand's breadth into the air. So they embraced, on the crest of Gargarus, covered by a golden cloud from which cool, sparkling dew dripped upon their naked bodies; until Zeus dozed off, conquered by the arts of Love and Sleep, still clasping Hera to his breast.

XVII [426–40] *Achilles' horses weep*

Meanwhile Achilles' horses, having escaped from the mêlée, stood weeping beside the river – they had wept ever since they saw Hector kill Patroclus. Automedon, son of Diores, tried to rouse them with blows of the whip, shouts, words of endearment; but they would not budge.

> Staunch as a head-stone on the tomb
>   Of man or woman dead,
> Each creature stood oppressed by gloom:
> In anguish at Patroclus' doom,
>   Abasing his proud head.
>
> Large mournful tears from every eye
>   Trickled without a sound;
> Their golden names, once flaunted high
> Above the yoke, drooped dismally
>   Upon the marshy ground.

XXI [97–136] *Achilles to Lycaon*

Achilles answered implacably: 'I reject this childish plea for mercy, and will accept no ransom. Until Patroclus died, I often spared suppliants, and sold them abroad; but now all Trojans whom I catch will die, especially all sons of King Priam! Yes,

friend, including you. Why bemoan your lot? Patroclus, a far better
fighter, is dead, too. And look at me! Did you ever see so strong or
so handsome a man? Yet, though my father was a hero, and my
mother a goddess, immediate death threatens me. Some day soon –
whether it will be morning, noon, or nightfall, and whether by
spear or arrow, nobody can foretell – I am doomed to fall in battle.'

Despair seized Lycaon, who let go Achilles' lance, and crouched
with arms outspread, awaiting the sword-sweep. Swiftly it descended,
sheering through collarbone and lungs. Lycaon tumbled prostrate,
and his lifeblood soaked the earth. Achilles took the corpse by
a foot and tossed it downstream, crying exultantly:

'Among the fish, Lycaon, lie!
Their dainty tongues your blood shall try;
Nor can Laothoë come near
To stretch your cold corpse on a bier,
With shrill lament; for there you go,
Borne on Scamander's rippling flow
To the salt bosom of the deep
Where dogfish hungrily shall leap
Through turbid waters, quick to tear
Strips from your white flesh floating there.

'So perish every man of Troy!
Whole squadrons now I will destroy,
Forcing the rest to flee pell-mell
Until I sack her Citadel.
Think not, my foes, that sacrifice
Of bulls, or other rich device –
Such as to toss a chariot-team
Alive into Scamander's stream –
Shall curb my vengeance-hungry blade!
An ample blood-price must be paid
For those who with Patroclus died
When, all too long, I nursed my pride.'

This speech enraged the River-god Xanthus   (1959)

ENNIS REES (b. 1925)

This version (Rees also translated the *Iliad*) aims 'at effective expression in the large area between the stilted and the vulgar and always with regard to dramatic context'. The form is that of a 'loose measure of five major stresses plus a varying number of relatively unaccented syllables'. It has its distinct lightness and narrative pace.

The Odyssey X [503–49] *Circe tells Odysseus of the voyage ahead*

   'To this the beautiful goddess answered at once:
"Zeus-sprung son of Laertes, resourceful Odysseus,
When you get to your ship, don't trouble yourself for a pilot,
But set up the mast, spread the white sail, and sit down,
While the North Wind carries her on. But when you have crossed
The stream of Oceanus, you'll come to a level shore
And the groves of Persephone – great poplars and fruit-dropping willows.
Draw your ship up on the beach by swirling Oceanus
And proceed to the moldering house of Hades. There
10   The River of Flaming Fire and the River of Wailing,
A branch of the waters of Styx, meet round a rock
And go thundering on into the waters of Acheron.
This is the spot, my lord, that I bid you find.
Then dig a pit something less than two feet on a side
And pour to every ghost a libation around it,
With milk and honey first, then with sweet wine,
And finally with water, sprinkling grains of white barley on all.
Then earnestly, fervently pray to the feeble dead,

Vowing that when you reach Ithaca, in the halls of home
20 You will sacrifice the best of your barren heifers and heap
The altar high with many good things, and that
To Tiresias alone you will offer a solid black ram,
The most outstanding ram in the flock. After
These promises and prayers to the ghostly nation, sacrifice
A ram and black ewe, holding their heads toward Erebus,
But your own in the other direction toward the stream of
       Oceanus.
Then many ghosts of those who are gone will come
       thronging.
Call to your men to flay and burn the sheep
That lie there victims of the ruthless bronze, and to pray
30 For all they are worth, especially to powerful Hades
And dread Persephone. As for you, draw your sharp sword
From beside your thigh and sit there, and do not allow
The strengthless dead any nearer the blood until
You have talked with Tiresias. That seer, O leader of men,
Will soon appear and tell you the way of return
And how far you have to go on the fish-full sea."
    'So she spoke, and shortly thereafter came Dawn
Of the golden throne. Then Circe gave me a tunic
And cloak to put on, while she slipped into a shimmering
40 White gown — long, lovely, and very sheer.
Round her waist she put an exquisite golden sash
And arranged a veil high up on her head. I went
Through the palace and gently aroused my men, saying
To each of them:
    '"Enough of sweet sleep. It is time
To get up and go. For at last my lady Circe
Has given the word."'   (1960)

THOM GUNN (b. 1929)

Of modern Homeric 'echoes', these two poems are among the best known. 'The Wound' has passed into the school syllabus. There are, in Thom Gunn's art and persona, elements which accord almost naturally with the distant epic source.

The Wound

The huge wound in my head began to heal
About the beginning of the seventh week.
Its valleys darkened, its villages became still:
For joy I did not move and dared not speak,
Not doctors would cure it, but time, its patient skill.

And constantly my mind returned to Troy.
After I sailed the seas I fought in turn
On both sides, sharing even Helen's joy
Of place, and growing up – to see Troy burn –
10 As Neoptolemus, that stubborn boy.

I lay and rested as prescription said.
Maneuvered with the Greeks, or sallied out
Each day with Hector. Finally my bed
Became Achilles' tent, to which the lout
Thersites came reporting numbers dead.

I was myself: subject to no man's breath:
My own commander was my enemy.
And while my belt hung up, sword in the sheath,
Thersites shambled in and breathlessly
20 Cackled about my friend Patroclus' death.

I called for armor, rose, and did not reel.
But, when I thought, rage at his noble pain
Flew to my head, and turning I could feel
My wound break open wide. Over again
I had to let those storm-lit valleys heal.   (1961)

Moly

Nightmare of beasthood, snorting, how to wake.
I woke. What beasthood skin she made me take?

Leathery toad that ruts for days on end,
Or cringing dribbling dog, man's servile friend,

Or cat that prettily pounces on its meat,
Tortures it hours, then does not care to eat:

Parrot, moth, shark, wolf, crocodile, ass, flea.
What germs, what jostling mobs there were in me.

   These seem like bristles, and the hide is tough.
10 No claw or web here: each foot ends in hoof.

Into what bulk has method disappeared?
Like ham, streaked. I am gross – gray, gross, flap-eared.

The pale-lashed eyes my only human feature.
My teeth tear, tear. I am the snouted creature

That bites through anything, root, wire, or can.
If I was not afraid I'd eat a man.

Oh a man's flesh already is in mine.
Hand and foot poised for risk. Buried in swine.

I root and root, you think that it is greed,
20   It is, but I seek out a plant I need.

Direct me, gods, whose changes are all holy,
To where it flickers deep in grass, the moly:

Cool flesh of magic in each leaf and shoot,
From milky flower to the black forked root.

From this fat dungeon I could rise to skin
And human title, putting pig within.

I push my big gray wet snout through the green,
Dreaming the flower I have never seen.   (1971)

ROBERT FITZGERALD (1910–85)

Robert Fitzgerald's *Odyssey* is one of the major achievements in the
canon. It is the work of a distinguished poet, who attains to the first
rank in this act of translation. The blank verse is highly organized
around a basic iambic beat against which it varies length and
cadence. Like few other versions, this *Odyssey* reflects the narrative
constancy of the original, its complex tactics of self-reference and
the halo of humane sadness which so many other translations fail to
render. Note also the 'lyrics' within the narration.

The Odyssey IV [351–93] *Meneláos' account of Proteus'*
daughter Eidothea

During my first try at a passage homeward
the gods detained me, tied me down to Egypt –
for I had been too scant in hekatombs,

and gods will have the rules each time remembered.
There is an island washed by the open sea
lying off Nile mouth – seamen call it Pharos –
distant a day's sail in a clean hull
with a brisk land breeze behind. It has a harbor,
a sheltered bay, where shipmasters
10   take on dark water for the outward voyage.
Here the gods held me twenty days becalmed.
No winds came up, seaward escorting winds
for ships that ride the sea's broad back, and so
my stores and men were used up; we were failing
had not one goddess intervened in pity –
Eidothea, daughter of Proteus,
the Ancient of the Sea. How I distressed her!
I had been walking out alone that day –
my sailors, thin-bellied from the long fast,
20   were off with fish hooks, angling on the shore –
then she appeared to me, and her voice sang:

'What fool is here, what drooping dance of dreams?
Or can it be, friend, that you love to suffer?
How can you linger on this island, aimless
and shiftless, while your people waste away?'

To this I quickly answered:

                                        'Let me tell you,
goddess, whatever goddess you may be,
these doldrums are no will of mine. I take it
the gods who own broad heaven are offended.
30   Why don't you tell me – since the gods know everything –
who has me pinned down here?
How am I going to make my voyage home?'

Now she replied in her immortal beauty:

'I'll put it for you clearly as may be, friend.

The Ancient of the Salt Sea haunts this place,
immortal Proteus of Egypt; all the deeps
are known to him; he serves under Poseidon,
and is, they say, my father.
If you could take him by surprise and hold him,
40   he'd give you course and distance for your sailing
homeward across the cold fish-breeding sea.
And should you wish it, noble friend, he'd tell you
all that occurred at home, both good and evil,
while you were gone so long and hard a journey.'

Fitzgerald is supreme in the Nekya.

XI [477–565] *Odysseus' meeting with the shades of Achilles
and of Ajax*

'Akhilleus, Peleus' son, strongest of all
among the Akhaians, I had need of foresight
such as Teiresias alone could give
to help me, homeward bound for the crags of Ithaka.
I have not yet coasted Akhaia, not yet
touched my land; my life is all adversity.
But was there ever a man more blest by fortune
than you, Akhilleus? Can there ever be?
We ranked you with immortals in your lifetime,
10   we Argives did, and here your power is royal
among the dead men's shades. Think, then, Akhilleus:
you need not be so pained by death.'

To this
he answered swiftly:

'Let me hear no smooth talk
of death from you, Odysseus, light of councils.

Better, I say, to break sod as a farm hand
for some poor country man, on iron rations,
than lord it over all the exhausted dead.
Tell me, what news of the prince my son: did he
come after me to make a name in battle
20   or could it be he did not? Do you know
if rank and honor still belong to Peleus
in the towns of the Myrmidons? Or now, may be,
Hellas and Phthia spurn him, seeing old age
fetters him, hand and foot. I cannot help him
under the sun's rays, cannot be that man
I was on Troy's wide seaboard, in those days
when I made bastion for the Argives
and put an army's best men in the dust.
Were I but whole again, could I go now
30   to my father's house, one hour would do to make
my passion and my hands no man could hold
hateful to any who shoulder him aside.'

Now when he paused I answered:

                                                'Of all that —

of Peleus' life, that is — I know nothing;
but happily I can tell you the whole story
of Neoptólemos, as you require.
In my own ship I brought him out from Skyros
to join the Akhaians under arms.

                                          And I can tell you,

in every council before Troy thereafter
40   your son spoke first and always to the point;
no one but Nestor and I could out-debate him.
And when we formed against the Trojan line
he never hung back in the mass, but ranged
far forward of his troops — no man could touch him
for gallantry. Aye, scores went down before him
in hard fights man to man. I shall not tell

all about each, or name them all – the long
roster of enemies he put out of action,
taking the shock of charges on the Argives.
50   But what a champion his lance ran through
in Eurypulos the son of Télephos! Keteians
in throngs around that captain also died –
all because Priam's gifts had won his mother
to send the lad to battle; and I thought
Memnon alone in splendor ever outshone him.

But one fact more: while our picked Argive crew
still rode that hollow horse Epeios built,
and when the whole thing lay with me, to open
the trapdoor of the ambuscade or not,
60   at that point our Danaan lords and soldiers
wiped their eyes, and their knees began to quake,
all but Neoptólemos. I never saw
his tanned cheek change color or his hand
brush one tear away. Rather he prayed me,
hand on hilt, to sortie, and he gripped
his tough spear, bent on havoc for the Trojans.
And when we had pierced and sacked Priam's tall city
he loaded his choice plunder and embarked
with no scar on him; not a spear had grazed him
70   nor the sword's edge in close work – common wounds
one gets in war. Arês in his mad fits
knows no favorites.'

                                    But I said no more,
for he had gone off striding the field of asphodel,
the ghost of our great runner, Akhilleus Aiákidês,
glorying in what I told him of his son.

Now other souls of mournful dead stood by,
each with his troubled questioning, but one
remained alone, apart: the son of Télamon,

Aîas, it was – the great shade burning still
80   because I had won favor on the beachhead
in rivalry over Akhilleus' arms.
The Lady Thetis, mother of Akhilleus,
laid out for us the dead man's battle gear,
and Trojan children, with Athena,
named the Danaan fittest to own them. Would
god I had not borne the palm that day!
For earth took Aîas then to hold forever,
the handsomest and, in all feats of war,
noblest of the Danaans after Akhilleus.
90   Gently therefore I called across to him:

'Aîas, dear son of royal Télamon,
you would not then forget, even in death,
your fury with me over those accurst
calamitous arms? – and so they were, a bane
sent by the gods upon the Argive host.
For when you died by your own hand we lost
a tower, formidable in war. All we Akhaians
mourn you forever, as we do Akhilleus;
and no one bears the blame but Zeus.
100   He fixed that doom for you because he frowned
on the whole expedition of our spearmen.
My lord, come nearer, listen to our story!
Conquer your indignation and your pride.'

But he gave no reply, and turned away,
following other ghosts toward Erebos.
Who knows if in that darkness he might still
have spoken, and I answered?

XXIII [264–99] *Odysseus tells Penélopê of the last voyage to come*

                                                    'My strange one,
must you again, and even now,
urge me to talk? Here is a plodding tale;
no charm in it, no relish in the telling.
Teirêsias told me I must take an oar
and trudge the mainland, going from town to town,
until I discover men who have never known
the salt blue sea, nor flavor of salt meat –
strangers to painted prows, to watercraft
10   and oars like wings, dipping across the water.
The moment of revelation he foretold
was this, for you may share the prophecy:
some traveller falling in with me will say:
"A winnowing fan, that on your shoulder, sir?"
There I must plant my oar, on the very spot,
with burnt offerings to Poseidon of the Waters:
a ram, a bull, a great buck boar. Thereafter
when I come home again, I am to slay
full hekatombs to the gods who own broad heaven,
one by one.
20   Then death will drift upon me
from seaward, mild as air, mild as your hand,
in my well-tended weariness of age,
contented folk around me on our island.
He said all this must come.'

                                          Penélopê said:

'If by the gods' grace age at least is kind,
we have that promise – trials will end in peace.'

So he confided in her, and she answered.
Meanwhile Eurýnomê and the nurse together
laid soft coverlets on the master's bed,
30   working in haste by torchlight. Eurýkleia
retired to her quarters for the night,
and then Eurýnomê, as maid-in-waiting,
lighted her lord and lady to their chamber
with bright brands.

      She vanished.

            So they came

into that bed so steadfast, loved of old,
opening glad arms to one another.
Telémakhos by now had hushed the dancing,
40   hushed the women. In the darkened hall
he and the cowherd and the swineherd slept.   (1961)

By comparison, the *Iliad* (1974) is much less convincing. Fitzgerald
tires of the constant slaughter and public rhetoric. This is simply not
his poem. It is Achilles' shield that elicits the best in this task.

The *Iliad* XVIII [541–605] *Achilles' shield*

Upon the shield, soft terrain, freshly plowed,
he pictured: a broad field, and many plowmen
here and there upon it. Some were turning
ox teams at the plowland's edge, and there
as one arrived and turned, a man came forward
putting a cup of sweet wine in his hands.
They made their turns-around, then up the furrows
drove again, eager to reach the deep field's
limit; and the earth looked black behind them,
10   as though turned up by plows. But it was gold,
all gold – a wonder of the artist's craft.

He put there, too, a king's field. Harvest hands
were swinging whetted scythes to mow the grain,
and stalks were falling along the swath
while binders girded others up in sheaves
with bands of straw – three binders, and behind them
children came as gleaners, proffering
their eager armfuls. And amid them all
the king stood quietly with staff in hand,
20   happy at heart, upon a new-mown swath.
To one side, under an oak tree his attendants
worked at a harvest banquet. They had killed
a great ox, and were dressing it; their wives
made supper for the hands, with barley strewn.

A vineyard then he pictured, weighted down
with grapes: this all in gold; and yet the clusters
hung dark purple, while the spreading vines
were propped on silver vine-poles. Blue enamel
he made the enclosing ditch, and tin the fence,
30   and one path only led into the vineyard
on which the loaded vintagers took their way
at vintage time. Lighthearted boys and girls
were harvesting the grapes in woven baskets,
while on a resonant harp a boy among them
played a tune of longing, singing low
with delicate voice a summer dirge. The others,
breaking out in song for the joy of it,
kept time together as they skipped along.

The artisan made next a herd of longhorns,
40   fashioned in gold and tin: away they shambled,
lowing, from byre to pasture by a stream
that sang in ripples, and by reeds a-sway.
Four cowherds all of gold were plodding after
with nine lithe dogs beside them.

On the assault,
in two tremendous bounds, a pair of lions
caught in the van a bellowing bull, and off
they dragged him, followed by the dogs and men.
Rending the belly of the bull, the two
gulped down his blood and guts, even as the herdsmen
50   tried to set on their hunting dogs, but failed:
no trading bites with lions for those dogs,
who halted close up, barking, then ran back.

And on the shield the great bowlegged god
designed a pasture in a lovely valley,
wide, with silvery sheep, and huts and sheds
and sheepfolds there.

A dancing floor as well
he fashioned, like that one in royal Knossos
Daidalos made for the Princess Ariadnê.
Here young men and the most desired young girls
60   were dancing, linked, touching each other's wrists,
the girls in linen, in soft gowns, the men
in well-knit khitons given a gloss with oil;
the girls wore garlands, and the men had daggers
golden-hilted, hung on silver lanyards.
Trained and adept, they circled there with ease
the way a potter sitting at his wheel
will give it a practice twirl between his palms
to see it run; or else, again, in lines
as though in ranks, they moved on one another:
70   magical dancing! All around, a crowd
stood spellbound as two tumblers led the beat
with spins and handsprings through the company.   (1974)

ROBERT LOWELL (1917–77)

Seeking to reproduce '*a* tone rather than *the* tone' of the original, Lowell tries to achieve what his authors 'might have done if they were writing their poems now and in America'. In translating the grim passage of the maddened Achilles' slaying of Lykaon in Book XXI, Lowell begins with the opening lines of the whole epic. He does so in order to stress the Achillean *menis*, that boundless rage on which the *Iliad* turns. Lowell's violent *mania* is a brilliant stab at the singularity of Homer's usage.

The *Iliad* I [1–7], XXI [99–135]

The Killing of Lykaon

Sing for me, Muse, the mania of Achilles
that cast a thousand sorrows on the Greeks
and threw so many huge souls into hell,
heroes who spilled their lives as food for dogs
and darting birds. God's will was working out,
from that time when first fell apart fighting
Atrides, king of men, and that god, Achilles . . .

*

'Coward, do not speak to me of ransom!
Before the day of terror overtook Patroklos,
10   sparing Trojans was my heart's choice and rest –
thousands I seized alive and sold like sheep!
Now there's not one who'll run out with his life,
should the god throw him to me before Troy,
but none are more accursed than Priam's sons . . .
You too must die, my dear. Why do you care?
Patroklos, a much better man, has died.
Or look at me – how large and fine I am –

a goddess bore me, and my father reigned,
yet I too have my destiny and death:
20   either at sunrise, night, or at high noon,
some warrior will spear me down in the lines,
or stick me with an arrow through the heel.'

He spoke so, and Lykaon lost his heart,
his spear dropped, and he fluttered his two hands
begging Achilles to hold back his sword.
The sword bit through his neck and collarbone,
and flashed blue sky. His face fell in the dust,
the black blood spouted out, and soaked the earth.

Achilles hurled Lykaon by his heel
30   in the Skamander, and spoke these wingéd words:
'Lie with the fish, they'll dress your wounds, and lick
away your blood, and have no care for you,
nor will your mother groan beside your pyre
by the Skamander, nor will women wail
as you swirl down the rapids to the sea,
but the dark shadows of the fish will shiver,
lunging to snap Lykaon's silver fat.
Die, Trojans – you must die till I reach Troy –
you'll run in front, I'll scythe you down behind,
40   nor will the azure Skamander save your lives,
whirling and silver, though you kill your bulls
and sheep, and throw a thousand one-hoofed horse,
still living, in the ripples. You must die,
and die and die and die, until the blood
of Hellas and Patroklos is avenged,
killed by the running ships when I was gone.'   (1962)

CHRISTOPHER LOGUE (b. 1926)

Christopher Logue's fragments out of the *Iliad* (the *Patrocleia* appeared in 1962, *Pax* in 1967) are an act of genius. They raise the vexing question of the access of a translator to an original whose language has to be translated for him (cf. the comparable wonder of Pound's *Cathay*). At several points, Logue's transmutations of the *Iliad* into 'now' seem to us to match in 'purchase' and brilliance anything in this collection. Homer and his audience would, we imagine, have thrilled to that image of the forward rush of Achilles' immortal horses 'as in dreams or at Cape Kennedy'. 'Translation' blazing into great poetry. Further fragments of this translation are continuing to appear.

The *Iliad*. Based on Book XVI *Hector goes after Patroklos*

Rat,
pearl,
onion,
honey:
these colours came before the sun
    lifted above the ocean
                    bringing light
    alike to mortals and immortals.

    And through this falling brightness
10 through the by now
        mosque,
        eucalyptus,
        utter blue,
            came Thetis,
        gliding across the azimuth,

with armour the colour of moonlight laid on Her forearms,
   palms upturned towards the sun,
                     hovering above the fleet,
   Her skyish face towards her son,

20   Achilles,
gripping the body of Patroklos naked and dead against his own,
   weeping terribly,
             while Thetis spoke:
   '*Son . . .*'
The soldiers looking on;
   looking away from it; remembering their own:
'*Grieving will not change what Heaven has done.*
Suppose you throw your hate after Patroklos' soul,
Who besides Troy will be the gainers?
30   *See what I've brought.*'

And as she laid the moonlit armour on the sand
it chimed;
   and the sounds that came from it,
followed the light that came from it,
   like sighing,
         saying,
Made In Heaven.

And those who had the neck to watch Achilles weep
could not look now. Nobody looked. They were afraid.

40   Except Achilles. Looked,
lifted a piece of it between his hands; turned it;
tested the weight of it; then,
spun the holy tungsten like a star between his knees,
slitting his eyes against the flare, some said,
but others thought the hatred shuttered by his lids,
   made him protect the metal.

His eyes like furnace doors ajar.

When he had got its weight
and let its industry console his grief a bit,
50   'I'll fight'
he said. Simple as that. 'I'll fight.'

And so Troy fell.

'But while I fight what will become of this' –
Patroklos – 'Mother?
'Inside an hour a thousand slimy things will burrow.
And if the fight drags on his flesh will swarm like water
        boiling.'
    And She:
'*Son, while you fight*
        Nothing shall taint him,
60   *Sun will not touch him,*
        Nor the slimy things.'

Promising this she slid
rare ickors in the seven born openings of Patroklos' head,
    making his carrion radiant.
And her Achilles went to make amends,
walking alone beside the broken lace that hung
    over the sea's green fist.

The sea that is always counting.

    Ever since men began in time, time and
70   *Time again they met in parliaments,*
    Where, in due turn, letting the next man speak,
    With mouthfuls of soft air they tried to stop
    Themselves from ravening their talking throats;
    Hoping enunciated airs would fall
    With verisimilitude in different minds,
    And bring some concord to those minds, soft air

> *Between the hatred dying animals*
> *Monotonously bear toward themselves,*
> *Only soft air to underwrite the in-*
80 *Built violence of being and meld it to*
> *Something more civil, rarer than true forgiveness.*
> *No work was lovelier in history;*
> *And nothing failed so often: knowing this*
> *The Army came to hear Achilles say:*
> *'Pax, Agamemnon.' And Agamemnon's 'Pax.'*   (1962)

Based on Book XIX *Achilles sets out to avenge Patroklos after receiving his new arms and armour*

Achilles stands; stretches; turns on his heel,
punches the sunlight, bends, then – jumps! . . .
and lets the world turn fractionally beneath his feet.

Noon.
In the foothills melons roll out of their green hidings.
Heat.

He walks towards the chariot.
Greece waits.

Over the wells in Troy mosquitoes hover.

10   Beside the chariot.
Soothing the perfect horses; watching his driver cinch,
shake out the reins, fold, lay them across the rail;
dapple and white the horses are, perfect they are,
sneezing to clear their cool black muzzles.

He mounts.

The chariot's basket dips. The whip
fires in between the horses' ears,

and as in dreams or at Cape Kennedy they rise,
slowly it seems, their chests like royals, yet,
20 behind them in a double plume the sand curls up
a yellow canopy,
is barely dented by their flying hooves
and wheels that barely touch the world,
and the wind slams shut behind them.

'Fast as you are,' Achilles says,
'when twilight makes the armistice,
take care you don't leave me behind
as you left my Patroklos.'

And as he ran the white horse turned its tall face back
30 and said:

'Prince,
This time we will, this time we must, but this time cannot
        last.
And when we leave you not for dead, but dead,
God will not call us negligent as you have done.'

And Achilles, shaken, says:
'I know I will not make old bones.'

And lays his scourge along their racing flanks.

Someone has left a spear stuck in the sand.   (1967)

Based on Book XIX

Banner behind slatted banner,
Blue overwhelming gold, gold over blue,
It was Patroklos' turn to run
Wide-armed, staring into the fight, and desperate
To hide (to blind that voice) to hide

Behind the moving blades.
                              And as he ran
Apollo dressed as Priam's brother
Settled beside the inner gates
10   And strolled with Hector for a while, and took his arm
And, mentioning the ways of duty, love, good-conduct,
And the other perishable joys infecting men,
Dissolved his cowardice with promises.
Think of it: They stand like brothers, man and god,
Chatting together on the parapet that spans the inner gate.
The elder points. The other nods. And the plumes nod
Over them both. Patroclus cannot see
The Uncle's finger leading Hector's eye
Towards his heart. Nor does he hear Apollo whispering
20   '*Achilles' heart will break* . . .' And neither man
Imagines that a god discusses mortals with a mortal.

   So Hector mounts. Half of each pair of gates swings up,
And with the sun across his shoulders like a metal stole
   Hector comes out.

   The daylight weakens. Up on the hillside
Women waist-deep in dusk sing while working.
The first movement of sunset turns the blue air
   Darker blue.

   Patroclus fought like dreaming.
30   His head thrown up, his mouth – wide as a shrieking mask –
Sucked at the air to nourish his infuriated body,
And the Trojans seem to be drawn to him,
Locked round his waist, red water, washed against his chest,
And laid their tired necks beside his sword like birds,
– Is it a god? Divine? Needing no tenderness? –
Yet instantly they touch he butts them,
Cuts them back

You know from books and talking pictures,
How people without firearms set about
40 *Killing a tiger that has grown too old*
To prey on antelope or zebra and
Must confine its diet to the slower
Animals like man. Following its spoor,
They rig a long funnel of netting up
On spikes (like pointed clothes-props) and the lean
Striped beast is driven down its throat by gongs.
The net is shut. And when the beast is tired out
The humans kill it in their own good time.
But if the net breaks many humans die.

50 Likewise Patroclus broke among the Trojans.
A set of zealous bones covered with flesh,
Finished with bronze, dipped in blood,
And the whole being inspired by ferocity.

— Kill them!
My sweet Patroclus,

— Kill them!
As many as you can,
For
Coming behind you in the dusk you felt
60 – What was it? — felt the darkness part and then

Apollo!

Who had been patient with you,
Struck.   (1967)

ALBERT COOK (b. 1925)

Cook is both scholar and learned poet. He provides a line-by-line reading in which the formulaic texture of the original is respected. Other early Indo-European literary works are brought to bear on Cook's lively sense of the 'civilized subtlety' of Homer's figurative idiom.

The *Odyssey* XIII [59–138] *Odysseus heads for home from Alcinoos' court, but the rage of Poseidon persists*

'May you constantly fare well, my queen, till old age
And death come upon you, which do exist for men.
But I am going now. Enjoy yourself in this house,
With your children and your people and King Alcinoos.'
When he had said this, godly Odysseus went over the threshold.
Alcinoos in his might sent a herald along with him
To lead him to the swift ship and the strand of the sea.
And Arete sent serving women along with him,
One of whom held a well-washed mantle and tunic,
10 Another she sent with her to bring the stout chest along,
And still another was carrying bread and red wine.
And when they had come down to the ship and the sea,
At once his noble escorts took those things and placed them
Inside the hollow ship, all of the food and drink.
They spread out a blanket and linen cloth for Odysseus
On the deck of the hollow ship, so he might sleep without
     waking,
Upon the stern. He himself boarded too and lay down
In silence. Each of them sat down at the oarlocks
In order. They loosed the cable from the pierced stone.
20 As soon as they leaned on the oars and flung up salt water
     with the blade
For him there fell down upon his eyelids a balmy sleep,

Unwaking, most sweet, nearest in semblance to death.
As for the ship, the way four yoked stallions on a plain
All rush on together under the blows of a whip,
Leap up high, and pursue their journey rapidly;
So was her stern raised up, and behind her there surged
A great purple wave of the loud-roaring sea.
She ran safely and steadily, nor could the circling
Hawks, the nimblest of winged things, have kept up,
30   So rapidly did it run as it cut the waves of the sea
Carrying a man who had plans like those of the gods,
Who in time past had suffered very many pains in his heart,
Passing through the wars of men and the troublesome waves,
But at this time he slept without a tremor, forgetting what he
          had suffered.
When the brightest star rose up that most of all
Comes on to announce the light of early-born dawn,
At that time did the seafaring ship reach the island.
There is a certain harbor of Phorcys, the old man of the sea,
In the land of Ithaca; and there, jutting out on it,
40   Are two headlands broken off, sloping down to the harbor.
They give shelter against the great wave from hard-blowing
          winds
Outside. And inside of it well-timbered ships remain
Without a cable when they reach the measure of mooring.
At the head of the harbor is an olive with long leaves,
And close to that is a pleasant and shadowy cavern
Sacred to the nymphs who are called Naiades.
And in it there are mixing bowls and two-handled jars
Of stone. And the bees store up their honey in them.
There are very long stone looms in it, where the nymphs
50   Weave sea purple mantles, a wonder to behold,
And ever-flowing waters are there. It has two doors,
One toward the North Wind, accessible to men,
And the other one divine is toward the South Wind, nor
          may men
Approach by that one, but it is a path for immortals.

The men, who knew it beforehand, drove the ship in there;
And then she was beached on the mainland, half her whole
    length
As she ran in, so fast was she pushed on by the rowers' hands.
They got out of the well-benched ship onto dry land.
First they raised Odysseus out of the hollow ship,
60   The linen sheet and the glistening blanket and all;
They set him down on the sand overcome with sleep.
They lifted out the goods the noble Phaeacians had given
As he was going home through great-hearted Athene's help,
And then put them in a heap by the base of the olive tree,
Out of the path lest by chance some wayfaring man
Might find and despoil them before Odysseus woke up.
Then they started back homeward. Nor did the earth-shaker
Forget the curses he had made originally
Against godlike Odysseus. And he asked about Zeus's plan:
70   'Father Zeus, I myself shall no longer be honored
Among the immortal gods when mortals do not respect me,
The Phaeacians, who are of my very own descent.
For I just now said Odysseus would suffer many ills
Before he got home; I have never deprived him of a return
Entirely, since you promised this first and nodded agreement.
Yet these men have brought him asleep on the ocean in a
    swift ship,
Have set him down in Ithaca and given him prodigious gifts,
Bronze and gold and woven clothing aplenty,
Much more than Odysseus ever would have taken from Troy
80   If he had arrived unharmed with his share of booty.'   (1967)

EDWIN MORGAN (b. 1920)

Composed in 1968, this passage is typical of the robust, almost colloquial manner aimed at by verse-translations in the later 1960s.

The *Iliad* XVII [735-61] *The Greeks retreat to the ships*

See now the two Greeks stumbling on with Patroclus
out from the fight, towards the shelter of the ships,
with the war pulsing about them wild as a fire
that leaps up unannounced in a busy city
and fastens blazing on houses which melt away
in ruinous flames, to the howling of the wind –
so, back they went, under a burden of clamour
raised by the clash of men and horses without break.

See them like mules exerting all their strength to draw
10   downhill some log or some great plank for a shipyard,
tugging it by a crazy track, till strain and sweat
have almost burst their hearts – so they went stumbling on.
Behind them the Ajaxes held the enemy
as a wooded hogback of land bristling across
the open country will stem a flood, checking spates
of ruinous rivers, forcing them to turn back
down along the flatlands – impotently foaming
at that firm barrier. The Trojans still attacked,
the Ajaxes still defended the rear, but now
20   against two men who made the task hard: Aeneas
Anchises' son, Hector the dazzling. Imagine
a cloud of starlings or jackdaws clattering up
and crying out in panic at sight of a cruising hawk,
the sign of death to birds like them – so Greek with Greek
fled from Aeneas and Hector crying in fear,
careless of the fight. And the trench was littered round
with good Greek armour as they fled.   (1968)

HUGO MANNING

The opening of this long poem is as distant from any Homeric text
as the (flexible) limits of this anthology will allow. Yet there is in
this evocation of 'the sea-fox' uncertainly desperate for homecoming
a vivid inference of Odysseus at the hour of shipwreck.

The Secret Sea

I

Seen is the shellback who rides his sea –
Odysseus, child of animus he shares
With fishing bird, shore crab, samphire, dulse –,
Seen by starness, moon in the night,
That is motherness strange to lull and excite
Design he is, counterpoint, and flexuous skein:
The love and the fury that reveal and make
Fragmentations dying   this dying towards life:
Ineluctable felt in the trident's caring,
In the hurricane's rage, shell-trumpet's roar.
Here   is it here amidst earthbound waters,
The reflection and symbol of supernal great sea,
That he warriors a way to fulfil and to show
Homecoming always in the long and dire distance
From transcendence, Power, that gives rudder and compass
In his narrative of change, still points him to peace?
Returning, returning?   then is it return
From the search for terrene insufficient safety,
Security, sheet anchor, which does not exist
For long or too well in the world of dust
Where tocsin sounds and cordage rots?
Returning, returning   it is here that he moves
Through mist and misfortune as a changing towards
      changeless,

As unfurling of forever, eternal preparation
For what is Illimitable, the secret sea, shoreless
Ocean of light, Ocean, that awaits exploration
Yet is always present in Now, all-containing
Now, the imperishable encompassing living
Without separative shadow, supper and trance.
30 Here in earth-dream, operation he shares
With sea-scorpion, orache, boar-fish, tern,
He is harmed and heavied by a fear more unreal
Than gamesome image and the kraken's stare:
Fear that clings to nescience that claims
Like breastless mother in a wealth of want,
'I am your loneliness; I will never leave you',
Is threat far greater than wrecker's intent
And shudders him more than cry from the crow's-nest,
Great gale and danger to bowsprit and timbers.
40 Long seems peril that makes no plain sailing
Where sea-fox prowls to the chant of the deep . . .   (1968)

LAWRENCE DURRELL (1912–90)

'Adapted rather light-heartedly from Homer', these catchy numbers from *Ulysses Come Back: Sketches for a Musical* (1970) do cry for music. But where is it?

Yoo Hoo Ulysses (*Circe's Song*)

White clouds sailing
Sea birds a'hailing

OH YOO HOO   YOO HOO

ULYSSES

Twilight's falling
Voices a'calling

OH YOO HOO   YOO HOO

ULYSSES

I'm just a woman alone
On an island of dreams
By myself in the midst of the sea
Being a goddess is all very well for a spell
But I'd rather be you – hoo
10   I'd rather be me.

The sun is sinking
I can't help thinking

OH YOO HOO   YOO HOO

ULYSSES

Out of the Blue (*Circe's Song*)

I'm tired of late nights
Of forbidden delights
I'm so tired of the things that I knew
Now all of a sudden
The wind seems to change
And you come out of the blue

Like a song without words
Like a tree without birds
Like a cottage without any view
10   I was there all alone when
The wind seemed to change
And you came out of the blue.

Now every tick tock
Of the ocean's vast clock
Says you're wasting your time all alone
Try and find him
Then remind him
He needs a loving woman all of his own . . .

As Adam once thought of
20 The apple Eve brought
A longing he couldn't subdue,
I was all on my own when
The wind seemed to change
And you came out of the blue.

You're Bringing Out the Swine in Me

(U) You're bringing out the swine in me
By giving too much wine to me
Though all your promises sound fine to me

But Circe, I simply gotta go.

(C) O won't you stay and dine with me
O honey stay in line with me
Let's drink our nectar in close harmony

Don't ever let me go.

(U) You're bringing out the swine in me
10 And though you seem divine baby
And all alone and fancy free

Circe, I simply gotta go.

(C) What's eatin' of you, hairy man?
Come on take your pleasure while you can
Come on and act the gentleman

Honey, don't ever let me go.

(U) I must admit you pack a punch
Your kisses baby, are the crunch
It's clear we won't get up for lunch

20 Circe, I simply can't say no.

Time Out of Mind (*Ulysses' Song*)

Time out of mind
I hear the ocean
It's stronger than any magic potion

Oh I've got those deep green sea blues.

Nights of phosphorous
And days of fire
Almost settin' of the sails on fire

Oh I've got those deep green sea blues.

With the Pole Star above you
10 With no one to love you
Horizons of rock and roll
The water's enchantment
Will say all your heart meant
And utter a song in your soul.

Time out of mind
My heart is turning
Sure as a needle where the surf lies burning

Oh I've got those deep green sea blues.   (1970)

M. L. WEST (b. 1916)

West is a distinguished classical scholar. The model for this experiment in short verses with a trochaic beat (*Sing Me, Goddess, being the First Recitation of Homer's Iliad*) is the Finnish epic, the *Kalevala*. West aims at reproducing oral performance.

The *Iliad* I [148–205] *The enraged exchanges between Achilles and Agamemnon*

Swift Achilles answered frowning:
'So! Advantage is your liking,
brazenness your shoulders' mantle.
How should one of the Achaeans
willingly obey your bidding,
go a journey, or do battle?
I came not to fight in battles
on account of Trojan spearmen,
for I have no quarrel with them.
10   They have never stolen from me
cows or horses, they have never
harmed my crops in fertile Phthia:
great the distance that divides us,
sounding sea and shadowed mountains.
You, o brazen one, did bring us
for your joy, that Menelaus

and your shameless self might levy
restitution from the Trojans:
this you mind not and regard not.
20 Now you bid to take my trophy,
which to win I laboured greatly,
and the Achaeans gave it to me.
Never do I get a trophy
great as yours, when the Achaeans
sack a township of the Trojans.
My hands most in furious battle
work, but at a distribution
yours is much the greater trophy;
I go off with but a small one,
30 small and precious, to my vessels,
weary as I am of fighting.
Now I will return to Phthia:
better far to take my beaked ships
homeward, for I do not fancy
staying here, deprived of honour,
drawing you your wealth and riches.'
    Answered him king Agamemnon:
'Fly, if so your spirit urges.
I beseech you not, for my sake
40 here to dally; I have others
who will give my due of honour,
chiefly Zeus the counsel-maker.
Most of all the kings I loathe you;
you like quarrels, war, and fighting.
If you're strong, 'tis God's bestowing.
Go home with your ships and comrades,
over Myrmidons be monarch.
I care nothing for your anger;
and I give you now this warning:
50 Phoebus claims Chryseis from me;
her then with my ships and comrades
will I render; but for my part
I will come for fair Briseis,

take your trophy from your cabin,
teach you how I rank above you,
and another man shall tremble
to oppose me as my equal.'
    At his words the son of Peleus
suffered anguish; in his rough breast
60 did the heart two counsels ponder,
whether to draw forth the sharp sword
from his thigh, to rouse the men up,
and to slay the son of Atreus,
or to check his angry spirit.
Thus he pondered, mind and spirit,
grasped the great sword in his scabbard,
when Athena came from heaven:
white-armed Hera sent her thither,
troubled for her two dear warriors.
70 She behind the son of Peleus
stood and took him by his brown hair;
none but he alone might see her.
Then Achilles turned, astonished,
straightway recognized Athena –
dreadful were her eyes a-gleaming –
and in wingèd words addressed her.
'Child of Zeus that bears the aegis,
have you come to see the insults
of Atrides Agamemnon?
80 Let me tell you this prediction:
by his arrogant demeanour
he is like to leave his spirit.'   (1971)

THELMA SARGENT

To our mind, one of the most lucid and moving versions of these
uneven and, at times, intractable originals.

The Homeric Hymns II [393-458] *To Demeter*

'Tell me, my child, did you eat any food at all down
     below?
Speak out, and hide nothing from me, that we may both
     know.
For if not, you are free of the loathsome dominion of Hades,
And may dwell with me and your father, cloud-wrapped son
     of Cronos,
Held in honor by all of the immortal gods everlasting.
But if you have eaten, back you must go to the depths of the
     earth,
There to live for a third of the span of each year,
But the other two seasons with me and the other immortals.
But when the earth blooms with all kinds of sweet-smelling
     flowers
10 In springtime, you will come up again from the kingdom
Of shadows – a wonder indeed for gods and for mortal
     mankind.
But tell me how he carried you off to his shadowy kingdom,
The ruthless receiver of many. What bait did he use to
     ensnare you?'
   Then surpassingly lovely Persephone answered her, saying:
'Indeed I will tell you unerringly, mother, all that has
     happened.
When the swift courier, Hermes, the bringer of luck,
Came to me from the son of Cronos my father
And the other gods of the heavens, bidden to lead me
Out of Erebos, so that, beholding me with your eyes,
20 You would cease from your immortal wrath and terrible
     anger,
I jumped up rejoicing. But Hades secretly gave me
A seed of the red pomegranate, honey-sweet food,
And forced me, reluctant, to eat it. As for the rest –

How, through the shrewd plan of the son of Cronos my
     father,
He came and carried me down to the depths of the earth –
I will tell you the tale from beginning to end as you ask.
We were all playing there in the lovely green meadow –
Leucippe, Phaeno, Electra, Ianthe, Melita,
Iache, Rhodea, Callirhoë, Melobosis, Tyche,
30   Flower-faced Ocyrhoë, Chryseis, Ianeira, Acaste,
Admete and Rhodope, Pluto, charming Calypso,
Styx and Urania, darling Galaxaura, Pallas,
Rouser of battle, and Artemis, strewer of arrows –
Playing, and with our hands picking beautiful flowers:
Modest crocuses mingled with iris and hyacinth,
Rosebuds and lilies and, wondrous to see, a narcissus
That broad earth made to grow, just like a crocus.
In delight I picked the bright blossom, but earth underneath
Gave way, and the mighty lord, the receiver of many, rushed
     forth
40   And carried me off all unwilling deep underground
In his chariot of gold, and I cried out at the top of my voice.
Deeply grieved though I am, all this that I tell you is true.'
     Then all day long, with their hearts in agreement, they
          basked
In each other's presence, embracing with love and forgetful
     of sorrow,
And each received joy from the other and gave joy in return.
Then smooth-coifed Hecate came and lovingly kissed
The holy child of Demeter, and the queen from that time
Served as Persephone's priestess and faithful companion.
     Far-seeing Zeus of loud thunder then sent among them
50   As messenger lovely-haired Rhea to summon blue-robed
          Demeter
And lead her to the tribes of the gods, and he promised to
     give
Of honors among the immortals whatever she chose.
But with a nod he affirmed that her daughter must live

For a third part of the circling year in the shadowy kingdom,
But with her mother the rest of the year, and the other
    immortals.
So he spoke, and Rhea, obedient to Zeus,
Swiftly descended from the peaks of Olympus
And soon came to Rharos, once fertile and life-giving land,
Now lying fallow – unfruitful, all leafless, the white barley
    hidden
60 By the design of Demeter, delicate-ankled.
But soon, with the coming of spring, the grain would grow
    tall,
And, ripening, fill the rich furrows with tassels of gold,
To be gathered in sheaves at the harvest and bound with
    straw bands.
There Rhea alighted out of the sky's barren waste,
And mother and daughter, seeing each other, rejoiced in
    their hearts.   (1973)

SANFORD PINSKER (b. 1941)

No selection of recent American poetry on this (or any other)
theme would be complete without a touch of Yiddish. *Shlep* means
'to haul, to drag out'. Once again, we meet with the motif of
Homerus hebraizon.

Penelope's Reply (with apologies to Tennyson.)

Where does he get off with a line like
'It little profits that an idle king'?
Weaving in and out of this story is pain.
And twenty years of soiled togas and socks.
All Ithaca sees the dirty linen on the line.

But *I* am supposed to pack his bags in peace,
Shlep out Telemachus for a farewell kiss
and wax up the bloody floors again.
I said to him: 'Listen Ulysses, *what* "mariners"?

10   They're *dead*. Finished. At the bottom of
(You'll pardon the expression) a wine-dark sea.
Rest awhile. Have a little something to eat.
What you call "some three suns to store and hoard"
Hardly constitutes giving kingship a fair chance.
Besides, Telemachus tells me it's tough work
What with all the check and balances
(Put in, by the way, since you left)
And the referendum on monarchy coming up.'
But he just gave me the deaf ear he is famous for

20   And shoved off, muttering to an invisible crew.
As for me, it looks like the same old pattern:
Crafty sewing by day / crafty suitors by night.
I wonder what I should wear. A basic black?
Or, perhaps, my chartreuse shift with the lemon
trim . . .

(1979)

WALTER SHEWRING (b. 1906)

A 'rather free' translation in prose. Shewring respects Homeric formulae and repeated epithets. Archaizing is to be avoided.

The Odyssey XVI [154–212] *Odysseus reveals himself to his son*

Thus did he urge the need for haste; and the swineherd seized his sandals, put them on and made for the town. His going did not escape Athene, and now she drew near in likeness of a woman, tall and handsome and skilled in fine handiwork. She stood outside the cottage gateway, making herself visible to Odysseus. Telemachus did not see her before him or sense her coming, because it is not to every man that divinities make themselves manifest. Odysseus saw her; so did the dogs, and they did not bark, but fled away whining across the yard. She made a sign to Odysseus with her eyebrows; he saw it and went out from the room and past the big courtyard wall; there he stood facing her. Athene spoke: 'Royal son of Laertes, Odysseus of many wiles, now is the moment to tell your son the truth. Hide nothing; and then you two can devise the suitors' death and doom before you enter the town again. And I myself shall not be absent from you long: I burn for battle.'

She touched him then with her golden wand. First she put a fresh mantle and tunic over him, then made him more tall and young and lithe; his skin grew bronzed again and his cheeks filled out; the beard on his chin showed dark once more.

Having thus transformed him she went her way, and Odysseus returned into the cottage. His own son gazed at him in wonder, then turned his eyes away, terrified – was not this a god? His words hastened forth in rapid flight: 'Stranger, your likeness is other than what I saw before – the garments on you have changed, and your skin is of a different hue. Surely you are some god, one of those whose home is wide heaven itself. Be gracious to us, and let us offer you acceptable sacrifices and gifts of wrought gold. Only have compassion on us.'

Odysseus answered him: 'I am not a god. Why liken me to the Deathless Ones? I am your own father, the very man for whose sake you have grieved long and borne much and suffered the violences of men.'

With these words he kissed his son and let fall a tear from his cheeks to the ground, though until then he had been firm and tearless. But Telemachus could not yet believe that this was his own father, and therefore answered him thus again: 'You are not Odysseus, not my father; no, some god is beguiling me, only to make me grieve and despair the more. No mortal man could do such a thing by his own devising; it would need a god, no less, to intervene and make a man young or old – a god's wish makes such marvels easy.

A moment ago you were old and dressed in rags, but now you look like those divinities whose home is wide heaven itself.'

Subtle Odysseus answered him: 'Telemachus, you need not be much bewildered or much amazed at sight of your father at home again. No other Odysseus will come to this land for you after this; there is only I, such as you see me, after many trials and many wanderings, returning now to my own land in the twentieth year. Athene the goddess has transformed me; it is her way to make me, according to her all-powerful will, now like a beggar, now like a youth in handsome garments. To the gods whose home is heaven itself it is an easy thing to exalt a mortal or to abase him.   (1980)

DENISON BINGHAM HULL
(b. 1897)

A translation in unrhymed iambic pentameter. Hull seeks a 'language spoken by educated people'. This swift-moving yet closely attentive rendition seems to me unjustly neglected. It surpasses a number of more highly publicized recent exercises.

The Iliad IV [446–72] *In the thick of the struggle*

>   Now when at length they reached one place and met,
>   they flung together shields, spears and the might
>   of men in brazen breastplates; big-bossed shields
>   closed on each other, and the din grew great.
>   Then screams and shouts of triumph rose together
>   from killers and from killed; the earth ran blood.
>   As when two swollen streams flow from a mountain,
>   and cast together at a fork the water
>   from huge springs deep within the hollow stream bed,
> 10   and far away the shepherd hears their roaring –
>   such were their shouts and struggles when they met.

Antilochus was first to kill a Trojan,
a noble champion, Echepolus;
throwing first, he struck the crest of the helmet;
the bronze point stuck in his forehead, driven through
into the bone, and darkness covered his eyes.
He tumbled like a tower in cruel combat.
As he fell Chalcodon's son, Elephenor,
the chief of the Abantes, caught his feet,
20   and dragged him from beneath the arrows, in haste
to strip the armor off; his try was brief.
For when Agenor saw him drag the corpse,
exposing ribs beneath the shield when bending,
he stabbed with his bronze-pointed spear, and killed him.
His spirit left, but over him went on
the Trojans' and Achaeans' work; like wolves
who spring on one another, man charged man.

XVI [257–84] *The Myrmidons advance*

These armed with brave Patroclus marched in line,
planning a mighty charge against the Trojans.
They poured out fast like wasps along the roadside
which little boys habitually madden,
teasing them in their homes along the wayside,
the silly fools, for they hurt many people,
for if some traveler upon the road
stirs them unintentionally, they come swarming
in raging fury to defend their children.
10   So poured the Myrmidons out of the ships
with hearts enraged, making an awful din.
Patroclus from afar called to his comrades:
'O Myrmidons, companions of Achilles,
be men, my friends, remember your great courage,
so we, his fighting comrades by the ships,
may honor Peleus' son, the best of Argives,

so Atreus' son may recognize his madness
dishonoring the best of the Achaeans.'
    He spoke, and roused the spirit in each man,
20   and in a mass they fell upon the Trojans;
the ships around them echoed to their yelling.
    The Trojans, when they saw Menoetius' son
and his companions in their shining armor,
were shaken in their ranks beside the ships,
fearing it might be Peleus' son himself,
who put away his wrath, and caught up friendship,
and each one watched for some chance to escape.   (1982)

ROBERT FAGLES (b. 1933)

Via its brilliant recording on audiotape this version has reached a wide
public. It aims at narrative pace and oral resonance. A 'loose five-or-
six-beat' line, sometimes lengthening to seven, seeks to render the
interplay of norm and variety in the original. Fagles cites the magic of
'mass and movement both', of 'so much grace and speed in Homer'.

The Iliad III.146–219 [121–80] *Helen on the ramparts to view the warriors*

    And now a messenger went to white-armed Helen too,
Iris, looking for all the world like Hector's sister
wed to Antenor's son, Helicaon's bride Laodice,
the loveliest daughter Priam ever bred.
And Iris came on Helen in her rooms . . .
weaving a growing web, a dark red folding robe,
working into the weft the endless bloody struggles
stallion-breaking Trojans and Argives armed in bronze
had suffered all for her at the god of battle's hands.
10   Iris, racing the wind, brushed close and whispered,

'Come, dear girl, come quickly –
so you can see what wondrous things they're doing,
stallion-breaking Trojans and Argives armed in bronze!
A moment ago they longed to kill each other, longed
for heartbreaking, inhuman warfare on the plain.
Now those very warriors stand at ease, in silence –
the fighting's stopped, they lean against their shields,
their long lances stuck in the ground beside them.
Think of it: Paris and Menelaus loved by Ares
20   go to fight it out with their rugged spears –
all for you – and the man who wins that duel,
you'll be called his wife!'
                                        And with those words
the goddess filled her heart with yearning warm and deep
for her husband long ago, her city and her parents.
Quickly cloaking herself in shimmering linen,
out of her rooms she rushed, live tears welling,
and not alone – two of her women followed close behind,
Aethra, Pittheus' daughter, and Clymene, eyes wide,
and they soon reached the looming Scaean Gates.

30   And there they were, gathered around Priam,
Panthous and Thymoetes, Lampus and Clytius,
Hicetaon the gray aide of Ares, then those two
with unfailing good sense, Ucalegon and Antenor.
The old men of the realm held seats above the gates.
Long years had brought their fighting days to a halt
but they were eloquent speakers still, clear as cicadas
settled on treetops, lifting their voices through the forest,
rising softly, falling, dying away . . . So they waited,
the old chiefs of Troy, as they sat aloft the tower.
40   And catching sight of Helen moving along the ramparts,
they murmured one to another, gentle, winged words:
'Who on earth could blame them? Ah, no wonder
the men of Troy and Argives under arms have suffered
years of agony all for her, for such a woman.
Beauty, terrible beauty!

A deathless goddess – so she strikes our eyes!
                                   But still
ravishing as she is, let her go home in the long ships
and not be left behind . . . for us and our children
down the years an irresistible sorrow.'
                                   They murmured low
50   but Priam, raising his voice, called across to Helen,
'Come over here, dear child. Sit in front of me,
so you can see your husband of long ago,
your kinsmen and your people.
I don't blame you. I hold the gods to blame.
They are the ones who brought this war upon me,
devastating war against the Achaeans –
                                   Here, come closer,
tell me the name of that tremendous fighter. Look,
who's that Achaean there, so stark and grand?
Many others afield are much taller, true,
60   but I have never yet set eyes on one so regal,
so majestic . . . That man must be a king!'

And Helen the radiance of women answered Priam,
'I revere you so, dear father, dread you too –
if only death had pleased me then, grim death,
that day I followed your son to Troy, forsaking
my marriage bed, my kinsmen and my child,
my favorite, now full-grown,
and the lovely comradeship of women my own age.
Death never came, so now I can only waste away in tears.
70   But about your question – yes, I have the answer.
That man is Atreus' son Agamemnon, lord of empires,
both a mighty king and a strong spearman too,
and he used to be my kinsman, whore that I am!
There was a world . . . or was it all a dream?'

XII.464–512 [400–441] *The Trojans storm the Greek wall*

But Teucer and Ajax, aiming at him together,
shot! – Teucer's arrow hitting the gleaming belt
that cinched his body-shield around his chest –
but Zeus brushed from his son the deadly spirits:
not by the ships' high sterns would his Sarpedon die.
Ajax lunged at the man, he struck his shield but the point
would not pierce through, so he beat him back in rage
and he edged away from the breastwork just a yard.
Not that Sarpedon yielded all the way, never,
10   his heart still raced with hopes of winning glory,
whirling, shouting back to his splendid Lycians,
'Lycians – why do you slack your fighting-fury now?
It's hard for me, strong as I am, single-handed
to breach the wall and cut a path to the ships –
come, shoulder-to-shoulder!
The more we've got, the better the work will go!'

So he called, and dreading their captain's scorn
they bore down fiercer, massing round Sarpedon now
but against their bulk the Argives closed ranks,
20   packed tight behind the wall,
and a desperate battle flared between both armies.
Lycian stalwarts could not force the Achaeans back,
breach their wall and burst through to the ships,
nor could Achaean spearmen hurl the Lycians back,
clear of the rampart, once they'd made their stand.
As two farmers wrangle hard over boundary-stones,
measuring rods in hand, locked in a common field,
and fight it out on the cramped contested strip
for equal shares of turf – so now the rocky bastion
30   split the troops apart and across the top they fought,
hacked at each other, chopped the oxhides round their chests,
the bucklers full and round, skin-shields, tassels flying.

Many were wounded, flesh ripped by the ruthless bronze
whenever some fighter wheeled and bared his back
but many right through the buckler's hide itself.
Everywhere – rocks, ramparts, breastworks swam
with the blood of Trojans, Argives, both sides,
but still the Trojans could not rout the Argives.
They held tight as a working widow holds the scales,
40   painstakingly grips the beam and lifts the weight
and the wool together, balancing both sides even,
struggling to win a grim subsistence for her children.
So powerful armies drew their battle line dead even
till, at last, Zeus gave Hector the son of Priam
the greater glory – the first to storm the wall.
Hector loosed a piercing cry at his men:
'Drive, drive, my stallion-breaking Trojans!
Breach the Achaean rampart! Hurl your fire now –
a blazing inferno of fire against their ships!'

XX.553-69 [490-503] *Achilles lunges into battle*

                              Achilles now
like inhuman fire raging on through the mountain gorges
splinter-dry, setting ablaze big stands of timber,
the wind swirling the huge fireball left and right –
chaos of fire – Achilles storming on with brandished spear
like a frenzied god of battle trampling all he killed
and the earth ran black with blood. Thundering on,
on like oxen broad in the brow some field hand yokes
to crush white barley heaped on a well-laid threshing floor
10   and the grain is husked out fast by the bellowing oxen's
             hoofs –
so as the great Achilles rampaged on, his sharp-hoofed
             stallions
trampled shields and corpses, axle under his chariot splashed

with blood, blood on the handrails sweeping round the car,
sprays of blood shooting up from the stallions' hoofs
and churning, whirling rims – and the son of Peleus
charioteering on to seize his glory, bloody filth
splattering both strong arms, Achilles' invincible arms – (1990)

ALLEN MANDELBAUM (b. 1926)

Mandelbaum is both an academic and a tireless translator from
Italian, Latin, Greek. The effects aimed at are at once 'oral' and
'aural'. This sumptuously printed version, with its resort to moments
of American English and colloquialism, has been, perhaps unjustly,
neglected.

The Odyssey of Homer I [337–80] *Telemachus replies to his
mother's dismay at the song of the minstrel, Phemius*

'You, Phémius, know many other deeds
of men and gods – exploits that bring delight
to mortals, acts that singers celebrate.
Then, seated here among these suitors sing
of such things – while they drink their wine in silence.
But stop this dismal chant, for it consumes
the heart within my breast, since I have been
struck by a loss that cannot be forgotten.
Indeed, such was the man for whom I grieve
10   with endless memory, a man whose glory
is known through Hellas, Argos – all of Greece.'

This was Telémachus' astute reply:
'My mother, why not let the faithful singer
delight us as his heart impels? The singer
is not to blame; this grief was brought by Zeus,

he who assigns to those who feed on bread
the good or evil he alone decrees.
Do not fault Phémius if he would sing
the Dánaans' sorry doom: men hold most dear
20   whatever song is newest to their ears.
Allow your heart and soul to listen, for
Odysseus was not the only one
to lose in Troy the day of his return:
there many other warriors met their death.
But go now to your room; tend to your tasks,
the distaff and the loom; your women can
complete the work that they began. Leave speech
to men: to all those here and – most – to me;
within this house, I have authority.'

30   Amazed, while going to her room, she laid
to heart her son's wise words. Then, with her maids,
she reached the upper floor, and wept and wept
for her dear husband, her Odysseus,
until Athena, gray-eyed goddess, shed
sweet sleep upon her eyelids.
                        But the suitors
began to clamor in the shadowed hall:
each hoped that he might lie in bed with her.
For them Telémachus had these sharp words:

'How arrogant you are – beyond all measure –
40   you who would win my mother. Feast with pleasure
for now, but let there be no brouhaha:
to hear the song of one whose voice is like
the gods' – that is most fine. There will be time
tomorrow to assemble, one and all;
within that council I shall frankly call
on every one of you to quit my halls.
Just hold your future revels someplace else;
consume your own fine goods; let each for each

prepare, in turn – in his own house – a feast.
50   Or if you think it easier – better –
to eat your unpaid way through one man's wealth,
feast here indeed. But I shall then implore
the gods, who live forever, asking Zeus
to grant me my requital: all of you
would then die unavenged within these halls.'   (1990)

DEREK WALCOTT (b. 1930)

Walcott's metamorphic reading of the *Odyssey* is the great feat of
reanimating delight and penetration after Joyce. Walcott takes
literally, as it were, Borges's dictum that Homer now comes after
Joyce's *Ulysses*. Interleaving the Homeric characters and episodes
with the Caribbean setting, with the mythologies and *patois* of
Santa Lucia and West Africa, Walcott gives us a Homeric 'masque'
and carnival which reaffirms, smilingly, the universality of the
original epic.

Omeros, pp. 17–18

In which Joyce, his 'blind singer' (cf. our selection from the 'Sirens'
episode in *Ulysses*) and Homer are fused against the West Indian
background.

II

Ma Kilman had the oldest bar in the village.
Its gingerbread balcony had mustard gables
with green trim round the eaves, the paint wrinkled with
    age.

In the cabaret downstairs there were wooden tables
for the downslap of dominoes. A bead curtain
tinkled every time she came through it. A neon

sign endorsed Coca-Cola under the NO PAIN
CAFÉ ALL WELCOME. The NO PAIN was not her own
idea, but her dead husband's. 'Is a prophecy,'

10   Ma Kilman would laugh. A hot street led to the beach
past the small shops and the clubs and a pharmacy
in whose angling shade, his khaki dog on a leash,

the blind man sat on his crate after the pirogues
set out, muttering the dark language of the blind,
gnarled hands on his stick, his ears as sharp as the dog's.

Sometimes he would sing and the scraps blew on the wind
when her beads rubbed their rosary. Old St. Omere.
He claimed he'd sailed round the world. 'Monsieur Seven Seas'

they christened him, from a cod-liver-oil label
20   with its wriggling swordfish. But his words were not clear.
They were Greek to her. Or old African babble.

Across wires of hot asphalt the blind singer
seemed to be numbering things. Who knows if his eyes
saw through the shades, tapping his cane with one finger?

She helped him draw his veteran's compensation
every first of the month from the small Post Office.
He never complained about his situation

like the rest of them. The corner box, and the heat
on his hands would make him shift his box to the shade.
30   Ma Kilman saw Philoctete hobbling up the street,

so she rose from her corner window, and she laid
out the usual medicine for him, a flask of white
acajou, and a jar of yellow Vaseline,

a small enamel basin of ice. He would wait
in the No Pain Café all day. There he would lean
down and anoint the mouth of the sore on his shin.

Pp. 200–204

Again, the Joyce–Homer symbiosis, followed by a set of variations
on the Homeric tale of the voyage and of Circe.

III

I leant on the mossed embankment just as if he
bloomed there every dusk with eye-patch and tilted hat,
rakish cane on one shoulder. Along the Liffey,

the mansards dimmed to one indigo silhouette;
then a stroke of light brushed the honey-haired river,
and there, in black cloche hat and coat, she scurried faster

to the changing rose of a light. Anna Livia!
Muse of our age's Omeros, undimmed Master
and true tenor of the place! So where was my gaunt,

10   cane-twirling flaneur? I blest myself in his voice,
and climbed up the wooden stairs to the restaurant
with its brass spigots, its glints, its beer-brightened noise.

'There's a bower of roses by Bendemeer's stream'
was one of the airs Maud Plunkett played, from Moore
perhaps, and I murmured along with them; its theme,

as each felted oar lifted and dipped with hammer-
like strokes, was that of an adoring sunflower
turning bright hair to her Major. And then I saw him.

The Dead were singing in fringed shawls, the wick-low shade
20 leapt high and rouged their cold cheeks with vermilion
round the pub piano, the air Maud Plunkett played,

rowing her with felt hammer-strokes from my island
to one with bright doors and cobbles, and then Mr Joyce
led us all, as gently as Howth when it drizzles,

his voice like sun-drizzled Howth, its violet lees
of moss at low tide, where a dog barks 'Howth! Howth!' at
the shawled waves, and the stone I rubbed in my pocket

from the Martello brought one-eyed Ulysses
to the copper-bright strand, watching the mail-packet
30 butting past the Head, its wake glittering like keys.

Chapter XL

I

A snail gnawing a leaf, the mail-packet nibbles
the Aegean coast, its wake a caterpillar's
accordion. Then, becalmed by its own ripples,

sticks like a butterfly to its branch. The pillars,
the lizard-crossed terraces on the ruined hills
are as quiet as the sail. Storks crest the columns.

Gulls chalk the blue enamel and a hornet drills
the pink blossoms of the oleander and hums
at its work. In white villages with cracked plaster

40 walls, shawled women lean quietly on their shadows,
    remembering statues in their alabaster
    manhood, when their oiled hair was parted like the crow's

    folded wings. The flutes in the square and the sea-lace
    of bridal lilac; sawing fiddles that outlast
    the cicadas. On the scorched deck Odysseus

    hears the hill music through the wormholes of the mast.
    The sail clings like a butterfly to the elbow
    of an olive branch. A bride on her father's arm

    scared of her future. On its tired shadow,
50 the prow turns slowly, uncertain of its aim.
    He peels his sunburnt skin in maps of grey parchment

    which he scrolls absently between finger and thumb.
    The crew stare like statues at that feigned detachment
    whose heart, in its ribs, thuds like the galley-slaves' drum.

    II

    Hunched on their oars, they smile; 'This is we Calypso,
    Captain, who treat we like swine, you ain't seeing shore.
    Let this sun burn you black and blister your lips so

    it hurt them to give orders, fuck you and your war.'
    The mattock rests, idle. No oar lifts a finger.
60 Blisters flower on palms. The bewildered trireme

    is turning the wrong way, like the cloud-eyed singer
    whose hand plucked the sea's wires, back towards the dream
    of Helen, back to that island where their hunched spine

bristled and they foraged the middens of Circe,
when her long white arm poured out the enchanting wine
and they bucked in cool sheets. 'Cap'n, boy? Beg mercy

o' that breeze for a change, because sometimes your heart
is as hard as that mast, you dream of Ithaca,
you pray to your gods. May they be as far apart

70   from your wandering as ours in Africa.
Island after island passing. Still we ain't home.'
The boatswain lifted the mattock, and the metre

of the long oars slowly settled on a rhythm
as the prow righted. He saw a limestone palace
over his small harbour, he saw a sea-swift skim

the sun-harped water, and felt the ant of a breeze
crossing his forehead, and now the caterpillar's
strokes of the oars lifted the fanning chrysalis

of the full sails as a wake was sheared by the bow.
80   The quick mattock beat like the heart of Odysseus;
and if you have seen a butterfly steer its shadow

across a hot cove at noon or a rigged canoe
head for the horns of an island, then you will know
why a harbour-mouth opens with joy, why black crew,

slaves, and captain at the end of their enterprise
shouted in response as they felt the troughs lifting
and falling with their hearts, why rowers closed their eyes

and prayed they were headed home. They knew the drifting
Caribbean currents from Andros to Castries
90   might drag them to Margarita or Curaçao,

that the nearer home, the deeper our fears increase,
that no house might come to meet us on our own shore,
and fishermen fear this as much as Ulysses

until they see the single eye of the lighthouse
winking at them. Then the strokes match heartbeat to oar,
their blistered palms weeping for palms or olive trees.   (1990)

MICHAEL LONGLEY (b. 1939)

Born in 1939, this Northern Irish poet adverts to the ambiguities
and violence of Odysseus' homecoming as an 'allegory' of the
Belfast condition.

Gorse Fires, p. 31

Eurycleia

I

Eurycleia fetched a basin, poured cold water into it,
Added hot water, and got ready to wash his feet.
But Odysseus shifted out of the firelight, afraid
She might notice his scar, the key to his identity,
A wound a boar inflicted years back, a flesh-wound.
His wet-nurse cradled his foot in her hands and touched
The scar, and recognising him she let go of his leg
Which clattered into the basin – water everywhere,
Such pain and happiness, her eyes filling with tears,
10   Her old voice cracking as she stroked his beard and
         whispered
     'You are my baby boy for sure and I didn't know you
     Until I had fondled my master's body all over.'

II

I began like Odysseus by loving the wrong woman
Who has disappeared among the skyscrapers of New York
After wandering for thousands of years from Ithaca.
She alone remembers the coppice, dense and overgrown,
Where in a compost of dead leaves the boar conceals
Its bristling spine and fire-red eyes and white tusks.

P. 35

Anticleia

If at a rock where the resonant rivers meet, Acheron,
Pyriphlegethon, Cocytus, tributary of the Styx, you dig
A pit, about a cubit each way, from knuckles to elbow,
And sacrifice a ram and a black ewe, bending their heads
Towards the outer darkness, while you face the water,
And so many souls of the anaemic dead come crowding in
That you hold them back with your bayonet from the blood
Only to recognise among the zombies your own mother,
And if, having given her blood to drink and talked about
    home,
You lunge forward three times to hug her and three times
Like a shadow or idea she vanishes through your arms
And you ask her why she keeps avoiding your touch and
    weep
Because here is your mother and even here in Hades
You could comfort each other in a shuddering embrace,
Will she explain that the sinews no longer bind her flesh
And bones, that the irresistible fire has demolished these,
That the soul takes flight like a dream and flutters in the sky,
That this is what happens to human beings when they
    die?   (1991)

10

OLIVER TAPLIN (b. 1943)

Oliver Taplin is a distinguished classicist and translator. He has worked much on Homer. *The Wanderings of Odysseus* is among the rare versions for the stage.

The Odyssey V [388–450] *Odysseus swims desperately to reach land*

Narrator
Two days Odysseus was driven   and two nights over the
     waves;
often and often he feared   that his last hour was looming;
but when the curly locks   of dawn unfurled the third day,
the wind dropped down   and a calm came over. From the
     very top
of a swelling roller   he caught a quick glimpse of land.
As welcome as would be   the first signs of reviving life
to a family whose father   has lain suffering from fever,
weeks wasting away,   and loathed death has brushed by
     him,
yet one day – welcome –   the gods free him from disease,
10 so welcome the woods   and land seemed to Odysseus,
who swam with all his might   to get his feet on dry ground.

When he was as far off   as a loud shout would carry
and could hear the swash   as the sea smacked on the rocks –
for a heavy wave-swell   from the recent storm was still
roaring on the shore,   all cloaked in clouds of spray,
where there were no havens   or sheltered inlets,
but sharp promontories,   jagged rocks, ragged reefs –
then Odysseus' strength   and spirit collapsed, and he said
grimly to himself:

Odysseus

20   'Here's an irony,   when Zeus has shown
land so near, beyond   my dreams, after so long a swim,
and now there's no way   I can find out of the grey brine.
At the edge are jagged   rocks with the surf roughly
breaking about them,   then the shelf is sheer, and the sea
        deep,
so there's no way to win   a firm foothold out of trouble,
or to avoid a wave   catching me as I climb out
and shattering me on shore   – that would be a foolish
        landfall!
But if I make a circuit   swimming round to try to find
bays with beaches   or coves safe from the surf,
30   I'm afraid I shall find   the off-shore winds sweeping me out
in agony again   over the fish-infested sea.
Or some sea-monster   will be let loose on me –
I'm well aware how   Poseidon has sided against me.'

Narrator

Even while his mind was   turning these thoughts, a
        turbulent
wave swelling to break   was lifting him to the rough rocks,
where his flesh would have been flayed,   bones broken and
        crushed,
had not bright-eyed Athena   inspired the idea in his mind of
desperately grasping   a boulder with both his hands.
He gripped it in pain   while the crashing wave washed over.
40   He'd no sooner survived that   than the sucking backwash
        struck
with irresistible pull   and swept him way out to sea.
As clusters of stones   stick tight on the tentacle-
cups of an octopus   that's been plucked out of its lair,
so Odysseus' skin clung   stuck to the rock, scraped
from his strong grip.   And the vast wave covered him.

Then wretched Odysseus   might have gone under despite his
    destiny,
had not bright-eyed Athena   planted a plan in his mind:
battling clear of the breakers   that roared frothing towards
    land,
he stroked along beyond,   always searching the shore-line
50   to find bays with beaches   or coves safe from the surf.
And as he swam he came   to the mouth of a fresh-flowing
    stream,
which seemed the most promising spot,   free of threatening
    rocks
and away from the wind.   He prayed in his heart to the
    stream:

Odysseus
'Whatever your true title,   listen to me, lord of the stream,
I pray you for protection   from pursuit on the sea by
    Poseidon.
A helpless suppliant   human can command some mercy
even from a divinity,   if he's a homeless fugitive, as I am;
I've come after many   struggles to your welcome stream. So
pity me, mighty lord   – I throw myself on your mercy.'

                                (1994)

PETER READING (b. 1946)

A harsh but convincingly faithful rendition of the cruel epilogue to
the slaying of the suitors.

The Odyssey XXII [381–477]

Homeric

After Odysseus had slaughtered the Suitors he
    grimly surveyed them –

sprawling in crans in a welter of blood and
  muck, like the beached fish
dragged up by driftnetters onto the sand to
  gulp for the grey brine
till in the heat of the sun they expire, so
  lay the slain Suitors.

Calling Telemachus, devious-thinking
  wily Odysseus
asked for the nurse Eurycleia to be brought
  into his presence.

Rattling her door, Telemachus shouted
  old Eurycleia,
matron in charge of the servant women, to
  go to his father.

When she arrived, she discovered Odysseus
  striding through corpses,
10   spattered with offal and gore, like a lion
  leaving a farmstead
where he has feasted on cattle, the blood-gouts
  staining his body.

When she set eyes on the dead and the blood-bath,
  old Eurycleia
let out a triumphal yell but Odysseus
  stopped her with these words:
'Silence, old woman, for it is immoral to
  gloat over slain men;
justice was meted out to them by the
  gods for their evil,
they have been slain for their want of respect, their
  doom has been dreadful.
Now, let us talk of the women attendants –
  who has betrayed me?'

'Sir, of the fifty who serve in your household
     twelve should be punished
for their recalcitrance – even Penelope
     couldn't control them.'
20   'Go to those women who flouted decorum;
     summon them to me.'
These were his words, and the nurse was quick to
     muster the culprits.

Meanwhile Odysseus briefed his son and his
     two faithful herdsmen:
'Carry the carcasses out of here – order the
     women to help you.
Then swab the elegant chairs and tables with
     sponges and water.
Then, when the palace is cleansed and in order,
     take out the women,
lead them between the domed outhouse and the
     wall of the courtyard,
then with your long-bladed swords make sure you
     hack them to pieces –
end their lascivious memories of lewd
     nights with the Suitors.'

Howling, convulsively sobbing, the women were
     herded together.
30   Firstly they dragged out the carcasses, dumped them
     under the portal
(superintending, Odysseus forced their
     unwilling labour);
next, they attended to swabbing the elegant
     chairs and the tables;
meanwhile Telemachus worked with the pair of
     trustworthy herdsmen
scraping with shovels the crusted blood-clots
     out of the flooring,

ordered the women to carry away the
    loathsome detritus.

Now that the palace was cleansed and in order, the
        women were taken,
herded between the domed outhouse and the wall of the
        courtyard,
into a corner from which there could be no
        hope of escaping.
Worthy Telemachus next outlined his
        plan of disposal:
40 'Death by the sword is too good for these sluts who
        brought to this household
shameful dishonour and sully us by their
        wanton cavortings.'
Seizing a hawser, removed from the deck of some
        blue-prowed vessel,
ever-resourceful Telemachus lashed it
        high on a column,
slung it across the dome of the outhouse,
        tautened it so that
anyone strung from it wouldn't be able to
        reach for a foothold.
Then, in the same way as thrushes or doves dropping
        into a thicket,
seeking a roosting-place, find only snares set
        cruelly to kill them,
so did the women, their heads in a row of
        tightly-drawn nooses,
dangle and writhingly twitch until death had
        stilled their convulsions.

50 Next, through the gate they dragged the treacherous
        goatherd Melanthius
[trussed, he had been, by the hands and feet and
        roped to a roof-beam,

left there suspended and suffering since the
    heat of the battle].
Plying a keen-edged blade, they sawed his
    nose and his ears off,
carved off his genitals, tossed them aside as
    meat for the mongrels.
Finally, hacking his hands and his feet off, their
    fury was sated.   (1994)

WILLIAM LOGAN (b. 1950)

An American poet and critic who often draws on classical themes,
Logan has prepared these fragments from the *Odyssey* specifically
for this anthology. They are notable for their restrained intensity.

The Odyssey X

The Death of Elpenor X [551–60]

I brought my men away except Elpenor,
our little brother, no good at a sea knot
or in a sea fight, and with no sense at all.
Restless and drunk, he reeled away from the fire,
off to a dusty corner where he could drowse
away from the jabber, out in the sea breeze.
He found some straw on the flat roof of the palace.
At dawn he heard the noise of the other sailors,
joking and swearing, scraping their gear together,
10   forgot where he was, forgot the rickety ladder,
and half-asleep, walked blindly into the air.
His neckbone snapped like a dove's, and he was dead.

The Cattle of Helios XII [354-73]

They swayed. The fork-horned oxen cropped the weeds
beneath the shadow of the Greeks' black prow.
The dark Greeks waded through the herd, slapping their rumps,
and chased a pair of oxen up the beach.
Surrounding them, the Greeks spoke to their gods,
and stripped the new leaves from a bristling oak –
there was no barley left within the ship.
They slit the cattle's throats, one at a time,
and flayed their hides. The thick blood soaked the sand.
10   Cutting away the meat, they wrapped the thighs in fat,
and in the double folds laid gobbets of flesh.
They had no wine to pour on the steaming guts –
tipping a leather bucket of freezing brine,
they scorched the stinking guts in the low fire.
When the fatty thighs had burnt, and the guts were coals,
they spitted on their spears the bloody steaks.
I had been asleep. I wobbled down the shore,
back to the ship, and smelled an unfamiliar smell:
cooked meat. I knew what my hungry men had done,
20   and spoke to Zeus in all my gristly rage
for drugging me with sleep, and letting my companions
draw their bronze knives, and kill the sacred cattle.

The Return to Kharybdis XII [417-44]

The air reeked sulphur. Knocked overboard, my men
ghosted down the waves cawing like sea crows.
A dark god stole their lives and their passage home.
I staggered aft, where waves had torn out the keel.
The rigging was gone, except a rawhide backstay,
and with it I lashed the keel to the broken mast.
As the ship broke up, I rode them into the waves.

The west wind faltered, then the south picked up,
and back my crude raft drifted toward Kharybdis,
10 through the cold froth of tar-black night. At dawn,
the sun broke on the jagged rock of Skylla,
and below it the whirlpool, sucking down seawater.
I could just reach the bole of a sea fig –
as the mast dropped away, I hung like a bat,
the branches drooping far over the whirlpool,
the knotted mass of roots out of reach. I clung there,
and waited for Kharybdis to spew up the mast.
All day I dangled there, arms racked in their sockets,
almost till dark, when a man, still in his robes,
20 leaves the law court for supper, having judged
the dreary cases brought by angry young men
eager to sue their neighbors, even their friends –
then mast and keel, still tangled, burst to the surface.
I fell on them and weakly paddled away.

The Kidnap of Eumaios XV [459–83]

One of the mates appeared at my father's house
wearing a gold chain hung with amber teardrops.
He laid it in my mother's cool, soft hands.
Turning it over her fingers, she asked the price,
showing her servants how it caught the light –
and as it glowed, he nodded to my nurse.
Late in the day, she led me from the palace,
past the great table where my father's men
had drunk away the hours before the debates.
10 She slipped three hammered goblets in her robe –
I followed her in my cold innocence.
Late afternoon, the streets were long in shadow.
We took the rutted road to the flashing harbor,
where the Phoenician ship lay rocking at anchor,
like a carving knife. Traders took us aboard,

and we cut the salt-whipped sea on a trailing wind.
Days passed. A week. The coast was just in sight.
Clutching her chest, my nurse staggered as if shot,
and pitched face down in the bilge like a diving tern.
20   The sailors threw her corpse to the barking seals,
and brought me here to Ithaka, where I was sold.   (1994)

LIST OF TRANSLATORS
BY BOOK*

The *Iliad*

* This list is in principle restricted to direct translators of the original Greek.

The *Odyssey*

The *Homeric Hymns*

BIBLIOGRAPHICAL SOURCES

Anon., *A Burlesque Translation of Homer*, London, 1797

Anon., *The Iliad of Homer Translated into English Prose*, Oxford, 1821

Andrew, S. O., *Homer's Odyssey*, London, 1948

Arnold, Matthew, *On Translating Homer*, London, 1861

Auden, W. H., *The Shield of Achilles*, London, New York, 1952

Bates, Herbert, *The Odyssey of Homer*, New York, 1929

Brandreth, T. S., *The Iliad of Homer*, London, 1816

Browning, Robert, *Development*, London, c.1888–9

Bryant, W. Cullen, *The Odyssey of Homer*, Boston, Mass., 1873

Buckley, Thomas A., *The Odyssey of Homer*, London, 1874

Butcher, S. H., and Lang, A., *The Odyssey of Homer*, London, 1879

Butler, Samuel: *The Iliad of Homer*, London, 1898; *The Odyssey of Homer*, London, 1900

Calverley, Charles Stuart, *Translations into English and Latin*, London, 1866

Caulfield, Francis, *The Odyssey*, London, 1923

Caxton, William, Epilogue to Book III of *Recuyell of the Historyes of Troye*, in W. J. B. Crotch, ed., *The Prologues and Epilogues of William Caxton*, London, 1928/New York, 1973

Chapman, George, *Chapman's Homer*, ed. Allardyce Nicoll, New York, 1956

Chaucer, Geoffrey, *Troylus and Criseyde*, in J. H. Fisher, ed., *Chaucer: The Complete Poetry and Prose*, London/New York, 1977

Clark, Thomas, *The Iliad of Homer with an Interlinear Translation . . . on the Hamiltonian System as Improved by Thomas Clark*, New York, 1888, re-edited 1952

Cochrane, James Inglis, *Homer's Iliad*, Edinburgh, 1867

Cook, Albert, *The Odyssey*, 2nd edn, New York, 1967

Cotterill, H. B., *Homer's Odyssey: A Line-for-line Translation in the Metre of the Original*, London, 1911

Cowper, William, *The Iliad and Odyssey of Homer*, London, 1791

Dart, J. Henry, *The Iliad of Homer*, London, 1865

Day-Lewis, C., 'Nearing Again the Legendary Isle', *Collected Poems, 1929–1933*, New York, 1933

Derby, The Earl of, *Homer's Iliad*, London, 1862, 1864

Dryden, John, *Fables Ancient and Modern*, London, 1700

Dunbar, Henry, *Complete Concordance to the Odyssey and the Hymns of Homer*, London, 1880

Durrell, Lawrence, *Ulysses Comes Back: Sketches for a Musical*, London, 1970

Edgington, G. W., *The Odyssey of Homer*, London, 1869

Ernle, George, *The Wrath of Achilles*, Oxford, 1922

Fagles, Robert, *The Iliad*, New York, 1990

Fitzgerald, Robert: *The Odyssey*, New York, 1961; *The Iliad*, New York, 1974

Gladstone, W. E., *Studies on Homer and the Homeric Age*, Oxford, 1858

Graves, Robert, *The Anger of Achilles, Homer's Iliad*, New York, 1959

Gunn, Thom: *My Sad Captains*, London, 1961; *Jack Straw's Castle and Other Poems*, London, 1976

Hall, Arthur, *Tenne Bookes of the Iliades of Homer*, London, 1581, reprinted in H. G. Wright, *The Life and Works of Arthur Hall of Grantham*, Manchester, 1919

Henryson, Robert, *Poems*, ed. Charles Elliott, Oxford, 1974

Hewlett, Maurice, *The Iliad of Homer, The First Twelve Staves*, London, 1928

Hobbes, Thomas, *The Iliads and Odysses of Homer*, London, 1676

Hull, Denison Bingham, *Homer's Iliad*, Scottsdale, Ariz., 1932

Joyce, James, *Ulysses: The Corrected Text*, New York, 1986

Keats, John, *Poems*, London, 1817

Kitto, H. D. F., *The Greeks*, London, 1951

Lamb, Charles, *The Adventures of Ulysses*, London, 1808

Lang, A., Leaf, W., and Myers, E., *The Iliad of Homer*, London, 1882

Lattimore, Richmond: *The Iliad of Homer*, Chicago, 1951; *The Odyssey of Homer*, New York, 1965

Lawrence, D. H., 'The Argonauts', *Last Poems*, London/New York, 1933

Lockhart, J. G., 'The twenty-fourth book of Homer's Iliad', *Blackwood's Magazine*, March 1846

Logue, Christopher: *Patrocleia*, London, 1962; *Pax*, London, 1967

Longley, Michael, *Gorse Fires*, London, 1991

Lowell, Robert, *Imitations*, London, 1962

Lucas, F. L., *The Odyssey, Translated in Selection*, London, 1948

Lydgate, John, *The Troy Book*, ed. H. Bergen, London, 1906/New York, 1975

MacKail, J. W., *The Odyssey*, London, 1903–10

Macpherson, James, *The Iliad of Homer*, London, 1773

Maginn, William, *Homeric Ballads*, London, 1850

Mandelbaum, Allen, *The Odyssey of Homer*, Berkeley, Calif., 1990

Manning, Hugo, *The Secret Sea*, London, 1968

Meakin, Annette, *Nausikaa*, Versailles, 1926

Morgan, Edwin, 'The Greeks Retreat to the Ships', in M. Grant, ed., *Greek Literature, an Anthology*, London, 1976

Morris, William, *The Odyssey of Homer, Done into English Verse,* London, 1887

Murray, A. T.: *The Odyssey*, London, 1919; *The Iliad*, London, 1924–5

Musgrave, G., *The Odyssey of Homer*, London, 1865

Newman, F. W., *The Iliad of Homer*, London, 1856

Norgate, Thomas Starling, *The Iliad; or, Achilles' Wrath; At the Siege of Ilion*, London, 1864

Ogilby, John, *Homer's Iliads*, London, 1660

Palmer, George Herbert, *The Odyssey of Homer*, Cambridge, Mass., 1891/London, 1920

Picard, Barbara Leonie, *The Odyssey*, Oxford, 1952

Pinsker, Sanford, 'Penelope's Reply', *Salmagundi*, No. 26, spring 1974

Pope, Alexander, *The Iliad of Homer*, ed. Maynard Mack, New Haven, Conn., 1967

Pound, Ezra, *A Draft of XXX Cantos*, London, 1930, 1934

Reading, Peter, 'Homeric', *Last Poems*, London, 1994

Rees, Ennis, *The Odyssey of Homer*, New York, 1960

Richards, I. A., *The Wrath of Achilles, The Iliad of Homer Shortened and in a New Translation*, New York, 1950

Rieu, E. V.: *The Odyssey*, London, 1946; *The Iliad*, London, 1950

Rose, John Benson, *Homer's Iliad*, London, 1874

Rouse, W. H. D., *The Story of Odysseus*, London, 1932

Sargent, Thelma, *The Homeric Hymns*, New York, 1973

Shakespeare, William, *Troilus and Cressida*, First Quarto, London, 1609

Shaw, T. E., *The Odyssey of Homer*, New York, 1932/Oxford, 1935

Shelley, P. B., in *P. W.*, pub. Mrs Shelley, 2nd edn, 1839; reprinted in *Shelley/Poetical Works*, Oxford, 1967

Shewring, Walter, *Homer, The Odyssey*, Oxford, 1980

Simcox, Edwin W., *Homer's Iliad*, London, 1865

Smith, William Benjamin, and Miller, Walter, *The Iliad of Homer*, New York, 1945

Sotheby, William, *The Odyssey of Homer*, London, 1834

Sturt, Jemimah Makepiece, 'Penelope's Musings', Centersville, Ohio, 1875

Taplin, Oliver, 'Extract from *The Wanderings of Odysseus*', *Hellenic Studies Review*, No. 1, 1994, pp. 77–80

Tennyson, Alfred, Lord, *Poems*, 1832, p. 498

Tickell, Thomas, *The First Book of Homer's Iliad*, London, 1715

Walcott, Derek, *Omeros*, London, 1990

Way, A. S., *The Homeric Hymns*, London, 1934

West, M. L., *Sing Me, Goddess, being the First Recitation of Homer's Iliad*, London, 1971

Worsley, P. S., *The Odyssey of Homer*, London, 1861–2

ACKNOWLEDGEMENTS

Grateful thanks are due to Everyman's Library, David Campbell Publishers Ltd, for permission to reprint from *Homer's Odyssey* by S. O. Andrew (Dent, 1948); to Faber & Faber Ltd and Random House, Inc., for 'The Shield of Achilles' by W. H. Auden from *Collected Poems*, ed. Edward Mendelson (1976) (published by Random House, Inc., in *The Shield of Achilles*, copyright © 1955 by W. H. Auden); to W. W. Norton & Co., Inc., for *The Odyssey: A Norton Critical Edition*, 2nd edn, trans. and ed. Albert Cook (1993), copyright © 1967, 1974, 1993 by Albert Cook; to Chambers Harrap Publishers Ltd for *Homer's Odyssey: A Line-for-line Translation in the Metre of the Original* by H. B. Cotterill (Harrap, 1911); to Peters Fraser & Dunlop Group Ltd for 'Nearing Again the Legendary Isle' by C. Day-Lewis from *Collected Poems* (Jonathan Cape, 1954); to Oxford University Press for *The Wrath of Achilles* by George Ernle (1922); to Harvard University Press for Robert Fitzgerald's translations from *The Iliad* (1974) and *The Odyssey* (1961); to Carcanet Press Ltd for 'The Anger of Achilles' from *Homer's Iliad* by Robert Graves (1959); to Random House, Inc., for *Ulysses: The Corrected Text* by James Joyce, Preface by Richard Ellmann, Afterword by Hans Gabler, copyright © 1986 by Random House, Inc., reading text copyright © 1984 by The Trustees of the Estate of James Joyce; to Penguin Books Ltd for *The Greeks* by H. D. F. Kitto (Penguin Books, 1951, rev. edn 1957), copyright © H. D. F. Kitto, 1951, 1957; to Viking Penguin, a division of Penguin Books USA, Inc., for 'The Argonauts' by D. H. Lawrence from *The Complete Poems of D. H. Lawrence*, ed. V. de Sola Pinto and F. W. Roberts, copyright © 1964, 1971 by Angelo Ravagli and C. M. Weekley, Executors of the Estate of Frieda Lawrence Ravagli; to HarperCollins Publishers, Inc., for *The Odyssey of Homer* by Richmond Lattimore, copyright © 1965, 1967 by Richmond Lattimore, copyright renewed; to the University of Chicago Press for *The Iliad of Homer* by Richmond Lattimore (1951); to William Logan for 'The Death of Elpenor', 'The Cattle of Helios', 'The Return to Kharybdis' and 'The Kidnap of Eumaios' from *The Odyssey*, copyright © W. Logan, 1994; to

Aitken, Stone & Wylie and Faber & Faber Ltd for 'Patrocleia' and 'Pax' by Christopher Logue from *War Music*; to Peters Fraser & Dunlop Group Ltd for *Gorse Fires* by Michael Longley (Secker & Warburg, 1991); to Faber & Faber Ltd for 'The Killing of Lykaon' by Robert Lowell from *Imitations* (1962); to the Folio Society for *The Odyssey, Translated in Selection* (1948) and *The Iliad* (1950) by F. L. Lucas; to John Murray (Publishers) Ltd for *The Odyssey* by J. W. MacKail; to Bantam Books, a division of Bantam Doubleday Dell Publishing Group, Inc., for *The Odyssey of Homer* by Allen Mandelbaum, translation copyright © 1990 by Allen Mandelbaum; to I. J. Percal for *The Secret Sea* by Hugo Manning (Trigram Press, 1968); to Harvard University Press and Loeb Classical Library for *The Odyssey* (Heinemann, 1919) and *The Iliad* (Heinemann, 1924–5) by A. T. Murray; to Oxford University Press for *The Odyssey of Homer*, retold by Barbara Leonie Picard (1952); to Faber & Faber Ltd and New Directions Publishing Corporation for 'Canto I' by Ezra Pound from *The Cantos of Ezra Pound*, copyright © 1934 by Ezra Pound; to Penguin Books Ltd for *The Iliad* by E. V. Rieu (Penguin Classics, 1950), copyright © the Estate of E. V. Rieu, 1950, and *The Odyssey* by E. V. Rieu, rev. D. C. H. Rieu (Penguin Classics, 1946, rev. edn 1991), copyright © E. V. Rieu, 1946, rev. trans. copyright © the Estate of the late E. V. Rieu and D. C. H. Rieu, 1991; to W. W. Norton & Co., Inc., for *The Homeric Hymns: A Verse Translation*, by Thelma Sargent, copyright © 1973 by W. W. Norton & Co., Inc.; to Oxford University Press for *Homer, The Odyssey* by Walter Shewring (1980); to Simon & Schuster, Inc., for *The Iliad of Homer* by William Benjamin Smith and Walter Miller, copyright 1944 by Macmillan Publishing Co., renewed 1972 by Edith Miller Crowe; to Oliver Taplin for *The Wanderings of Odysseus* (published in *Dialogos*, 1, 1994), copyright © Oliver Taplin, 1994; to Faber & Faber Ltd for *Omeros* by Derek Walcott (1990); to Duckworth (Publishers) Ltd for *Sing Me, Goddess, Being the First Recitation of Homer's Iliad*, by M. L. West (1971).

Every effort has been made to trace or contact all copyright-holders. The publishers will be glad to make good any omissions brought to their attention.

READ MORE IN PENGUIN

In every corner of the world, on every subject under the sun, Penguin represents quality and variety – the very best in publishing today.

For complete information about books available from Penguin – including Puffins, Penguin Classics and Arkana – and how to order them, write to us at the appropriate address below. Please note that for copyright reasons the selection of books varies from country to country.

In the United Kingdom: Please write to *Dept. EP, Penguin Books Ltd, Bath Road, Harmondsworth, West Drayton, Middlesex UB7 ODA*

In the United States: Please write to *Consumer Sales, Penguin USA, P.O. Box 999, Dept. 17109, Bergenfield, New Jersey 07621-0120*. VISA and MasterCard holders call 1-800-253-6476 to order Penguin titles

In Canada: Please write to *Penguin Books Canada Ltd, 10 Alcorn Avenue, Suite 300, Toronto, Ontario M4V 3B2*

In Australia: Please write to *Penguin Books Australia Ltd, P.O. Box 257, Ringwood, Victoria 3134*

In New Zealand: Please write to *Penguin Books (NZ) Ltd, Private Bag 102902, North Shore Mail Centre, Auckland 10*

In India: Please write to *Penguin Books India Pvt Ltd, 706 Eros Apartments, 56 Nehru Place, New Delhi 110 019*

In the Netherlands: Please write to *Penguin Books Netherlands bv, Postbus 3507, NL-1001 AH Amsterdam*

In Germany: Please write to *Penguin Books Deutschland GmbH, Metzlerstrasse 26, 60594 Frankfurt am Main*

In Spain: Please write to *Penguin Books S. A., Bravo Murillo 19, 1° B, 28015 Madrid*

In Italy: Please write to *Penguin Italia s.r.l., Via Felice Casati 20, I–20124 Milano*

In France: Please write to *Penguin France S. A., 17 rue Lejeune, F–31000 Toulouse*

In Japan: Please write to *Penguin Books Japan, Ishikiribashi Building, 2–5–4, Suido, Bunkyo-ku, Tokyo 112*

In Greece: Please write to *Penguin Hellas Ltd, Dimocritou 3, GR–106 71 Athens*

In South Africa: Please write to *Longman Penguin Southern Africa (Pty) Ltd, Private Bag X08, Bertsham 2013*

PENGUIN AUDIOBOOKS

A Quality of Writing that Speaks for Itself

Penguin Books has always led the field in quality publishing. Now you can listen at leisure to your favourite books, read to you by familiar voices from radio, stage and screen. Penguin Audiobooks are ideal as gifts, for when you are travelling or simply to enjoy at home. They are produced to an excellent standard, and abridgements are always faithful to the original texts. From thrillers to classic literature, biography to humour, with a wealth of titles in between, Penguin Audiobooks offer you quality, entertainment and the chance to rediscover the pleasure of listening.

You can order Penguin Audiobooks through Penguin Direct by telephoning (0181) 899 4036. The lines are open 24 hours every day. Ask for Penguin Direct, quoting your credit card details.

Published or forthcoming:

Emma by Jane Austen, read by Fiona Shaw

Persuasion by Jane Austen, read by Joanna David

Pride and Prejudice by Jane Austen, read by Geraldine McEwan

The Tenant of Wildfell Hall by Anne Brontë, read by Juliet Stevenson

Jane Eyre by Charlotte Brontë, read by Juliet Stevenson

Villette by Charlotte Brontë, read by Juliet Stevenson

Wuthering Heights by Emily Brontë, read by Juliet Stevenson

The Woman in White by Wilkie Collins, read by Nigel Anthony and Susan Jameson

Heart of Darkness by Joseph Conrad, read by David Threlfall

Tales from the One Thousand and One Nights, read by Souad Faress and Raad Rawi

Moll Flanders by Daniel Defoe, read by Frances Barber

Great Expectations by Charles Dickens, read by Hugh Laurie

Hard Times by Charles Dickens, read by Michael Pennington

Martin Chuzzlewit by Charles Dickens, read by John Wells

The Old Curiosity Shop by Charles Dickens, read by Alec McCowen

PENGUIN AUDIOBOOKS

Crime and Punishment by Fyodor Dostoyevsky, read by Alex Jennings

Middlemarch by George Eliot, read by Harriet Walter

Silas Marner by George Eliot, read by Tim Pigott-Smith

The Great Gatsby by F. Scott Fitzgerald, read by Marcus D'Amico

Madame Bovary by Gustave Flaubert, read by Claire Bloom

Jude the Obscure by Thomas Hardy, read by Samuel West

The Return of the Native by Thomas Hardy, read by Steven Pacey

Tess of the D'Urbervilles by Thomas Hardy, read by Eleanor Bron

The Iliad by Homer, read by Derek Jacobi

Dubliners by James Joyce, read by Gerard McSorley

The Dead and Other Stories by James Joyce, read by Gerard McSorley

On the Road by Jack Kerouac, read by David Carradine

Sons and Lovers by D. H. Lawrence, read by Paul Copley

The Fall of the House of Usher by Edgar Allan Poe, read by Andrew Sachs

Wide Sargasso Sea by Jean Rhys, read by Jane Lapotaire and Michael Kitchen

The Little Prince by Antoine de Saint-Exupéry, read by Michael Maloney

Frankenstein by Mary Shelley, read by Richard Pasco

Of Mice and Men by John Steinbeck, read by Gary Sinise

Travels with Charley by John Steinbeck, read by Gary Sinise

The Pearl by John Steinbeck, read by Hector Elizondo

Dr Jekyll and Mr Hyde by Robert Louis Stevenson, read by Jonathan Hyde

Kidnapped by Robert Louis Stevenson, read by Robbie Coltrane

The Age of Innocence by Edith Wharton, read by Kerry Shale

The Buccaneers by Edith Wharton, read by Dana Ivey

Mrs Dalloway by Virginia Woolf, read by Eileen Atkins

READ MORE IN PENGUIN

A CHOICE OF CLASSICS

Aeschylus	**The Oresteian Trilogy**
	Prometheus Bound/The Suppliants/Seven Against Thebes/The Persians
Aesop	**Fables**
Ammianus Marcellinus	**The Later Roman Empire (AD 354–378)**
Apollonius of Rhodes	**The Voyage of Argo**
Apuleius	**The Golden Ass**
Aristophanes	**The Knights/Peace/The Birds/The Assemblywomen/Wealth**
	Lysistrata/The Acharnians/The Clouds
	The Wasps/The Poet and the Women/The Frogs
Aristotle	**The Art of Rhetoric**
	The Athenian Constitution
	Ethics
	The Politics
	De Anima
Arrian	**The Campaigns of Alexander**
St Augustine	**City of God**
	Confessions
Marcus Aurelius	**Meditations**
Boethius	**The Consolation of Philosophy**
Caesar	**The Civil War**
	The Conquest of Gaul
Catullus	**Poems**
Cicero	**Murder Trials**
	The Nature of the Gods
	On the Good Life
	Selected Letters
	Selected Political Speeches
	Selected Works
Euripides	**Alcestis/Iphigenia in Tauris/Hippolytus**
	The Bacchae/Ion/The Women of Troy/Helen
	Medea/Hecabe/Electra/Heracles

READ MORE IN PENGUIN

A CHOICE OF CLASSICS

READ MORE IN PENGUIN

A CHOICE OF CLASSICS

Plautus	**The Pot of Gold and Other Plays**
	The Rope and Other Plays
Pliny	**The Letters of the Younger Pliny**
Pliny the Elder	**Natural History**
Plotinus	**The Enneads**
Plutarch	**The Age of Alexander** (Nine Greek Lives)
	The Fall of the Roman Republic (Six Lives)
	The Makers of Rome (Nine Lives)
	The Rise and Fall of Athens (Nine Greek Lives)
	Plutarch on Sparta
Polybius	**The Rise of the Roman Empire**
Procopius	**The Secret History**
Propertius	**The Poems**
Quintus Curtius Rufus	**The History of Alexander**
Sallust	**The Jugurthine War/The Conspiracy of Cataline**
Seneca	**Four Tragedies/Octavia**
	Letters from a Stoic
Sophocles	**Electra/Women of Trachis/Philoctetes/Ajax**
	The Theban Plays
Suetonius	**The Twelve Caesars**
Tacitus	**The Agricola/The Germania**
	The Annals of Imperial Rome
	The Histories
Terence	**The Comedies (The Girl from Andros/The Self-Tormentor/The Eunuch/Phormio/The Mother-in-Law/The Brothers)**
Thucydides	**History of the Peloponnesian War**
Virgil	**The Aeneid**
	The Eclogues
	The Georgics
Xenophon	**Conversations of Socrates**
	A History of My Times
	The Persian Expedition

READ MORE IN PENGUIN

A CHOICE OF CLASSICS

St Anselm	**The Prayers and Meditations**
St Augustine	**Confessions**
Bede	**Ecclesiastical History of the English People**
Geoffrey Chaucer	**The Canterbury Tales**
	Love Visions
	Troilus and Criseyde
Marie de France	**The Lais of Marie de France**
Jean Froissart	**The Chronicles**
Geoffrey of Monmouth	**The History of the Kings of Britain**
Gerald of Wales	**History and Topography of Ireland**
	The Journey through Wales and **The Description of Wales**
Gregory of Tours	**The History of the Franks**
Robert Henryson	**The Testament of Cresseid and Other Poems**
Walter Hilton	**The Ladder of Perfection**
Julian of Norwich	**Revelations of Divine Love**
Thomas à Kempis	**The Imitation of Christ**
William Langland	**Piers the Ploughman**
Sir John Mandeville	**The Travels of Sir John Mandeville**
Marguerite de Navarre	**The Heptameron**
Christine de Pisan	**The Treasure of the City of Ladies**
Chrétien de Troyes	**Arthurian Romances**
Marco Polo	**The Travels**
Richard Rolle	**The Fire of Love**
François Villon	**Selected Poems**

READ MORE IN PENGUIN

A CHOICE OF CLASSICS

ANTHOLOGIES AND ANONYMOUS WORKS

The Age of Bede
Alfred the Great
Beowulf
A Celtic Miscellany
The Cloud of Unknowing and Other Works
The Death of King Arthur
The Earliest English Poems
Early Irish Myths and Sagas
Egil's Saga
English Mystery Plays
Eyrbyggja Saga
Hrafnkel's Saga
The Letters of Abelard and Heloise
Medieval English Verse
Njal's Saga
Roman Poets of the Early Empire
Seven Viking Romances
Sir Gawain and the Green Knight